KICKING THE SACRED COW

KICKING THE SACRED COW

Questioning the Unquestionable and Thinking the Impermissible

JAMES P. HOGAN

A Baen Books Original

Baen Publishing Enterprises
P.O. Box 1403
Riverdale, NY 10471
www.baen.com

ISBN: 0-7434-8828-8

Cover art by Allan Pollack

First printing, July 2004

Library of Congress Cataloging-in-Publication Data

Hogan, James P.
    Kicking the sacred cow : questioning the unquestionable and thinking the
    impermissible / by James P. Hogan.
        p. cm.
    Includes bibliographical references.
    ISBN 0-7434-8828-8 (HC)
    1. Science I. Title.

    Q158.5.H65 2004
    500--dc22

                                                                    2004009764

Distributed by Simon & Schuster
1230 Avenue of the Americas
New York, NY 10020

Production by Windhaven Press, Auburn, NH
Printed in the United States of America

10 9 8 7 6 5 4 3 2 1

DEDICATION

TO HALTON ARP, PETER DUESBERG—

AND ALL OTHER SCIENTISTS OF INTEGRITY WHO FOLLOWED

WHERE THE EVIDENCE POINTED, AND STOOD BY THEIR

CONVICTIONS.

ACKNOWLEDGMENTS

The help and advice of the following people is gratefully acknowledged—for generously giving their time in describing their work and answering questions; providing invaluable material without which the book would not have been possible; giving more of their time to reading, criticizing, and offering suggestions; and in some cases for the plain, simple moral support of wanting to see it finished. A few words at the front never seems enough to repay this kind of cooperation.

John Ackerman, Firmament & Chaos, Philadelphia, PA; Halton Arp, Max-Planck Institut für Astrophysik, Germany; Russell T. Arndts; Andre Assis, Universidade Estadual del Campinas-Unicamp, São Paulo, Brazil; Petr Beckmann, Professor Emeritus of Electrical Engineering, University of Colorado, Boulder; Michael J. Bennett; Tom Bethell, Hoover Institution, Stanford, CA, and *American Spectator*, Washington, DC; Anthony Brink, South African Bar, Pietermaritzburg, South Africa; Candace Crandall, Science & Environmental Policy Project, Arlington, VA; David Crowe, Reappraising AIDS Society, Alberta, Canada; Peter Duesberg, Department of Molecular & Cell Biology, University of California, Berkeley; Fintan Dunne, AIDS Watch, Dublin, Ireland; Hugh Ellsaesser, visiting scientist, Lawrence Livermore Laboratories, Livermore, CA; Scott Fields; Charles Ginenthal, *The Velikovskian*, Queens, NY; Tim Gleason, Unionville, CT; Larry Gould, Department of Physics, University of Connecticut, Storrs; Tina Grant, Venice, CA; Lewis Greenberg, *Kronos*, Deerfield Beach, FL; Sheryl Guffrey, Tulsa, OK; Ron Hatch, GPS Consultant, Wilmington, CA; Howard Hayden, Professor Emeritus of Physics, University of Connecticut, Storrs; Marjorie Hecht, 21st Century Science Associates, Leesburg, VA; Alex Hogan; Jackie Hogan; Joe Hogan; Mike Hogan; Bob Holznecht, Auto Air, Coco Beach, FL; Kent Hovind, Pensacola, FL; Les Johnson, NASA, Marshall Spaceflight Center, Huntsville, AL; Phillip Johnson, Professor of Law, University of California, Berkeley; Jeff Kooistra, Champagne, IL; Eric Lerner, Princeton, NJ; Robert Lightfoot, Chattanooga, TN; Anthony Liversidge, New York, NY; Scott Lockwood, Lubbock, TX; Christine Maggiore, Alive & Well, Venice, CA; George Marklin, Houston, TX; Paul Marmet, University of Ottawa, Canada; Mike Miller, Quackgrass Press; Bill Nichols, Seattle, WA; Mike Oliver, Carson City, NV; Henry Palka, Farmington,

CT; Robert Pease, Professor Emeritus of Physical Climatology at the University of California, Riverside; Peter Perakos; Thomas E. Phipps Jr., Urbana, IL; C. J. Ransom, Colleyville, TX; Lynn E. Rose, Solana Beach, CA; Peter Saint-Andre, Monadnock, NH; S. Fred Singer, SEPP, Arlington, VA; Michael Sisson, Tampa, FL; Patrick Small; Toren Smith, Studio Proteus, San Francisco, CA; E. D. Trimm, Covington, GA; Valendar Turner, Royal Perth Hospital, Australia; Ruyong Wang, St. Cloud State University, MN; Brent Warner, NASA, Goddard Spaceflight Center, Greenbelt, MD; Jonathan Wells, Olympia, WA; Eleanor Wood, Spectrum Literary Agency, New York, NY.

CONTENTS

LIST OF ILLUSTRATIONS

INTRODUCTION

Engineering and the Truth Fairies

Science really doesn't exist. Scientific beliefs are either proved wrong, or else they quickly become engineering. Everything else is untested speculation.   —JPH

My interest in science began at an early age, as a boy growing up in postwar England. One of my older sisters, Grace—I was the baby by a large gap in a family with four children, two boys and two girls—was married to a former Royal Air Force radio and electronics technician called Don. He was one of the practical kind that people described as "good with his hands," capable of fixing anything, it seemed. The shelves, additions to the house, and other things that he created out of wood were always true and square, with the pieces fitting perfectly. He would restore pieces of machinery that he had come across rusting in the local tip, and assemble a pile of electrical parts and a coil wound on a cardboard custard container into a working radio. I spent long summer and Christmas vacations at Grace and Don's, learning the art of using and taking care of tools ("The job's not finished until they're cleaned and put away" was one of his maxims), planning the work through ("Measure twice; cut once" was another), and talking with people across the world via some piece of equipment that he'd found in a yard sale and refurbished. Kids today take such things for granted, but there was no e-mail then. Computers were unheard of. Don would never pass by a screw or a bolt lying on the roadside that might be useful for something one day. His children once told me ruefully that they never got to play with their presents on Christmas Day because the paint was never dry.

Although Don was not a scientist, working with him imbued in me an attitude of mind that valued the practicality of science as a way of dealing with life and explaining much about the world. Unlike all of the other creeds, cults, and ideologies that humans had been coming up with for as long as humanity had existed, here was a way of distinguishing between beliefs that were probably true and beliefs that were probably not in ways that gave observable results that could be repeated. Its success was attested to by the new world that had come into existence in—what?— little more than a century. From atoms to galaxies, phenomena were made comprehensible and predictable that had remained cloaked in superstition and ignorance through thousands of years of attempts at inquiry by other means. Airplanes worked; magic carpets didn't. Telephones, radio, and TV enabled anyone, at will, anytime, to accomplish things which before had been conceivable only as miracles. The foot deformities that I had been born with were corrected by surgery, not witch doctoring, enabling me later to enjoy a healthy life mountain hiking and rock climbing as a teenager. Asimov's nonfiction came as a topping to the various other readings I devoured in pursuit of my interest: Science was not only effective and made sense; it could actually be *fun* too!

I would describe science as formalized common sense. We all know how easily true believers can delude themselves into seeing what they want to see, and even appearances reported accurately are not always to be relied upon. (My older brother was something of a card sharp, so there was nothing particularly strange in the idea of things sometimes not being what they seemed.) What singled science out was its recognition of objective reality: that whatever is true will remain true, regardless of how passionately someone might wish things to be otherwise, or how many others might be induced to share in that persuasion. A simple and obvious enough precept, one would have thought. Yet every other belief system, even when professing commitment to the impartial search for truth, acted otherwise when it came to recruiting a constituency. And hence, it seemed, followed most of the world's squabbles and problems.

So it was natural enough for me to pursue a career in the Royal Aircraft Establishment, Farnborough—a few miles from where Grace and Don lived—after passing the requisite three days of qualifying examinations, as a student of electrical, mechanical, and aeronautical engineering. On completion of the general course I went on to specialize in electronics. Later, I moved from design to sales, then into computers, and ended up working with scientists and engineers across-the-board in just about every discipline and area of application. Seeing the way they went about things confirmed the impressions I'd been forming since those boyhood days of working with Don.

The problems that the world had been getting itself into all through history would all be solved straightforwardly once people came around to seeing things the right way. Wars were fought over religions, economic resources, or political rivalries. Well, science showed that men made gods, not vice versa. Sufficiently advanced technologies could produce plenty of resources for everybody, and once those two areas were taken care of, what was there left to create political rivalries over? Then we could be on our way to the stars and concern ourselves with things that were truly interesting.

When I turned to writing in the mid seventies—initially as a result of an office bet, then going full-time when I discovered I liked it—a theme of hard science-fiction with an upbeat note came naturally. I was accused (is that the right word?) of reinventing the genre of the fifties and sixties from the ground up, which was probably true to a large degree, since I had read very little of it, having come into the field from a direction diametrically opposed to that of most writers. The picture of science that I carried into those early stories reflected the idealization of intellectual purity that textbooks and popularizers portray. Impartial research motivated by the pursuit of knowledge assembles facts, which theories are then constructed to explain. The theories are tested by rigorous experiment; if the predicted results are not observed, the theories are modified accordingly, without prejudice, or abandoned. Although the ideal can seldom be achieved in practice, free inquiry and open debate will detect and correct the errors that human frailty makes inevitable. As a result, we move steadily through successively closer approximations toward the Truth.

Such high-flying fancy either attains escape velocity and departs from the realities of Earth totally, or it comes back to ground sometime. My descent from orbit was started by the controversy over nuclear energy. It wasn't just political activists with causes, and journalists cooking a story who were telling the public things that the physicists and engineers I knew in the nuclear field insisted were not so. Other scientists were telling them too. So either scientists were being knowingly dishonest and distorting facts to promote political views; or they were sincere, but ideology or some other kind of bias affected what they were willing to accept as fact; or vested interests and professional blinkers were preventing the people whom I was talking to from seeing things as they were. Whichever way, the ideal of science as an immutable standard of truth where all parties applied the same rules and would be obliged to agree on the same conclusion was in trouble.

I quickly discovered that this was so in other fields too. Atmospheric scientists whom I knew deplored the things being said about ozone holes. Chemists scoffed at the hysteria over carcinogens. A curious thing I noticed, however, was that specialists quick to denounce the misinformation and sensationalized reporting concerning their own field would accept uncritically what the same information sources and media said with regard to other fields. Nuclear engineers exasperated by the scares about radiation nevertheless believed that lakes formed in some of the most acidic rock on the continent had been denuded of fish (that had never lived there) by acid rain; climatologists who pointed out that nothing could be happening to the ozone layer since surface ultraviolet was not increasing signed petitions to ban DDT; biologists who knew that bird populations had thrived during the DDT years showed up to picket nuclear plants; and so it went on. Clearly, other factors could outweigh the objective criteria that are supposed to be capable of deciding a purely scientific question.

Browsing in a library one day, I came across a creationist book arguing that the fossil record showed the precise opposite of what evolutionary theory predicts. I had never had reason to be anything but a staunch supporter of Darwinism, since that was all I'd been exposed to, and everyone knew the creationists were strange anyway. But I checked the book out and took it home, thinking it would be good for a laugh. Now, I didn't buy their Scriptural account of how it all began, and I still don't. But contrary to the ridicule and derision that I'd been accustomed to hearing, to my own surprise I found the evidence that they presented for finding huge problems with the Darwinian theory to be solid and persuasive. So, such being my bent, I ordered more books from them out of curiosity to look a bit more deeply into what they have to say. Things got more interesting when I brought my findings up with various biologists whom I knew. While some would fly into a peculiar mix of apoplexy and fury at the mere mention of the subject—a distinctly unscientific reaction, it seemed—others would confide privately that they agreed with a lot of it; but things like pressures of the peer group, the politics of academia, and simple career considerations meant that they didn't talk about it. I was astonished. This was the late-twentieth-century West, not sixteenth-century Spain.

Shortly afterward, I met Peter Duesberg, one of the nation's leading molecular biologists, tipped by many to be in line for a Nobel Prize, suddenly professionally ostracized and defunded for openly challenging the mainstream dogma on AIDS. What was most disturbing about it after talking with him and his associates and reading their papers was that what they were saying made sense; the official party line didn't. Another person I got to know was the late Petr Beckmann, professor emeritus of electrical engineering, whose electrical interpretation of the phenomena conventionally explained by the Einstein Relativity Theory (ERT) is equally compatible with all the experimental results obtained to date, simpler in its assumptions, and more powerful predictively— but it is ignored by the physics community. I talked to an astrophysicist in NASA who believed that Halton Arp—excommunicated from American astronomy for presenting evidence contradicting the accepted interpretation of the cosmic redshifts that the Big Bang theory rests on—was "onto something." But he would never say so in public, nor sign his name to anything to that effect on paper. His job would be on the line, just as Arp's had been.

Whatever science might be as an ideal, scientists turn out to be as human as anyone else, and they can be as obstinate as anyone else when comfortable beliefs solidify into dogma. Scientists have emotions—often expressed passionately, despite the myths—and can be as ingenious as any senator at rationalizing when a reputation or a lifetime's work is perceived to be threatened. They value prestige and security no less than anyone else, which inevitably fosters convergences of interests with political agendas that control where the money and the jobs come from. And far from least, scientists are members of a social structure with its own system of accepted norms and rewards, commanding loyalties that at times can approach fanaticism, and with rejection and ostracism being the ultimate unthinkable.

This book is not concerned with cranks or simple die-hards, who are entitled to their foibles and come as part of life's pattern.

Rather, it looks at instances of present-day orthodoxies tenaciously defending beliefs in the face of what would appear to be verified fact and plain logic, or doggedly closing eyes and minds to ideas whose time has surely come. In short, where scientific authority seems to be functioning more in the role of religion protecting doctrine and putting down heresy than championing the spirit of the free inquiry that science should be.

The factors bringing this about are various. Massive growth of government funding and the direction of science since World War II have produced symbiotic institutions which, like the medieval European Church, sell out to the political power structure as purveyors of received truth in return for protection, patronage, and prestige. Sometimes vested commercial interests call the tune. In areas where passions run high, ideology and prejudice find it easy to prevail over objectivity. Academic turf, like any other, is defended against usurpers and outside invasion. Some readily trade the anonymity and drudgery of the laboratory for visibility as celebrities in the public limelight. Peer pressure, professional image, and the simple reluctance to admit that one was wrong can produce the same effects at the collective level as they do on individuals.

I used to say sometimes in flippant moments that science was the only area of human activity in which it actually matters whether or not what one believes is actually true. Nowadays, I'm not so sure. It seems frequently to be the case that the cohesiveness that promotes survival is fostered just as effectively by shared belief systems within the social-political structures of science, whether those beliefs be true or not. What practical difference does it make to the daily routine and budget of the typical workaday scientist, after all, if the code that directs the formation and behavior of the self-assembling cat wrote itself out of random processes or was somehow inspired by a Cosmic Programmer, or if the universe really did dance out of the head of a pin? Scientific truth can apparently be an elusive thing when you try to pin it down, like the Irish fairies.

So today, I reserve the aphorism for engineering. You can fool yourself if you want, and you can fool as many as will follow for as long as you can get away with it. But you can't fool reality. If your design is wrong, your plane won't fly. Engineers don't have the time or the inclination for highfalutin' theories. In fact, over-elaborate theories that try to reach too far, I'm beginning to suspect, might be the biggest single menace affecting science. Maybe that's why I find that the protagonists of the later books that I've written, now that I look back at them and think about it, have tended to be engineers.

ONE
HUMANISTIC RELIGION

The Rush to Embrace Darwinism

I think a case can be made that faith is one of the world's great evils, comparable to the smallpox virus but harder to eradicate.
—Richard Dawkins, professor of zoology,
Oxford University

History will judge neo-Darwinism a minor twentieth-century religious sect within the sprawling religious persuasion of Anglo-Saxon biology.
— Lynn Margulis, professor of biology,
University of Massachusetts

Science, Religion, and Logic

Science and religion are both ways of arriving at beliefs regarding things that are true of the world. What distinguishes one from the other? The most common answer would probably be that religion derives its teaching from some kind of supreme authority, however communicated, which must not be questioned or challenged, whereas science builds its world picture on the available facts as it finds them, without any prior commitment to ideas of how things ought to be.

This is pretty much in accord with our experience of life, to be sure. But I would submit that, rather than being the primary differentiating quality in itself, it comes about as a consequence of something more fundamental. The difference lies in the relationship between the things that are believed and the reasons for believing them. With a religion, the belief structure comes first as an article of faith, and whatever the recognized authority decrees is accepted as being true. Questioning such truth is not permitted. Science begins by finding out what's true as impartially as can be managed, which means accepting what we find whether we like it or not, and the belief structure follows as the best picture that can be made as to the reasons for it all. In this case, questioning a currently held truth is not only permissible but encouraged, and when necessary the belief structure is modified accordingly. Defined in that way, the terms encompass more than the kinds of things that go on in the neighborhood church or a research laboratory, and take on relevance to just about all aspects of human belief and behavior. Thus, not walking under ladders because it brings bad luck (belief in principle, first; action judged as bad, second) is "religious"; doing the same thing to avoid becoming a victim of a dropped hammer or splashed paint (perceiving the world, first; deciding there's a risk, second) is "scientific."

Of course, this isn't to say that scientific thinking never proceeds according to preexisting systems of rules. The above two paths to belief reflect, in a sense, the principles of deductive and inductive logic. Deduction begins with a set of premises that are taken to be incontestably true, and by applying rules of inference derives the consequences that must necessarily follow. The same inference rules can be applied again to the conclusions to generate a second level of conclusions, and the procedure carried on as far as one wants. Geometry is a good example, where a set of initial postulates considered to be self-evident (Euclid's five, for example) is operated on by the rules of logic to produce theorems, which in turn yield further theorems, and so on. A deductive system cannot originate new knowledge. It can only reveal what was implicit in the assumptions. All the shelves of geometry textbooks simply make explicit what was implied by the choice of axioms. Neither can deduction prove anything to be true. It demonstrates merely that certain conclusions necessarily follow from what was assumed. If it's assumed that all crows are black, and given that Charlie is a crow, then we may conclude that Charlie is black.

So deduction takes us from a general rule to a particular truth. Induction is the inverse process, of inferring the general rule from a limited number of particular instances. From observing what's true of part of the world, we try to guess on the basis of intuition and experience—in other words, to "generalize"—what's probably true of all of it. "Every crow I've seen has been black, and the more of them I see, the more confident I get that they're all black." However, inductive conclusions can never be proved to be true in the rigorous way that deductions can be shown to follow from their premises. Proving that all crows are black would require every crow that exists to be checked, and it could never be said with certainty that this had been done. One disconfirming instance, on the other hand—a white crow—would be sufficient to prove the theory false.

This lack of rigor is probably why philosophers and logicians, who seek precision and universally true statements, have never felt as comfortable with induction as they have with deduction, or accorded it the same respectability. But the real world is a messy place of imperfections and approximations, where the art of getting by is more a case of being eighty percent right eighty percent of the time, and doing something now rather than waste any more time. There are no solid guarantees, and the race doesn't always go to the swift nor the battle to the strong—but it's the way to bet.

Deduction operates within the limits set by the assumptions. Induction goes beyond the observations, from the known to the unknown, which is what genuine innovation in the sense of acquiring new knowledge must do. Without it, how could new assertions about the world we live in ever be made? On the other hand, assertions based merely on conjecture or apparent regularities and coincidences—otherwise known as superstition—are of little use without some means of testing them against actuality. This is where deduction comes in—figuring out what consequences should follow in particular instances if our general belief is correct. This enables ways to be devised for determining whether or not they in fact do, which of course forms the basis of the scientific experimental method.

DARWINISM AND THE NEW ORDER

THE TRIUMPH OF THE ENLIGHTENMENT

Scientific method played the central role in bringing about the revolutionary world view ushered in by such names as Roger Bacon, Descartes, and Galileo, which by the time of the seventeenth-century "Age of Enlightenment" had triumphed as the guiding philosophy of Western intellectual culture. No longer was permissible Truth constrained by interpretation of the Scriptures, readings of Aristotle and the classics, or logical premises handed down from the medieval Scholastics. Unencumbered by dogma and preconceptions of how reality had to be, Science was free to follow wherever the evidence led and uncover what it would. Its successes were spectacular indeed. The heavenly bodies that had awed the ancients and been regarded by them as deities were revealed as no different from the matter that makes up the familiar world, moved by the same forces. Mysteries of motion and form, winds and tides, heat and light were equally reduced to interplays of mindless, mechanical processes accessible to reason and predictable by calculation. The divine hand whose workings had once been invoked to explain just about everything that happened was no longer necessary. Neither, it seemed to many, were the traditional forms of authority that presented themselves as interpreters of its will and purpose. The one big exception was that nobody had any better answers to explain the baffling behavior of living things or where they could have come from.

THE ORIGINAL IN "ORIGINS": SOMETHING FOR EVERYONE

A widely held view is that Charles Darwin changed the world by realizing that life could appear and diversify by evolution. This isn't really the way it was, or the reason he caused so much excitement. The notion of life appearing spontaneously through some natural process was not in itself new, being found in such places as the Babylonian creation epic, *Enuma Elish*, and ancient Chinese teachings that insects come from nothing on the leaves of plants. Ideas of progressive development are expressed in the philosophies of Democritus and Epicurus, while Amaximander of Miletus (550 B.C.) held that life had originated by material processes out of sea slime— in some ways anticipating modern notions of a prebiotic soup. Empedocles of Ionia (450 B.C.) proposed a selection-driven process to account for adaptive complexity, in which all kinds of monstrosities were produced from the chance appearance of various combinations of body parts, human and animal, out of which only those exhibiting an inner harmony conducive to life were preserved and went on to multiply. The line continues down through such names as Hume, who speculated that the random juggling of matter must eventually produce ordered forms adapted to their environment; Lamarck, with his comprehensive theory of evolution by the inheritance of characteristics acquired through the striving of the parents during life; to Charles Darwin's grandfather, Erasmus Darwin, who studied the similarities of anatomy between species and speculated on common ancestry as the reason.

The full title of Charles Darwin's celebrated 1859 publication was *The Origin of Species By Means of Natural Selection or the Preservation of Favoured Races in the Struggle for Life*. The case it presents hardly needs to be elaborated here. Essentially, species improve and diverge through the accumulation of selected modifications inherited from common ancestors, from which arise new species and eventually all of the diversity that makes up the living world. The solution that Darwin proposed was simple and elegant, requiring three premises that were practically self-evident: that organisms varied; that these variations were inherited; and that organisms were engaged in a competition for the means of survival, in the course of which the better equipped would be favored. Given variations, and given that they could be inherited, selection and hence adaptive change of the group as a whole was inevitable. And over sufficient time the principle could be extrapolated indefinitely to account for the existence of anything.

None of the ingredients was especially new. But in bringing together his synthesis of ideas that had all been around for some time, Darwin provided for the first time a plausible, intellectually acceptable naturalistic and materialist explanation for the phenomenon of life at a time when many converging interests were desperately seeking one. Enlightenment thinkers, heady with the successes of the physical sciences, relished the opportunity to finish the job by expelling the last vestiges of supernatural agency from their world picture. The various factions of the new political power arising out of commerce and manufacturing found common ground from which to challenge the legitimacy of traditional authority rooted in land and Church, while at the same time, ironically, the nobility, witnessing the specter of militant socialist revolution threatening to sweep Europe, took refuge in the doctrine of slow, imperceptible change as the natural way of things. Meanwhile, the forces of exploitation and imperialism, long straining against the leash of moral restraint, were freed by the reassurance that extermination of the weak by the strong, and domination as the reward for excellence were better for all in the long run.

There was something in it for everyone. Apart from the old order fighting a rearguard action, the doctrine of competitive survival, improvement, and growth was broadly embraced as the driving principle of all progress—the Victorian ideal—and vigorously publicized and promoted. Science replaced the priesthood in cultural authority, no longer merely serving the throne but as supreme interpreter of the laws by which empires and fortunes flourish or vanish. Darwin's biographer, Gertrude Himmelfarb, wrote that the theory could only have originated in laissez-faire England, because "Only there could Darwin have blandly assumed that the basic unit was the individual, the basic instinct self-interest, and the basic activity struggle."[1]

A CULTURAL MONOPOLY

Since then the theory has become established as a primary guiding influence on deciding social values and shaping relationships among individuals and organizations. Its impact extends across all institutions and facets of modern society, including philosophy, economics, politics, science, education, and religion. Its advocates pronounce it to be no longer theory but incontestable fact, attested to by all save the simple-minded or willfully obtuse. According to Daniel Dennett, Director of the Center for Cognitive Studies at Tufts University and a staunch proponent of Darwinism, "To put it bluntly but fairly, anyone today who doubts that the variety of life on this planet was produced by a process of evolution is simply ignorant—inexcusably ignorant."[2]

And from Oxford University's professor of zoology, Richard Dawkins, one of the most vigorous and uncompromising popularizers of Darwinism today: "It is absolutely safe to say that, if you meet somebody who claims not to believe in evolution, that person is ignorant, stupid or insane (or wicked, but I'd rather not consider that)."[3]

Dennett also expresses reservations about the suitability of anyone denying Darwinism to raise children.[4]

Like the majority of people in our culture, I suppose, I grew up accepting the Darwinian picture unquestioningly because the monopoly treatment accorded by the education system and the scientific media offered no alternative, and the authority images that I trusted at the time told me there wasn't one. And nothing much had happened to change that by the time of my own earlier writings. The dispute between Hunt and Danchekker in *Inherit the Stars* [5] isn't over whether or not the human race evolved, but where it happened. And eleven years later I was still militantly defending the theory. [6] By that time, however, my faith in many of the things that "everyone knows" was being eroded as a result of getting to know various people with specialized knowledge in various fields, who, in ways I found persuasive, provided other sides to many public issues, but which the public weren't hearing. Before long I found myself questioning and checking just about everything I thought I knew.

SWEEPING CLAIMS—AND RESERVATIONS

As far as I recall, doubts about evolution as it was taught began with my becoming skeptical that natural selection was capable of doing everything that it was supposed to. There's no question that it happens, to be sure, and that it has its effects. In fact, the process of natural selection was well known to naturalists before Darwin's day, when the dominant belief was in Divine Creation. It was seen, however, as a conservative force, keeping organisms true to type and stable within limits by culling out extremes. Darwin's bold suggestion was to make it the engine of innovation. Observation of the progressive changes brought about by the artificial selection applied in animal and plant breeding led him—a pigeon breeder himself—to propose the same mechanism, taken further, as the means for transforming one species into another, and ultimately to something else entirely.

But on rereading *Origin*, I developed the uneasy feeling of watching fancy flying away from reality, as it is all too apt to do when not held down by the nails of evidence. The changes that were fact and discussed in great detail were all relatively minor, while the major transitions that constituted the force and substance of the theory were entirely speculative. No concrete proof could be shown that even one instance of the vast transformations that the theory claimed to explain had actually happened. And the same pattern holds true of all the texts I consulted that are offered today. Once the fixation on survival to the exclusion of all else sets in, a little imagination can always suggest a way in which any feature being considered "might" have conferred some advantage. Dull coloring provides camouflage to aid predators or protect prey, while bright coloring attracts mates. Longer beaks reach more grubs and insects; shorter beaks crack tougher seeds. Natural selection can explain anything or its opposite. But how do you test if indeed the fittest survive, when by definition whatever survives is the "fittest"?

BY SCAFFOLDING TO THE MOON

All breeders know there are limits beyond which further changes in a characteristic can't be pushed, and fundamental innovations that can never be induced to any degree. Some varieties of sheep are bred to have a small head and small legs, but this can't be carried to the point where they reduce to the scale of a rat. You can breed a larger variety of carnation or a black horse, but not a horse with wings. A given genome can support a certain amount of variation, giving it a range of adaptation to alterations in circumstances—surely to be expected for an organism to be at all viable in changeable environments. But no amount of selecting and crossing horses will produce wings if the genes for growing them aren't there. As Darwin himself had found with pigeons, when extremes are crossed at their limit, they either become nonviable or revert abruptly to the original stock.

Horizontal variations within a type are familiar and uncontroversial. But what the theory proposes as occurring, and to account for, are vertical transitions from one type to another and hence the emergence of completely new forms. It's usual in the literature for these two distinct types of change to be referred to respectively as "microevolution" and "macroevolution." I'm not happy with these terms, however. They suggest simply different degrees of the same thing, which is precisely the point that's at issue. So I'm going to call them "adaptive variation" and "evolutionary transition," which as a shorthand we can reduce to "adaption" and "evolution." What Darwin's theory boils down to is the claim that given enough time, adaptive variations can add up to become evolutionary transitions in all directions to an unlimited degree. In the first edition of *Origin* (later removed) he said, "I can see no difficulty in a race of bears being rendered, by natural selection, more and more aquatic in their habits, with larger and larger mouths, till a creature was produced as monstrous as a whale." But, unsubstantiated, this is the same as seeing no difficulty in adding to scaffolding indefinitely as a way to get to the Moon, or changing a Chevrolet a part at a time as a workable way of producing a Boeing 747. Regarding the generally held contention that there are limits to natural variation, he wrote, "I am unable to discover a single fact on which this belief is grounded."[7] But there wasn't a single fact to support the belief that variation could be taken beyond what had been achieved, either, and surely it was on this side that the burden of proof lay.

And the same remains true to this day. The assurance that adaptations add up to evolution, presented in textbooks as established scientific fact and belligerently insisted on as a truth that can be disputed only at the peril of becoming a confessed imbecile or a sociopath, is founded on faith. For decades researchers have been selecting and subjecting hundreds of successive generations of fruit flies to X rays and other factors in attempts to induce faster rates of mutation, the raw material that natural selection is said to work on, and hence accelerate the process to observable dimensions. They have produced fruit flies with varying numbers of bristles on their abdomens, different shades of eye colors, no eyes at all, and grotesque variations with legs growing out of their heads instead of antennas. But the results always remain fruit flies. Nothing comes out of it suggestive of a house fly, say, or a mosquito. If selection from variations were really capable of producing such astounding transformations as a bacterium to a fish or a reptile to a bird, even in the immense spans of time that the theory postulates, then these experiments should have revealed some hint of it.

ROCKS OF AGES—THE FOSSIL RECORD

Very well, if neither the undisputed variations that are observed today, nor laboratory attempts to extend and accelerate them provide support for the kind of plasticity that evolution requires, what evidence can we find that it nevertheless happened in the past? There is only one place to look for solid testimony to what actually happened, as opposed to all the theorizing and excursions of imagination: the fossil record. Even if the origin of life was a one-time, nonrepeatable occurrence, the manner in which it took place should still yield characteristic patterns that can be predicted and tested.

SLOW-MOTION MIRACLES—THE DOCTRINE OF GRADUALISM

Transforming a fish into a giraffe or a dinosaur into an eagle involves a lot more than simply switching a piece at a time as can be done with Lego block constructions. Whole systems of parts have to all work together. The acquisition of wolf-size teeth doesn't do much for the improvement of a predator if it still has rat-size jaws to fit them in. But bigger jaws are no good without stronger muscles to close them and a bigger head to anchor the muscles. Stronger muscles need a larger blood supply, which needs a heavier-duty circulatory system, which in turn requires upgrades in the respiratory department, and so it goes. For all these to all come about together in just the right amounts—like randomly changing the parts of a refrigerator and ending up with a washing machine—would be tantamount to miraculous, which was precisely what the whole theory was intended to get away from.

Darwin's answer was to adopt for biology the principle of "gradualism" that his slightly older contemporary, the Scottish lawyer-turned-geologist, Sir Charles Lyell, was arguing as the guiding paradigm of geology. Prior to the mid nineteenth century, natural philosophers—as investigators of such things were called before the word "scientist" came into use—had never doubted, from the evidence they found in abundance everywhere of massive and violent animal extinctions, oceanic flooding over vast areas, and staggering tectonic upheavals and volcanic events, that the Earth had periodically undergone immense cataclysms of destruction, after which it was repopulated with radically new kinds of organisms. This school was known as "catastrophism," its leading advocate being the French biologist Georges Cuvier, "the father of paleontology." Such notions carried too much suggestion of Divine Creation and intervention with the affairs of the world, however, so Lyell dismissed the catastrophist evidence as local anomalies and proposed that the slow, purely natural processes that are seen taking place today, working for long enough at the same rates, could account for the broad picture of the Earth as we find it.

This was exactly what Darwin's theory needed. Following the same principles, the changes in living organisms would take place imperceptibly slowly over huge spans of time, enabling all the parts to adapt and accommodate to each other smoothly and gradually. "As natural selection acts solely by accumulating slight, successive, favourable variations, it can produce no great or sudden modifications; it can act only by short and slow steps." [8] Hence, enormous numbers of steps are needed to get from things like invertebrates protected by external shells to vertebrates with all their hard parts inside, or from a bear- or cowlike quadruped to a whale. It follows that the intermediates marking the progress over the millions of years leading up to the present should vastly outnumber the final forms seen today, and have left evidence of their passing accordingly. This too was acknowledged freely throughout *Origin* and in fact provided one of the theory's strongest predictions. For example:

"[A]ll living species have been connected with the parent-species of each genus, by differences not greater than we see between the natural and domestic varieties of the same species at the present day; and these parent species, now generally extinct, have in turn been similarly connected with more ancient forms; and so on backwards, always converging to the common ancestor of every great class. So that the number of intermediate and transitional links, between all living and extinct species, must have been inconceivably great. But assuredly, if this theory be true, such have lived upon the earth." [9]

LIFE'S UPSIDE-DOWN TREE: THE FIRST FAILED PREDICTION

The theory predicted not merely that transitional forms would be found, but implied that the complete record would consist *mainly* of transitionals; what we think of as fixed species would turn out to be just arbitrary—way stations in a process of continual change. Hence, what we should find is a treelike branching structure following the lines of descent from a comparatively few ancient ancestors of the major groups, radiating outward from a well-represented trunk and limb formation laid down through the bulk of geological time as new orders and classes appear, to a profusion of twigs showing the diversity reached in the most recent times. In fact, this describes exactly the depictions of the "Tree of Life" elaborately developed and embellished in Victorian treatises on the wondrous new theory and familiar to museum visitors and anyone conversant with textbooks in use up to quite recent times.

But such depictions figure less prominently in the books that are produced today—or more commonly are omitted altogether. The reason is that the story actually told by the fossils in the rocks is the complete opposite. The Victorians' inspiration must have stemmed mainly from enthusiasm and conviction once they *knew* what the answer had to be. Species, and all the successively higher groups composed of species—genus, family, order, class, phylum—appear abruptly, fully differentiated and specialized, in sudden epochs of innovation just as the catastrophists had always said,

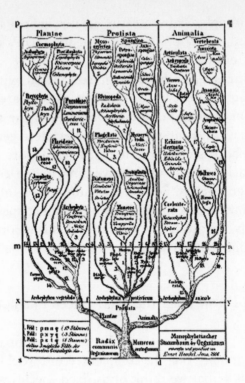

The "Tree of Life" as envisioned in a Victorian textbook.

without any intermediates leading up to them or linking them together. The most remarkable thing about them is their stability thereafter—they remain looking pretty much the same all the way down to the present day, or else they become extinct. Furthermore, the patterns seen after the appearance of a new population are not of divergence from a few ancestral types, but once again the opposite of what such a theory predicted. Diversity was most pronounced early on, becoming less, not greater with time as selection operated in the way previously maintained, weeding out the less suited. So compared to what we would expect to find, the tree is nonexistent where it should be in the greatest evidence, and what does exist is upside down.

Darwin and his supporters were well aware of this problem from the ample records compiled by their predecessors. In fact, the most formidable opponents of the theory were not clergymen but fossil experts. Even Lyell had difficulty in accepting his own ideas of gradualism applied to biology, familiar as he was with the hitherto undisputed catastrophist interpretation. But ideological fervor carried the day, and the generally agreed answer was that the fossil record as revealed at the time was incomplete. Now that the fossil collectors knew what to look for, nobody had any doubt that the required confirming evidence would quickly follow in plenitude. In other words, the view being promoted even then was a *defense against* the evidence that existed, driven by prior conviction that the real facts had to be other than what they seemed.

Well, the jury is now in, and the short answer is that the picture after a century and a half of assiduous searching is, if anything, worse now than it was then. Various ad hoc reasons and speculations have been put forward as to why, of course. These include the theory that most of the history of life consists of long periods of stasis during which change was too slow to be discernible, separated by bursts of change that happened too quickly to have left anything in the way of traces ("punctuated equilibrium"); that the soft parts that weren't preserved did the evolving while the hard parts stayed the

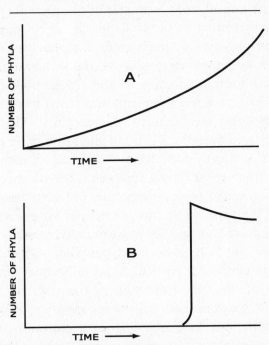

Increase in the number of animal phyla with time as predicted from Darwin's theory, A, compared to the pattern shown by the fossil evidence, B. Almost all types appear abruptly at the time of the "Cambrian Explosion," the number declining thereafter due to extinctions.

same ("mosaic evolution"); that fossilization is too rare an occurrence to leave a reliable record; and a host of others. But the fact remains that if evolution means the gradual transformation of one kind of organism into another, the outstanding feature of the fossil record is its absence of evidence for evolution. Elaborate gymnastics to explain away failed predictions are almost always a sign of a theory in trouble. Luther Sunderland describes this as a carefully guarded "trade secret" of evolutionary theorists and refers to it as "Darwin's Enigma" in his book of the same name, which reports interviews conducted during the course of a year with officials of five natural history museums containing some of the largest fossil collections in the world. [10]

The plea of incompleteness of the fossil record is no longer tenable. Exhaustive exploration of the strata of all continents and across the ocean bottoms has uncovered formations containing hundreds of billions of fossils. The world's museums are filled with over 100 million fossils of 250,000 species. Their adequacy as a record may be judged from estimates of the percentage of known, living forms that are also found as fossils. They suggest that the story that gets preserved is much more complete than many people think. Of the 43 living orders of terrestrial vertebrates, 42, or over 97 percent are found as fossils. Of the 329 families of terrestrial vertebrates the figure is 79 percent, and when birds (which tend to fossilize poorly) are excluded, 87 percent.[11] What the record shows is clustered variations around the same basic designs over and over again, already complex and specialized, with no lines of improvement before or links in between. Forms once thought to have been descended from others turn out have been already in existence at the time of the ancestors that supposedly gave rise to them. On average, a species persists fundamentally unchanged for over a million years before disappearing—which again happens largely in periodic mass extinctions rather than by the gradual replacement of the ancestral stock in the way that gradualism requires. This makes nonsense of the proposition we're given that the bat and the whale evolved from a common mammalian ancestor in a little over 10 million years, which would allow at the most ten to fifteen "chronospecies" (a segment of the fossil record judged to have changed so little as to have remained a single species) aligned end to end to effect the transitions.[12]

FLIGHTS OF FANCY: THE BIRDS CONTROVERSY

It goes without saying that the failure to find connecting lines and transitional forms hasn't been from want of trying. The effort has been sustained and intensive. Anything even remotely suggesting a candidate receives wide acclaim and publicity. One of the most well-known examples is *Archaeopteryx*, a mainly birdlike creature with fully developed feathers and a wishbone, but also a number of skeletal features such as toothed jaws, claws on its wings, and a bony, lizardlike tail that at first suggest kinship with a small dinosaur called *Compsognathus* and prompted T. H. Huxley to propose originally that birds were descended from dinosaurs. Presented to the world in 1861, two years after the publication of *Origin*, in Upper Jurassic limestones in Bavaria conventionally dated at 150 million years, its discovery couldn't have been better timed to encourage the acceptance of Darwinism and discredit skeptics. Harvard's Ernst Mayr, who has been referred to as the "Dean of Evolution," declared it to be "the almost perfect link between reptiles and birds," while a paleontologist is quoted as calling it a "holy relic . . . The First Bird."[13]

Yet the consensus among paleontologists seems to be that there are too many basic structural differences for modern birds to be descended from *Archaeopteryx*. At best it could be an early member of a totally extinct group of birds. On the other hand, there is far from a consensus as to what might have been *its* ancestors. The two evolutionary theories as to how flight might have originated are "trees down," according to which it all began with exaggerated leaps leading to parachuting and gliding by four-legged climbers; and "ground up," where wings developed from the insect-catching forelimbs of two-legged runners and jumpers. Four-legged reptiles appear in the fossil record well before *Archaeopteryx* and thus qualify as possible ancestors by the generally accepted chronology, while the two-legged types with the features that would more be expected of a line leading to birds don't show up until much later.

This might make the trees-down theory seem more plausible at first sight, but it doesn't impress followers of the relatively new school of biological classification known as "cladistics," where physical similarities and the inferred branchings from common ancestors are all that matters in deciding what gets grouped with what. (Note that this makes the fact of evolution an axiom.) Where the inferred ancestral relationships conflict with fossil sequences, the sequences are deemed to be misleading and are reinterpreted accordingly. Hence, by this scheme, the animals with the right features to be best candidates as ancestors to *Archaeopteryx* are birdlike dinosaurs that lived in the Cretaceous, tens of millions of years after *Archaeopteryx* became extinct. To the obvious objection that something can't be older than its ancestor, the cladists respond that the ancestral forms must have existed sooner than the traces that have been found so far, thus reintroducing the incompleteness-of-the-fossil-record argument but on a scale never suggested even in Darwin's day. The opponents counter that in no way could the record be that incomplete, and so the dispute continues. In reality, therefore, the subject abounds with a lot more contention than pronouncements of almost-perfection and holy relics would lead the outside world to believe.

The peculiar mix of features found in *Archaeopteryx* is not particularly conclusive of anything in itself. In the embryonic stage some living birds have more tail vertebrae than *Archaeopteryx*, which later fuse. One authority states that the only basic difference from the tail arrangement of modern swans is that the caudal vertebrae are greatly elongated, but that doesn't make a reptile.[14] There are birds today such as the Venezuelan hoatzin, the South African touraco, and the ostrich that have claws. *Archaeopteryx* had teeth, whereas modern birds don't, but many ancient birds did. Today, some fish have teeth while others don't, some amphibians have teeth and others don't, and some mammals have teeth but others don't. It's not a convincing mark of reptilian ancestry. I doubt if many humans would accept that the possession of teeth is a throwback to a primitive, reptilian trait.

So how solid, really, is the case for *Archaeopteryx* being unimpeachable proof of reptile-to-bird transition, as opposed to a peculiar mixture of features from different classes that happened upon a fortunate combination that endured in the way of the duck-billed platypus, but which isn't a transition toward anything in the Darwinian sense (unless remains unearthed a million years from now are interpreted as showing that mammals evolved from ducks)? Perhaps the fairest word comes from Berkeley law professor Phillip Johnson, no champion of Darwinism, who agrees that regardless of the details, the *Archaeopteryx* specimens could still provide important clues as to how birds evolved. "[W]e therefore have a possible bird ancestor rather than a certain one," he grants, " . . . on the whole, a point for the Darwinists." [15] But he then goes on to comment, "Persons who come to the fossil evidence as convinced Darwinists will see a stunning confirmation, but skeptics will see only a lonely exception to a consistent pattern of fossil disconfirmation." It was Darwin himself who prophesied that incontestable examples would be "inconceivably great."

LINES OF HORSES

The other example that everyone will be familiar with from museum displays and textbooks is the famous "horse series," showing with what appears to be incontrovertible clarity the 65-million-year progression from a fox-sized ungulate of the lower Eocene to the modern-day horse. The increase in size is accompanied by the steady reduction of the foreleg toes from four to one, and the development of relatively plain leaf-browsing teeth into high-crowned grazing ones. Again, this turns out to be a topic on which the story that scientists affirm when closing ranks before the media and the public can be very different from that admitted off the record or behind closed doors.[16]

The first form of the series originated from the bone collections of Yale professor of paleontology O. C. Marsh and his rival Edward Cope, and was arranged by the director of the American Museum of Natural History (AMNH), Henry Fairfield Osborn, in 1874. It contained just four members, beginning with the four-toed *Eohippus*, or "dawn horse," and passing through a couple of three-toed specimens to the single-toed *Equus* of modern times, but that was sufficient for Marsh to declare that "the line of descent appears to have been direct and the remains now known supply every important form." More specimens were worked into the system and the lineage filled in to culminate in a display put on by the AMNH in 1905 that was widely photographed and reproduced to find its way as a standard inclusion in textbooks for generations afterward. By that time it was already becoming apparent to professionals that the real picture was more complicated and far from conclusive. But it was one of those things that once rooted, takes on a life of its own.

In the first place, given the wide diversity of life and the ubiquity of the phenomenon known as convergence—which evolutionists interpret as the arrival of closely similar forms from widely separated ancestral lines, for example sharks and porpoises, or marsupial and placental dogs—inferring closeness of relationships purely from skeletal remains is by no means a foolproof business. The coelancanth, an early lobe-finned fish, was once confidently thought to have been a direct ancestor of the types postulated to have invaded the land and given rise to the amphibians. And then the surprise discovery of living specimens in the 1930s and thereafter showed from examination of previously unavailable soft parts that the assumptions based on the fossil evidence alone had been incorrect, and the conclusion was no longer tenable. Hence, if the fossil record is to provide evidence for evolutionary continuity as opposed to the great divisions of nature seen by Cuvier, it is not sufficient that two groups merely resemble each other in their skeletal forms. Proof that it had actually happened would require at least to show one unambiguous continuum of transitional species possessing an incontestable progression of graduations from one type to another. Such a stipulation does, of course, invite the retort that every filling of a gap creates two more gaps, and no continuity could ever be demonstrated that would be capable of pleasing a sufficiently pedantic critic. But a Zeno-like reductio ad absurdum isn't necessary for an acceptance of the reality of continuity beyond reasonable doubt to the satisfaction of common sense and experience. As an analogy, suppose that the real numbers were scattered over the surface of the planet, and a survey of them was conducted to test the theory that they formed a continuum of infinitesimally small graduations. If the search turned up repeated instances of the same integers in great amounts but never a fraction, our knowledge of probabilities would soon cast growing suspicion that the theory was false and no intermediates between the integers existed. A more recent study of the claim of evolutionary transition of types, as opposed to the uncontroversial fact of variation within types stated: "The known fossil record fails to document a single example of phyletic (gradual) evolution accomplishing a major morphologic transition and hence offers no evidence that the gradualistic school can be valid." [17]

Later finds and comparisons quickly replaced the original impressive linear progression into a tangled bushlike structure of branches from assumed common ancestors, most of which led to extinction. The validity of assigning the root genus, *Eohippus*, to the horse series at all had been challenged from the beginning. It looks nothing like a horse but was the name given to the North American animal forming the first of Osborn's original sequence. Subsequently, it was judged to be identical to a European genus already discovered by the British anatomist and paleontologist, Robert Owen, and named *Hyracotherium* on account of its similarities in morphology and habitat to the *Hyrax* running around alive and well in the African bush today, still equipped with four fore-toes and three hind ones, and more closely related to tapirs and rhinoceroses than anything horselike. Since *Hyracotherium* predated the North American discovery, then by the normally observed custom *Eohippus* is not the valid name. But the suggestiveness has kept it entrenched in conventional horse-series lore. Noteworthy, however, is that *Hyracotherium* is no longer included in the display at Chicago's Museum of Natural History.

In the profusion of side branches, the signs of relentless progress so aptly discerned by Victorians disappear in contradictions. In some lines, size increases only to reduce again. Even with living horses, the range in size from the tiny American miniature ponies to the huge English shires and Belgian warhorse breeds is as great as that collected from the fossil record. *Hyracotherium* has 18 pairs of ribs, the next creature shown after it has 19, then there is a jump to 15, and finally a reversion back to 18 with *Equus*. Nowhere in the world are fossils of the full series as constructed found in successive strata. The series charted in school books comes mainly from the New World but includes Old World specimens where the eye of those doing the arranging considered it justified. In places where successive examples do occur together, such as the John Day formation in Oregon, both the three-toed and one-toed varieties that remain if the doubtful *Hyracotherium* is ignored are found at the same geological levels. And even more remarkable on the question of toes, of which so much is made when presenting the conventional story, is that the corresponding succession of ungulates in South America again shows distinctive groupings of full three-toed, three-toed with reduced lateral toes, and single-toed varieties, but the trend is in the reverse direction, i.e., from older single-toed to later three-toed. Presumably this was brought about by the same forces of natural selection that produced precisely the opposite in North America.

KEEPING NATURALISM PURE: ORTHOGENESIS WARS

The perfection and complexity seen in the adaptations of living things are so striking that even among the evolutionists in Darwin's day there was a strong, if not predominant belief that the process had to be directed either by supernatural guidance or the imperative of some yet-to-be identified force within the organisms themselves. (After all, if the result of evolution was to cultivate superiority and excellence, who could doubt that the ultimate goal at the end of it all was to produce eminent Victorians?)

The view that some inner force was driving the evolutionary processes toward preordained goals was known as "orthogenesis" and became popular among paleontologists because of trends in the fossil record that it seemed to explain—the horse series being one of the most notable. This didn't sit well with the commitment to materialism a priori that dominated evolutionary philosophy, however, since to many it smacked of an underlying supernatural guidance one step removed from outright creationism. To provide a purely materialist source of innovation, Darwin maintained that some random agent of variation had to exist, even though at the time he had no idea what it was. A source of variety of that kind would be expected to show a radiating pattern of trial-and-error variants with most attempts failing and dying out, rather than the linear progression of an inner directive that knew where it was going. Hence, in an ironic kind of way, it has been the efforts of the Darwinians, particularly since the 1950s, that have contributed most to replacing the old linear picture of the horse series with the tree structure in their campaign to refute notions of orthogenesis.

But even if such a tree were to be reconstructed with surety, it wouldn't prove anything one way or the other; the introduction of an element of randomness is by no means inconsistent with a process's being generally directed. The real point is that the pattern was constructed to promote acceptance of a preexisting ideology, rather than from empirical evidence. Darwin's stated desire was to place science on a foundation of materialistic philosophy; in other words, the first commitment was to the battle of ideas. Richard Dawkins, in the opening of his book *The Blind Watchmaker*, defines biology as "the study of complicated things that give the appearance of having been designed for a purpose."[18] The possibility that the suggestion of design might be anything more, and that appearances might actually mean what they say is excluded as the starting premise: "I want to persuade the reader, not just that the Darwinian worldview *happens* to be true, but that it is the only known theory that *could*, in principle, solve the mystery of our existence." The claim of a truth that must be so "in principle" denotes argument based on a philosophical assumption. This is not science, which builds its arguments from facts. The necessary conclusions are imposed on the evidence, not inferred from it.

Left to themselves, the facts tell yet again the ubiquitous story of an initial variety of forms leading to variations about a diminishing number of lines that either disappear or persist to the present time looking much the same as they always did. And at the end of it all, even the changes that are claimed to be demonstrated through the succession are really quite trivial adjustments when seen against the background of equine architecture as a whole. Yet we are told that they took sixty-five million years to accomplish. If this is so, then what room is there for the vastly more complex transitions between forms utterly unlike one another, of which the evidence shows not a hint?

ANYTHING, EVERYTHING, AND ITS OPPOSITE: NATURAL SELECTION

DISSENT IN THE RANKS: LOGICAL FALLACY AND TAUTOLOGY

Norman Macbeth's concise yet lucid survey of the subject, *Darwin Retried*, began when he used some idle time while convalescing in Switzerland to read a volume of essays commemorating the 1959 centenary of *Origin*'s publication. His conclusion after the several years of further research that his first impressions prompted was that "in brief, classical Darwinism is no longer considered valid by qualified biologists." [19] They just weren't telling the public. One of the most startling things Macbeth discovered was that while natural selection figured almost as a required credo on all the lists of factors cited in the experts' writings as contributing to evolution, the importance they assigned to it ranged from its being "*the* only effective agency," according to Julian Huxley, to virtually irrelevant in the opinions of others—even though it was just this that formed the substantive part of the title to Darwin's book.

The reason for this backing off from what started out as the hallmark of the theory is that while mechanisms showing the effectiveness of natural selection can be readily constructed in imaginative speculations, any actual example of the process in action in the real world proceeds invisibly. Early Darwinians were carried away into concluding that every aspect of an animal down to the number of its spots or bristles was shaped by natural selection and thus was "adaptive," i.e., relevant to survival. Purporting to explain how the selective value of a particular, possibly trivial characteristic arose became something of a game among the enthusiasts, leading to such wild flights of just-so-story fancy and absurd reasoning that the more serious-minded gave up trying to account for the specifics, which were observable, while retaining undiminished faith in the principle, which wasn't.

Put another way, it was claimed that natural selection worked because the results said to follow from it were evident all around. But this is the logical fallacy of saying that because A implies B, B must imply A. If it rained this morning, the grass will necessarily be wet. But finding the grass wet doesn't mean necessarily that it rained. The sprinklers may have been on; the kids could have been playing with the hose; a passing UFO might have vented a coolant tank, and so on. Confirming the deductions from a theory only lends support to the theory when they can be shown to follow from it uniquely, as opposed to being equally consistent with rival theories. If only naturalistic explanations are allowed by the ground rules, then that condition is satisfied automatically since no explanation other than natural selection, even with its problems, has been offered that comes even close to being plausible. But being awarded the prize through default after all other contenders have been disqualified is hardly an impressive performance.

The Darwinists' reaction to this entanglement was to move away from the original ideas of struggle and survival, and redefine evolution in terms of visible consequences, namely that animals with certain features did well and increased in numbers, others declined, while yet others again seemed to stay the same. Although perpetuating the same shaky logic, this had the benefit of making the theory synonymous with facts that couldn't be denied, without the burden of explaining exactly how and why they came about, which had been the original intention. In the general retreat from what Darwinism used to mean, "evolution" became a matter of the mathematics of gene flows and population dynamics, in a word *differential reproduction*, in the course of which "natural selection" takes on the broader meaning of being simply anything that brings it about. [20] So evolution is defined as change brought about by natural selection, where natural selection, through a massive circularity, arrives back at being anything that produces change. What Macbeth finds staggering in this is the ease with which the leaders of the field not only accept such tautologies blithely as inherent in their belief system, but are unable to see anything improper in tautological reasoning or the meaninglessness of any conclusions drawn from it. [21]

MOTH MYTHS. THE CROWNING PROOF?

A consequence of such illogic is that simple facts which practically define themselves become celebrated as profound revelations of great explanatory power. Take as an example the case of the British peppered moth, cited in virtually all the textbooks as a perfect demonstration of "industrial melanism" and praised excitedly as living proof of evolution in action before our eyes. In summary, the standard version of the story describes a species of moth found in the British Midlands that were predominantly light-colored in earlier times but underwent a population shift in which a dark strain became dominant when the industrial revolution arrived and tree trunks in the moths' habitat were darkened by smoke and air pollution. Then, when cleaner air resulted from the changes and legislation in modern times and the trees lightened again, the moth population reverted to its previous balance. The explanation given is that the moths depend on their coloring as camouflage to protect them from predatory birds. When the tree barks were light, the lighter-colored variety of moths was favored, with darker barks the darker moths did better, and the changing conditions were faithfully mirrored in the population statistics. Indeed, all exactly in keeping with the expectations of "evolution" as now understood.

The reality, however, is apparently more complicated. Research has shown that in at least some localities the darkening of the moths *precedes* that of the tree barks, suggesting that some common factor—maybe a chemical change in the air—affects both of them. Further, it turns out that the moths don't normally rest on the trunks in daylight in the way textbook pictures show, and in conditions not artificially contrived for experiments, birds in daylight are not a major influence. The pictures were faked by gluing dead moths to tree trunks. [22]

But even if the facts were as presented, what would it all add up to, really? Light moths do better against a light background, whereas dark moths do better against a dark background. This is the Earth-shattering outcome after a century and a half of intensive work by some of the best-known names in science developing a theory that changed the world? Both light strains and dark strains of moth were already present from the beginning. Nothing changed or mutated; nothing genetically new came into existence. If we're told that of a hundred soldiers sent into a jungle wearing jungle camouflage garb along with a hundred in arctic whites, more of the former were still around a week later, are we supposed to conclude that one kind "evolved" into another, or that anything happened that wouldn't have been obvious to common sense?

If that's what we're told "evolution" in the now-accepted use of the word means, then so be it. But now we'll need a different word to explain how moths came into existence in the first place. Yet along with such examples as *Archaeopteryx* and the horse series, the peppered moth is offered as proof that sets the theory on such incontestable grounds that to question it is evidence of being dim-witted or malicious. While other sciences have progressed from sailing clippers to spaceships, Morse telegraph to satellite nets, steam engines to nuclear reactors, these constitute the best evidence that can be mustered after a hundred and fifty years.

THE ORIGIN OF ORIGINALITY?
GENETICS AND MUTATION

RECOMBINATION: ANSWERING THE WRONG QUESTION

Natural selection in itself originates nothing. It can only select out of what is already present to be selected from. In order to be the driving engine of evolution, it needs a source of new raw material to be tested and either preserved for further experimentation or rejected. Much is written about genetic transposition and recombination—the insertion, deletion, and duplication of the genes carried by the chromosomes, and their rearrangement into new permutations. And it is true that an enormous variety of altered programs for directing the form that an organism will assume can be produced in this way—far greater than could ever be realized in an actual population. Lee Spetner, a former MIT physicist and information scientist who has studied the mathematics of evolution for forty years, calculates that the number of possible variations that could occur in a typical mammalian genome to be in the order of one followed by 24 million zeros. [23] (Yes, I did get that right. Not 24 orders of magnitude; 24 *million* orders of magnitude.) Of this, the fraction that could be stored in a population of a million, a billion, ten billion, or a hundred billion individuals—it really doesn't make much difference—is so close to zero as to be negligible. And indeed this is a huge source of potential variety. But the attention it gets is misleading, since it's the same sleight of hand we saw before of presenting lots of discussion and examples of adaptive variations that nobody doubts, and assuming evolutionary transitions to be just more of the same. The part that's assumed is precisely what the exercise is supposed to be proving. For all that's going on, despite the stupendous number of combinations it can come up with, is reshuffling the genes that already make up the genome of the species in question. Recombination is a very real and abundant phenomenon, taking place through sexual mixing whenever a mating occurs and well able to account for the variation that we see—it's theoretically possible for two siblings to be formed from exactly complementary gametes (the half set of parental genes carried by a sperm or egg cell) from each parent, and thus to not share one gene in common. But it can't work beyond the species level, where inconceivably greater numbers of transitions are supposed to have happened, that we don't see.

RANDOM MUTATION: FINALLY, THE KEY TO NEW THINGS UNDER THE SUN

The source of original variation that Darwin sought was eventually identified as the mechanism of genetic mutation deduced from Mendel's studies of heredity, which was incorporated into

Darwinian theory in what became known in the 1930s as the neo-Darwinian synthesis. By the 1940s the nucleic acid DNA was known to be the carrier of hereditary information, and in 1953 James Watson and Francis Crick determined the molecule's double-helix structure with its "cross-rungs" of nucleotide base pairs that carry the genetic program. This program is capable of being misread or altered, leading the molecular biologist Jacques Monod, director of the Pasteur Institute, to declare in 1970 that "the mechanism of Darwinism is at last securely founded." [24] Let's take a deeper look, then, at what was securely founded.

AN AUTOMATED MANUFACTURING CITY

Sequences of DNA base pairs—complementary arrangements of atoms that bridge the gap between the molecule's two "backbones" like the steps of a helical staircase—encode the instructions that direct the cellular protein-manufacturing machinery to produce the structural materials for building the organism's tissues, as well as molecules like hormones and enzymes to regulate its functioning. The operations that take place in every cell of the body are stupefyingly complex, embodying such concepts as realtime feed-back control, centralized databanks, error-checking and correcting, redundancy coding, distributed processing, remote sensing, pre-fabrication and modular assembly, and backup systems that are found in our most advanced automated factories. Michael Denton describes it as a miniature city:

> To grasp the reality of life as it has been revealed by molecular biology, we must magnify a cell a thousand million times until it is twenty kilometers in diameter and resembles a giant airship large enough to cover a great city like London or New York. What we would then see would be an object of unparalleled complexity and adaptive design. On the surface of the cell we would see millions of openings, like the port holes of a vast space ship, opening and closing to allow a continual stream of materials to flow in and out. If we were to enter one of these openings we would find ourselves in a world of supreme technology and bewildering complexity. We would see endless highly organized corridors and

conduits branching in every direction away from the perimeter of the cell, some leading to the central memory bank in the nucleus and others to assembly plants and processing units. The nucleus itself would be a vast spherical chamber more than a kilometer in diameter, resembling a geodesic dome inside of which we would see, all neatly stacked together in ordered arrays, the miles of coiled chains of the DNA molecules. . . . We would see all around us, in every direction we looked, all sorts of robot-like machines. We would notice that the simplest of the functional components of the cell, the protein molecules, were astonishingly complex pieces of molecular machinery, each one consisting of about three thousand atoms arranged in highly organized 3-D spatial conformation. We would wonder even more as we watched the strangely purposeful activities of these weird molecular machines, particularly when we realized that, despite all our accumulated knowledge of physics and chemistry, the task of designing one such molecular machine—that is one single functional protein molecule—would be completely beyond our capacity at present and will probably not be achieved until at least the beginning of the next century." [25]

And this whole vast, mind-boggling operation can replicate itself in its entirety in a matter of hours. When this happens through the cell dividing into two daughter cells, the double-stranded DNA control tapes come apart like a zipper, each half forming the template for constructing a complete copy of the original DNA molecule for each of the newly forming cells. Although the copying process is monitored by error-detection mechanisms that surpass anything so far achieved in our electronic data processing, copying errors do occasionally happen. Also, errors can happen spontaneously or be induced in existing DNA by such agents as mutagenic chemicals and ionizing radiation. Once again the mechanism for repairing this kind of damage is phenomenally efficient—if it were not, such being the ravages of the natural environment, no fetus would ever remain viable long enough to be born—but at the end of the day, some errors creep through to become part of the genome written into the DNA. If the cell that an error occurs in happens to be a germ cell (sperm or egg), the error will be heritable and appear in all the cells of the offspring it's passed on to. About 10 percent of human DNA actually codes for structural and regulatory proteins; the function of the rest is not known. If the inherited copying error is contained in that 10 percent, it could (the code is highly redundant; for example, several code elements frequently specify the same protein, so that mutating one into another doesn't alter anything) be expressed as some physical or behavioral change.

THE BLIND GUNMAN: A LONG, HARD LOOK AT THE ODDS

Such "point mutations" of DNA are the sole source of innovation that the neo-Darwinian theory permits to account for all life's diversity. The theory posits the accumulation of tiny, insensible fluctuations to bring about all major change, since large variations would cause too much dislocation to be viable. They must occur frequently enough for evolution to have taken place in the time available; but if they occur too frequently no two generations would be the same, and no "species" as the basis of reproducing populations could exist. The key issue, therefore, is the *rate* at which the mutations that the theory rests on take place. More specifically, the rate of favorable mutations conferring some adaptive benefit, since harmful ones obviously contribute nothing as far as progress toward something better is concerned.

And here things run into trouble straight away, for beneficial mutations practically never happen. Let's take some of the well-known mutations that have been cataloged in studies of genetic diseases as examples.

All body cells need a certain amount of cholesterol for their membranes. It is supplied in packages of cholesterol and certain fats manufactured by the liver and circulated via the cardiovascular system. Too much of it in circulation, however, results in degeneration and narrowing of the large and medium-size arteries. Cholesterol supply is regulated by receptor proteins embedded in the membrane wall that admit the packages into the cell and send signals back to the liver when more is needed. The gene that controls the assembly of this receptor protein from 772 amino acids is on chromosome 19 and consists of about 45,000 base pairs. Over 350 mutations of it have been described in the literature. Every one of them is deleterious, producing some form of disease, frequently fatal. Not one is beneficial.

Another example is the genetic disease cystic fibrosis that causes damage to the lungs, digestive system, and in males the sperm tract. Again this traces to mutations of a gene coding for a transmembrane protein, this time consisting of 1,480 amino acids and regulating chloride ion transport into the cell. The controlling gene, called CFTR, has 250,000 base pairs to carry its instructions, of which over 200 mutations are at present known, producing conditions that range from severe lung infections leading to early deaths among children, to lesser diseases such as chronic pancreatitis and male infertility. No beneficial results have ever been observed.

"The Blind Gunman" would be a better description of this state of affairs. And it's what experience would lead us to expect. These programs are more complex than anything running in the PC that I'm using to write this, and improving them through mutation would be about as likely as getting a better word processor by randomly changing the bits that make up the instructions of this one.

The mutation rates per nucleotide that Spetner gives from experimental observations are between 0.1 and 10 per billion transcriptions for bacteria and 0.01 to 1 per billion for other organisms, giving a geometric mean of 1 per billion. [26] He quotes G. Ledyard Stebbins, one of the architects of the neo-Darwinian theory, as estimating 500 successive steps, each step representing a beneficial change, to change one species into another. To compute the probability of producing a new species, the next item required would be the fraction of mutations that are beneficial. However, the only answer here is that nobody knows for sure that they occur at all, because none has ever been observed. The guesses found here and there in the evolutionary literature turn out to be just that—postulated as a hypothetical necessity for the theory to stand. (Objection: What about bacteria mutating to antibiotic-resistant strains? A well-documented fact. Answer: It can't be considered meaningful in any evolutionary sense. We'll see why later.)

But let's follow Spetner and take it that a potentially beneficial mutation is available at each of the 500 steps, and that it spreads into the population. The first is a pretty strong assumption to make, and there's no evidence for it. The second implies multiple cases of the mutation appearing at each step, since a single occurrence is far more likely to be swamped by the gene pool of the general population and disappear. Further, we assume that the favorable mutation that exists and survives to spread at every step is dominant, meaning that it will be expressed even if occurring on only one of the two parental chromosomes carrying that gene. Otherwise it would be recessive, meaning that it would have to occur simultaneously in a male and a female, who would then need to find each other and mate.

Even with these assumptions, which all help to oil the theory along, the chance that the postulated mutation will appear and survive in one step of the chain works out at around 1 in 300,000, which is less than that of flipping 18 coins and having them all come up heads. For the comparable thing to happen through all 500 steps, the number becomes one with more than 2,700 zeros.

Let's slow down for a moment to reflect on what that means. Consider the probability of flipping 150 coins and having them all come up heads. The event has a chance of 1 in 2^{150} of happening, which works out at about 1 in 10^{45} (1 followed by 45 zeros, or 45 orders of magnitude). This means that on average you'd have to flip 150 coins 10^{45} times before you see all heads. If you were superfast and could flip 150 coins, count them, and pick them up again all in one second you couldn't do it in a lifetime. Even a thousand people continuing nonstop for a hundred years would only get through 3 trillion flips, i.e., 3×10^{12}—still a long, long way from 10^{45}.

So let's try simulating it on a circuit chip that can perform each flip of 150 coins in a trillionth of a second. Now build a super-computer from a billion of these chips and then set a fleet of 10 billion such supercomputers to the task . . . and they should be getting there after somewhere around 3 million years. Well, the odds that we're talking about, of producing just one new species even with favorable assumptions all the way down the line, is over two thousand orders of magnitude *more* improbable than that.

BUT IT HAPPENED! SCIENCE OR FAITH?

This is typical of the kinds of odds you run into everywhere with the idea that life originated and developed by accumulated chance. Spetner calculates odds of 1 in 600 orders of magnitude against the occurrence of any instance of "convergent evolution," which is invoked repeatedly by evolutionists to explain physical similarities that by no stretch of the imagination can be attributed to common ancestry. The British astronomer Sir Fred Hoyle gives as 5 in 10^{19}

the probability that one protein could have evolved randomly from prebiotic chemicals, and for the 200,000 proteins found in the human body, a number with 40,000 zeros. [27] The French scientist Lecomte de Nouy computed the time needed to form a single protein in a volume the size of the Earth as 10^{243} years. [28] These difficulties were already apparent by the mid sixties. In 1967 a symposium was held at the Wistar Institute in Philadelphia to debate them, with a dazzling array of fifty-two attendees from the ranks of the leading evolutionary biologists and skeptical mathematicians. Numbers of the foregoing kind were produced and analyzed. The biologists had no answers other than to assert, somewhat acrimoniously from the reports, that the mathematicians had gotten their science backward: Evolution *had* occurred, and therefore the mathematical problems in explaining it had to be only apparent. The job of the mathematicians, in other words, was not to assess the plausibility of a theory but to rubber-stamp an already incontestable truth.

LIFE AS INFORMATION PROCESSING

EVOLUTION MEANS ACCUMULATING INFORMATION

The cell can be likened to a specialized computer that executes the DNA program and expresses the information contained in it. Cats, dogs, horses, and *Archaeopteryxes* don't really evolve, of course, but live their spans and die still being genetically pretty much the same as they were when born. What evolves, according to the theory, is the package of genetic information that gets passed down from generation to generation, accumulating and preserving beneficial innovations as it goes. The species that exists at a given time is a snapshot of the genome expressing itself as it stands at the point it has reached in accumulating information down the line of descent from the earliest ancestor. Although the process may be rapid at times and slow at others, every mutation that contributes to the process adds something on average. This is another way of saying that to count as a meaningful evolutionary step, a mutation must add some information to the genome. If it doesn't, it contributes nothing to the building up of information that the evolution of life is said to be.

No mutation that added information to a genome has ever been observed to occur, either naturally or in the laboratory. This is the crucial requirement that disqualifies all the examples that have been presented in scientific papers, reproduced in textbooks, and hyped in the popular media as "evolution in action." We already saw that the case of the peppered moth involves no genetic innovation; what it demonstrates is an already built-in adaptation capacity, not evolution. This isn't to say that mutations never confer survival benefits in some circumstances. Such occurrences are rare, but they do happen. However, every one that has been studied turns out to be the result of information being lost from a genome, not gained by it. So what's going on in such situations is just part of the normal process of existing organisms shuffling and jostling in their own peculiar ways for a better place in the sun, but not turning into something new.

BACTERIAL IMMUNITY CLAIMS: A FALSE INFORMATION ECONOMY

A frequently cited example is that of bacteria gaining resistance to streptomycin and some other mycin drugs, which they are indeed able to do by a single-point mutation. The drug molecule works by attaching to a matching site on a ribosome (protein-maker) of the bacterium, rather like a key fitting into a lock, and interfering with its operation. The ribosome strings the wrong amino acids together, producing proteins that don't work, as a result of which the bacterium is unable to grow, divide, or propagate, and is wiped out. Mammalian ribosomes don't have similar matching sites for the drug to attach to, so only the bacteria are affected, making such drugs useful as antibiotics. However, several mutations of the bacterial genome are possible that render the drug's action ineffective. In a population where one of them occurs, it will be selected naturally to yield a resistant strain which in the presence of the antibiotic indeed has a survival benefit.

But the "benefit" thus acquired turns out to be a bit like gaining immunity to tooth decay by losing your teeth. Every one of the resistance-conferring mutations does so by altering one part or another of the ribosome "lock" in such a way that the drug's molecular "key" will no longer match. This is another way of saying that the specific set of lock parts that enables the key fit is replaced by one of several randomly determined alternative sets that it won't fit. The significant point is that a single, unique state is necessary to bring about the first condition, "key fits," whereas any one of a number of states is sufficient to produce the second condition, "key doesn't fit." Thinking of it as a combination lock, only one combination of all digits will satisfy the first condition, but altering any digit (or more) meets the second. This makes a number *less specific*—such as by changing 17365 to 173X5, where X can be any digit. Loss of specificity means a *loss* of information. The same applies to pests becoming resistant to insecticides such as DDT. Although a survival benefit may be acquired in certain circumstances, the mutant strains invariably show impairment in more general areas, such as by slowed metabolism or sluggish behavior. Hence, they turn out to be not "super species" at all, as the media love to sensationalize, but genetic degenerates which if the artificial conditions were taken away would rapidly be replaced by the more all-round-rugged wild types.

Losing the genes that control the growth of teeth might produce a strain of survivors in a situation where all the food that required chewing was poisoned and only soup was safe. But it couldn't count as meaningful in any evolutionary sense. If evolution means the gradual accumulation of information, it can't work through mutations that lose it. A business can't accumulate a profit by losing money a bit at a time.

Neither can it do so through transactions that break even. Some bacteria can become resistant through infection by a virus carrying a gene for resistance that the virus picked up from a naturally resistant variety. Some insects seem to get their uncannily effective camouflage by somehow having acquired the same color-patterning genes as are possessed by the plants they settle on. [29] Similar results can also be achieved artificially by genetic engineering procedures for transferring pieces of DNA from one organism to another. Although it is true that information is added to the recipient genomes in such cases, there is no gain for life as a whole in the sense of a new genetic program being written. The program to direct the process in question was already in existence, imported from somewhere else. Counting it as contributing to the evolution of life would be like expecting an economy to grow by having everyone take in everyone else's laundry. For an economy to grow, wealth must be created somewhere. And as we've seen, considerations of the probabilities involved, limitations of the proposed mechanisms, and all the evidence available, say that theories basing large-scale evolution on chance don't work.

MORE BACTERIA TALES: DIRECTED MUTATION

Cases of adaptations occurring not through selection of random changes but being directed by cues in the environment have been reported for over a century. [30] But since any suggestion of nonrandom variation goes against the prevailing beliefs of mainstream biology, they have largely been ignored. Take, for example, the backup feeding system that the laboratory staple bacterium *E. coli* is able to conjure up on demand. [31]

The normal form of *E.coli* lives on the milk sugar lactose and possesses a set of digestive enzymes tailored to metabolize it. A defective strain can be produced that lacks the crucial first enzyme of the set, and hence cannot utilize lactose. However, it can be raised in an alternative nutrient. An interesting thing now happens when lactose is introduced into the alternative nutrient. Two independent mutations to the bacterium's genome are possible which together enable the missing first step to be performed in metabolizing lactose. Neither mutation is any use by itself, and the chances of both happening together is calculated to be vanishingly small at 10^{-18}. For the population size in a typical experiment, this translates into the average waiting time for both mutations to happen together by chance being around a hundred thousand years. In fact, dozens of instances are found after just a few days. *But only when lactose is present in the nutrient solution.* In other words, what's clearly indicated in experiments of this kind—and many have been described in the literature [32]—is that the environment itself triggers precisely the mutations that the organism needs in order to exploit what's available.

AND SO, BACK TO FINCHES

The forms of adult animal bone-muscle systems are influenced to a large degree by the forces that act on them while they are growing. Jaws and teeth have to bear the forces exerted when the animal chews its food, and these forces will depend in strength and direction on the kind of food the animal eats. The adult form of jaws and teeth that develops in many rodents, for example, can

vary over wide ranges with changes in diet, brought about possibly by environmental factors or through a new habit spreading
culturally through a population. If the new conditions or behavior become established, the result can be a permanent change in
the expressed phenotype of the animal.

In 1967, a hundred or so finches of the same species were
brought from Laysan, an island in the Pacific about a thousand miles
northwest of Hawaii, forming part of a U.S. government bird res-
ervation, to a small atoll called Southeast Island, somewhat southeast
of Midway, which belongs to a group of four small islands all within
about ten miles of each other. Twenty years later, the birds had
dispersed across all the islands and were found to have given rise
to populations having distinct differences, particularly with regard
to the shapes and sizes of their beaks. [33] Clearly this wasn't the
result of randomly occurring mutations being naturally selected over
many generations. The capacity to switch from one form to another
was already present in the genetic program, and the program was
switched to the appropriate mode by environmental signals. The
ironic aspect of this example, of course, is that observations of precisely this type of variety in beak forms among finches of the
Galapagos Islands led Darwin to the notion that he was witnessing the beginnings of new species.

CONFRONTING THE UNTHINKABLE

By the above, if a population of rodents, say, or maybe horses,
were to shift their diet abruptly, the phenotype would change
abruptly even though the genotype does not. The fossil record
would show abrupt changes in tooth and bone structure, even
though there had been no mutation and no selection. Yet the
evolution read into the fossil record is inferred largely from bones
and teeth. In his reconstruction of the story of horse evolution,
Simpson tells that when the great forests gave way to grassy plains,
Mesohippus evolved into *Merychippus*, developing high-crowned
teeth through random mutation and selection, for "It is not likely
to be a coincidence that at the same time grass became common,
as judged by fossil grass seeds in the rocks." [34]

It may indeed have been no coincidence. But neither does it have
to be a result of the mechanism that Simpson assumes. If these
kinds of changes in fossils were cued by altered environments acting

on the developing organisms, then what has been identified as clear examples of evolution could have come about without genetic modification being involved, and with random mutation and selection playing no role at all.

Should this really be so strange? After all, at various levels above the genetic, from temperature regulation and damage repair to fighting or fleeing, organisms exhibit an array of mechanisms for sensing their environment and adjusting their response to it. The suggestion here is that the principle of sensing and control extends down also to the genetic level, where genes can be turned on and off to activate already-existing program modules, enabling an organism to live efficiently through short-term changes in its environment. Nothing in the genome changes. The program is *set up* for the right adaptive changes in the phenotype to occur when they are needed.

The problem for Darwinism, and maybe the reason why suggestions of directed evolution are so fiercely resisted, is that if there was trouble enough explaining the complexity of genetic programs before, this makes it immeasurably worse. For now we're implying a genome that consists not only of all the directions for constructing and operating the self-assembling horse, but also all the variations that can be called up according to circumstances, along with all the reference information to interpret the environmental cues and alter the production specification accordingly. Fred Hoyle once observed that the chances of life having arisen spontaneously on Earth were about on a par with those of a whirlwind blowing through a junkyard containing all the pieces of a 747 lying scattered in disarray, and producing an assembled aircraft ready to fly. What we're talking about now is a junkyard containing parts for the complete range of Boeing civil airliners, and a whirlwind selecting and building just the model that's best suited to the current situation of cost-performance economics and projected travel demands.

INTELLIGENCE AT WORK? THE CRUX OF IT ALL

So finally we arrive at the reason why the subject is not just a scientific issue but has become such a battle of political, moral, and philosophic passions. At the root of it all, only two possibilities exist: Either there is some kind of intelligence at work behind what's going on, or there is not. This has nothing to do with the world's being six thousand years old or six billion. A comparatively young world—in the sense of the surface we observe today—is compatible with unguided Catastrophist theories of planetary history, while many who are of a religious persuasion accept orthodox evolution as God's way of working. What's at the heart of it is naturalism and materialism versus belief in a creative intelligence of some kind. Either these programs which defy human comprehension in their effectiveness and complexity wrote themselves accidentally out of mindless matter acting randomly; or something wrote them for a reason. There is no third alternative.

DARWIN'S BLACK BOX OPENED:
BIOCHEMISTRY'S IRREDUCIBLE COMPLEXITY

At the time Darwin formulated his original theory, nothing was known of the mechanism of heredity or the internal structures of the organic cell. The cell was known to possess a dark nucleus, but the inner workings were pretty much a "black box," imagined to be a simple unit of living matter, and with most of the interesting things taking place at higher levels of organization. With the further development of sciences leading to the molecular biology that we see today, this picture has been dramatically shattered and the cell revealed as the stupendous automated factory of molecular machines that we glimpsed in Michael Denton's description earlier. The complexity that has been revealed in the last twenty years or so of molecular biochemistry is of an order that dwarfs anything even remotely imagined before then.

These findings prompted Michael Behe, professor of biochemistry at Lehigh University in Pennsylvania, to write what has become an immensely popular and controversial book, *Darwin's Black Box*,[35] in which he describes systems ranging from the rotary bearings of the cilia that propel mobile cells, to vision, the energy metabolism, and the immune system, which he argues *cannot* have come into existence by any process of evolution from something simpler. His basis for this assertion is the property they all share, of exhibiting what he terms "irreducible complexity." The defining feature is that every one of the components forming such a system is essential for its operation. Take any of them away, and the system is not merely degraded in some way but totally incapable of functioning in any way at all. Hence, Behe maintains, such systems cannot have arisen from anything simpler, because nothing simpler— whatever was supposed to have existed before the final component was added—could have done anything; and if it didn't do anything, it couldn't have been selected for any kind of improvement. You either have to have the whole thing—which no variation of evolution or any other natural process could bring into existence in one step—or nothing.

The example he offers to illustrate the principle is the common mousetrap. It consists of five components: a catch plate on which the bait is mounted; a holding bar that sets and restrains the hammer; a spring to provide the hammer with lethal force; and a platform for mounting them all on and keeping them in place. Every piece is essential. Without any one, nothing can work. Hence, it has to be built as a complete, functioning unit. It couldn't assume its final form by the addition of any component to a simpler model that was less efficient.

An example of reduced complexity would be a large house built up by additions and extensions from an initial one-room shack. The improvements could be removed in reverse order without loss of the essential function it provides, though the rendering of that function would be reduced in quality and degree.

Here, from Behe's book, are the opening lines of a section that sketches the process of vision at the biochemical level. Nobody has been able to offer even a speculation as to how the system could function at all if even one of its molecular cogs were removed.

> When light first strikes the retina a photon interacts with a molecule called 11-*cis*-retinal, which rearranges within picoseconds [a picosecond is about the time light takes to cross the width of a human hair] to *trans*-retinal. The change in the shape of the retinal molecule forces a change in the shape of the protein rhodopsin, to which the retinal is tightly bound. The protein's metamorphosis alters its behavior. Now called metarhodopsin II, the protein sticks to another protein, called transducin. Before bumping into metarhodopsin II, transducin had tightly bound a small molecule called GDP. But when transducin interacts with metarhodopsin II, the GDP falls off, and a molecule called GTP binds to transducin.

Concluding, after three long, intervening paragraphs of similar intricacy:

> *Trans*-retinal eventually falls off rhodopsin and must be reconverted to 11-*cis*-retinal and again bound by rhodopsin to get back to the starting point for another visual cycle. To accomplish this, *trans*-retinal is first chemically modified by an enzyme called *trans*-retinol—a form containing two more hydrogen atoms. A second enzyme then converts the molecule to 11-*cis*-retinol. Finally, a third enzyme removes the previously added hydrogen atoms to form 11-*cis*-retinal, a cycle is complete. [36]

The retinal site is now ready to receive its next photon.

Behe gives similarly comprehensive accounts of such mechanisms as blood clotting and the intracellular transport system, where the functions of all the components and their interaction with the whole are known in detail, and contends that only purposeful ordering can explain them. In comparison, vague, less precisely definable factors such as anatomical similarities, growth of embryos, bird lineages, or the forms of horses become obsolete and irrelevant, more suited to discussion in Victorian drawing rooms.

The response from the evolutionists to these kinds of revelations has been almost complete silence. In a survey of thirty textbooks of biochemistry that Behe conducted, out of a total of 145,000 index entries, just 138 referred to evolution. Thirteen of the textbooks made no mention of the subject at all. As Behe notes, "No one at Harvard University, no one at the National Institutes of Health, no member of the National Academy of Sciences, no Nobel prize winner—no one at all can give a detailed account of how the cilium, or vision, or blood clotting, or any other complex biochemical process might have developed in a Darwinian fashion." [37]

Behe unhesitatingly sees design as the straightforward conclusion that follows from the evidence itself—not from sacred books or sectarian beliefs. He likens those who refuse to see it to detectives crawling around a body lying crushed flat and examining the floor with magnifying glasses for clues, while all the time ignoring the elephant standing next to the body—because they have been told to "get their man." In the same way, Behe contends, mainstream science remains doggedly blind to the obvious because it has fixated on finding only naturalistic answers. The simplest and most obvious reason why living systems should show over and over again all the signs of having been designed—is that they were.

ACKNOWLEDGING THE ALTERNATIVE: INTELLIGENT DESIGN

Others whom we have mentioned, such as Denton, Hoyle, Spetner, express similar sentiments—not through any prior convictions but purely from considerations of the scientific evidence. Interest in intelligent design has been spreading in recent years to include not just scientists but also mathematicians, information theoreticians, philosophers, and others dissatisfied with the Darwinian theory or opposed to the materialism that it implies. Not surprisingly, it attracts those with religious interpretations too, including fundamentalists who insist on a literal acceptance of Genesis. But it would be a mistake to characterize the whole movement by one constituent group with extreme views in a direction that isn't really relevant, as many of its opponents try to do—in the same way that it would be to belittle the notion of extraterrestrial intelligence because UFO abduction believers happen to subscribe to it. As Phillip Johnson says, "ID is a big tent" that accommodates many diverse acts. All that's asserted is that the evidence indicates a creative intelligence of some kind. In itself, the evidence says nothing about the nature of such an intelligence nor what its purpose, competence, state of mind, or inclination to achieve what we think it should, might be.

The argument is sometimes put forward that examples of the apparent lack of perfection in some aspects of biological function and adaptation mean that they couldn't be the work of a supreme, all-wise, all-knowing creator. This has always struck me as curious grounds for scientists to argue on, since notions of all-perfect creators were inventions of opponents more interested in devising means for achieving social control and obedience to ruling authorities than interpreting scientific evidence. Wrathful gods who pass judgments on human actions and mete out rewards or retribution make ideal moral traffic policemen, and it seems to be only a matter of time (I put it at around 200–300 years) before religions founded perhaps on genuine insights for all I know are taken over by opportunists and sell out to, or are coopted by, the political power structure. In short, arguments are made for the reality of some kind of creative intelligence; human social institutions find that fostering belief in a supreme moral judge is to their advantage. Nothing says that the two have to be one and the same. If the former is real, there's no reason why it needs to possess attributes of perfection and infallibility that are claimed for the latter. Computers and jet planes are products of intelligence, but nobody imagines them to be perfect.

Those who are persuaded by religious interpretations insist on the need for a perfect God to hand down the absolute moral standards which they see as the purpose in creating the world—and then go into all kinds of intellectual convolutions trying to explain why the world clearly isn't perfect. I simply think that if such an intelligence exists it would do things for its reasons not ours, and I don't pretend to know what they might be—although I could offer some possibilities. An analogy that I sometimes use is to imagine the characters in a role-playing game getting complex enough to become aware that they were in an environment they hadn't created, and which they figure couldn't have created itself. Their attempts to explain the reason for it all could only be framed in terms of the world that they know, that involves things like finding treasures and killing monsters. They could have no concept of a software writer creating the game to meet a specification and hold down a job in a company that has a budget to meet, and so on.

I sometimes hear the remark that living things don't look like the products of design. True enough, they don't look very much like the things we're accustomed to producing. But it seems to me that anyone capable of getting self-assembling protein systems to do the work would find better things to do than spend their existence bolting things together in factories. Considering the chaotically multiplying possibilities confronting the development of modules of genetic code turned loose across a range of wildly varying environments to make what they can of themselves, what astounds me is that they manage as well as they do.

These are all valid enough questions to ask, and we could spend the rest of the book speculating about them. But they belong in such realms of inquiry as theology and philosophy, not science.

Is Design Detectable?

How confident can we be that design is in fact the necessary explanation, as opposed to some perhaps unknown natural process—purely from the evidence? In other words, how do you detect design? When it comes to nonliving objects or arrangements of things, we distinguish without hesitation between the results of design and of natural processes: a hexagonal, threaded nut found among pebbles on a beach; the Mount Rushmore monument as opposed to a naturally weathered and eroded rock formation; a sand castle on a beach, distinguished from mounds heaped by the tide. Exactly what is it that we are able to latch on to? If we can identify what we do, could we apply it to judging biological systems? William Dembski, who holds doctorates in mathematics and philosophy from the Universities of Chicago and Illinois, has tackled the task of setting out formally the criterion by which design is detected. [38] His analysis boils down to meeting three basic conditions.

The first is what Dembski terms "contingency": that the system being considered must be compatible with the physics of the situation but not required by it. This excludes results that follow automatically and couldn't be any other way. Socrates, for example, believed that the cycles of light and darkness, or the progressions of the seasons pointed toward design. But what else could follow day except night? What could come after cold but warming, or after drought other than rain?

Second is the condition that most people would agree, that of "complexity," which is another way of describing a situation that has a low probability of occurring. Of all the states that the components of a watch might assume from being thrown in a pile or joined together haphazardly, if I see them put together in precisely the configuration necessary for the watch to work, I have no doubt that someone deliberately assembled them that way.

But complexity in itself isn't sufficient. This is the point that people whom I sometimes hear from—and others writing in books, who should know better—miss when they argue that the information content of a genome is nothing remarkable, since there's just as much information in a pile of sand. It's true that spelling out the position and orientation of every sand grain to construct a given pile of sand would require a phenomenal amount of information. In fact it would be a maximum for the number of components involved, for there's no way of expressing a set of random numbers in any shorter form such as a formula or the way a computer program of a few lines of code could be set up to generate, say, all the even numbers up to ten billion. But the only thing the numbers would be good for is to reconstruct that *specific* pile of sand. But the specificity means nothing, since for the purposes served by a pile of sand on the ground, one pile is as good as another and so you might as well save all the bother and use a shovel. But the same can't be said of the sequences of DNA base pairs in a genome.

Suppose someone comes across a line of Scrabble tiles reading METHINKS IT IS LIKE A WEASEL, with spaces where indicated. Asked to bet money, nobody would wager that it was the result of the cat knocking them out of the box or wind gusting through the open window. Yet it's not the improbability of the arrangement that forces this conclusion. The sequence is precisely no more or no less probable than any other of twenty-eight letters and spaces. So what is it? The typical answer, after some chin stroking and a frown, is that it "means something." But what does that mean? This is what Dembski was possibly the first to recognize and spell out formally. What we apprehend is that the arrangement, while not only highly improbable, *specifies a pattern* that is intelligible by a convention separate from the mere physical description. Knowledge of this convention—Dembski calls this "side information"—enables the arrangement to be constructed independently of merely following physical directions. In this case the independent information is knowledge of the English language, Shakespeare, and awareness of a line spoken by Hamlet. Dembski's term for this third condition is "specificity," which leads to "specified complexity" as the defining feature of an intelligently contrived arrangement.

Specifying a pattern recognizable in English enables the message to be encoded independently of Scrabble tiles, for example into highly improbable configurations of ink on paper, electron impacts on a screen, magnetic dots on a VHS sound track, or modulations in a radio signal. Michael Behe's irreducible complexity is a special case of specified complexity, where the highly improbable organizations of the systems he describes specify independent patterns in the form of unique, intricate biological processes that the components involved, like the parts of a watch, could not perform if organized in any other way.

PHILOSOPHERS' FRUIT-MACHINE FALLACY

A process that Richard Dawkins terms "cumulative complexity" is frequently put forward as showing that Darwinian processes are perfectly capable of producing such results. An example is illustrated in the form of a contrived analogy given by the philosopher Elliott Sober that uses the same phrase above from *Hamlet*. [39] The letters are written on the edges of randomly spun disks, one occupying each position of the target sentence like the wheels of a slot machine. When a wheel happens to come up with its correct letter it is frozen thereafter until the sentence is complete. Ergo, it is claimed, pure randomness and selection can achieve the required result surprisingly rapidly. The idea apparently comes from Richard Dawkins and seems to have captured the imagination of philosophers such as Michael Ruse and Daniel Dennett, who also promote it vigorously.

But their enthusiasm is hard to understand, for the model shows the *opposite* of what it purports to. Who is deciding which disks to freeze, and why? What the analogy demonstrates is an intelligence directing the assembly of a complex system toward a preordained target already constructed independently of the mechanics by other means—in this case the creativity of Shakespeare. Yet the whole aim of Darwinism was to produce a *non*teleological explanation of life, i.e., one in which purpose played no role. Hence, either these advocates don't understand their own theory, or they fail to register that they've disproved their assumptions.

TESTING FOR INTELLIGENCE

Given that little if anything in life is perfect, how confident could we be in a test using these principles to detect the signature of intelligence in nature? As with a medical test it can err in two ways: by giving a "false positive," indicating design when there isn't any, or a "false negative," by failing to detect design when it was actually present.

We live with false negatives all the time. When the information available is simply insufficient to decide—a rock balanced precariously on another; a couple of Scrabble tiles that happen to spell IT or SO—our tendency is to favor chance, since the improbabilities are not so high as to rule it out, but we're sometimes wrong. Such instances are specific, yes, but not complex enough to prove design. Intelligence can also mimic natural processes, causing us to let pass as meaningless something encrypted in an unrecognized code or to accept as an accident what had been set up to appear as such when in fact it was arson or a murder. Although we have entire professions devoted to detecting such false negatives, such as police detectives, forensic scientists, and insurance claim investigators, we can get by with imperfection.

False positives are another thing entirely. A test that can discern design where there is none is like reading information into entrails, tea leaves, or flights of birds that isn't there, which makes the test totally useless. Hence, a useful test needs to be heavily biased toward making false negatives, rejecting everything where there's the slightest doubt and claiming a positive only when the evidence is overwhelming. Thinking of it as a net, we'd rather it let any number of false negatives slip through. But if it catches something, we want to be sure that it's a real positive. How sure can we be?

What the criterion of specified complexity is saying is that once the improbabilities of a situation become too vast (27^{28} possible combinations of the Scrabble example above), and the specification too tight (one line from Hamlet), chance is eliminated as a plausible cause, and design is indicated. Just where is the cutoff where chance becomes unacceptable? The French mathematician Emile Borel proposed 10^{-50} as a universal probability bound below which chance could be precluded—in other words a *specified event* as improbable as this could not be attributed to chance. [40] This is equivalent to saying it can be expressed in 166 bits of information. How so? Well, Imagine a binary decision tree, where the option at each branch point is to go left or right. The first choice can be designated by "0" or "1," which is another way of saying it encodes one bit of information. Since each branch leads to a similar decision point, the number of branches at the next level will be four, encoded by two bits: 00, 01, 10, and 11. By the time the tree gets to 166 levels, it will have sprouted 10^{50} branches. The information to specify the path from the starting point to any one of the terminal points increases by one bit for each decision and hence can be expressed as a binary number of 166 bits.

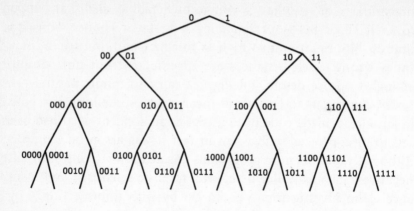

Binary Decision Tree.

The criterion that Dembski develops applies a bound of 10^{-150}. That's 100 zeros more stringent than the limit beyond which Borel said chance can be discounted. This translates into 500 bits of information. [41] According to Dembski's criterion, specified information of greater than 500 bits cannot be considered as having come about via chance processes. The bacterial cilium that Behe presents as one of his cases of irreducible complexity is a whiplike rotary paddle used for propulsion, driven by an intricate molecular machine that includes an acid-powered engine, stator housing, O-rings, bushings, and a drive shaft, and is built from over 40 interacting proteins, every one of them essential. Its complex specified information is well above 500 bits. So are those of all the other cases Behe gives. And we've already come across improbabilities that are way beyond this bound, such as Fred Hoyle's figure for the likelihood of the full complement of human proteins arising through chance, or Lee Spetner's for speciation and convergence. Many other examples could be cited.

But those who commit a priori to a philosophy that says the universe consists of nothing but matter and motion *must* accept evolution. The worldview that they have stated as fact leaves no alternative. Things like fossils, genetics, probabilities, and complexity have no real bearing apart from a need for being somehow interpreted to fit, because the issue has already been decided independently of any evidence.

So, to repeat what we said above, either mindless, inanimate matter has the capacity to organize itself purposelessly into the things we've been talking about, or some kind of intelligence caused it to be organized. Now let's go back to the question posed right at the beginning. Based on what we see today, which belief system constrains permissible answers only to those permitted by a pre-specified dogma, and which simply follows the evidence, without prejudice, to wherever it seems to be leading? Which, in other words, is the religion, and which is the science?

Some defenders of the Darwinist view evade the issue by defining science as the study of naturalistic, materialistic phenomena and the search for answers to all things only in those terms. But what if the simple reality is that some questions don't have answers in those terms? One response is that science could only be enriched by abandoning that restrictive philosophy and opening its horizons in the way the spirit of free inquiry was supposed to. The alternative could be unfortunate. For in taking such a position, science could end up excluding itself from what could well be some of the most important questions confronting us.

Section Notes

1 Himmelfarb, 1962
2 Dennett, 1995, p. 46
3 *New York Times*, April 9, 1989, Sec 7, p. 34
4 Dennett, 1995, pp. 515–516
5 Hogan, 1977
6 Hogan, 1988
7 Darwin, 1859, p.184
8 *The Origin of Species*, 1872, 6th edition, John Murry, London, p. 468
9 *The Origin of Species*, 1872, 6th edition, John Murray, London, p. 309
10 Sunderland, 1998
11 Denton, 1985, p. 190
12 Johnson, Phillip, 1991, p.51
13 Wells, 2000, Chapter 6
14 Sunderland, 1998, p. 86
15 Johnson, 1991, p. 79
16 See, for example, Sunderland, 1998, p. 94
17 Stanley, 1979, p. 39
18 Dawkins, 1986, p. 1
19 Macbeth, 1971, p. 5
20 According to Simpson, "anything tending to produce systematic, heritable change in populations between one generation and the next." Quoted in Macbeth, 1971, p. 48
21 Macbeth, 1971, p. 48
22 See Wells, 2000, Chapter 7 for more details and a discussion on the implications of needing to falsify textbooks when we're assured that the evidence for evolution is "overwhelming." A full account of the story is available online at the Nature Institute, http://www.netfuture.org/ni/misc/pub/moth.html
23 Spetner, 1997, p. 63
24 Judson, 1979, p. 217
25 Denton, 1985, pp. 328–29
26 Spetner, 1997, p. 92
27 Hoyle, 1983, pp. 12–17
28 Sunderland, 1996, p. 152

29 Hoyle, 1983, Chapter 5

30 For examples of reviews see Ho and Saunders, 1979; Cook, 1977; Rosen and Buth, 1980

31 Original research reported in Hall, 1982

32 See Spetner, 1997, Chapter 7 for more examples

33 Spetner, 1997, p. 204

34 Simpson, 1951, p. 173

35 Behe, 1996

36 Behe, 1996, p. 20

37 Behe, 1996. p. 187

38 Dembski 1998, 1999, 2002

39 Sober, 1993

40 Borel, 1962, p. 28

41 Dembski, 1998, Section 6.5

TWO
OF BANGS AND BRAIDS
Cosmology's
Mathematical Abstractions

It's impossible that the Big Bang is wrong.
—Joseph Silk, astrophysicist

Can we count on conventional science always choosing the incorrect alternative between two possibilities? I would vote yes, because the important problems usually require a change in paradigm, which is forbidden to conventional science.
—Halton Arp, observational astronomer

MATHEMATICAL WORLDS— AND THIS OTHER ONE

Mathematics is purely deductive. When something is said to be mathematically "proved," it means that the conclusion follows rigorously and necessarily from the axioms. Of itself, a mathematical system can't show anything as being "true" in the sense of describing the real world. All the shelves of volumes serve simply to make explicit what was contained in the assumptions. If some mathematical procedures happen to approximate the behavior of certain real-world phenomena over certain ranges sufficiently closely to allow useful predictions to be made, then obviously that can be of immense benefit in gaining a better understanding of the world and applying that knowledge to practical ends. But the only measure of if, and if so to what degree, a mathematical process does in fact describe reality can be actual observation. Reality is in no way obligated to mimic formal systems of symbol manipulation devised by humans.

COSMOLOGIES AS MIRRORS

Advocates of this or that political philosophy will sometimes point to a selected example of animal behavior as a "natural" model that is supposed to tell us something about humans—even if their rivals come up with a different model exemplifying the opposite. I've never understood why people take much notice of things like this. Whether some kinds of ape are social and "democratic," while others are hierarchical and "authoritarian" has to do with apes, and that's all. It's not relevant to the organizing of human societies. In a similar kind of way, the prevailing cosmological models adopted by societies throughout history—the kind of universe they believe they live in, and how it originated—tend to mirror the political, social, and religious fashion of the times.

Universes in which gods judged the affairs of humans were purpose-built and had beginnings. Hence, the Greek Olympians with their creation epics and thunderbolts, and mankind cast in a tragedy role, heroic only in powers to endure whatever fate inflicted. These also tend to be times of stagnation or decline, when the cosmos too is seen as running downhill from a state of initial perfection toward ruin that humans are powerless to avert. Redemption is earned by appeasing the supernatural in such forms as the God of Genesis and of the Christendom that held sway over Europe from the fall of the Roman Empire to the stirring of the Renaissance.

But in times of growth and confidence in human ability to build better tomorrows, the universe too evolves of itself, by its own internal powers of self-organization and improvement. Thoughts turn away from afterlives and retribution, and to things of the here and now, and the material. The gods, if they exist at all, are at best remote, preoccupied with their own concerns, and the cosmos is conceived as having existed indefinitely, affording time for all the variety and complexity of form to have come about through the operation of unguided natural forces. Thus, with Rome ruling over the known world, Lucretius expounded the atomism of Epicurus, in which accidental configurations of matter generated all of sensible physical reality and the diversity of living things. A millennium later, effectively the same philosophy reappeared in modern guise as the infinite machine set up by Newton and Laplace to turn the epochal wheels for Lyell and Darwin. True, Newton maintained a religious faith that he tried to reconcile with the emerging scientific outlook; but the cosmos that he discovered had no real need of a creator, and God was reduced to a kind of caretaker on the payroll, intervening occasionally to tweak perturbed orbits and keep the Grand Plan on track as it unfolded.

Even that token to tradition faded, and by the end of the nineteeth century, with Victorian exultation of unlimited Progress at its zenith, the reductionist goal of understanding all phenomena from the origin of life to the motions of planets in terms of the mechanical operations of natural processes seemed about complete. This was when Lord Kelvin declared that the mission of science was as good as accomplished, and the only work remaining was to determine the basic constants to a few more decimal places of accuracy.

That world and its vision self-destructed in the trenches of

1914–18. From the aftermath emerged a world of political disillusionment, roller-coaster economics, and shattered faith in human nature. Mankind and the universe, it seemed, were in need of some external help again.

MATTERS OF GRAVITY: RELATIVITY'S UNIVERSES

In 1917, two years after developing the general relativity theory (GRT), Albert Einstein formulated a concept of a finite, static universe, into which he introduced the purely hypothetical quantity that he termed the "cosmological constant," a repulsive force increasing with the distance between two objects in the way that the centrifugal force in a rotating body increases with radius. This was necessary to prevent a static universe from collapsing under its own gravitation. (Isaac Newton was aware of the problem and proposed an infinite universe for that reason.) But the solution was unstable, in that the slightest expansion would increase the repulsive force and decrease gravity, resulting in runaway expansion, while conversely the slightest contraction would lead to total collapse.

Soon afterward, the Dutch astronomer, Willem de Sitter, found a solution to Einstein's equations that described an expanding universe, and the Russian mathematician Alexander Friedmann found another. Einstein's static picture, it turned out, was one of three special cases among an infinity of possible solutions, some expanding, some contracting. Yet despite the excitement and publicity that the General Theory had aroused—publication of Einstein's special relativity theory in 1905 had made comparatively little impact; his Nobel Prize of that year was awarded for a paper on the photoelectric effect—the subject remained confined to the circle of probably not more than a dozen or so specialists who had mastered its intricacies until well into the 1920s. Then the possible significance began being recognized of observational data that had been accumulating since 1913, when the astronomer V. M. Slipher (who, as is often the case in instances like this, was looking for something else) inferred from redshifts of the spectra of about a dozen galaxies in the vicinity of our own that the galaxies were moving away at speeds ranging up to a million miles per hour.

AN ASIDE ON SPECTRA AND REDSHIFTS

A spectrum is the range of wavelengths over which the energy carried by a wave motion such as light, radio, sound, disturbances on a water surface, is distributed. Most people are familiar with the visible part of the Sun's spectrum, ranging from red at the low-frequency end to violet at the high-frequency end, obtained by separating white sunlight into its component wavelengths by means of a prism. This is an example of a continuous, or "broadband" spectrum, containing energy at all wavelengths in the range. Alternatively, the energy may be concentrated in just a few narrow bands within the range.

Changes in the energy states of atoms are accompanied by the emission or absorption of radiation. In either case, the energy transfers occur at precise wavelength values that show as "lines," whose strength and spacings form patterns—"line spectra"—characteristic of different atomic types. Emission spectra consist of bright lines at the wavelengths of the emitted energy. Absorption spectra show as dark lines marking the wavelengths at which energy is absorbed from a background source—for example, of atoms in the gas surrounding a star, which absorb certain wavelengths of the light passing through. From the line spectra found for different elements in laboratories on Earth, the elements present in the spectra from stars and other astronomical objects can be identified.

A "redshifted" spectrum means that the whole pattern is displaced from its normal position toward the red—longer wavelength—end. In other words, all the lines of the various atomic spectra are observed to lie at longer wavelength values than the "normal" values measured on Earth. A situation that would bring this about would be one where the number of waves generated in a given time were stretched across more intervening space than they "normally" would be. This occurs when the source of the waves is receding. The opposite state of affairs applies when the source is approaching and the wavelengths get compressed, in which case spectra are "blue-shifted." Such alteration of wavelength due to relative motion between the source and receiver is the famous Doppler shift. [43] Textbooks invariably cite train whistles as an example at this point, so I won't.

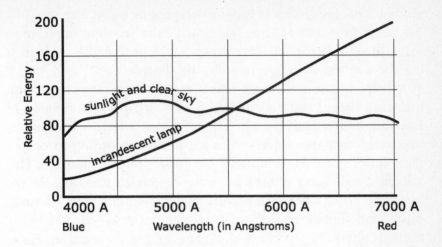

Spectra. Above, continuous spectra showing energy distribution with wavelength for sunlight and an incandescent lamp. Below, atomic line spectrum for barium.

LINE SPECTRUM OF BARIUM

A UNIVERSE IN THE RED AND LEMAÎTRE'S PRIMEVAL ATOM

By 1924 the reports of redshifts from various observers had grown sufficiently for Carl Wirtz, a German astronomer, to note a correlation between the amounts of galactic redshift and their optical faintness, which was tentatively taken as a measure of distance. The American astronomer Edwin Hubble had recently developed a new method for measuring galactic distances using the known brightnesses of certain peculiar variable stars, and along with his assistant, Milton Humason, conducted a systematic review of the data using the 60-inch telescope at the Mount Wilson Observatory in California, and later the 100-inch—the world's largest at that time. In 1929 they announced what is now known as Hubble's Law: that the redshift of galaxies increases steadily with distance. Although Hubble himself always seemed to have reservations, the shift was rapidly accepted as a Doppler effect by the scientific world at large, along with the startling implication that not only is the universe expanding, but that the parts of it that lie farthest away are receding the fastest.

A Belgian priest, Georges Lemaître, who was conversant with Einstein's theory and had studied under Sir Arthur Eddington in England, and at Harvard where he attended a lecture by Hubble, concluded that the universe was expanding according to one of the solutions of GRT in which the repulsive force dominated. This still left a wide range of options, including models that were infinite in extent, some where the expansion arose from a state that had existed indefinitely, and others where the universe cycled endlessly through alternating periods of expansion and contraction. However, the second law of thermodynamics dictated that on balance net order degenerates invariably, one way or another, to disorder, and the process is irreversible. The organized energy of a rolling rock will eventually dissipate as heat in the ground as the rock is brought to a halt by friction, but the random heat motions of molecules in the ground never spontaneously combine to set a rock rolling. This carries the corollary that eventually everything will arrive at the same equilibrium temperature everywhere, at which point all further change must cease. This is obviously so far from being the case with the universe as seen today that it seemed the universe could only have existed for a limited time, and it must have arrived at its present state from one of minimum disorder, or "entropy." Applying these premises, Lemaître developed his concept of the "primeval atom," in which the universe exploded somewhere between 10 billion and 20 billion years ago out of an initial point particle identified with the initial infinitely large singularity exhibited by some solutions to the relativistic equations. According to this "fireworks model," which Lemaître presented in 1931, the primeval particle expanded and split up into progressively smaller units the size of galaxies, then stars, and so forth in a process analogous to radioactive decay.

This first version of a Big Bang cosmology was not generally accepted. The only actual evidence offered was the existence of cosmic rays arriving at high energies from all directions in space, which Lemaître argued could not come from any source visible today and must be a leftover product of the primordial breakdown. But this was disputed on the grounds that other processes were known which were capable of providing the required energy, and this proved correct. Cosmic-ray particles were later shown to be accelerated by electromagnetic forces in interstellar space. The theory was also criticized on the grounds of its model of stellar evolution based on a hypothetical process of direct matter-to-energy annihilation, since nuclear fusion had become the preferred candidate for explaining the energy output of stars, and Willem de Sitter showed that it was not necessary to assume GRT solutions involving a singularity. Further, the gloomy inevitability of a heat death was rejected as not being necessarily so, since whatever might seem true of the second law locally, nothing was known of its applicability to the universe as a whole. Maybe the world was deciding that the period that had brought about such events as the Somme, Verdun, and the end of Tsarist Russia had been an aberration, and was recovering from its pessimism. Possibly it's significant, then, that the resurrection of the Big Bang idea came immediately following World War II.

After the Bomb: The Birth of the Bang

Gamow's Nuclear Pressure-Cooker

In 1946, Russian-born George Gamow, who had worked on the theory of nuclear synthesis in the 1930s and been involved in the Manhattan Project, conjectured that if an atomic bomb could, in a fraction of a millionth of a second, create elements detectable at the test site in the desert years later, then perhaps an explosion on a colossal scale could have produced the elements making up the universe as we know it. Given high enough temperatures, the range of atomic nuclei found in nature could be built up through a succession starting with hydrogen, the lightest, which consists of one proton. Analysis of astronomical spectra showed the universe to consist of around 75 percent hydrogen, 24 percent helium, and the rest a mix continuing on through lithium, beryllium, boron and so on of the various heavier elements. Although all of the latter put together formed just a trace in comparison to the amount of hydrogen and helium, earlier attempts at constructing a theoretical model had predicted far less than was observed—the discrepancy being in the order of ten orders of magnitude in the case of intermediate mass elements such as carbon, nitrogen, and oxygen, and getting rapidly worse (in fact, exponentially) beyond those.

Using pointlike initial conditions of the GRT equations, Gamow, working with Ralph Alpher and Robert Herman, modeled the explosion of a titanic superbomb in which, as the fireball expanded, the rapidly falling temperature would pass a point where the heavier nuclei formed from nuclear fusions in the first few minutes would cease being broken down again. The mix of elements that existed at that moment would thus be "locked in," providing the raw material for the subsequently evolving universe. By adjusting the parameters that determined density, Gamow and his colleagues developed a model that within the first thirty minutes of the Bang yielded a composition close to that which was observed.

Unlike Lemaître's earlier proposal, the Gamow theory was well received by the scientific community, particularly the new generation of physicists versed in nuclear technicalities, and became widely popularized. Einstein had envisaged a universe that was finite in space but curved and hence unbounded, as the surface of a sphere is in three dimensions. The prevailing model now became one that was also finite in time. Although cloaked in the language of particle physics and quantum mechanics, the return to what was essentially a medieval worldview was complete, raising again all the metaphysical questions about what had come before the Bang. If space and time themselves had come into existence along with all the matter and energy of the universe as some theorists maintained, where had it all come from? If the explosion had suddenly come about from a state that had endured for some indefinite period previously, what had triggered it? It seemed to be a one-time event. By the early 1950s, estimates of the total amount of mass in the universe appeared to rule out the solutions in which it oscillated between expansion and contraction. There wasn't enough to provide sufficient gravity to halt the expansion, which therefore seemed destined to continue forever. What the source of the energy might have been to drive such an expansion—exceeding all the gravitational energy contained in the universe—was also an unsolved problem.

HOYLE AND SUPERNOVAS AS "LITTLE BANG" ELEMENT FACTORIES

Difficulties for the theory mounted when the British astronomer Fred Hoyle showed that the unique conditions of a Big Bang were not necessary to account for the abundance of heavy elements; processes that are observable today could do the job. It was accepted by then that stars burned by converting hydrogen to helium, which can take place at temperatures as low as 10 million degrees—attainable in a star's core. Reactions beyond helium require higher temperatures, which Gamow had believed stars couldn't achieve. However, the immense outward pressure of fusion radiation balanced the star's tendency to fall inward under its own gravity. When the hydrogen fuel was used up, its conversion to helium would cease, upsetting the balance and allowing the star to collapse. The gravitational energy released in the collapse would heat the core further, eventually reaching the billion degrees necessary to initiate the fusion of helium nuclei into carbon, with other elements appearing through neutron capture along the lines Gamow had proposed. A new phase of radiation production would ensue, arresting the collapse and bringing the star into a new equilibrium until the helium was exhausted. At that point another cycle would repeat in which oxygen could be manufactured, and so on through to iron, in the middle of the range of elements, which is as far as the fusion process can go. Elements heavier than iron would come about in the huge supernova explosions that would occur following the further collapse of highly massive stars at the end of their nuclear burning phase—"little bangs" capable of supplying all the material required for the universe without need of any primordial event to stock it up from the beginning.

This model also accounted for the observational evidence that stars varied in their makeup of elements, which was difficult to explain if they all came from the same Big Bang plasma. (It also followed that any star or planet containing elements heavier than iron—our Sun, the Earth, indeed the whole Solar System, for example—must have formed from the debris of an exploded star from an earlier generation of stars.) Well, the images of starving postwar Europe, shattered German cities, Stalingrad, and Hiroshima were fading. The fifties were staid and prosperous, and confidence in the future was returning. Maybe it was time to rethink cosmology again.

THE STEADY-STATE THEORY

Sure enough, Fred Hoyle, having dethroned the Big Bang as the only mechanism capable of producing heavy elements, went on, with Thomas Gold and Herman Bondi, to propose an alternative that would replace it completely. The Hubble redshift was still accepted by most as showing that the universe we see is expanding away in all directions to the limits of observation. But suppose, Hoyle and his colleagues argued, that instead of this being the result of a one-time event, destined to die away into darkness and emptiness as the galaxies recede away from each other, new matter is all the time coming into existence at a sufficient rate to keep the overall density of the universe the same. Thus, as old galaxies disappear beyond the remote visibility "horizon" and are lost, new matter being created diffusely through all of space would be coming together to form new galaxies, resulting in a universe populated by a whole range of ages—analogous to a forest consisting of all forms of trees, from young saplings to aging giants.

The rate of creation of new matter necessary to sustain this situation worked out at one hydrogen atom per year in a cube of volume measuring a hundred meters along a side, which would be utterly undetectable. Hence, the theory was not based on any hard observational data. Its sole justification was philosophical. The long-accepted "cosmological principle" asserted that, taken at a large-enough scale, the universe looked the same anywhere and in any direction. The Hoyle-Bondi-Gold approach introduced a "perfect cosmological principle" extending to time also, making the universe unchanging. It became known, therefore, as the steady-state theory.

The steady-state model had its problems too. One in particular was that surveys of the more distant galaxies, and hence ones seen from an earlier epoch because of the delay in their light reaching Earth, showed progressively more radio sources; hence the universe hadn't looked the same at all times, and so the principle of its maintaining a steady, unvarying state was violated. But it attracted a lot of scientists away from the Big Bang fold. The two major theories continued to rival each other, each with its adherents and opponents. And so things remained through into the sixties.

Then, in 1965, two scientists at Bell Telephone Laboratories, Arno

Penzias and Robert Wilson, after several months of measurement and double-checking, confirmed a faint glow of radiation emanating evenly from every direction in the heavens with a frequency spectrum corresponding to a temperature of 2.7°K. [44] This was widely acclaimed and publicized as settling the issue in favor of the Big Bang theory.

THE COSMIC BACKGROUND RADIATION: NEWS BUT NOTHING NEW

Big Bang had been wrestling with the problem of where the energy came from to drive the expansion of the "open" universe that earlier observations had seemed to indicate—a universe that would continue expanding indefinitely due to there being too little gravitating mass to check it. Well, suppose the estimates were light, and the universe was in fact just "closed"—meaning that the amount of mass was just enough to eventually halt the expansion, at which point everything would all start falling in on itself again, recovering the energy that had been expended in driving the expansion. This would simplify things considerably, making it possible to consider an oscillating model again, in which the current Bang figures as simply the latest of an indeterminate number of cycles. Also, it did away with all the metaphysics of asking who put the match to whatever blew up, and what had been going on before.

A group at Princeton looked into the question of whether such a universe could produce the observed amount of helium, which was still one of Big Bang's strong points. (Steady state had gotten the abundance of heavier elements about right but was still having trouble accounting for all the helium.) They found that it could. With the conditions adjusted to match the observed figure for helium, expansion would have cooled the radiation of the original fireball to a diffuse background pervading all of space that should still be detectable—at a temperature of 30°K. [45] Gamow's collaborators, Ralph Alpher and Robert Herman, in their original version had calculated 5°K for the temperature resulting from the expansion alone, which they stated would be increased by the energy production of stars, and a later publication of Gamow's put the figure at 50°K. [46]

The story is generally repeated that the discovery of the 2.7°K microwave background radiation confirmed precisely a prediction of the Big Bang theory. In fact, the figures predicted were an order of magnitude higher. We're told that those models were based on an idealized density somewhat higher than that actually reported by observation, and (mumble-mumble, shuffle-shuffle) it's not really too far off when you allow for the uncertainties. In any case, the Big Bang proponents maintained, the diffuseness of this radiation across space, emanating from no discernible source, meant that it could only be a relic of the original explosion.

It's difficult to follow the insistence on why this had to be so. A basic principle of physics is that a structure that emits wave energy at a given frequency (or wavelength) will also absorb energy at the same frequency—a tuning fork, for example, is set ringing by the same tone that it sounds when struck. An object in thermal equilibrium with—i.e., that has reached the same temperature as—its surroundings will emit the same spectrum of radiation that it absorbs. Every temperature has a characteristic spectrum, and an ideal, perfectly black body absorbing and reradiating totally is said to be a "blackbody" radiator at that temperature. The formula relating the total radiant energy emitted by a blackbody to its temperature was found experimentally by Joseph Stefan in 1879 and derived theoretically by Ludwig Boltzmann in 1889. Thus, given the energy density of a volume, it was possible to calculate its temperature.

Many studies had applied these principles to estimating the temperature of "space." These included Guillaume (1896), who obtained a figure of 5°–6° K, based on the radiative output of stars; Eddington (1926), 3.18° K; Regener (1933), 2.8° K, allowing also for the cosmic ray flux; Nernst (1938), 0.75° K; Herzberg (1941), 2.3° K; Finlay-Freundlich (1953 and 1954), using a "tired light" model for the redshift (light losing energy due to some static process not involving expansion), 1.9° K to 6° K. [47] Max Born, discussing this last result in 1954, and the proposal that the mechanism responsible for "tiring" the light en route might be photon-photon interactions, concluded that the "secondary photons" generated to carry away the small energy loss suffered at each interaction would be in the radar range. The significant thing about all these results is that they were based on a static, nonexpanding universe, yet consistently give figures closer to the one that Arno Penzias and Robert Wilson eventually measured than any of the much-lauded predictions derived from Big Bang models.

Furthermore, the discrepancy was worse than it appeared. The amount of energy in a radiation field is proportional to the fourth power of the temperature, which means that the measured background field was *thousands* of times less than was required by the theory. Translated into the amount of mass implied, this measurement made the universe even more diffuse than Gamow's original, nonoscillating model, not denser, and so the problem that oscillation had been intended to solve—where the energy driving the expansion had come from—became worse instead of better.

An oscillating model was clearly ruled out. But with some modifications to the gravity equations—justified by no other reason than that they forced an agreement with the measured radiation temperature—the open-universe version could be preserved, and at the same time made to yield abundances for helium, deuterium, and lithium which again were close to those observed. The problem of what energy source propelled this endless expansion was still present—in fact exacerbated—but quietly forgotten. Excited science reporters had a story, and the *New York Times* carried the front-page headline SIGNALS IMPLY A BIG BANG UNIVERSE.

Resting upon three pillars of evidence—the Hubble redshifts, light-element abundance, and the existence of the cosmic background radiation—Big Bang triumphed and became what is today the accepted standard cosmological model.

QUASAR AND SMOOTHNESS ENIGMAS: ENTER, THE MATHEMATICIANS.

At about this time, a new class of astronomical objects was discovered that came to be known as quasars, with redshifts higher than anything previously measured, which by the conventional interpretation of redshift made them the most distant objects known. To be as bright as they appeared at those distances they would also have to be astoundingly energetic, emitting up to a hundred thousand times the energy radiated by an entire galaxy. The only processes that could be envisaged as capable of pouring put such amounts of energy were ones resulting from intense gravity fields produced by the collapse of enormous amounts of mass. This was the stuff of general relativity, and with Big Bang now the reigning cosmology, the field became dominated by mathematical theoreticians. By 1980, around ninety-five percent of papers published on the subject were devoted to mathematical models essentially sharing the same fundamental assumptions. Elegance, internal consistency, and preoccupation with technique replaced grounding in observation as modelers produced equations from which they described in detail and with confidence what had happened in the first few fractions of a millionth of a second of time, fifteen billion years ago. From an initial state of mathematical perfection and symmetry, a new version of Genesis was written, rigorously deducing the events that *must* have followed. That the faith might be . . . well, wrong, became simply inconceivable.

But in fact, serious disagreements were developing between these idealized realms of thought and what astronomers surveying reality were actually finding. For one thing, despite all the publicity it had been accorded as providing the "clincher," there was still a problem with the background radiation. Although the equations could be made to agree with the observed temperature, the observed value itself was just too uniform—everywhere. An exploding ball of symmetrically distributed energy and particles doesn't form itself into the grossly uneven distribution of clustered matter and empty voids that we see. It simply expands as a "gas" of separating particles becoming progressively more rarified and less likely to interact with each other to form into anything. To produce the galaxies and clusters of galaxies that are observed, some initial unevenness would have to be present in the initial fireball to provide the focal points where condensing matter clouds would gravitate together and grow. Such irregularities should have left their imprint as hot spots on the background radiation field, but it wasn't there. Observation showed the field to be smooth in every direction to less than a part in ten thousand, and every version of the theory required several times that amount. (And even then, how do galaxies manage to collide in a universe where they're supposed to be rushing apart?)

Another way of stating this was that the universe didn't contain enough matter to have provided the gravitation for galaxies to form in the time available. There needed to be a hundred times more of it than observation could account for. But it couldn't simply be ordinary matter lurking among or between the galaxies in some invisible form, because the abundance of elements also depended critically on density, and increasing density a hundredfold would upset one of the other predictions that the Big Bang rested on, producing far too much helium and not enough deuterium and lithium. So another form of matter—"dark matter"—was assumed to be there with the required peculiar properties, and the cosmologists turned to the particle physicists, who had been rearing their own zoo of exotic mathematical creations, for entities that might fill the role. Candidates included heavy neutrinos, axions, a catch-all termed "weakly interacting massive particles," or "WIMPS," photinos, strings, superstrings, quark nuggets, none of which had been observed, but had emerged from attempts at formulating unified field theories. The one possibility that was seemingly impermissible to consider was that the reason why the "missing mass" was missing might be that it wasn't there.

Finally, to deal with the smoothness problem and the related "flatness" problem, the notion of "inflation" was introduced, whereby the universe began in a superfast expansion phase of doubling in size every 10^{-35} seconds until 10^{-33} seconds after the beginning, at which point it consisted of regions flung far apart but identical in properties as a result of having been all born together, whereupon the inflation suddenly ceased and the relatively sluggish Big Bang rate of expansion took over and has been proceeding ever since.

Let's pause for a moment to reflect on what we're talking about here. We noted in the section on evolution that a picosecond, 10^{-12} seconds, is about the time light would take to cross the width of a human hair. If we represent a picosecond by the distance to the nearest star, Alpha Centauri (4.3 light-years), then, on the same scale, 10^{-35} seconds would measure around half a micron, or a quarter the width of a typical bacterium—far below the resolving power of the human eye. Fine-tuning of these mathematical models reached such extremes that the value of a crucial number expressed as a part in fifty-eight decimal places at an instant some 10^{-43} seconds into the age of the universe made the difference between its collapsing or dispersing in less than a second.

But theory had already dispersed out of sight from reality anyway. By the second half of the 1980s, cosmic structures were being discovered and mapped that could never have come into being since the time of the Big Bang, whatever the inhomogeneities at the beginning or fast footwork in the first few moments to smooth out the background picture. The roughly spherical, ten-million-or-so-light-year-diameter clusters of galaxies themselves turned out to be concentrated in ribbonlike agglomerations termed superclusters, snaking through space for perhaps several hundred million light-years, separated by comparatively empty voids. And then the superclusters were found to be aligned to form planes, stacked in turn as if forming parts of still larger structures—vast sheets and "walls" extending for billions of light-years, in places across a quarter of the observable universe. The problem for Big Bang is that relative to the sizes of these immense structures, the component units that form them are moving too slowly for these regularities to have formed in the time available. In the case of the largest void and shell pattern identified, 150 billion light-years would have been needed at least—eight times the longest that Big Bang allows. New ad-hoc patches made their appearance: light had slowed down, so things had progressed further than we were aware; another form of inflation had accelerated the formation of the larger, early structures, which had then been slowed down by hypothetical forces invented for the purpose. But tenacious resistance persisted to any suggestion that the theory could be in trouble.

Yet the groundwork for an alternative picture that perhaps explains all the anomalies in terms of familiar, observable processes had been laid in the 1930s.

THE PLASMA UNIVERSE

HANNES ALFVÉN, THE PIONEER: COSMIC CYCLOTRONS.

Hannes Alfvén studied the new field of nuclear physics at the University of Uppsala, in Sweden, and received his doctorate in 1934. Some of his first research work was on cosmic rays, which Lemaître had wrongly attributed to debris from the primeval atom in his first version of a Big Bang theory. Although such renowned names as America's Robert Millikan and Britain's Sir James Jeans were still ascribing them to some kind of nuclear fission or fusion, Alfvén followed the line of the Norwegian experimental scientist Kristian Birkeland in proposing electromagnetic processes. This set the tone of what would characterize his approach to science through life: reliance on observation in the laboratory as a better guide to understanding the real world than deduction from theory, and a readiness to question received wisdom and challenge the authority of prestigious scientists.

That decade had seen the development of the cyclotron accelerator for charged particles, which uses an electric field to get them up to speed and a magnetic field to confine them in circular paths. (Electrical dynamics are such that a particle moving through a magnetic field experiences a force at right angles to the direction of motion—like that of a ship's rudder.) It had been established that the Sun possesses a magnetic field, which seemed likely to be the case with other stars also. A binary system of two stars orbiting each other—of which there are many—could form, Alfvén theorized, the components of a gigantic natural cyclotron capable of accelerating particles of the surrounding plasma to the kinds of energies measured for cosmic rays. This would also explain why they arrived equally from all directions, until then taken as indicating that their source lay outside the galaxy. The streams of high-energy particles would form huge electrical currents flowing through space—Alfvén estimated them to be typically in the order of a billion amperes—which would generate magnetic fields traversing the galaxy. These in turn would react back on the cosmic ray particles, sending them into all manner of curving and spiraling paths, with the result that those happening to arrive at the Earth could appear to have come from anywhere.

It would be twenty years—not until the fifties—before the electromagnetic acceleration of cosmic rays was generally accepted. The existence of large-scale plasma currents was not confirmed until the seventies. At the time Alfvén put forward his ideas, virtually all scientists believed that space had to be an empty, nonconducting vacuum. One reason why they resisted the notion of an electrically active medium was that it complicated the elegant, spherically symmetrical mathematics of fields constrained to isolated bodies. It often happens when ideas come before their time that when they are eventually accepted, the person who originated them gets forgotten. Ten years after Alfvén's paper, the electromagnetic acceleration of cosmic rays was proposed by Enrico Fermi and has since been known as the Fermi process.

Alfvén next applied these concepts to the aurora, which had also interested Birkeland, and explained the effect as the result of plasma currents from the Sun being deflected to the Earth's poles by its magnetic field, where they produce displays of light by ionizing atoms in the upper atmosphere. (The same process takes place in a neon tube, where the applied voltage creates an ionizing current through a gas. The gas atoms absorb energy from the current and reemit it as visible light.) Although noncontroversial today, this was again resisted for a long time by a mathematically indoctrinated orthodoxy who thought of space in terms of an idealized vacuum and refused to accept that it could conduct electricity. Alfvén used mathematics more in the mode of an engineer—as a tool for quantifying and understanding better what is observed, not as something to determine what reality is allowed to be. On one occasion, in a visit to Alfvén's home in Sweden, the Cambridge theoretician Sydney Chapman, who had steadfastly opposed Alfvén's views and declined to debate them, refused to go down to the basement to observe a model that Alfvén had constructed in the hope of swaying him. Alfvén commented, "It was beneath his dignity as a mathematician to look at a piece of laboratory apparatus!" [48]

The tradition of the professors who wouldn't look through Galileo's telescope was alive and well, it seemed. It wasn't until the mid 1960s that satellites began detecting the highly localized incoming currents in the auroral zones that proved Alfvén to have been correct.

THE SOLAR SYSTEM AS A FARADAY GENERATOR

But Alfvén was already turning to larger things. The currents that produced the aurora led back to the Sun, where the rotating vortexes that appear as sunspots act as generators in the Sun's magnetic field, accelerating plasma particles outward in flares and prominences that can cause displays extending for hundreds of thousands of miles above the surface. According to the conventional picture of how the Solar System had formed, which went back to Pierre-Simon Laplace, the Sun and planets condensed out of a spinning disk of gas and dust as it contracted under gravity. But there were two problems with this. The first was that as a rotating body contracts it speeds up (conservation of angular momentum), and calculation showed that the outwardly directed centrifugal force would balance any further collapse long before the core region became dense enough to form a star. To reach the form it is in today, Laplace's disk needed to get rid of the greater part of the angular momentum it had started out with—in fact, about 99.9 percent of it. Second, of the amount that remained, most ought to have ended up concentrated in the Sun, causing it to rotate in something like thirteen hours instead of the twenty-eight days that is found. In fact, most of the angular momentum in the Solar System lies with the planets—75 percent of it in Jupiter, 27 percent Saturn, 1 percent distributed among the remaining rubble—leaving only 2 percent in the Sun itself. How, then, did the bulk of the angular momentum get transferred to where it is?

If the central region, rotating faster as it contracts, develops a magnetic field, the field will sweep through the surrounding cloud of plasma, inducing currents to flow inward toward the core. Because the currents are in a magnetic field, they will experience a force accelerating the plasma in the direction of the rotation, in other words, transferring angular momentum from the central region, allowing it to collapse further. Following the field lines, the currents will complete a return path back via the proto-Sun, the effect there being to slow its rotation. A metal disk rotated in a magnetic field shows the same effect and is known as a homopolar generator. Michael Faraday demonstrated it in the middle of the nineteenth century.

A SKATER'S WALTZ AMONG THE PLANETS

Two parallel wires carrying currents flowing in the same direction experience a force that draws them together. If the conducting medium is a plasma rather than wires, the plasma will tend to pull itself together into filaments. But the movement of charged plasma particles toward each other also constitutes a current that generates its own magnetic field, with the result that the filaments tend to twist around each other like the braided strands of a thread. These filamentary structures are seen clearly in laboratory plasma discharges, solar prominences, and the shimmering draperies of the aurora, kinking and writhing unpredictably under their own internally generated fields, as fusion researchers trying to contain plasmas have learned to their consternation. This braiding repeats on a larger scale like threads twisting to form ropes, creating inhomogeneity and complexity as an inherent tendency of plasma structures.

This mechanism also accounted for the origin of the angular momentum of a planetary system, which straightforward collapse under gravitation had never really been able to explain. Any two forces that are not in alignment and not directed in parallel in the same direction, applied to a rigid object, will cause it to rotate about some center, and are said to possess "torque," or turning moment, about that point. Two bodies moving along the lines of action of those forces possess angular momentum about that point, even though they are traveling in straight lines. This can be seen with two skaters approaching each other on paths that are slightly offset. If they link arms as they pass, they will go into a spin about each other; angular momentum has to be conserved, and so it must have been there all along. In a plasma made up of particles of differing masses such as electrons and protons, a magnetic field will accelerate the masses at different rates, concentrating them into polarized regions of opposite charge. When two current filaments are pulled together under their mutual interaction, the forces acting are not center-to-center but offset, like the courses of the skaters. This is what causes filaments to twist around each other and braid into more complex forms.

By the sixties Alfvén was proposing this as the basis of the formation of the entire Solar System. It was generally rejected on the grounds that electrical currents could not be supported in such plasmas. Ironically, the reason that was given went back to work on solar electrodynamics that Alfvén himself and a few colleagues had done during the early years of World War II, in which Sweden remained neutral. For an electrical current to flow, there must be an electric field maintaining a voltage difference to drive it, in the same way that for a water current to flow, a pipe must have a gradient to maintain a pressure difference. But, it was argued, a conducting plasma would short out any electric field that tried to form, preventing any voltage difference from developing, and so no current could be driven.

This does come close to being true in the Sun, and the success of Alfvén's own theory in representing solar phenomena was used as justification for treating all plasma models the same way. Alfvén tried to point out that the limitation on electric fields only applied to *dense* plasmas, but it was in vain. Whereas before his ideas had been opposed on the grounds of space being a mathematically idealized insulator, now the criticism was that he couldn't be right because the space he described was assumed to be a perfect conductor. Nevertheless, his earlier work had been so thoroughly vindicated, providing much of what became standard reference material for plasma work, that in 1970 Alfvén was awarded a Nobel Prize, particular mention being made of the very theory whose limitations he had been trying to get the physics community to appreciate. He probably made history by being the only recipient of the prize to criticize, at the award ceremony, the reasons for which his own work was being recognized. "But it is only the plasma that does not understand how beautiful the theories are," he said, "and absolutely refuses to obey them." [49]

Space probes pushing out to Jupiter, Saturn, then Uranus through the end of the seventies and into the eighties confirmed the whole system of magnetic fields, ionization belts, and twisting plasma currents that Alfvén had theorized. This time the initial proponent of the ideas that led to it all was not overlooked. The vast plasma circuits extending across space are known today as Birkeland currents.

SOLAR SYSTEM TO GALAXY

After spending a short while by invitation in the Soviet Union, in 1967 Alfvén moved to the U.S.A. and settled in San Diego. Electrical forces, not gravity, he was by now convinced, had been the primary influence in shaping the Solar System. Gravitation became a significant factor only later, when the natural tendency of plasmas to organize coherent structures out of a diffuse medium at much faster rates had already produced higher-density regions— the "clumpiness" that Big Bang cosmologists had been unable to bring about by means of gravity alone. Only when matter cooled sufficiently for electrically neutral atoms to form could objects like planets arise that moved essentially in response to gravity alone and which allowed the familiar celestial dynamics that worked well enough within the local neighborhood of the Solar System. But local behavior couldn't be extrapolated to describe a universe existing 99 percent in the form of plasma in stars at temperatures of millions of degrees or charged particles streaming through space.

Wasn't the disk-shaped galaxy little more than scaled-up Solar-System geometry? A proto-galaxy rotating in an intergalactic magnetic field would generate electric fields in the same way, which in turn would produce filamentary currents flowing inward through the galactic plane to the center, and then up along the rotational axis to loop back in a return path reentering around the rim. As in the case of the Solar System, the self-"pinching" effect would compress these currents into twisting vortexes sweeping around the galaxy like immense fan blades and gathering the matter together into high-density regions along which proto-stars would form as subvortexes. However, it will be a long time yet before man-made probes are able to venture out into the galactic disk with instruments to test such theories.

PERATT'S MODELS AND SIMULATIONS: GALAXIES IN THE LABORATORY

Encouragement came, nevertheless, from a different direction. In 1979, Anthony Peratt, who had been a graduate student of Alfvén's ten years previously, was working with the aerospace defense contractor Maxwell Laboratories on a device called Black-jack V, which generated enormous pulses of electrical power—10 trillion watts!—to vaporize wires into filaments of plasma, producing intense bursts of X rays. The purpose was to simulate the effects of the electromagnetic pulse produced by a hydrogen bomb on electronics and other equipment. High-speed photographs showed the filaments of plasma moving toward each other under the attraction of their magnetic fields, and then wrapping around each other in tight spiral forms strikingly suggestive of familiar astronomical pictures of galaxies. Computer simulations of plasma interactions that Peratt performed later at the Los Alamos National Laboratory duplicated with uncanny faithfulness the features of all known galaxy types. By varying the parameters of the simulations, Peratt was able to match the result with every one of the pictures shown in Halton Arp's *Atlas of Peculiar Galaxies* and guess with confidence just what electromagnetic forces were shaping the galaxies.

These simulations also suggested a possible answer to another mystery that astronomers had been debating for a long time. In a galaxy held together purely by gravity, the velocity of the component stars about the center as it rotates should decrease with distance from it—as with the Solar System, in which the outer planets move more slowly in their orbits around the Sun. Observations, however, show that the speeds of stars orbiting the

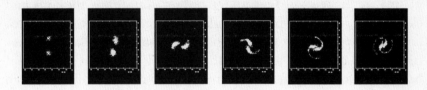

Simulation of plasma currents merging into a galaxy-like spiral structure.

---

galactic center remain fairly constant regardless of distance. This is just what the simulations showed would be expected of an electrically formed galaxy, where the spiral arms form coherent structures that trail back like the cords of a gigantic Weed Eater, moving with the same velocity along their whole length. Conventional theory had been forced to postulate an invisible halo of the strange gravitating but otherwise noninteracting dark matter surrounding a galaxy— there for no other reason than to produce the desired effect. But with electromagnetic forces, behaving not peculiarly but in just the way they are observed to on Earth, the effect emerges naturally.

AN EXPLANATION FOR X-RAY FLASHES

The most intense X-ray emission in the Blackjack V plasmas came from center of the spiral form. This was evocative of the high-energy bursts from galactic centers that cosmologists were trying to explain in terms of black holes and other exotic concepts. Blackjack V didn't use black holes. But there was a way in which sudden explosive releases of energy could come about from purely electrical causes—the same that sometimes cause the plug of an appliance to spark when it's pulled out of a wall socket.

An electric field that drives currents and accelerates particles in a cyclotron, a neon light, or a TV tube is produced by a changing magnetic field (in other words, not by a steady one). A magnetic field accompanies an electric current. In the late fifties, Alfvén had been called in by the Swedish power company ASEA to investigate a problem they were having with explosions in mercury arc rectifiers used in the transmission grid. The rectifiers used a low-pressure mercury vapor cell containing a current-carrying plasma. It turned out that under certain conditions the ions and electrons forming the plasma could separate in a positive-feedback process that created a rapidly widening gap in the plasma, interrupting the current. The fall in the magnetic field that the current had been supporting generated an electric field that built up a high voltage, accelerating the electrons to the point where the ensuing heat caused an explosion.

Alfvén's work had shown that analogous effects involving suddenly collapsing magnetic fields could also operate at larger scales to produce such results as solar flares. The energy released in such an event is nonlocal in that it derives not just from the conditions pertaining at the point where the current break occurs, but from the magnetic field sustained around the entire circuit. The energy stored in a galactic circuit thousands of light-years long and carrying ten million trillions of amperes can be a staggering 10^{57} ergs—as much energy as a typical galaxy generates in 30 million years. The electric fields produced by that kind of release could accelerate electrons to enormous velocities, approaching that of light. Accelerated charges radiate electromagnetic waves. Black-hole-density concentrations of gravity are not necessary to generate jets of radio brilliance that can be heard on the far side of the universe.

ERIC LERNER AND THE PLASMA FOCUS

Peratt published his findings in a small astronomy journal, *Astrophysics and Space Science,* in 1983, [50] and the following year in the more widely read amateur magazine *Sky and Telescope.* [51] Little reaction came from mainstream astrophysicists. Then, toward the end of 1984, he was contacted by Eric J. Lerner, a theoretician who had been pursuing a parallel line of thought, though not within the recognized establishment. Lerner's interest in the subject had been stimulated at an early age by an illustration in an astronomy book of all the trains that would be needed to haul the billions of tons of coal whose burning would equal the Sun's output in one second. He studied physics at Columbia University and the University of Maryland, with an emphasis on nuclear fusion, and in the mid seventies formed an association with Winston Bostick, who was working on an approach to controlled fusion known as the plasma focus.

Invented independently in the sixties by a Soviet, N. V. Filippov, and an American, Joseph Mather, the device first compresses electrical energy a millionfold into a sub-millimeter-size donut of filamentary plasma called a plasmoid, and then collapses the associated magnetic field to shoot out two intense, high-energy beams, each in the order of a micron (one ten-thousandth of a centimeter) wide—electrons in one direction and ions in the other. In the course of this, some of the confined ions are heated to sufficient temperatures to fuse.

Bostick too thought that filamentary processes might be involved in galaxy formation, and this led Lerner to wonder if something like the energy concentration mechanism of the plasma focus might account for the distant, highly energetic, yet compact quasars mentioned earlier. Since 1980, the new Very Large Array (VLA) radio telescope, consisting of twenty-seven dish antennas spread over miles of the New Mexico desert, had revealed enormously energetic jets of energy emanating from quasars, similar to the ones already known to power the emissions of radio galaxies, which Alfvén's work attributed to collapsing magnetic fields. If the visible core region of a typical radio galaxy is pictured as a spinning dime, two narrow jets of particles shoot out along the axis in opposite directions for a distance of about a foot before cooling and dissipating into football-size "lobes," where the energy is radiated away as radio waves. The same processes occur at lesser intensity in the jets created by ordinary galaxies also. In the case of quasars, conventional theory postulated charged particles spiraling inward in the intense gravity fields of black holes as the source. Maybe black holes weren't needed.

The radio galaxy Cygnus A. High-energy jets from the central object power radio emissions from the two "lobes."

GOING ALL THE WAY: GALAXIES TO THE UNIVERSE

A plasma focus can increase the power density of its emission by a factor of ten thousand trillion over that of energy supplied. (Power signifies concentration in time; density, concentration in space.) The flow of current inward along a galaxy's spiral arms, out along the axis, and looping back around via the rim reproduced the geometry of the plasmoid—the same that Alfvén had arrived at about four years earlier. But the suggestion of structures produced via electrical processes didn't stop there. Astronomers were producing maps showing the galaxies to be not distributed uniformly across space but in clusters strung in "superclusters" along lacy, filament-like threads running through vast voids—scaled-up versions of the filaments that Lerner had visualized as forming within galaxies, from which stars formed as matter densities increased and gravitation broke them up. These larger filaments—vast rivers of electricity flowing through space—would create the magnetic fields that galaxies rotated in, enabling them to become generators; indeed, it would be from the initial drawing together and twisting of such large-scale filaments that galaxies formed in the first place.

To establish some kind of firm foundation for his ideas, Lerner needed to know the scaling laws that related laboratory observations to events occurring on a galactic scale—the relationships that changed as the scale of the phenomenon increased, and the ones that remained invariant. This was when a colleague introduced him to Alfvén's *Cosmic Electrodynamics*, first published in 1963, which set out the scaling laws that Alfvén had derived. These laws provided quantitative support for the hierarchical picture that Lerner had envisaged—a series of descending levels, each repeating the same basic process of plasma twisting itself into vortex filaments that grow until self-gravitation breaks them up.

Few outside a small circle were receptive to such ideas, however. The majority of astrophysicists didn't believe that such currents could flow in space because a plasma's resistance is too low and would dissipate them—the same objection that Alfvén had encountered two decades before, now reiterated at the galactic level. Then bundles of helically twisted filaments a light-year across and a hundred light-years long, looping toward the center and arcing out along the axis of our galaxy and—the sizes predicted by Lerner's model—were mapped with the VLA telescope by a Columbia University graduate student, Farhad Yusef-Zadeh, and carried on the cover of the August 1984, issue of *Nature*. Yusef-Zadeh's colleague, Mark Morris, later confirmed that magnetic forces, not gravity, must have controlled their formation. Encouraged, and at Peratt's suggestion, Lerner submitted a paper describing his theory to *Astrophysics and Space Science*, the journal that Peratt had published in, but it was rejected, the reviewer dismissing the analogy between galaxies and the plasma focus as absurd. The black-hole explanation of quasars and the cores of energetic galaxies is still favored, sometimes being invoked to account for Yusef-Zadeh's filaments. Lerner's paper did finally appear in *Laser and Particle Beams* in 1986. [52]

The scaling laws implied that the smaller an object is in the hierarchy, the more isolated it will be from neighboring objects of the same kind in terms of the ratio of size to distance. Thus stars are separated from each other by a distance of 10 million times their diameters, galaxies by thirty times their diameters, clusters by ten times their diameters. Hence there was nothing strange about space being so filled in some places and empty in others. Far from being a mystery in need of explanation, the observed clumpiness was inevitable.

An upper size limit also emerged, beyond which filaments will fail to form from a homogenous plasma because of the distortion of particle paths by internal gravitation. The maximum primordial filament would be in the order of ten billion light-years in diameter and compress itself down to around a fifth that size before breaking into several dozen smaller filaments spaced 200 million light-years apart—which corresponded well with the observed values for the superclusters. Beyond this, therefore, there should exist a further, larger structure of elongated, filamentary form, a billion or so light-years in radius and a few billion light-years long. It turned out to have contracted a bit more than Lerner's calculations said. Brent Tully's 1986 paper in *Astrophysical Journal* announcing the discovery of "supercluster complexes" put their radius at around six hundred million light-years.

OLDER THAN THE BIG BANG

These were far too massive and ancient to have formed since the Big Bang, requiring a trillion years or more for the primordial filaments to differentiate themselves. Although this news caused a sensation among cosmologists, the plasma-universe alternative remained virtually unknown, since papers on it had been rejected by recognized astrophysical journals, while the few journals in which they had appeared were not read by astrophysicists. However, through contacts in the publishing world Lerner was invited to write a specialized science article for the *New York Times Magazine* and promptly proposed one on Alfvén and the plasma universe. Alfvén had been skeptical of the Big Bang theory ever since he first came across it in 1939. Nevertheless, in discussing the *New York Times* offer with Lerner, he cautioned that in his opinion an article challenging the Big Bang would be premature; instead it should focus on the electrical interpretation of more familiar and observable phenomena to prepare the ground. "Wait a year," he advised. "I think the time will be riper next year to talk about the Big Bang." [53]

But Lerner couldn't let such an opportunity pass, and after further consulting with Peratt and much editing and rewriting, he submitted an article giving a full exposition to his theory. It was not only accepted by the editorial staff but scheduled as the cover story for the October 1986 edition. Lerner was elated. But Alfvén's experience of the business turned out to be well rooted, and his advice prescient. Upon routine submission to the science section of the daily paper for review the article was vetoed on the grounds that Alfvén was a maverick, without support in the scientific community. (Being awarded a Nobel Prize apparently counts for little against entrenched dogma.) A revised version of Lerner's article did eventually appear in *Discover* magazine in 1988. [54]

OTHER WAYS OF MAKING LIGHT ELEMENTS . . .

The existence of large-scale structures posed difficulties for Big Bang. But it still rested solidly on its two other pillars of helium abundance and microwave background ratiation—at least, as far as the general perception went. We've already seen that the widespread acceptance of the background radiation was a peculiar business, since it had been predicted more accurately without any

Big Bang assumptions at all. More recently conducted work showed that it wasn't necessary to account for the helium abundance either.

The larger a star, the hotter its core gets, and the faster it burns up its nuclear fuel. If the largest stars, many times heavier than the Sun, tended to form in the earlier stages of the formation of our galaxy, they would long ago have gone through their burning phase, producing large amounts of helium, and then exploded as supernovas. Both in Lerner's theoretical models and Peratt's simulations, the stars forming along the spiral arms as they swept through the plasma medium would become smaller as the density of the medium increased. As the galaxy contracted, larger stars would form first, and smaller, longer-lived ones later. The smaller, more sedate stars—four to ten times larger than the Sun—would collapse less catastrophically at the end of the burning phase, blowing off the outer layers where the helium had been formed initially, but not the deeper layers where heavier elements would be trapped. Hence the general abundance of helium would be augmented to a larger degree than of the elements following it; there is no need for a Big Bang to have produced all the helium in a primordial binge.

Critics have argued that this wouldn't account for the presence of light elements beyond helium such as lithium and boron, which would be consumed in the stellar reactions. But it seems stars aren't needed for this anyway. In June 2000, a team of astronomers from the Universities of Austin, Texas, and Toledo, Ohio, using the Hubble Space Telescope and the McDonald Observatory, described a process they termed "cosmic-ray spallation," in which energetic cosmic rays consisting mainly of protons traveling near the speed of light break apart nuclei of elements like carbon in interstellar space. The team believed this to be the most important source of the lighter elements. [55]

AND OF PRODUCING EXPANSION

That pretty much leaves only the original Hubble redshift as the basis for the Big Bang. But as we've already seen, the steady-state theory proposed another way in which it could be explained. And back in the early sixties, Alfvén gave some consideration to another.

A theory put forward by an old colleague and teacher of his, Oskar Kleine, had proposed antimatter as the energy source responsible. Antimatter had been predicted from quantum mechanics in the 1920s, and its existence subsequently confirmed in particle experiments. For every type of elementary particle, there also exists an "antiparticle," identical in all properties except for carrying the opposite electrical charge (assuming the particle is charged). If a particle and its antiparticle meet, they annihilate each other and are converted into two gamma rays equal in energy to the total masses of the particles that created them, plus the kinetic energy they were carrying. (The thermonuclear reaction in a hydrogen bomb converts about one percent of the reacting mass to energy.) Conversely, sufficiently energetic radiation can be converted into particles. When this occurs, it always produces a particle-antiparticle pair, never one of either kind on its own.

This fact leads to the supposition that the universe too ought to consist of equal amounts of both particles and antiparticles. Kleine hypothesized that in falling together under gravity, a particle-antiparticle mixture (too rarified to undergo more than occasional annihilating collisions) would separate according to mass; at the same time, if the motion were in a magnetic field, positive charges would be steered one way and negative charges the other. The result would be to produce zones where either matter or antimatter dominated, with a layer of energetic reactions separating them and tending to keep them apart while they condensed into regions of galaxies, stars, and planets formed either from ordinary matter, as in our own locality, or of antimatter elsewhere.

Should such matter and antimatter regions later meet, the result would be annihilation on a colossal scale, producing energy enough, Kleine conjectured, to drive the kind of expansion that the redshift indicated. This would make it a "Neighborhood Bang" rather than *the* Bang, producing a localized expansion of the part of the universe we see which would be just part of a far vaster total universe that had existed for long before. Although this allows time for the formation of large structures, there are questions as to how they could have been accelerated to the degree they apparently have without being disrupted, and others that require a lot more observational data, and so the idea remains largely speculative.

REDSHIFT WITHOUT EXPANSION AT ALL

MOLECULAR HYDROGEN: THE INVISIBLE ENERGY-ABSORBER

The steady-state and Kleine's antimatter theories both accepted the conventional interpretation of the redshift but sought causes for it other than the Big Bang. But what if it has nothing to do with expansion of the universe at all? We already saw that Finlay-Freundlich's derivation of the background temperature in the early fifties considered a "tired light" explanation that Born analyzed in terms of photon-photon interactions. More recently, the concept has found a more substantial grounding in the work of Paul Marmet, a former physicist at the University of Ottawa, and before that, senior researcher at the Herzberg Institute of Astrophysics of the National Research Council of Canada.

It has long been known that space is permeated by hydrogen, readily detectable by its 21-centimeter emission line, or absorption at that wavelength from the background radiation. This signal arises from the spin of the hydrogen atom. Monatomic hydrogen, however, is extremely unstable and reacts promptly to form diatomic hydrogen molecules, H_2. Molecular hydrogen is very stable, and once formed does not easily dissociate again. Hence, if space is pervaded by large amounts of atomic hydrogen, then molecular hydrogen should exist there too—according to the calculations of Marmet and his colleagues, building up to far greater amounts than the atomic kind. [56] Molecular hydrogen, however, is extraordinarily difficult to detect—in fact, it is the most transparent of diatomic molecules. But in what seems a peculiar omission, estimates of the amount of hydrogen in the universe have traditionally failed to distinguish between the two kinds and reported only the immediately detectable atomic variety.

Using the European Space Agency's Infrared Space Observatory, E. A. Valentijn and P. P. van der Werf recently confirmed the existence of huge amounts of molecular hydrogen in NGC891, a galaxy seen edge-on, 30 million light-years away. [57] This discovery was based on new techniques capable of detecting the radiation from rotational state transitions that occur in hydrogen molecules excited to relatively hot conditions. Cold molecular hydrogen is still undetectable, but predictions from observed data put it at five to fifteen times the amount of atomic hydrogen that has long been confirmed. This amount of hitherto invisible hydrogen in the universe would have a crucial effect on the behavior of light passing through it.

Most people having a familiarity with physics have seen the demonstration of momentum transfer performed with two pendulums, each consisting of a rod weighted by a ball, suspended adjacently such that when both are at rest the balls just touch. When one pendulum is moved away and released, it stops dead on striking the other, which absorbs the momentum and flies away in the same direction as the first was moving. The collision is never perfectly "elastic," meaning that some of the impact energy is lost as heat, and the return swing of the second pendulum will not quite reverse the process totally, bringing the system eventually to rest.

Something similar happens when a photon of light collides with a molecule of a transparent medium. The energy is absorbed and reemitted in the same, forward direction, but with a slight energy loss—about 10^{-13} of the energy of the incoming photon. [58] (Note this is not the same as the transverse "Rayleigh scattering" that produces angular dispersion and produces the blueness of the sky, which is far less frequent. The refractive index of a transparent medium is a measure of light's being slowed down by successive forward re-emissions. In the case of air it is 1.0003, indicating that photons traveling 100 meters are delayed 3 centimeters, corresponding to about a billion collisions. But there is no noticeable fuzziness in images at such distances.)

What this means is that light traveling across thousands, or millions, or billions of light-years of space experiences innumerable such collisions, losing a small fraction of its energy at each one and hence undergoing a minute reddening. The spectrum of the light will thus be shifted progressively toward the red by an amount that increases with distance—a result indistinguishable from the distance relationship derived from an assumed Doppler effect. So no expansion of the universe is inferred, and hence there's no call for any Big Bang to have caused it.

Two further observations that have been known for a long time lend support to this interpretation. The Sun has a redshift not attributable to gravity, which is greater at the edges of the disk than in the center. This could be explained by sunlight from the edge having to pass through a greater thickness of lower solar atmosphere, where more electrons are concentrated. (It's the electrons in H_2 molecules that do the absorbing and reemitting.) Second, it has been known since 1911 that the spectra of hot, bright blue OB-type stars—blue-white stars at the hot end of the range that stars come in—in our galaxy show a slight but significant redshift. No satisfactory explanation has ever been agreed. But it was not concluded that we are located in the center of an expanding shell of OB stars.

So the redshift doesn't have to imply an expansion of the universe. An infinite, static universe is compatible with other interpretations—and ones, at that, based on solid bodies of observational data rather than deduction from assumptions. However, none of the models we've looked at so far questions the original Hubble relationship relating the amount of the shift to distance (although the value of the number relating it has been reappraised several times). But what if the redshifts are not indicators of distance at all?

THE ULTIMATE HERESY: QUESTIONING THE HUBBLE LAW

The completely revolutionary threat to toppling the last of Big Bang's supporting pillars came not from outside mavericks or the fringes, but from among the respected ranks of the professionals. And from its reactions, it seems that the Establishment reserves its most savage ire for insiders who dare to question the received dogma by putting observation before theory and seeing the obvious when it's what the facts seem to say.

HALTON ARP'S QUASAR COUNTS

Halton Arp comes from a background of being one of America's most respected and productive observational astronomers, an old hand at the world-famous observatories in California and a familiar face at international conferences. *Arp's Atlas of Peculiar Galaxies* has become a standard reference source. Then, in the 1960s and '70s, "Chip" started finding excess densities of high-redshift quasars concentrated around low-redshift galaxies.

A large redshift is supposed to mean that an object is receding rapidly away from us; the larger the shift, the greater the recession velocity and the distance. With the largest shifts ever measured, quasars are by this reckoning the most distant objects known, located billions of light-years away. A galaxy showing a moderate shift might be thousands or millions of times less. But the recurring pattern of quasars lying conspicuously close to certain kinds of bright galaxies suggested some kind of association between them. Of course, chance alignments of background objects are bound to happen from time to time in a sky containing millions of galaxies. However, calculating how frequently they should occur was a routine statistical exercise, and what Arp was saying was that they were being found in significantly greater numbers than chance could account for. In other words, these objects *were* associated in some kind of way. A consistently recurring pattern was that the quasars appeared as pairs straddling a galaxy.

The first reactions from the orthodoxy were simply to reject the observations as being incorrect—because they *had* to be. Then a theoretician named Claude Canizares suggested an explanation whereby the foreground galaxy acted as a "gravitational lens," magnifying and displacing the apparent position of a background quasar. According to Einstein's theory, light rays passing close to a massive body will be bent by its gravity (although, as discussed later in the section on relativity, other interpretations see it as regular optical refraction). So imagine a massive foreground galaxy perfectly aligned with a distant quasar as viewed from Earth. As envisaged by the lensing explanation, light from the quasar that would otherwise pass by around the galaxy is pulled inward into a cone—just like light passing through a convex optical lens—and focused in our vicinity. Viewed back along the line of sight, it would be seen ideally as a magnified ring of light surrounding the galaxy. Less than ideal conditions would yield just pieces of the ring, and where these happened to be diametrically opposed they would create the illusion of two quasars straddling the intervening galaxy. In other cases, where the alignment is less than perfect, the ring becomes a segment of arc to some greater or lesser degree, offset to one side—maybe just a point. So quasar images are found close to galaxies in the sky more often than you'd expect.

But the locations didn't match fragmented parts of rings. So it became "microlensing" by small objects such as stars and even planets within galaxies. But for that to work, either the number of background quasars would need to increase sharply with faintness, whereas actual counts showed the number flattening off as they got fainter. Such a detail might sound trivial to the lay public, but it's the kind of thing that can have immense repercussions within specialist circles. When Arp submitted this fact to *Astronomy and Astrophysics* the editor refused to believe it until it was substantiated by an acknowledged lens theorist. When Arp complied with that condition, he was then challenged for his prediction as to how the counts of quasars should vary as a function of their apparent brightness. By this time Arp was becoming sure that regardless of the wrecking ball it would send through the whole cosmological edifice, the association was a real, physical one, and so the answer was pretty easy. If the quasars were associated with bright, nearby galaxies, they would be distributed in space the same way. And the fit between the curves showing quasar counts by apparent magnitude and luminous Sb spiral galaxies such as M31 and M81—galaxies resembling our own—was extraordinarily close, matching even the humps and minor nonlinearities. [59]

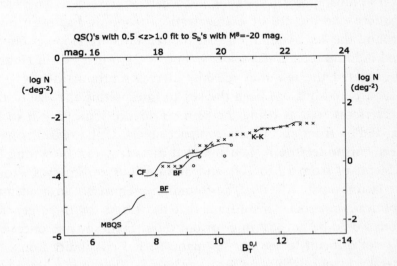

Counts of highly luminous nearby galaxies, crosses, compared to quasar counts, solid lines, according to apparent magnitude. The relationship indicates that they are distributed similarly in space.

Arp's paper detailing all this, giving five independent reasons why gravitational lensing could not account for the results and demonstrating that only physical association with the galaxies could explain the quasar counts, was published in 1990. [60] It should have been decisive. But four years later, papers were still reporting statistical associations of quasars with "foreground" galaxy clusters. Arp quotes the authors of one as stating, "We interpret this observation as being due to the statistical gravitational lensing of background QSO's [Quasi-Stellar Objects, i.e., quasars] by galaxy clusters. However, this . . . overdensity . . . cannot be accounted for in any cluster lensing model . . ." [61]

You figure it out. The first part is obligatory, required by custom; the second part is unavoidable, demanded by the data. So I suppose the only answer is to acknowledge both with an Orwellian capacity to hold two contradictory statements and believe both of them. Arp's paper conclusively disproving lensing was not even referenced. Arp comments wearily, "As papers multiply exponentially one wonders whether the end of communication is near."

Taking on an Established Church

It's probably worth restating just what's at stake here. The whole modern-day picture of extragalactic astronomy has been built around the key assumption that the redshifts are Doppler effects and indicate recessional velocity. Since 1929, when Edwin Hubble formulated the law that redshift increases proportionally with distance, redshift has been the key to interpreting the size of the universe as well as being the prime evidence indicating it to be expanding from an initially compact object. If the redshifts have been misunderstood, then inferred distances can be wrong by a factor of from 10 to 100, and luminosities and masses wrong by factors up to 10,000. The founding premise to an academic, political, and social institution that has stood for three generations would be not just in error but catastrophically misconceived. It's not difficult to see why, to many, such a possibility would be literally inconceivable. As inconceivable as the thought once was that Ptolemy could have been wrong.

It began when Arp was studying the evolution of galaxies and found a consistent pattern showing pairs of radio sources sitting astride energetic, disturbed galaxies. It seemed that the sources had been ejected from the galaxies, and the ejection had caused the disturbance. This was in line with accepted thinking, for it had been acknowledged since 1948 that galaxies eject radio-emitting material in opposite directions. Then came the shock that time and time again the sources turned out to be quasars, often showing other attributes of matter in an excited state, such as X-ray emissions and optical emission lines of highly energized atoms. And the galaxies they appeared to have been ejected from were not vastly distant from our own, but close by.

These associations had been accumulating since the late sixties, but in that time another kind of pattern made itself known also. A small group of Arp's less conformist colleagues, who even if perhaps not sharing his convictions totally, remained sufficiently open-minded to be sympathetic. From time to time one of them would present observational data showing another pair of radio or X-ray sources straddling a relatively nearby low-redshift galaxy which coincided with the optical images of Blue Stellar Objects— quasar candidates. To confirm that they were quasars required allocation of observation time to check their spectra for extreme quasar redshifts. At that point a dance of evasion would begin of refusals to look through the telescopes—literally. The requests would be turned down or ignored, even when they came from such figures as the director of the X-Ray Institute. When resourceful observers cut corners and made their own arrangements, and their findings were eventually submitted for publication, hostile referees would mount delaying tactics in the form of finicky fussing over detail or petty objections that could hold things up for years.

In the 1950s, the American astronomer Karl Seyfert had discovered a class of energetic galaxies characterized by having a sharp, brilliant nucleus with an emission line spectrum signifying that large amounts of energy were being released there. Arp found their association with quasar pairs to be so strong that it could almost be said to be a predictable attribute of Seyfert galaxies. Spectroscopically, quasars look like pieces of Seyfert nuclei. One of the most active nearby spiral galaxies, known by the catalog reference NGC4258, has a Seyfert nucleus from which the French astronomer G. Courtès, in 1961, discovered a pair of proto-spiral arms emerging, consisting of glowing gaseous matter also emitting the "synchrotron" radiation of high-energy electrons spiraling in magnetic fields. An X-ray astronomer called Wolfgang Piestch established that the arms of gas led like rocket trails to a pair of X-ray sources coinciding perfectly with two Blue Stellar Objects. When the ritual of obstructionism to obtain the spectra of the BSOs ensued, Margaret Burbridge, a Briton with over fifty years of observational experience, bypassed the regular channels to make the measurement herself using the relatively small 3-meter reflector telescope on Mount Hamilton outside San Jose in California, and confirmed them to be quasars. Arp put the probability of such a chance pairing as being less than 1 in 2.5 million.

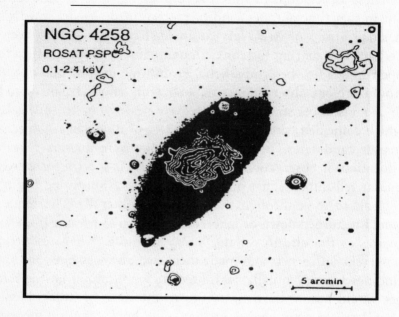

One of Halton Arp's quasar pairs, left, above center, and right, below center, ejected from the central Seyfert galaxy. The contours are of X-ray emission.

His paper giving all the calculations deemed to be scientifically necessary, along with four other examples each with a chance of being coincidental that was less than one in a million, was not even rejected—just put on indefinite hold and never acted upon since. When the number of examples continued growing, as did Arp's persistence, his tenure was suddenly terminated and he was denied further access to the major American observatories. After facing censorship from the journals and ferocious personal attacks in public by prestigious figures at conferences, he left the U.S. in 1984 to join the Max-Planck-Institut für Astrophysik in Germany, who he says have been cooperative and hospitable.

EYES CLOSED AND EYES OPEN: PROFESSIONALS AND AMATEURS

A new generation of high-resolution telescopes and more-sensitive instruments produced further examples of gaseous bridges emitting in the X-ray bands, connecting the quasars to their source galaxies. The configurations could be *seen* as a composite, physically connected object. But the response of those trained to the orthodox view was not to see them. They were dismissed as artifacts of random noise or instrument errors. I've witnessed this personally. On mentioning Arp's work to a recent astrophysics graduate I was cut off with, "Those are just background noise," although I hadn't mentioned bridges. I asked him if he'd seen any of the pictures. He replied stonily, "I haven't read anything of Arp's, but I have read the critics." Whence, knowing the approved answers is presumably all that is needed. Shades of the Scholastics.

In 1990, the Max-Planck-Institut für Extraterrestrische Physik (MPE) launched the X-ray telescope ROSAT (Röntgen Observatory Satellite Telescope), which was later used to look for a filament connecting the violently disrupted spiral galaxy NGC4319 to the quasarlike object Markarian 205, whose association had been disputed since 1971. Although the prime aim failed (Arp thinks the connection is probably too old now to show up at the energies searched for), it did reveal two new X-ray filaments coming out of Mark205 and leading to point-like X-ray sources. So the high redshift, quasarlike Seyfert ejected from the low redshift spiral was itself ejecting a pair of yet-higher-redshift sources, which turned out to be quasars.

The NGC4319-Mark205 connection was subsequently established by a high-school teacher, when the NASA announced a program making 10 percent of the time on the orbiting Hubble Space Telescope available to the community of amateur astronomers. It seems that the amateur community—for whom Halton Arp has an extremely high regard—had taken a great interest in his work and were arranging more investigations of nearby quasar connections, drawing their subject matter mainly from Arp's 1987 book, *Quasars, Redshifts, and Controversies,* which the NASA committees that allocated observation time had been avoiding like the plague. After another amateur used his assigned time for a spectroscopic study of an Arp connecting filament, the Space Telescope Science Institute suspended the amateur program on the grounds that it was "too great a strain on its expert personnel." No doubt.

QUASAR CASCADES: REDSHIFTS AS A MEASURE OF GALAXY AGE

On this basis, quasars turn out to be young, energetic, high-redshift objects ejected recently, typically from Seyfert galaxies of lower-redshift—in fact, high-resolution X-ray images of the Seyfert galaxy NGC4151 show clearly proto-quasars forming in its nucleus prior to being ejected.

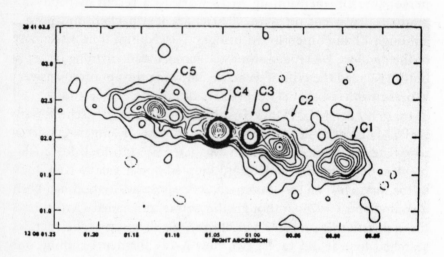

Radio map of the nucleus of the Seyfert galaxy NGC4151. C4 is believed to be the central nucleus, and the objects aligned across it, proto-quasars forming prior to ejection.

The quasars are not very luminous but grow in brightness as they age and evolve. The enormous brightness that's convention-ally attributed to them arises from incorrectly assigned distances that place them on the edge of the observable universe. Arp found that on charts showing quasar positions, pairing the quasars by redshift almost always leads to finding a cataloged Seyfert close to the center point between them.

The process can be taken further. The Seyferts in turn usually occur in matched pairs about some larger, still-lower-redshift galaxy from which they appear to have been originally ejected. This yields a cascade in which large, older galaxies have ejected younger material that has formed into younger companion galaxies around it. The younger galaxies in turn eject material as quasars, which evolve through a sequences of stages eventually into regular galaxies. Corresponding to the age hierarchy at every step is the hierarchy of redshifts reducing as the associated objects become older. Such cascades lead back to massive central spiral galaxies whose advanced age is marked by their large populations of old, red stars. Typically they are found with smaller companion galaxies at the ends of the spiral arms. Companion galaxies are found to be systematically redshifted with respect to the central galaxy, indicating them to be first-generation descendants. The same pattern extends to groupings of galaxies in clusters and of clusters in superclusters.

Our own Milky Way galaxy is a member of the Local Group, centered on the giant Sb spiral M31, known as the "Andromeda" galaxy, which is the most massive of the group. All members of the group, including our galaxy, are redshifted with respect to M31, indicating it to be the source from which the rest were ejected as young, high-energy objects at some time. So, when gazing at the immense disk of M31, now about a million light-years away, familiar from almost every astronomy book, we're looking back at our "parent" galaxy—and indeed, we see M31 as having a slight negative redshift, or "blueshift," indicating it to be older.

The next nearest major group to us is the M81 group, again centered on the same kind of massive Sb spiral galaxy as M31. Once more, every major companion to M81 is redshifted with respect to it. In fact there are many clusters like the M31 and M81 groups, which together form the Local Supercluster. At its center one finds the Virgo Cluster, which consists of the full range of morphological galaxy types, the smaller ones showing a systematic redshift with respect to the giant spirals. Apart from M31, only six other major galaxies show a negative redshift. All six are in the Virgo Cluster and consist of giant spiral types of galaxy, marking them as the older and originally dominant members. It's quite possible, therefore, that these are the origin of M31 and our entire Local Group. So with Virgo we are looking back at our "grandparent."

On a final note, all the way down, this hierarchy has exhibited the pattern of new objects being produced in pairs. The Virgo Supercluster itself, viewed in terms of the configuration of its dominant originating galaxies and the clusters of groups they have spawned, turns out to be a virtual twin of the Fornax Supercluster, seen from the Southern Hemisphere.

WHAT HAPPENS TO THE DISTANCES?

If redshift isn't a measure of a recessional velocity at all, and hence not of distance either, what does this do to the scale of distances that has been constructed, mapping structures out to 10 billion or more light-years away? Although the observational evidence has been there for twenty years, conventional astronomy has never really accepted that the redshifts are quantized, and has tried strenuously to find arguments to show that there is no quantization. Quantized means that the values are not continuous through the range like heights of points on a hill from bottom to top, but occur in a series of jumps like a staircase. Since, in general, an object can be moving in any direction relative to us, the radial components of the velocities, i.e., the part of the motion that is directly toward or directly away (which is what the Doppler effect measures) should, if redshift indicates velocity, come in all values. Hence, the conventional theory can't allow it not to.

If redshift correlates with galaxy ages, then what quantization would imply is that the ejections of new generations of proto-galaxies in the form of quasars occur episodically in bursts, separated by periods of quiescence—rather like the generations of cell division in a biological culture. This fits with the kind of way we'd imagine a cascade model of the kind we've sketched would work. It also has the interesting implication that interpreting the red-shift as distance instead of age would give the appearance of galaxies occurring in sheets separated by empty voids, which of course is what the conventional picture shows.

So what happens to the immense distances? it appears that they largely go away. Arp's studies indicate that on an age interpreta-tion basis, the Local Supercluster becomes a far more crowded place than is commonly supposed, with all of the quasars and other objects that we feel we know much about existing within it, and

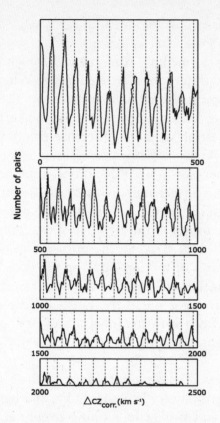

Numbers of galaxies plotted by redshift, showing them to be clustered at regularly spaced intervals. Conventional theory denies that any quantization exists.

---

not very much at all beyond. So suddenly the universe shrinks back to something in the order of the size it was before Hubble (or, more correctly, the Hubble advocates who grabbed his constant and ran with it) detonated it. No wonder the Establishment puts Arp in the same league as the medieval Church did Giordano Bruno.

WHAT CAUSES REDSHIFT? MACHIAN PHYSICS AND THE GENERALIZATION OF GRT

Through the last several pages we've been talking about a hierarchy in which redshift correlates inversely with the ages of galaxies and other cosmological objects—i.e., as redshift increases, they become younger. Is it possible, then, to say what, exactly, redshift is indicating? In short, what causes it?

Isaac Newton performed an experiment in which he suspended a pail containing water on a twisted rope. When the pail is released it spins, and the centrifugal force causes the water to pile up toward the sides, changing the shape of the surface from flat to curved. The question is, in an otherwise empty universe, how would the water "know" whether to assume a flat surface or a curved one? In other words, what determines rotation—or for that matter, accelerations in general? Ernst Mach, an Austrian physicist who lived around the turn of the twentieth century, argued that the only sense in which the term has meaning is with respect to the "fixed," or distant stars. So the property an object exhibits when it resists changes of motion—its "inertial mass"—arises from its interacting with the total mass of the universe. It "senses" that the rest of the universe is out there. Einstein believed that Mach was correct and set out with the intention of developing GRT on a fully Machian basis, but somewhere along the way it turned into a "local" theory.

Jayant Narlikar is director of the Inter University Center for Astronomy and Astrophysics in Pune, India, and has collaborated with Fred Hoyle and others in looking deeply at some of the fundamental issues confronting physics. In 1977 he rewrote the equations of GRT in a more general form, yielding solutions in which mass is not a constant but can take the form of a quantity that increases with time. [62] Now, the way mathematics is taught is that the proper way to solve an equation is to derive the general form first, and *then* make any simplifications or approximations that might be appropriate to a particular problem. The approximations that Aleksandr Friedmann used in 1922 in solving the GRT equations to produce the expanding universe solution were made in such a way as to force any changes in mass to be expressed in the geometry of the situation instead. This is what leads to the models involving the curved spacetime that helps give relativity its reputation for incomprehensibility, and which science-fiction writers have so much fun with. But with the full range of dynamical expressions that permit mass to vary, curved spacetime isn't needed.

According to Narlikar's version, a newly created particle, new to the universe, begins its existence with zero mass. That's because it doesn't "know" yet of the existence of any other mass out there, which is necessary for it to begin exhibiting the properties of mass. Its "awareness" grows as an ever-widening sphere of interaction with other masses, and as it does so the particle's own mass proceeds to increase accordingly, rapidly at first and leveling off exponentially. Note, this isn't the same process as pair production in an accelerator, which is matter *conversion* from already existing (and hence "aged") energy. It represents the introduction of new mass-energy into the universe, induced in the vicinity of concentrations of existing matter—in the form of short-lived "Planck particles," which according to quantum mechanical dynamics rapidly decay into the more familiar forms.

This, then, is what's going on in the nuclei of energetic galaxies like Seyferts. New matter is coming into existence and being ejected at high velocities because of its low initial mass. As the mass increases it slows to conserve momentum, forming the sequence of quasars, BL Lac Objects (highly variable radio and X-Ray sources transitional between quasars and more regular galaxies), BSOs, and the like, eventually evolving into the galaxy clusters that we see. The universe thus grows as a pattern of new generations appearing and maturing before giving rise to the next, unfolding from within itself. This is certainly no more bizarre than a Big Bang that has all the matter in the universe being created at once in a pinpoint. Furthermore, its fundamental process is one of continual production and ejection of material, which is what's seen everywhere we look, unlike exotic mechanisms built around black holes whose function is just the opposite. And to survive as a theory it doesn't have to depend on the burying and suppression of observational data.

But here's the really interesting thing. Consider an electron in some remote part of the universe (in the Local Supercluster if that's all there is to it), that's still relatively new and therefore of low mass. If it has joined with a nucleus to become part of an atom, and if it makes a transition from one energy state to another, the energy of the transition will be less than that of the same transition measured in a laboratory here on Earth, because the mass involved is less. Thus the emitted or absorbed photon will be lower in energy, which means longer in wavelength, i.e., redder. So the correlation between the age hierarchy and the redshift hierarchy is explained. The reason why young objects like quasars have high redshifts is that high redshifts mean exactly that: recently created matter. Redshifts don't measure velocities; they measure youth, decreasing as matter ages. And for objects that are even older than the massive, luminous spiral that we inhabit, such as its parent, Andromeda, or the dominant galaxies in Virgo that are of the generation before that, it becomes a blueshift.

THE GOD OF THE MODERN CREATION MYTH

We've looked briefly at several alternatives that have been developed to the Big Bang model of cosmology that dominates the thinking of our culture at the present time. In many ways the alternatives seem better supported by the way reality is observed to work at both the laboratory and astronomical scale. Certainly, some of the alternatives might appear to be in conflict; yet in other ways they could turn out to be complementary. I don't pretend to have all the answers. I doubt if anyone has.

The Alfvén-Lerner plasma universe builds larger structures up from small, while Arp-Narlikar's cascade of "mini-bangs" produces enlarging, maturing objects from compact, energetic ones. Conceivably they could work together, the magnetic fields and currents of the former shaping and ordering into coherent forms the violently ejected materials that would otherwise disperse chaotically.

Paul Marmet's molecular hydrogen produces a redshift that increases with distance, preserving the conventional scale and structure without involving expansion velocities or a finite time. But this could be compatible with an age-related redshift too. Quasars appear to be enveloped in extremely fuzzy, gaseous clouds. If this comes with the matter-creation process, subsequent sweeping and "cleaning up" of the area by gravity could give an initially high absorption redshift that reduces with time. Nothing says that the redshift has to be the result of one single cause. It could be a composite effect, with several factors contributing.

Some critics assert that Lerner's electrical forces simply wouldn't be strong enough to confine stars in their orbits and hold galaxies together. Marmet points out that the existence of ten times as much virtually undetectable molecular hydrogen as the measured amount of atomic hydrogen—readily attainable by his estimation—

would provide all the gravity that's needed, without resorting to exotic forms of "missing mass." And another possibility is that the law of gravitation assumed to be universal but which has only been verified locally could turn out to be just an approximation to something more complex that deviates more with increasing distance.

The point is that enormous opportunities surely exist for cross-fertilizations of ideas and a willingness to consider innovative answers that admit all the evidence, instead of a closed-minded adherence to sacred assumptions that heretics deny on pain of excommunication. Surely it's a time for eclecticism, not ecclesiasticism. Maybe the metaphor is more than superficial.

We noted at the outset that there seems to be a historical correlation between creation-type cosmologies being favored at times when things seem in decline and gods are in vogue, and unguided, evolutionary cosmologies when humanity feels in control and materialism prevails. Well, the philosophy dominating the age we currently live in is probably about as reductionist and materialist as it gets. It seems curious that at a time when an ageless plasma universe or a self-regenerating matter-creation universe should, one would think, be eagerly embraced, what has to be the ultimate of creation stories should be so fiercely defended. An age that has disposed of its creator God probably more thoroughly than any in history produces a cosmology that demands one. The throne is there, but there's nobody to sit on it.

Or is there?

Maybe there's some kind of a Freudian slip at work when the cardinals of the modern Church of Cosmology make repeated allusions to "glimpsing the mind of God" in their writings, and christen one of their exotic theoretical creations the "God Particle."

The servant, Mathematics, who was turned into a god, created the modern cosmos and reveals Truth in an arcane language of symbols accessible only to the chosen, promising ultimate fulfillment with the enlightenment to come with the promised day of the Theory of Everything.

To be told that if they looked through the telescope at what's really out there, they'd see that the creator they had deified really wasn't necessary, would make the professors very edgy and angry indeed.

Section Notes

43 Often referred to as Doppler frequency shift. Frequency is inversely related to wavelength, longer wavelength corresponding to lower frequency.

44 Kelvin—a temperature scale using degrees the same size as centigrade but with its 0° at absolute zero, which is as cold as you can get, when all thermal motion ceases. 0°C, the freezing point of water, corresponds to 273.15°K.

45 Dicke, R. H., P.J.E. Peebles, P. G. Roll, and D. T. Wilkinson, 1965, *Astrophysical Journal*, 142, 414–19

46 Assis and Neves, 1995

47 All figures from Assis and Neves, 1995

48 Lerner, 1991, p. 185

49 Lerner, 1991, p. 204

50 Peratt and Green, 1983

51 Peratt, 1983

52 Lerner, 1986

53 Lerner, 1991, p. 265

54 Lerner, 1988

55 "Interstellar Clouds Yield Clues to the Origin of the Element Lithium," McDonald Observatory, The University of Texas at Austin, news release, June 21, 2000.

56 Marmet, 2000

57 Valentijn and van der Werf, 1999

58 Marmet, 1990

59 Arp, 1998, p. 170

60 *Astronomy and Astrophysics*, pp. 229, 93, 1990

61 Arp, 1998, p.171

62 *Annals of Physics*, pp. 107, 325

THREE
DRIFTING IN THE ETHER

Did Relativity Take A Wrong Turn?

Nature and Nature's laws lay hid in night: God said Let Newton
be! And all was light.
— Alexander Pope. Epitaph intended for Sir Isaac Newton

It did not last. The Devil, shouting, Ho! Let Einstein be! restored
the status quo.
— Unknown

It is generally held that few things could be more solidly grounded than Einstein's theory of relativity which, along with quantum mechanics, is usually cited as one of the twin pillars supporting modern physics. Questioning is a risky business, since it's a subject that attracts cranks in swarms. Nevertheless, a sizeable body of well-qualified, far-from-crankish opinion exists which feels that the edifice may have serious cracks in its foundations. So, carried forth by the touch of recklessness that comes with Irish genes, and not having any prestigious academic or professional image to anguish about, I'll risk being branded as of the swarms by sharing some of the things that my wanderings have led me to in connection with the subject.

The objections are not so much to the effect that relativity is "wrong." As we're endlessly being reminded, the results of countless experiments are in accord with the predictions of its equations, and that's a difficult thing to argue with. But neither was Ptolemy's model of the planetary system "wrong," in the sense that if you want to make the Earth the center of everything you're free to, and the resulting concoction of epicycles within epicycles correctly describes the heavenly motions as seen from that vantage point. Coming up with a manageable force law to account for them, however, would be monumentally close to an impossibility. [63] Put the Sun at the center, however, and the confusion reduces to a simplicity that reveals Keplerian order in a form that Newton was able to explain concisely in a way that was intuitively satisfying, and three hundred years of dazzlingly fruitful scientific unification followed.

In the same kind of way, critics of relativity maintain that the premises relativity is founded on, although enabling procedures to be formulated that correctly predict experimental results, nevertheless involve needlessly complicated interpretations of the way things are. At best this can only impede understanding of the kind that would lead to another explosion of enlightenment reminiscent of that following the Newtonian revolution. In other words, while the experimental results obtained to date are consistent with relativity, they do not *prove* relativity in the way we are constantly being assured, because they are not unique to the system that follows from relativity's assumptions. Other interpretations have been proposed that are compatible with all the cited observations, but which are conceptually and mathematically simpler. Moreover, in some cases they turn out to be more powerful predictively, able to derive from basic principles quantities that relativity can only accept as givens. According to the criteria that textbooks and advocates for the scientific method tell us are the things to go by, these should be the distinguishing features of a preferred theory.

However, when the subject has become enshrined as a doctrine founded by a canonized saint, it's not quite that simple. The heliocentric ideas of Copernicus had the same thing going for them too, but he circulated them only among a few trusted friends until he was persuaded to publish in 1543, after which he became ill and died. What might have happened otherwise is sobering to speculate. Giordano Bruno was burned at the stake in 1600 for combining similar thoughts with indiscreet politics. The Copernican theory was opposed by Protestant leaders as being contrary to Scriptural teachings and declared erroneous by the Roman Inquisition in 1616. Galileo was still being silenced as late as 1633, although by then heliocentricism was already implicit in Kepler's laws, enunciated between 1609 and 1619. It wasn't until 1687, almost a century and a half after Copernicus's death, that the simpler yet more-embracing explanation, unburdened of dogma and preconceptions, was recognized openly with the acceptance of Newton's *Principia*.

Fortunately, the passions loosed in such issues seem to have abated somewhat since those earlier times. I experienced a case personally at a conference some years ago, when I asked a well-known physicist if he'd gotten around to looking at a book I'd referred him to on an alternative interpretation to relativity, written by the late Czech professor of electrical engineering Petr Beckmann [64] (of whom, more later). Although a friend of many years, his face hardened and changed before my eyes. "I have not read the book," he replied tightly. "I have no intention of reading the book. Einstein cannot be wrong, and that's the end of the matter."

SOME BASICS

REFERENCE FRAMES AND TRANSFORMS

The principle of relativity is not in itself new or something strange and unfamiliar, but goes back to the physics of Galileo and Newton. It expresses the common experience that some aspects of the world look different to observers who are in motion relative to each other. Thus, somebody on the ground following a bomb released from an aircraft will watch it describe a steepening curve (in fact, part of an ellipse) in response to gravity, while the bomb aimer in the plane (ignoring air resistance) sees it as accelerating on a straight line vertically downward. Similarly, they will perceive different forms for the path followed by a shell fired upward at the plane and measure different values for the shell's velocity at a given point along it.

So who's correct? It doesn't take much to see that they both are when speaking in terms of their own particular viewpoint. Just as the inhabitants of Seattle and Los Angeles are both correct in stating that San Francisco lies to the south and north respectively, the observers on the ground and in the plane arrive at different but equally valid conclusions relative to their own frame of reference. A frame of reference is simply a system of x, y, and z coordinates and a clock for measuring where and when an event happens. In the above case, the first frame rests with the ground; the other moves with the plane. Given the mathematical equation that describes the bomb's motion in one frame, it's a straightforward process to express it in the form it would take in the other frame. Procedures for transforming events from the coordinates of one reference frame to the coordinates of another are called, logically enough, coordinate transforms.

On the other hand, there are some quantities about which the two observers will agree. They will both infer the same size and weight for the bomb, for example, and the times at which it was released and impacted. Quantities that remain unvarying when a transform is applied are said to be "invariant" with respect to the transform in question.

Actually, in saying that the bomb aimer in the above example would see the bomb falling in a straight line, I sneaked in an assumption (apart from ignoring air resistance) that needs to be made explicit. I assumed the plane to be moving in a straight line and at constant speed with respect to the ground. If the plane were pulling out of a dive or turning to evade ground fire, the part-ellipse that the ground observer sees would transform into something very different when measured within the reference frame gyrating with the aircraft, and the bomb aimer would have to come up with something more elaborate than a simple accelerating force due to gravity to account for it.

But provided the condition is satisfied in which the plane moves smoothly along a straight line when referred to the ground, the two observers will agree on another thing too. Although their interpretations of the precise motion of the bomb differ, they will still conclude that it results from a constant force acting in a fixed direction on a given mass. Hence, the *laws* governing the motions of bodies will still be the same. In fact they will be Newton's familiar Laws of Motion. This is another way of saying that the equations that express the laws remain in the same form, even though the terms contained in them (specific coordinate readings and times) are not themselves invariant. Equations preserved in this way are said to be *covariant* with respect to the transformation in question. Thus, Newton's Laws of Motion are covariant with respect to transforms between two reference frames moving relative to one another uniformly in a straight line. And since any airplane's frame is as good as another's, we can generalize this to all frames moving uniformly in straight lines relative to each other. There's nothing special about the frame that's attached to the ground. We're accustomed to thinking of the ground frame as having zero velocity, but that's just a convention. The bomb aimer would be equally justified in considering his own frame at rest and the ground moving in the opposite direction.

INERTIAL FRAMES

Out of all the orbiting, spinning, oscillating, tumbling frames we can conceive as moving with the various objects, real and imaginable, that fill the universe, what we've done is identify a particular set of frames within which all observers will deduce the same laws of motion, expressed in their simplest form. (Even so, it took two thousand years after Aristotle to figure them out.) The reason this is so follows from one crucial factor that all of the observers will agree on: Bodies not acted upon by a force of any kind will continue to exist in a state of rest or uniform motion in a straight line—even though what constitutes "rest," and which particular straight line we're talking about, may differ from one observer to another. In fact, this is a statement of Newton's first law, known as the law of inertia. Frames in which it holds true are called, accordingly, "inertial frames," or "Galilean frames." What distinguishes them is that there is no relative acceleration or rotation between them. To an observer situated in one of them, very distant objects such as the stars appear to be at rest (unlike from the rotating Earth, for example). The procedures for converting equations of motion from one inertial frame to another are known as Galilean transforms. Newton's laws of motion are covariant with respect to Galilean transforms.

And, indeed, far more than just the laws of motion. For as the science of the eighteenth and nineteenth centuries progressed, the mechanics of point masses was extended to describe gravitation, electrostatics, the behavior of rigid bodies, then of continuous deformable media, and so to fluids and things like kinetic theories of heat. Laws derived from mechanics, such as the conservation of energy, momentum, and angular momentum, were found to be covariant with respect to Galilean transforms and afforded the mechanistic foundations of classical science. Since the laws formulated in any Galilean frame came out the same, it followed that no mechanical experiment could differentiate one frame from another or single out one of them as "preferred" by being at rest in absolute space. This expresses the principle of "Galilean-Newtonian Relativity." With the classical laws of mechanics, the Galilean transformations, and the principle of Newtonian relativity mutually consistent, the whole of science seemed at last to have been integrated into a common understanding that was intellectually satisfying and complete.

EXTENDING CLASSICAL RELATIVITY

PROBLEMS WITH ELECTRODYNAMICS

As the quotation at the beginning of this section says, it couldn't last. To begin with, the new science of electrostatics appeared to be an analog of gravitation, with the added feature that electrical charges could repel as well as attract. The equations for electrical force were of the same form as Newton's gravitational law, known to be covariant under Galilean transform, and it was expected that the same would apply. However, as the work of people like André-Marie Ampère, Michael Faraday, and Hans Christian Oersted progressed from electrostatics to electrodynamics, the study of electrical entities in motion, it became apparent that the situation was more complicated. Interactions between magnetic fields and electric charges produced forces acting in directions other than the straight connecting line between the sources, and which, unlike the case in gravitation and electrostatics, depended on the velocity of the charged body as well as its position. Since a velocity in one inertial frame can always be made zero in a different frame, this seemed to imply that under the classical transformations a force would exist in one that didn't exist in the other. And since force causes mass to accelerate, an acceleration could be produced in one frame but not in the other when the frames themselves were not accelerating relative to each other—which made no sense. The solution adopted initially was simply to exclude electrodynamics from the principle of classical relativity until the phenomena were better understood.

But things got worse, not better. James Clerk Maxwell's celebrated equations, developed in the period 1860–64, express concisely yet comprehensively the connection between electric and magnetic quantities that the various experiments up to that time had established, and the manner in which they affect each other across intervening space. (Actually, Wilhelm Weber and Neumann derived a version of the same laws somewhat earlier, but their work was considered suspect on grounds, later shown to be erroneous, that it violated the principle of conservation of energy, and it's Maxwell who is remembered.) In Maxwell's treatment, electrical and magnetic effects appear as aspects of a combined "electromagnetic field"—the concept of a field pervading the space around a charged or magnetized object having been introduced by Faraday—and it was by means of disturbances propagated through this field that electrically interacting objects influenced each other.

An electron is an example of a charged object. A moving charge constitutes an electric current, which gives rise to a magnetic field. An accelerating charge produces a changing magnetic field, which in turn creates an electric field, and the combined electromagnetic disturbance radiating out across space would produce forces on other charges that it encountered, setting them in motion—a bit like jiggling a floating cork up and down in the water and creating ripples that spread out and jiggle other corks floating some distance away. A way of achieving this would be by using a tuned electrical circuit to make electrons surge back and forth along an antenna wire, causing sympathetic charge movements (i.e., currents) in a receiving antenna, which of course is the basis of radio. Another example is light, where the frequencies involved are much higher, resulting from the transitions of electrons between orbits within atoms rather than oscillations in an electrical circuit.

MAXWELL'S CONSTANT VELOCITY

The difficulty that marred the comforting picture of science that had been coming together up until then was that the equations gave a velocity of propagation that depended only on the electrical properties of the medium through which the disturbance traveled, and was the same in every direction. In the absence of matter, i.e., in empty space, this came out at 300,000 kilometers per second and was designated by c, now known to be the velocity of light. But the appearance of this value in the laws of electromagnetism meant that the laws were not covariant under Galilean transforms between inertial frames. For under the transformation rules, in the same way that our airplane's velocity earlier would reduce to zero if measured in the bomb aimer's reference frame, or double if measured in the frame of another plane going the opposite way, the same constant velocity (depending only on electrical constants pertaining to the medium) couldn't be true in all of them. If Maxwell's equations were to be accepted, it seemed there could only exist one "absolute" frame of reference in which the laws took their standard, simplest form. Any frame moving with respect to it, even an inertial frame, would have to be considered "less privileged."

Putting it another way, the laws of electromagnetism, the classical Galilean transforms of space and time coordinates, and the principle of Newtonian relativity, were not compatible. Hence the elegance and aesthetic appeal that had been found to apply for mechanics didn't extend to the whole of science. The sense of completeness that science had been seeking for centuries seemed to have evaporated practically as soon as it was found. This was not very intellectually satisfying at all.

One attempt at a way out, the "ballistic theory," hypothesized the speed of light (from now on taken as representing electromagnetic radiation in general) as constant with respect to the source. Its speed as measured in other frames would then appear greater or less in the same way as that of bullets fired from a moving airplane. Such a notion was incompatible with a field theory of light, in which disturbances propagate at a characteristic rate that has nothing to do with the movement of their sources, and was reminiscent of the corpuscular theory that interference experiments were thought to have laid to rest. But it was consistent with the relativity principle: Light speed would transform from one inertial frame, that of the source, to any other just like the velocity of a regular material body.

However, observations ruled it out. In binary star systems, for example, where one star is approaching and the other receding, the light emitted would arrive at different times, resulting in distortions that should have been unmistakable but which were not observed. A series of laboratory experiments [65] also told against a ballistic explanation. The decisive one was probably one with revolving mirrors conducted by A. A. Michelson in 1913, which also effectively negated an ingenious suggestion that lenses and mirrors might reradiate incident light at velocity c with respect to themselves—a possibility that the more orthodox experiments hadn't taken into account.

Another thought was that whenever light was transmitted through a material medium, this medium provided the local privileged frame in which c applied. Within the atmosphere of the Earth, therefore, the speed of light should be constant with respect to the Earth-centered frame. But this runs into logical problems. For suppose that light were to go from one medium into another moving relative to the first. The speeds in the two domains are different, each being determined by the type of medium and their relative motion. Now imagine that the two media are progressively rarified to the point of becoming a vacuum. The interaction between matter and radiation would become less and less, shown as a steady reduction of such effects as refraction and scattering to the point of vanishing, but the sudden jump in velocity would still remain without apparent cause, which is surely untenable.

Once again, experimental evidence proved negative. For one thing, there was the phenomenon of stellar aberration, known since James Bradley's report to Newton's friend Edmond Halley, in 1728. Bradley found that in the course of a year the apparent position of a distant star describes an ellipse around a fixed point denoting where it "really" is. The effect results from the Earth's velocity in its orbit around the Sun, which makes it necessary to offset the telescope angle slightly from the correct direction to the star in order to allow for the telescope's forward movement while the light is traveling down its length. It's the same as having to tilt an umbrella when running, and the vertically falling rain appears to be coming down at a slant. If the incoming light were swept along with the atmosphere as it entered (analogous to the rain cloud moving with us), the effect wouldn't be observed. This was greeted by some as vindicating the corpuscular theory, but it turns out that the same result can be derived from wave considerations too, although not as simply. And in similar vein, experiments such as that of Armand Fizeau (1851), which measured the speed of light through fast-flowing liquid in a pipe, and Sir George Airy (1871), who repeated Bradley's experiment using a telescope filled with water and showed aberration didn't arise in the telescope tube, demonstrated that the velocity of light in a moving medium could not be obtained by simple addition in the way of airplanes and machine-gun bullets or as a consequence of being dragged by the medium.

Relativity is able to provide interpretations of these results—indeed, the theory would have had a short life if it couldn't. But the claim that relativity is thereby "proved" isn't justified. As the Dutch astronomer M. Hoek showed as early as 1868, attempts at using a moving material medium to measure a change in the velocity of light are defeated by the effect of refraction, which cancels out the effects of the motion. [66]

MICHELSON, MORELY, AND THE ETHER THAT WASN'T

These factors suggested that the speed of light was independent of the motion of the radiation source and of the transmitting medium. It seemed, then, that the only recourse was to abandon the relativity principle and conclude that there was after all a privileged, universal, inertial reference frame in which the speed of light was the same in all directions as the simplest form of the laws required, and that the laws derived in all other frames would show a departure from this ideal. The Earth itself cannot be this privileged frame, since it is under constant gravitational acceleration by the Sun (circular motion, even at constant speed, involves a continual change of direction, which constitutes an acceleration) and thus is not an inertial frame. And even if at some point its motion coincided with the privileged frame, six months later its orbit would have carried it around to a point where it was moving with double its orbital speed with respect to it. In any case, whichever inertial frame was the privileged one, sensitive enough measurements of the speed of light in orthogonal directions in space, continued over six months, should be capable of detecting the Earth's motion with respect to it.

Many interpreted this universal frame as the hypothetical "ether" that had been speculated about long before Maxwell's electromagnetic theory, when experiments began revealing the wave nature of light. If light consisted of waves, it seemed there needed to be something present to be doing the "waving"—analogous to the water that carries ocean waves, the air that conducts sound waves, and so on. The eighteenth to early nineteenth centuries saw great progress in the development of mathematics that dealt with deformation and stresses in continuous solids, and early notions of the ether sought an interpretation in mechanical terms. It was visualized as a substance pervading all space, being highly rigid in order to propagate waves at such enormous velocity, yet tenuous enough not to impede the motions of planets. Maxwell's investigations began with models of fields impressed upon a mechanical ether, but the analogy proved cumbersome and he subsequently dispensed with it to regard the field itself as the underlying physical reality. Nevertheless, that didn't rule out the possibility that an "ether" of some peculiar nature might still exist. Perhaps, some concluded, the universal frame was none other than that within which the ether was at rest. So detection of motion with respect to it could be thought of as measuring the "ether wind" created by the Earth's passage through it in its movement through space.

The famous experiment that put this to the test, repeated and refined in innumerable forms since, was performed in 1887 by

Albert Michelson and Edward Morley. The principle, essentially, was the same as comparing the round-trip times for a swimmer first crossing a river and back, in each case having to aim upstream of the destination in order to compensate for the current, and second covering the same distance against the current and then returning with it. The times will not be the same, and from the differences the speed of the current can be calculated. The outcome was one of the most famous null results in history. No motion through an ether was detected. No preferred inertial reference frame could be identified that singled itself out from all the others in any way.

So now we have a conundrum. The elaborate experimental attempts to detect a preferred reference frame indicated an acceptance that the relativity principle might have to be abandoned for electromagnetism. But the experimental results failed to identify the absolute reference frame that this willingness allowed. The laws of electromagnetism themselves had proved strikingly successful in predicting the existence of propagating waves, their velocity and other quantities, and appeared to be on solid ground. And yet an incompatibility existed in that they were not covariant under the classical transforms of space and time coordinates between inertial frames. The only thing left to question, therefore, was the process involving the transformations themselves.

LORENTZ'S TRANSFORMS FOR ELECTROMAGNETICS

Around the turn of the twentieth century the Dutch theoretical physicist Hendrick Lorentz followed the path of seeking alternative transformation laws that would do for electromagnetics what the classical transforms had done for mechanics. Two assumptions that few people would question were implicit in the form of the Galilean transforms: (1) that observers in all frames will measure time the same, as if by some universal clock that ticks the same everywhere; and (2) while the space coordinates assigned to points on a rigid body such as a measuring rod might differ, the distance between them would not. In other words, time intervals and lengths were invariant.

In the Lorentz Transforms, as they came to be called, this was no longer so. Time intervals and lengths measured by an observer in one inertial frame, when transformed to another frame, needed to be modified by a factor that depended on the relative motion between them. Lorentz's system retained the notion of an absolute frame in which the ether is at rest. But the new transforms resulted in distances being reduced in the direction of motion relative to it, and it was this fact which, through an unfortunate coincidence of effects, made detection of the motion unobservable. As a matter of fact, an actual physical shrinkage of precisely this form—the "Fitzgerald Contraction"—had been proposed to explain the Michelson-Morley result as due to a shortening of the interferometer arms in the affected direction. Some textbook writers are of the opinion that Lorentz himself took the contractions as real; others, that he used them simply as mathematical formalisms, symbolizing, as it were, some fictitious realm of space and time that applied to electromagnetic phenomena. I don't claim to know what Lorentz thought. But here was a system which acknowledged a preferred frame as required by Maxwell's equations (defined by the constancy of *c*), yet at the same time observed the relativity that the optical experiment seemed to demand. Okay, maybe things were a bit messy in that a different system applied to mechanics. But everything more or less worked, and maybe that was just the way things from now on would have to be.

Except that somebody called Albert Einstein wasn't happy with it.

THE NEW RELATIVITY

EINSTEIN: TRANSFORMING ALL OF PHYSICS

Neither mechanics nor—regardless of the constant in Maxwell's equations— electromagnetics had revealed an absolute frame of reference. All experiments seemed to indicate that any inertial frame was as good as another. What this suggested to Einstein was that some kind of relativity principle was in evidence that applied across the whole of science, according to which physics should be the same for all observers. Or putting it another way, the equations expressing all physical laws should be covariant between inertial frames. Following Lorentz, but with an aim that was general and not restricted to a subset of physics, Einstein set out to discover a system of transforms that would make this true. Two postulates formed his starting point. (1) The relativity principle applies for all of physics across all inertial frames, which was what the intuitively satisfying solution he was searching for required. (2) The velocity of light, c, is the same for observers in all inertial frames regardless of their state of motion relative to each other. For that's what Maxwell's equations said, and being a physical law, it had to apply in all frames for (1) to be true.

And what he did in his paper on special relativity, published in 1905, was rediscover the Lorentz Transforms. This was hardly surprising, since they gave the right answers for electromagnetism—hence anything saying otherwise would have been wrong. But there was a crucial difference. Whereas Lorentz's application of them had been restricted to the special area of electromagnetism, Einstein maintained that they applied to everything—mechanics as well.

But, wait a minute. If the relativity principle was to be observed, and the new transforms applied, how could they still be compatible with Newton's long-established mechanics, which was enthroned as being consistent with the classical Galilean transforms, not with the new Lorentzian ones?

The only answer could be that Newtonian mechanics wasn't as invincibly established as everyone thought it was. Recall the two assumptions we mentioned earlier that the Galilean transforms imply: that space and time intervals are invariant. What Einstein proposed was that the velocity-dependencies deduced by Lorentz were not part of some fudge-factor needed for electromagnetism, but that they expressed fundamental properties of the nature of space and time that were true universally, and hence called for a revision of mechanics. However, the new mechanics could hardly render invalid the classical results that centuries of experimenting had so strongly supported. And indeed, this turned out to be so; at the low velocities that classical science had been confined to, and which shape the common sense of everyday experience, the equations of the new mechanics merged into and became indistinguishable for all practical purposes from the Newtonian ones.

Relativity's Weird Results

Where the two systems began departing significantly was when very high velocities were involved—of the order of those encountered in electromagnetism and late-nineteenth-century experiments on fast-moving particles, where it had already become clear that classical mechanics couldn't be correct. Space and time were no longer fixed and unchanging but behaved weirdly at extremes of velocity that everyday experience provided no schooling for, with consequences that Newtonian mechanics hadn't anticipated. These are well-enough known now to require no more than that they be listed. All have been verified by experiment.

Addition of velocities. In classical mechanics, a bullet fired from an airplane will hit a target on the ground ahead with a velocity equal to that of the plane relative to the ground plus that of the bullet relative to the plane. But according to relativity (henceforth the "special relativity theory," or "SRT"), what appears to be obvious isn't exactly so. The velocity in the target's frame doesn't equal the sum of the two components—although at the speeds of planes and bullets you'd never notice the difference. The higher the velocities, the greater the discrepancy, the relationship being such that the bullet's velocity in the target's frame never manages to exceed c, the speed of light. Thus even if the plane is coming in at 90% c and fires a bullet that leaves the plane at 90% c, the bullet's velocity measured by the target will be 90% c plus something, but not greater than c itself. (In fact it will be 99.45% c.) In the limit, when the bullet leaves the plane at c, the resultant, bizarre as it sounds, is still c. It has become a photon of light. Its speed is the same in both the frame of the airplane (source) and that of the target (receiver). Add two velocities—or as many as you like—each equal to c, and the result still comes out at c. And that's what all the Michelson-Morley-type experiments confirm.

Relativity of simultaneity. The upper limit on velocity makes it impossible to devise a method for synchronizing clocks in a way that enables different frames to agree on whether two events happen simultaneously. Some arbitrary frame could be chosen as a reference, of course—such as the Sun-centered frame—and a correction applied to decide if two events were simultaneous as far as that frame was concerned, but it wouldn't mean much. One person's idea of simultaneity would still be no better or worse than any other's, and the term loses any real significance. Establishing absolute simultaneity without a privileged frame would require an infinitely fast synchronizing signal, which SRT says we don't have.

Mass increase. Mass measures the amount of resistance that an object exhibits to being accelerated—that is, having its state of motion (speed and/or direction) changed. A cannon ball has a large mass compared to a soccer ball of the same size, as kicking or trying to stop one of each will verify. Though unobservable at everyday levels, this resistance to being accelerated increases as an object moves with higher speed. In particle accelerators, far more energy is required to nudge the velocity of a particle an additional tenth of a percent *c* faster when it is already moving at, say, 90% *c* than to accelerate it the first tenth of a percent from rest.

Mass-energy equivalence. As the velocity of a body increases, it stores more kinetic energy. From the preceding paragraph, it also exhibits an increase in mass. This turns out to be more than just coincidence, for according to relativity mass and energy become equivalent and can be converted one into the other. This is true even of the residual mass of an object not moving at all, which still has the energy equivalent given by the famous equation $E = m_0 \cdot c^2$, where E is the energy and m_0 the object's mass when at rest. All energy transitions thus involve changes in mass, but the effect is usually noticeable only in nuclear processes such as the mass deficit of particles bound into a nucleus or the yield of fission and fusion bombs; also the mass-energy balances observed in particle creation and annihilation events.

Time dilation. Time, and hence processes that are time-dependent, runs slower in a moving frame than in one at relative rest. An example is the extended lifetimes shown by muons created by bombardment of the upper atmosphere by protons from the Sun. The muons reach the Earth's surface in numbers about nine times greater than their natural decay time (half-life 2.2 microseconds) says they should. This is explained by time in the muon's moving frame being dilated as measured from the surface, giving a longer decay period than would be experienced by a muon at rest. High-accuracy clocks on rocket sleds run slower than stationary clocks.

The mathematician Hermann Minkowski developed the Einstein theory further by showing that it entailed a reality consisting not of the three-dimensional space and separate time that are ordinarily perceived, but of a strange, non-Euclidian, four-dimensional merging of the two known since as spacetime. Only from the local standpoint of a particular Galilean frame do they separate out into the space and time of everyday life. But the space and time that they resolve into is different in different frames—which is what the transforms of SRT are saying.

UNIFYING PHYSICS

Although many might remain unconvinced, this kind of thing is what scientists regard as a simplification. When phenomena that were previously thought to be distinct and independent—such as space and time in the foregoing—turn out to be just different aspects of some more fundamental entity, understanding of what's going on is deepened even if the techniques for unraveling that understanding take some work in getting used to. In the same kind of way, momentum and energy become unified in the new four-dimensional world, as do the classical concepts of force and work, and electric current and charge.

This also throws light (pun unintended, but not bad so I'll let it stand) on the interdependence of the electric and magnetic field quantities in Maxwell's equations. In Maxwell's classical three-dimensional space the electromagnetic field is formed from the superposition of an electric field, which is a vector field, and a magnetic field, which is a tensor field. In Minkowski's spacetime these merge into a single four-dimensional tensor called the electromagnetic tensor, and the four three-dimensional equations that Maxwell needed to describe the relationships reduce to two four-dimensional ones. Hence the interdependence of electric and magnetic fields, which in the classical view had to be simply accepted as a fact of experience, becomes an immediate consequence of their being partial aspects of the same underlying electromagnetic entity.

In SRT, Minkowski's four-dimensional spacetime is considered to be "flat"—uncurved, like the classical Euclidian space of Newton. An object's "world-line"—the path showing its history in spacetime—will be a straight line when the object is in a state of rest or uniform motion. What differentiates accelerating frames is that their world-lines become curved. In developing his general theory of relativity (GRT), Einstein sought to remove the restriction of inertial frames and extend the principle to frames in general. In doing so he proposed that a region of space subject to gravitation is really no different from a reference frame undergoing acceleration. Inside an elevator, for example, there's no way of telling if a pen falling to the floor does so because the elevator is accelerating upward or because the floor is attracting it downward. [67]

If a gravitational field is equivalent to acceleration, motions associated with it will also be represented by curved world-lines in spacetime. Hence, in GRT gravitation is interpreted geometrically. Instead of somehow attracting bodies like planets to move in curved paths through flat space, the presence of the Sun's mass itself warps the geometry of spacetime such that the paths they naturally follow become curved. An analogy often used to illustrate this is a stretched rubber sheet, representing undeformed space. Placing a heavy object like a bowling ball on the sheet creates a "well," with sides steepening toward the center, that the ball sits in, but which would be indiscernible to a viewer vertically above who had no knowledge of a dimension extending in that direction. If a marble is now rolled across the sheet, its trajectory will be deflected exactly as if the sheet were flat and the ball exerted an attraction. In the absence of any friction, the marble could be trapped in a closed path where the tendencies to fall down the well and to be lifted out of it by centrifugal force balance, causing it to orbit the bowling ball endlessly.

If spacetime itself is curved in the vicinity of masses, then not just massive objects but anything that moves through space will also follow paths determined by the nonflat geometry. So stars, for instance, should "attract" light, not just material bodies. That this is so is verified by the observed deflection of starlight passing close to the Sun. So once again, all forms of energy exhibit the equivalence to a property of mass.

Finally we're back to a situation where we have the principle of relativity, a universal statement of the laws of physics (the new mechanics, which subsumes electrodynamics), and a system of transformations that are mutually consistent. Science has been integrated into a common understanding that's found to be intellectually satisfying and complete. Its successes are celebrated practically universally as the crowning achievement of twentieth-century science. So what are some people saying is wrong with it?

DISSIDENT VIEWPOINTS

As we said at the beginning, it's not so much a case of being "wrong." When a theory's predictions accord with the facts as far as can be experimentally determined, it obviously can't be rejected as an invalid way of looking at things. But that isn't enough to make it the only valid way. And if other ways that can be shown to be equally valid by according with the same facts are able to do so more simply, they deserve consideration. The objection is more to the confident assurances that we now have all the answers, no way of doing better is conceivable, and the book is closed. When claims to a revelation of final Truth are heard, with all moves toward criticism being censured, ridiculed, or dismissed out of hand, then what's going is drifting toward becoming intolerant dogmatism rather than science. Einstein would probably have been one of the first to agree. One of his more endearing quotes was that "I only had two original ideas in my life, and one of them was wrong." I don't think he would object at all to our taking a long, hard look at the other one too.

ELEGANT, YES. BUT IS IT REALLY USEFUL?

Not everyone is as enamored that the disappearance of such fundamental concepts as space and time into abstractions of mathematical formalism helps our understanding of anything or sees it as necessary. Traditionally, length, time, and mass have constituted the elements of physics from which all other quantities, such as acceleration, force, energy, momentum, and so on, are derived. Elevating a velocity (length divided by time) to a privileged position as Nature's fundamental reality, and then having to distort space and time to preserve its constancy, just has the feel about it, to many, of somehow getting things the wrong way around. This isn't to say that what's familiar and apparently self-evident can always be relied upon as the better guide. But a physics of comprehension built on a foundation of intuition that can be trusted is surely preferable to one of mere description that results from applying formalized procedures that have lost all physical meaning. We live in a world inhabited not by four-dimensional tensors but by people and things, and events that happen in places and at times. A map and a clock are of more use to us than being told that an expression couched in terms of components having an obscure nature is invariant. If other interpretations of the facts that relativity addresses can be offered that integrate more readily with existing understanding, they deserve serious consideration.

LORENTZ'S ETHER REVISITED

A good place to start might be with Lorentz's ether theory (LET). Recall that it was compatible with all the electromagnetic results that SRT accounts for but postulated a fixed ether as the propagating medium, which is what the c in Maxwell's equations referred to. In another reference frame the velocity of light will be c plus or minus that frame's velocity relative to the privileged frame defined by the ether. "But measurements don't show c plus or minus anything. They show c." Which was where all the trouble started. Well, yes, that's what measurements show. But measurements are based on standards like meter-rules and clocks. While SRT was willing to give up the Lorentzian assumptions of space and time being immutably what they had always been, the proponents of an LET interpretation point out that SRT itself carries an assumption that would seem far closer to home and more readily open to question, namely that the measuring standards themselves are immutable. Before consigning the entire structure of the universe to deformities that it hasn't recovered from since, wouldn't it be a good idea to make sure that it wasn't the rules and clocks that were being altered?

If this should be so, then the rest frame of the ether is the one the electromagnetic laws are correct in, which the c in Maxwell's equations refers to. In frames that are moving relative to it, the speed of light will be different. However, motion through the ether alters physical structures in such a way that the standards used will still measure it as c. So nobody can detect their motion with respect to the ether frame, and the same experimental results as are derived from SRT follow. But space and time remain what they've always been, and light retains the same property as every other wave phenomenon in physics in that its velocity is a constant with respect to the medium that it's traveling through.

If motion relative to the ether frame could be established, the notion of absolute simultaneity would be restored. The velocity of light within that frame is known, and it would be meaningful to say, for example, that signals sent from the ends of a measured distance arrive at the midpoint at the same time. Velocities in other frames could then be corrected with respect to that standard. The situation would be similar to using sound signals to synchronize a clock on the ground with one carried on a moving vehicle.

It might seem a remarkable coincidence that the distortions induced in the measuring standards should be of just the right amount to keep the apparent value of c at that given by Maxwell's equations. But it isn't really, since the Lorentz Transforms that yield the distortions were constructed to account for those experimental results in the first place.

Lorentz himself conducted theoretical investigations of the flattening of electrons, assumed to be normally symmetrical, in their direction of motion through the ether. If basic particles can be affected, the notion of physical objects being distorted becomes less difficult to accept. After all, "matter" comprises a volume of mostly empty space—or ether in the context of the present discussion—defined by a highly dispersed configuration of electrical entities linked by forces. (Think of those models made up from balls connected by webs of springs that you see in science displays in museums and high-school laboratories to represent molecules.) Maybe the idea that objects moving fast through the ether could ever *not* be distorted is what really needs explaining.

Such distortions would perturb the energy dynamics of electron shell structures and atomic nuclei, with consequent modifications to emitted frequencies and other time-dependent processes, and hence any measuring techniques based on them. So the assumption of immutable clocks stands or falls on the same ground.

An introduction to the arguments favoring an LET model, and to the philosophical considerations supporting it is given concisely by Dr. George Marklin. [68] The LET interpretation can also be extended to include gravitational effects by allowing the ether to move differentially. Such a general ether theory has been developed by Ilja Schmelzer. [69] It is mathematically equivalent to GRT but uses Euclidean space and absolute time. Schmelzer gives the ether a density, velocity and pressure tensor and satisfies all the appropriate conservation equations, but it's a fairly recent development and there are still unresolved issues.

A comprehensive treatment that covers all the ground of SRT

and GRT as well as addressing the controversial experimental issues that are argued both ways, such as the interpretation of results from rotating frames, transporting of atomic clocks around the world, and the calibrating of GPS satellite ranging is Ronald Hatch's "modified Lorentz ether theory," MLET. [70] The "modified" part comes from its extension of using the same ether to account for material particles in the form of standing waves. The theory and its ramifications are explored in detail in Hatch's book *Escape from Einstein*. [71]

ENTRAINING THE ETHER

The concept of a fixed ether pervading all of space uniformly like a placid ocean was perhaps something of an idealization that owed more to Aristotlean notions of perfection than the messy, turbulent world we find ourselves living in. The Michelson-Morely result showed that no motion through such an ether can be detected—at least not by present methods—from which one conclusion is that it might as well not be there, and therefore to all practical purposes it doesn't exist. This is the path that SRT develops. However, the same result would be obtained if the ether in the vicinity of the Earth moved with it in its orbit around the Sun, accompanying it as a kind of "bubble" inside which the Earth and the local ether remain at rest relative to each other. Such an "entrained ether" interpretation was in fact favored by Michelson himself, who never accepted the SRT explanation. The general consensus, however, was it was incompatible with the aberration effect on starlight described earlier, and it was rejected accordingly.

But aberration turns out, on closer examination, to be a more complex business than is often acknowledged. The typical SRT textbook explanation attributes the effect to relative velocity, for example: " . . . the direction of a light ray depends essentially on the velocity of the light source relative to the observer. . . . This apparent motion is simply due to the fact that the observed direction of the light ray coming from the star depends on the velocity of the earth relative to the star." [72]

This can't be so, however, since stars in general possess velocities that vary wildly with respect to the Earth. Pointing a telescope at any patch of sky constrained sufficiently to signify direction should still capture a representative sample of them, which should display a spread of aberration displacements accordingly. But that isn't what's found. They turn out to be all the same.

Then again, let's consider what are known as spectroscopic binary stars, that is, double stars too close together to be resolved separately but which can be distinguished by their Doppler-shifted spectra. If aberration depended on velocity, the very difference in velocities that produces the Doppler shifts would be sufficient to separate the images resolvably—in which case they would no longer be spectroscopic binaries!

And further, even for a star that was not moving with respect to the Earth at all, the atoms in the star's photosphere that do the actual emitting of light, and which therefore constitute its true sources, will be moving thermally in all directions randomly. If aberration were due to their velocities, the compound effect would be sufficient to expand the points seen in the sky to a size that could be discerned with a good pair of binoculars.

There is an apparent displacement of planets, also called aberration, unfortunately, that results from the delay of light in reaching the Earth. It does depend on source velocity, but this isn't the quantity that we're talking about. Its effect reduces with distance and is effectively zero for things like stars. According to Thomas E. Phipps Jr., Einstein used the wrong one. [73] Howard Hayden, professor emeritus of physics at the University of Connecticut, Storrs, arrives at the same conclusion. [74]

Stellar aberration affects all stars in a locally surveyed region equally and varies systematically with an annual cycle. The velocity that it depends on is clearly the orbital velocity of the Earth, which would seem to imply velocity with respect to the Sun's frame. But there's a difficulty. Suppose there was a streetlamp beyond the telescope, directly in line with the star being observed. If some kind of motion through an ether were responsible, you'd think that light from one would follow the same path as the light from the other, and the same aberration should be observed. It isn't. No measurable effect occurs at all. Relativists chuckle and say, "We told you so. It's because there's no relative motion between the street light and the observer." But the considerations above are enough to say that can't be true either. It's more as if different ethers were involved, one containing the Earth and the streetlamp, inside which there is no aberration, the other extending out to somewhere less than the Sun's distance such that its annual motion within the Sun's frame produces the effect on starlight. There are further complications too, such as why long-baseline radio telescope arrays should detect aberration when there's no tube for photons to move sideways in, and the theories and arguments currently doing the rounds to try and account for them could bog us down for the rest of this book. I've dwelt on it this far to show that the whole subject of aberration is a lot more involved than the standard treatments that dismiss it in a few lines would lead one to believe.

FIELD-REFERRED THEORIES

Petr Beckmann, a Czech professor of electrical engineering at the University of Colorado, developed an alternative theory in which the second of SRT's two founding premises—that the speed of light is constant with respect to all observers everywhere—is replaced by its speed being constant with respect to the dominant local force field through which it propagates. (SRT's first premise was the relativity principle, by which the same laws of physics apply everywhere.) For most of the macroscopic universe in which observers and laboratories are located, this means the gravitational field that happens to dominate wherever one happens to be. On the surface of the Earth it means the Earth's field, but beyond some distance that gives way to the Sun's field, outside which the field of the local part of the galactic realm dominates, and so on. This gives a more tangible form to the notion of embedded "ether bubbles," with light propagating at its characteristic speed within fields that move relative to each other—like the currents and drifts and doldrums that make up a real ocean, as opposed to a universally static, glassy abstraction. And since, as with any conservative vector field (one in which energy potentials can be defined), any point of a gravity field is described by a line of force and the equipotential passing through it, the field coordinate system can serve as a local standard of rest.

Does this mean, then, that the gravitational field is, in fact, the long sought-for "ether"? Beckmann asks, in effect, who cares? since the answers come out the same. Marklin is more of a purist, insisting on philosophical grounds that whatever its nature finally turns out to be, a physically real medium must exist. A "field," he pointed out when I visited him at his home in Houston while researching this book, is simply a mathematical construct describing what a medium does. The smile can't exist without the Cheshire cat. I'm not going to attempt to sit in judgment on heavyweights like Petr and George. The purpose of this essay is simply to inform interested readers on some of the ideas that are out there.

The cause of all the confusion, Beckmann argues, is that what experiments have been telling us about motion relative to the field has been mistakenly interpreted as meaning motion relative to observers who have always been attached to it. Since every experiment cited to date as supporting or "proving" relativity has been performed in a laboratory solidly at rest on the Earth's surface, the same experiments are consistent with either theory. Both theories account equally well for the same results. Except that doing the accounting can be a far more involved business in one case than in the other. As an example of how the same result is explained simply and straightforwardly by one theory but requires elaborate footwork from the other, let's consider the Michelson-Gale experiment of 1925, which rarely finds its way into the textbooks. [75]

Michelson-Morley had failed to detect any motion of the Earth relative to an ether in its orbit around the Sun. This could be because there is no ether (SRT), or there is but the distortion of measuring standards obscures it (LET), or because the local ether moves with the Earth (Beckmann-type field-referred theories). Does the local ether bubble rotate with the Earth also, or does the Earth spin inside it?

Michelson and Gale set up an experiment to try to answer this at Clearing, Ilinois, using a rectangular interferometer large enough to detect the difference in velocity between the north and south arms due to the southern one's being slightly nearer the equator and hence moving slightly faster. It was a magnificent affair measuring over 2,000 feet east-west and 1,100 feet north-south, with evacuated pipes 12 inches across to carry the beams, and concrete boxes for the mirrors, lenses, and beam splitters. Two hundred sixty-nine measurements were taken in sets representing various conditions.

And fringe shifts *were* observed—not only of a magnitude consistent with the "hypothesis of a fixed ether" (Michelson's words) within the limits of observational error, but from which the experimenters were able accurately to calculate the rotation speed of the Earth.

Beckmann's theory predicts this on the theoretical argument that if the gravitational field describes an outward propagation, the effect would "decouple" from the source as soon as it leaves, somewhat like bullets from a rotating machine gun still radiating outward in straight lines. In other words, the field's effects shouldn't share the source's rotation, and hence the speeds of the light beams in the two arms of the interferometer will be different. This doesn't contradict Einstein, though, where the General Theory is invoked to arrive at the same result on the grounds that each beam has its own idea of time. But whereas Beckmann's conclusion follows from Galilean principles and a few lines of high-school algebra, GRT requires multidimensional tensors in spacetime and non-Euclidian geometry.

ELECTROMAGNETIC MASS—INCREASE WITHOUT EINSTEIN

The law of inertia says that a mass tends to keep its momentum constant, i.e., it resists external forces that try to change that momentum. That's what the definition of mass is. The same is true of an electromagnetic field. A steady electric current produces a steady magnetic field. If the field is changed by changing the current, it will, by Faraday's law, induce an electric field that will seek to restore the current and its field to its original value—all familiar to electrical engineers as Lenz's laws of self-inductance, mutual inductance, and so forth. Similarly, a steady electric field is produced by a steady distribution of charge. If the charge sources are moved to change the field, the resulting "displacement current" gives rise to a magnetic field, and the changing magnetic field induces an electric field that opposes the movement of the charges. This is sometimes known as the "inertia" of the electromagnetic field, manifesting an "electromagnetic momentum."

It turns out that the electromagnetic counterpart to momentum also carries precisely its counterpart to mass. The electromagnetic mass of a charged body is an additional factor by which it resists physical acceleration *beyond* the resistance normally exhibited by the uncharged mechanical mass. This was known to the classical physicists of the nineteenth century. It comes out as a constant that multiplies velocity to add a further parcel of momentum in the same way that regular Newtonian mass does.

At least, it does when the electric (Coulomb) field carried by the charged body is spherically symmetrical, as would be the case when it's at rest—and near enough when it isn't moving very fast. The direction of the electric field at any point around a charged body—the line of voltage gradient—lies perpendicular (orthogonal) to the surfaces of equipotential. For a charge at rest the equipotential surfaces are concentric spheres like the skins of an onion, across which the field lines radiate straight and symmetrically in all directions like sea-anemone spikes.

However, Maxwell's equations and the relativity principle—and nothing more—indicate that when the body moves, the charge distribution will change as the charge begins to partly "catch up" with its own equipotentials, causing them to bunch up ahead and spread out behind. The result is that the orthogonal field lines are no longer straight but become curves. (This was what prompted Lorentz to conclude that electrons contract in the direction in which they move.)

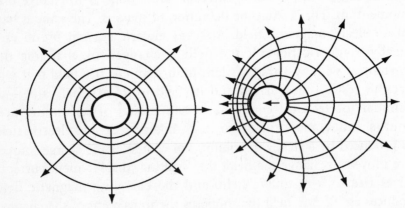

Equipotential surfaces and orthogonal field lines around a charged body when at rest, left, and in motion, right.

Now it gets interesting. The expression for the electromagnetic mass of a body depends on the distribution of its electric field in space. When the rearrangement that takes place with increasing velocity is taken into account, the electromagnetic mass increases from its value at rest. The formula that the classical physicists of the nineteenth century derived to describe it is the same as the SRT equation for mass increase. The difference is that instead of rearranging the field distribution, SRT rearranged space and time, then applied the result to *all* masses, electromagnetic or mechanical, charged or neutral. It would appear that SRT's way of getting there wasn't necessary.

Page, for example showed in 1912 [76] that Coulomb's law of electrostatic attraction and the Lorentz transforms are sufficient to derive Maxwell's equations—from which everything supporting SRT follows. But Coulomb's law is formally identical with Newton's law of gravitation. Hence, Page's method must lead to formally identical results—a "Maxwell" law that holds for mechanical, electrically neutral mass. By this argument *all mass* is shown to be velocity-dependent from classical principles, invoking none of the observer-dependence of SRT. (Objection. "But it's right there in the textbooks. Force equals mass times acceleration. $F = m \cdot dv/dt$. Mass is a constant. You can't get away from it." Answer: "True, that's what most textbooks show. But Newton never said it. His force was always given by the change in *momentum*: $d(m \cdot v)/dt$. It allowed for the possibility of mass being velocity dependent. Mark of a careful scientist.") And since both masses, neutral and electromagnetic, respond to velocity in the same way, they can be combined into a single inertial reaction—a force that resists changes in momentum—increasing with velocity. There's nothing especially remarkable about velocity-dependent forces. Hydraulic friction and aerodynamic drag are everyday examples.

When the mass expressed as a function of c is used to calculate the work done in accelerating a body from rest to velocity v, the resulting expression for kinetic energy reduces to the familiar $1/2mv^2$ when v is small. At rest, a residual energy E_0 remains that's related to the mass m_0 by, yes, you've guessed, $E_0 = m_0 \cdot c^2$. You can do it without Einstein.

In his book *Einstein Plus Two* Beckmann goes on to show that all of the experiments usually cited as confirming the Einsteinian formulas for mass, energy, and momentum are equally consistent with the field-referred theory. Similar arguments were presented following the publication of Einstein's original SRT paper in 1905—see, for example, Lewis, 1908, which derives the velocity-dependent relationships showing mass tending to infinity as its velocity approaches that of light, from considerations of conservation when a mass is accelerated by radiation pressure.

From the theory based on the real, physical deformation of forces in motion through the locally dominant field, Beckmann is also able to derive from first principles the line spacing of the spectrum of the hydrogen atom, a first approximation to the Schrödinger equation of quantum mechanics, and the Titius-Bode series giving the distances between planetary orbits, which relativity must simply accept as given. Doesn't this make it a more powerful candidate predictively? In the latter connection, Beckmann also correctly deduces the precession of the perihelion of Mercury's orbit, usually cited as one of the decisive tests for GRT, and shows that a German by the name of Paul Gerber was able to do so using purely classical considerations in 1898, seventeen years before publication of the Einstein General Theory in 1915.

In fact, it was more in connection with the General Theory that the word "relativity" caught the world's attention. SRT didn't really create that much of a stir—as mentioned earlier, Einstein's Nobel Prize was awarded for a different paper also published in 1905, on the photoelectric effect. But in 1919 it was announced that observations of the solar eclipse in the western Pacific by a team headed by the British physicist Sir Arthur Eddington had confirmed the GRT prediction of the bending of rays of starlight passing close to the Sun, which elevated Einstein to instant fame and retroactively the SRT, too, by association. Whether it was really a triumph of the magnitude popularly depicted has been questioned. Ian McCausland, for example, [77] shows that the measurements were not particularly accurate, the standard error being about 30 percent, while the various displacements ranged from half to twice what the theory predicted, and a lot of fudging went on to come up with an average of the order that was needed. But in any case, if the local gravitational field is effectively the propagating ether, the speed of a traveling disturbance will vary with its density, and the same result can be arrived at by treating it as a refractive medium in uncurved space. [78]

GRAVITY AND ELECTROMAGNETICS

Why have we been postulating the local gravitational field as the possible propagating medium, when everything we've been talking about refers to electromagnetics? Well, the reference frame that Beckmann's theory actually postulates is the dominant local *force* field. For most practical purposes it reduces to the same thing. The magnetic force between moving charges is so small compared to the electric force between them (one of those relationships like that of mass with energy, involving c^2) that it can't even be measured unless the electric field is neutralized.

The example Beckmann gives to illustrate this is two lines of negative charges—electrons, say—moving past a stationary observer like parallel columns of soldiers. The moving charges constitute currents moving in the same direction, which accordingly generate a magnetic attraction between them. But this attractive force will be completely overshadowed by the electrostatic repulsion of the charges. To reveal the magnetic effect, it's first necessary to neutralize this repulsion, which could be achieved by adding a row of stationary positive charges like fence posts along the line of march of at least one of the columns. This is exactly what happens with the ionized atoms inside a conductor. What this says is that to demonstrate a magnetic force, at least one of the currents must flow in a normally neutral conductor such as a wire.

In the macroscopic world of neutral matter that we live in and build instruments out of for investigating electromagnetic phenomena, therefore, the dominant force field that's left after the electric fields have been eliminated by positive and negative charges that neutralize each other is that of gravitation. Or perhaps we should say "almost neutralize each other." Some fascinating work is going on that interprets the gravitational force as a residual effect of electromagnetism—see, for example, Assis, 1992 and 1995. So certainly it might be the case that in other parts of the universe not dominated by neutral matter, some other definition of the local reference frame should apply.

Dr. Carl Zapffe in his *A Reminder on E = mc²* interprets the phenomena usually cited as relativistic in a field-referred theory using the magnetosphere, which also defines the local frame moving with the Earth—and in the process he provides three derivations using classical physics of the sanctified formula contained in the title. Plots derived from space probe data and other sources show the Earth's magnetopause—the boundary of the magnetosphere— as a huge, teardrop-shaped bubble compressed to a bowshock front on the sunward side and extending outward more than ten Earth radii, around which the solar wind streams like the airflow around the body of a plane. On our planet deep inside this bubble, we've been trying assiduously for over a century to measure our airspeed with our instruments inside the cabin. Zapffe offers a model of

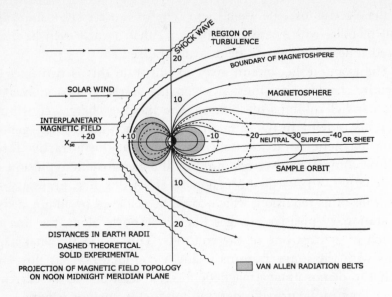

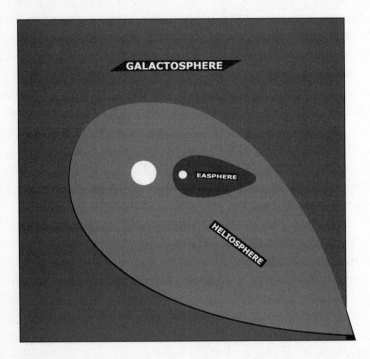

Above: General structure of the terrestrial magnetosphere. The Earth is the small circle in the center, at the origin of the coordinates. Below: The hierarchy of embedded magnetospheres. Each constitutes the local reference frame for electromagnetic propagation.

successively embedded domains in which the terrestrial magnetosphere riding with the Earth inside a "heliosphere," similarly formed
by its motion through the larger "galactosphere," and so on.

We can conduct a conversation effortlessly with another passenger in a plane because our entire acoustic environment is moving
with us. Trying it sitting out on the wing would be a different
matter, swiftly disposing of any notions we might have formed
that air doesn't exist. It might be revealing to perform experiments along the lines of Michelson-Morley on a space platform
outside the Earth's magnetosphere, under conditions that have
never been tested before, in motion relative to the local frame
as defined by the Sun.

DOES "TIME" DILATE? OR DO CLOCKS RUN SLOWER?

When we're assured of something to the effect that "relativity
is confirmed routinely in laboratories all around the world thousands of times every day," one of the instances usually cited is the
verifying of time dilation. The example given earlier was of muon
decay, where more muons from the upper atmosphere survive long
enough to reach the ground than should be able to. According to
relativity, it's because time in the muon's moving frame runs slower
than the time in the observer's frame, which includes the ground,
the atmosphere, and the whole of the path followed in the particle's
flight down. But a crucial question isn't being asked about another
possible state of affairs that would produce the same result.

Is some semi-abstract quantity called "time" actually being
dilated? Or is it simply that a difference in the internal dynamics (increased mass, for example) of moving clocks—meaning time-
varying processes in general—makes them run slower? What's the
difference? The difference is fundamental if by "moving" we mean
with respect to some privileged reference frame such as a general
Lorentzian ether, the local gravity field, or whatever. Simply put,
a clock moving in that frame runs slower—a physical reality, not
some trick of appearances or mathematical acrobatics—than a
clock that's at rest in it. The laboratory is at rest in the Earth's
frame while the muon isn't, and so the muon's clock actually
runs slower.

As an illustration of the principle (one which has nothing to
do with relativity), consider an ordinary pendulum clock being

flown around the world in an eastbound direction. The rate of a pendulum clock depends on g, the acceleration due to gravity. The Earth's rotation generates an upward centrifugal force that acts against g, reducing it slightly. Since an eastbound clock is adding to the Earth's rotation speed, this effect will be increased, causing the airborne clock to run marginally slower. This isn't due to *time* in the aircraft "dilating," but a real, physical effect arising from its motion. Hayden discusses this distinction and provides references to relevant experiments. [79]

This is also the answer that LET or field-referred-type theories give to the famous "twins paradox," where two young twins are separated by a motion that can be regarded as symmetrical and then reunited, upon which one or the other or neither is found to be older, depending which argument you buy.

"One's frame had to be accelerated somehow in order to bring them back together again, and therein lies the difference," runs one line. Response: "But the difference in ages increases with the time that the traveling one has been traveling. Yet exactly the same process of stopping and reversing will eventually return him whatever the duration of the trip. How can the same acceleration sequence cause different results?"

"It's the reversal of direction of one of them that does it. Even with the ingenious arrangements that have been proposed for effectively synchronizing oppositely moving, constant-speed conveyors." [80] Response: "But the SRT equations don't anything about direction. They only involve velocity."

"Acceleration is involved one way or the other, so SRT doesn't apply. You need to go to GRT." Response: "So why was it given as an example of an SRT effect in the first place?"

And so it goes. The debate has gone on for as long as the theory of relativity has existed. Careers have been toppled by it. [81] According to LET and its equivalents, the twin who does the most moving through the preferred reference frame (or the local preferred frames at the places he passed through) will age more, and that's the end of it.

In principle there is a way to resolve this. Going back to the muon, relativity says that only the velocity with respect to the observer matters, so the muon is just as entitled to argue that it's the laboratory that's moving. Thus, by the muon's frame of reckoning, the laboratory's time should be running slower. What we need is an observer sitting on the muon as it passes through the lab to tell us once and for all if the laboratory clock runs faster (Lorentz, Beckmann, field-referred) or slower (Einstein). This has never been done, of course. But eventually the ingenuity of experimenters will no doubt come up with an equivalent.

Perhaps the closest that anyone has come to actually testing this is the Hafele-Keating experiment in 1972, where cesium atomic clocks were transported east and west in commercial jets and their rates compared to a standard on the ground at the U.S. Naval Observatory in Washington, D.C. It's not uncommon to hear the result dismissed blandly with, "The moving clocks ran slower, just as relativity says they should." And it's true that they did—referred to a fictitious standard that didn't figure anywhere in the experiment. And they did so at different rates. The fact was that relative to the stated ground reference in Washington, D.C., the westbound clock ran *faster*, gaining 273 nanoseconds, whereas the eastbound one lost 59 nanoseconds. In a fast-foot shuffle to accommodate this awkward state of affairs, the relativists decided that everything should be referred to a nonrotating Earth-centered frame, relative to which everything was moving east, and hence it was possible to describe the three clocks as moving "slow" (westbound), "slower" (Washington, D.C.), and "slowest" (eastbound). But that still doesn't rescue the theory, which says, clearly, that as far as Washington, D.C., is concerned, as with any observer, lightspeed is constant and moving clocks are slowed *irrespective of* direction. Those who regard the clocks as moving with regard to an absolute local reference have no problem. Apparently, R. L. Keating himself was surprised by the result [82] but accepted the explanation that astronomers always use the Earth's frame for local phenomena. But they use a solar barycentric frame for other planetary phenomena in order to get results that agree with relativity. Interesting, eh?

THE FAMOUS FASTER-THAN-LIGHT QUESTION

So what about the consequence that comes out of it all that "nothing"—no kind of energy or other causal influence—can travel faster than light? It's probably the most popularly quoted line whenever relativity is mentioned, and so some words on it wouldn't be out of order here, although they are necessarily speculative.

The limit follows from the form of the equations that express velocity as a fraction of the speed of light—you can't have anything greater than a hundred percent of itself. Put that way it sounds a bit trite, rather than expressing anything especially profound. The same fraction forms the basis of all the velocity-dependence equations, such as that for mass, which increases to infinity as velocity approaches lightspeed, and time, which tends to a standstill. So accelerating a massive object to lightspeed would require an infinite input of energy, and since that's impossible the implication is you can't get there. All experiments on fast-moving particles confirm the predictions, and as far as some kinds of minds are concerned, those that seem to need limits and restrictions to guide their lives, that closes the subject. If all of the human race thought that way we'd never have bothered trying to build flying machines because the eminences who knew better had proved them impossible.

One person who didn't think that way was the aerospace engineer, science-fact and science-fiction writer G. Harry Stine. [83] As Stine pointed out, and we have spent space enough being reminded of here, relativity theory derives primarily from Maxwell's equations of electromagnetics, and the evidence supporting it comes from a narrow range of experiments using charged particles accelerated by electric or magnetic fields. The way mass is determined (or, strictly speaking, the mass-charge ratio) is by measuring the reaction to other fields or the momentum transfer of impacts with other particles. It's an extremely restricted sample for building overall pictures of the world.

Maxwell's equations, in essence, state that a charged particle, (a) at rest possesses an electric field; (b) moving at a steady velocity generates a magnetic field; (c) accelerating, radiates away some of the applied energy, i.e., not all of the accelerating energy will appear as motion of the particle. The theory derived from those statements and the experiments designed to test it say that the "deficit" not appearing as acceleration increases with velocity. It's as if energy is being supplied faster than the system can absorb it by changing its state motion. It sheds the excess by radiation, and the faster it moves the greater a proportion it has to get rid of until it's radiating all of it, at which point it can't be accelerated further. Interestingly, the equations of aerodynamics for propeller-driven aircraft take the same form, approaching a limit at the speed of sound through air. As a plane approaches the speed of sound, more of the propulsion energy goes into generating shock waves that radiate it away, and accelerating the plane further becomes progressively harder. It exhibits an increase of "aerodynamic mass."

In his general field equations, Einstein theorized that a gravitational "charge" (mass) would produce a field analogous to the magnetic field when in motion. Furthering the analogy, it should produce a gravitational radiation when accelerated. This would be true, for example, of any spinning mass. What is the nature, Stine wonders, of the peculiar forces we're all familiar with that hold gyros at strange angles when intuition says they ought to fall over, and play havoc when you try to carry them around corners? All of the second-derivative Newtonian forces are already accounted for, since a rotating mass undergoes constant acceleration. [Second-derivative of space with respect to time, hence d^2x/dt^2, or d/dt(momentum).] Stine hypothesizes a Newtonian-like third-derivative force that's proportional to rate of change of acceleration (d^3x/dt^3)—a quantity referred to as "surge"—and associated with it, a combined gravitational and inertial "GI" field playing a role comparable to the electromagnetic field, but one derivative step up from the counterpart in the charged domain. This field is also able to accept excess energy beyond the ability of an accelerating body to absorb quickly enough. But in the case of a charged body, electromagnetic reactions account for all the energy supplied by the time lightspeed is reached, and no further acceleration beyond that limit is possible.

But if that "barrier" could be overcome, the GI field would still be available to continue absorbing excess energy, meaning that acceleration could be pushed further. In other words, only *charged* particles—the magnetic-propeller-driven kinds used in all our relativistic experiments—are limited to lightspeed. Uncharged matter—providing you had a means of accelerating it—would have a limiting velocity set by the currently unknown properties of GI propagation. What might that be? Anybody's guess, really. But Stine cites an estimate made in 1961 by William Davis, S. A. Korff, and E. L. Victory, based on the apparent stability and relative sizes of structures from binary stars, up through galaxies, to the entire universe, that gave a range of from 10,000 to 15,000 times lightspeed. He gives them the unit "Mikes," after A. A. Michelson.

In considering possibilities of this kind, mention should also be made of the intriguing "field distortion theory" (FDT) developed by Steve Dinowitz. [84] As with other alternatives that we've looked at, the classical Galilean transforms hold, and the same experimental results are expected that support SRT. FDT begins with a model of propagation in which the field lines around a charged body such as an electron behave like radial compressible springs (recalling the charge redistribution treated by Beckmann) and exhibit an aerodynamic-like distortion when the source moves through a gravitational field. The body's inertial mass is then related to this distortion of its field, resulting in an expression for mass in which the determining factor is the motion through the locally dominant gravitational field and the field's energy density. As a consequence, mass-increase and time-slowing are not pure velocity effects but also depend on the comparative field energy densities of the body being accelerated and other bodies in the vicinity. These effects would not occur to anywhere near the degree expressed by the relativistic limits when the gravitational field due to the accelerated body predominates. This condition is never realized on the Earth's surface, where the gravitation of accelerated particles like electrons or protons is vanishingly small compared to the Earth's, and the equations of FDT reduce to those of SRT. But it would occur naturally in the case of, say, a spacecraft leaving the Solar System.

Little of this impresses the custodians of the sacred dogma, however. Heretical findings have been reported in connection with things like experiments performed on rotating platforms where light beams seem clearly to be traveling around in opposite directions at different speeds—the basic operating principle of the laser-ring gyro, which works just fine—and the synchronization of GPS satellites. [85] True enough, a relativistic explanation can usually be produced eventually—typically in the form of wheeling in GRT to account for a contradiction of something that SRT said in the first place—but always after the event, uncomfortably suggestive of the way in which with enough ingenuity a new epicycle could always be added to Ptolemy's hopelessly over-elaborate system to explain the latest data. Otherwise the problem is declared "meaningless." But if the underlying premises of relativity are inconsistent as some have argued it's really immaterial, since it can be proved that logic based on inconsistent premises can be made to agree with *any* conclusion. [86]

As with the Church of old, it seems to be "political" scientists of an authoritarian bent who end up directing and bureaucratizing the system. This becomes particularly true of "Big" science, where so much of what will be rewarded by recognition, funding, and appointments depends on political approval. But good science works best when left to muddle through in its own sloppy and democratic ways. Maybe what we need is a Constitutional amendment separating Science and State. Government should no more be deciding what good science shall be than dictating or suppressing religion.

Section Notes

63 In place of the familiar $F = m \cdot A$, where F is force, m is mass, and A is acceleration, the law becomes $F = m \cdot A$ + centrifugal force + Coriolis force + Euler force. Newton would still have been working to make sense of it.

64 Beckmann, 1987

65 For example Tolman, 1912, and Majorana, 1918 and 1919, both described in Beckmann, 1987, pp. 37–38

66 See Beckmann 1987, p. 34

67 Pedants might object that in the case of gravitation the lines of force will converge minutely toward the Earth's center, but the point rests.

68 Collection of papers available at
http://home.earthlink.net/~marklin/

69 Also online, at http://get.ilja-schmelzer.net/

70 Hatch, 2000

71 Hatch, 1999

72 Møller, 1952

73 Phipps, 1989 and 1994

74 Hayden, 1993

75 Michelson and Gale, 1925. Also discussed in Beckmann, 1987, p. 42 ff.

76 Discussed in Beckmann, 1987, p. 205

77 McCausland, 1999

78 See, for example, Hayden, 1990

79 Hayden, 1991

80 For example Renshaw, 1995

81 The most well-known case is probably that of the British physicist-philosopher Herbert Dingle. See Dingle, 1972, for an exposition of his views. Discussed in Chang, 1993

82 Van Flandern, 1998. More on Hafele-Keating at Hayden, 1991

83 Stine, 1980

84 Dinowitz, 1996

85 For example, Wang 2000 and 2000(a)

86 Sutliff, 1991

FOUR
CATASTROPHE OF ETHICS

The Case for Taking Velikovsky Seriously

Once one has experienced the desperation with which clever and conciliatory men of science react to the demand for a change in the thought pattern, one can only be amazed that such revolutions in science have actually been possible at all.
—Werner Heisenberg

I believe we must look for salvation from the non-specialists, amateurs and interdisciplinary thinkers—those who form judgments on the general thrust of the evidence, those who are skeptical about any explanation, particularly official ones, and above all are tolerant of other people's theories.
— Halton Arp

In the earlier section dealing with evolution, we saw that by the late nineteenth century the doctrine of uniformitarianism had been established as the officially recognized mechanism of geological and biological change. Ideas of catastrophism, previously unquestioned, were quickly relegated to obscurity. They carried too much suggestion of divine intervention and biblical retribution, which didn't fit with the new world view. Evidence that had long been accepted as pointing clearly to the occurrence of immense cataclysms in the course of Earth's history disappeared from the classrooms and the textbooks to be replaced by lyrical accounts of Nature rendering its works insensibly but tirelessly over huge spans of time. And the same spirit extended to the realm of astronomy, where the regularities of celestial motions were no longer seen as a choreography of God, but as the working of a vast, endlessly repeating, cosmic machine obeying the mechanical lawfulness revealed by Copernicus, Kepler, Newton, and their followers. Although rigorous observation had been limited to just a couple of centuries, the reigning philosophy of gradualism put no restraint on extrapolating the current conditions backward, creating a picture of the past that remained essentially unchanged. The possibility was never seriously entertained that even back in epochs long before humans existed, the skies might have been different in any significant way from the ones we see today.

As a teenager I was enthralled by the writings of Immanuel Velikovsky. But when the scientific authorities which at that time I didn't question did such a superb job of misrepresenting his work and dismissed him as a crank, I largely forgot about the subject. It was not until forty or so years later, in the 1990s, that I came across a remarkable book by Charles Ginenthal entitled *Carl Sagan and Immanuel Velikovsky*, [87] collecting together findings from the space missions and later developments in astronomy, geology, archeology, ancient history, and other areas, that were consistent with Velikovsky's ideas and basic theory, while refuting just about everything that had been said by the experts who vilified him. This was enough to revive my interest in the subject of catastrophism generally.

Early Work: The Makings of an Iconoclast

Immanuel Velikovsky was born in Vitebsk, Russia, in 1905, and graduated from the Medvednikov Gymnasium in Moscow in 1913. He completed premedical studies in France and Scotland, returned to Moscow during World War I to study law and ancient history, and received a medical degree in 1921. He then moved to Berlin, where he helped found and published a series of monographs by prominent Jewish scholars, known as *Scripta Universitatis*, which was instrumental in forming the Hebrew University at Jerusalem. The volume on mathematics and physics was edited by Albert Einstein. In 1923 Velikovsky married Elisheva Kramer, a violinist from Hamburg, and the following year moved to Palestine to become a general medical practitioner and psychiatrist.

How It All Began: A Small Question About the Exodus

In the summer of 1939 Velikovsky came with his family to the United States to complete his research for a proposed book on ancient history. The period he was interested in covered the time of the Hebrew Exodus from Egypt, and in comparing records it struck him as curious that an event that figured so prominently in Hebrew history, with all its attendant troubles and plagues, seemed to have no corresponding account in the Egyptian records. This had been a longstanding problem for historians, who because of the incongruities involved had never even been able to agree on who the pharaoh at the time of the Exodus had been. It turned out to be only one of many examples of major historical events in the Hebrew account with no correlating Egyptian counterpart, which had led some historians to dismiss Hebrew history as largely fictional. On the other hand, its claims received substantial support from archeological findings.

Further investigation led to a translation of an obscure papyrus written by an Egyptian sage called Ipuwer, kept at the museum of Leiden, in Holland, that described a time of rivers turning to blood, falling stones, sickness, darkness, and other events uncannily like those recounted in Exodus, in the aftermath of which the land fell into ruin and civil war, to be overrun by Asiatic tribes from the east. A papyrus preserved at the Hermitage in Leningrad told a similar tale of the Egyptian empire perishing in a period of natural disasters and falling prey to desert nomads.

It seemed that the missing Egyptian corroboration had been found. However, such considerations as language style and certain historical references indicated the time of these events to be the collapse of the Egyptian Middle Kingdom, conventionally dated around five hundred years before the Exodus, the latter being identified with the expulsion from Egypt of a people referred to as the Hyksos. Velikovsky began to suspect that this equating of the Hyksos with the Hebrews was an error, and the Hyksos were in fact the desert tribe that had invaded Egypt at the time the Middle Kingdom ended and the Hebrews left—and were then driven out themselves at a later date. This would mean that the Middle Kingdom ended more recently than the accepted chronology holds, leading Velikovsky to reexamine the entire Egyptian-Hebrew historical record. Since Egyptian chronology was taken as the standard by which the histories of other cultures in the region were correlated and dated, any error found in it would have widespread repercussions. And Velikovsky's conclusion was that the grounds the standard rested on were a lot shakier than was confidently supposed.

The ancient Egyptians did not use an absolute time scale as we do today, of dating all events with respect to a chosen reference year. They chronicled events occurring during the reign of each ruler separately, dating them from the beginning of that period—a bit like saying that the great San Francisco earthquake happened in the second year of Theodore Roosevelt, and then having to start over again with William Taft. This created many uncertainties for later scholars, first by being unclear about exactly what was meant in such cases as a co-regency by father and son, and second by frequently leaving no definite indication of how long a reign lasted. In addition to these, the list of dynasties drawn up by the historian-priest Manetho, which is used as the key in many accepted reconstructions, has been passed down in two recorded versions that don't agree, both apparently having been exaggerated by the inclusion of extraneous years and dynasties. Sometimes this stemmed from the practice of giving the same person different names, leading to acts of the same pharaoh being attributed to different individuals; at others it seemed deliberately contrived to show Egypt's civilization as going back farther than rivals such as the Greek or Assyrian-Babylonian.

Resorting to astronomical evidence to provide an absolute time scale frequently leads to the same kind of circularity as we found with Darwinism. The historians and the astronomers each believe that the other has accurate data to support the conventional chronology, and hence their own *speculations* must be true. A. H. Gardiner, the original translator of the Ipuwer papyrus, commented that "what is proudly advertised as Egyptian history is merely a collection of rags and tatters."[88] Velikovsky's response was to go with what the weight of evidence seemed to say and concluded that Egyptian history was padded to the extent of making events seem 500 to 800 years further away from the present than they had in fact been. To bring things into line, he proposed moving the end of the Middle Kingdom and invasion by the Hyksos down 500 years to accord with the Hebrew date for the Exodus of around 1450 B.C. When this was done, a whole set of what had been other anomalies were found to line up, too.

The biblical account of the Queen of Sheba's royal visit to Jerusalem after hearing of the fame and wisdom of King Solomon has always had something of a mysterious air, not the least being that the identity of this majestic sovereign and the location of her domain have never been established. She is described elsewhere as queen of Egypt and Ethiopia, but conventional chronology has no female pharaohs in Egypt during this period. But 600 years before the accepted biblical date, practically the inverse story is told in Egyptian records. Queen Hatshepsut, a female pharaoh, journeyed with a large entourage to a land to the east called Punt, described by one official as being associated with Byblos, the old capital of Phoenicia, its ruins today lying eighteen miles north of Beirut. Descriptions of the route overland from Thebes to the Red Sea coast, and by sea to the Gulf of Aqaba, returning via the Mediterranean and back up the Nile, tally. On her return, Hatshepsut built a temple patterned after the one she had visited in Punt, its wall decorated by reliefs commemorating her visit. The gifts from the ruler of Punt that they record closely match those that the Hebrew texts list as Solomon's to the Queen of Sheba. One of the features of Solomon's temple that especially impressed the Queen of Sheba was its terraces planted with algum trees. Hatshepsut's temple at Thebes was laid out with similar terraces planted in the same way.

And so it goes. Hebrew history records that after Solomon's death his son and successor, Rehoboam, was conquered by a king of Egypt called Shishak. Hatshepsut's successor in Egypt was Thutmose III, who invaded Palestine. Topping the list made at Karnak of the 119 cities that he took—the place where the most important would normally be found—is one called Kadesh. Many Hebrew and Arabic writings give Kadesh as the name of Jerusalem, the capital of Judah. Conventional historians have always hesitated to make this connection, however, since by their chronology David didn't establish it as the capital until long after Thutmose. A number of the other cities listed as conquered by Thutmose III didn't even yet exist according to the orthodox chronology. But if Shishak and Thutmose III were one and the same, as Velikovsky maintained, then it all makes sense.

Velikovsky's revised chronology also explained many discrepancies in the histories of other cultures whose chronology is derived from the Egyptian standard. One example is in styles of pottery and tomb construction found in parts of Cyprus and the neighboring coast of Syria, where clear association between the two cultures is indicated. However, conventional dating puts the Syrian culture five hundred years earlier than the other—presumably implying that customs and influences took that long to propagate across sixty miles of water. Another is the "dark age" of ancient Greece that orthodox chronology is forced to postulate to make its dates match with the Egyptian, when progress in the development of Greek art and technology ceased for half a millennium for no apparent reason and then resumed again. What makes this even more perplexing is that the activity of the Greek olive industry that supplied oil for lamps, cooking, and so forth, as recorded in layers of pollen grains preserved on lake bottoms, indicates it to have been at a maximum during precisely this time This would be like archeologists of the future determining that U.S. oil production peaked before Columbus arrived. But under the revised scheme the Greek time line closes up as Egypt's is contracted, and the need for a dark age goes away.

The outline for Velikovsky's revised chronology was published in 1945 as a booklet, *Theses for the Reconstruction of Ancient History.* Later, a more detailed account of about half of this work would be published as a full book form, covering the period from the Exodus to the time of the pharaoh Akhnaton. [89]

IMPLICATIONS OF CATASTROPHISM

For Velikovsky this was only a beginning. The Exodus had been synchronized with the collapse of the Middle Kingdom at around 1450 B.C. However else the plagues and other disruptions attending these events might have been interpreted at the time, the most likely explanation was that they coincided with a period of natural disasters. This invited the questions, how widespread were they? and what caused them? Starting with the regions adjoining Egypt and Israel, Velikovsky began investigating the histories and received mythologies of other ancient cultures for indications of parallel events. It became apparent that the phenomenon had affected not just the entire Middle East but places far remote from it as well. In fact, it showed signs of being nothing less than a global catastrophe. Further, it hadn't been the first time such a thing had happened, and neither was it the last. [90]

The first affliction that the Bible describes as befalling the Egyptians was the rivers turning to blood and there being blood throughout the land, both of which Ipuwer echoed. Babylonian myth tells of the land being covered by the blood of the slain heavenly monster, Tiamat. Likewise, those of the Asiatic Tartars and the Central American Maya relate sagas of the world turning red, while the Finns say it was sprinkled with pink milk.

Then came "hail." The word chosen by the earlier translators was one that we associate with icy pellets and cold rains, but this might be because they could imagine little else falling from the sky. The original Hebrew word, *barad*, means hot rocks. Ipuwer describes falling stones and fire, which in a day, he says, turned all the fields to wastelands. Similar accounts of red-hot stones falling in torrents, frequently accompanied by crashing thunder and showers of a blazing, sticky substance that ran along the ground causing widespread death and destruction, appear in Buddhist texts on world cycles, Siberian legends, and tales handed down in places as far apart as Mexico and Siberia. The same kind of story can be told relating days of darkness so intense that people were unable to move from the spot they were at, worldwide hurricanes that swept away towns and forests, and earthquakes devastating entire regions.

According to Velikovsky, the familiar interpretation of the tenth plague as the smiting by the Angel of Death of the Egyptian "first-born" (Hebrew *bkhor*), which of course would require some supernatural agency, arises from a corruption of *bchor*, which means "chosen," or high-born. [91] Hence the reason why the Israelites fared better was probably that as slaves they lived in dwellings made of reeds and clay, whereas the brick and stone houses of the Egyptians were more susceptible to collapse by earthquake. Eminently reasonable in my opinion.

Finally, there are suggestions that the "parting of the waters" during the pursuit by the Egyptians could have been the local aspect of a tidal disruption of global dimensions. Chinese annals tell of a time when the world was in flames, after which the water of the oceans was piled to enormous heights and swept across the continent to fill the valleys between the mountains, taking decades to drain away. The traditions of the people of Peru hold that after five days of darkness the ocean left the shore and broke over the land with a terrible din, changing the appearance of the surface permanently. The Choctaw Indians of Oklahoma (not their original habitat) relate a time when the world was plunged in darkness until light appeared in the north; but the light turned out to be mountain-high waves of water rapidly approaching.

VENUS AND THE COSMIC CONNECTION

Repeatedly, these calamities were attributed to a malicious deity—almost invariably a goddess—coming to wreak havoc upon the Earth. Although the actual names naturally varied, the deity involved turned out time and time again to be the one that cultures worldwide associated with the object we know today as the planet Venus. But they didn't talk about it as if it were a planet; they described it as a comet. A Chinese text describes Venus as spanning the heavens, rivaling the Sun in brightness. Mexican astronomers referred to it as "the star that smokes," while on the opposite side of the world the same theme is found in the Hindu Vedas, the Hebrew Talmud, and the Egyptian description of Sekhmet. The Aztecs called Venus the "heart" of Quetzlcoatl, which in turn means "plumed serpent," with feathers that signify fire. The serpent or dragon is one of the most common figures used in the ancient world to signify "comet," examples being the Greek Typhon, Egyptian Set, Babylonian Tiamat, Hindu Vrta, all of whom raged across the sky and brought destruction upon the world.

The word "comet" comes from the Greek *coma*, meaning hair, and among ancient astronomers referred to a star with hair, or a beard. The same appellation was given to Venus. One of the Mexican names for Venus was "the mane"; the Peruvian name, *chaska*, means "wavy-haired"; the Arabs call Venus "the one with hair." One of the most vivid comet images is the Babylonian goddess Ishtar, recognized universally as representing Venus. Ishtar is described as being "the bright torch of heaven," "clothed in fire," and the "fearful dragon," while her heavenly manifestation is known as the "bearded star."

Another widespread association of Venus was with the figure of a cow or a bull, still recalled in many religious rites and cults today. If Venus did indeed once possess a cometary coma, the illuminated portions would at times be seen as a gigantic crescent in the same way as the crescent forms of planets and of the Moon, especially during close approaches to Earth. The curving shapes sprouting from the body of the comet would be suggestive of a bull's head and horns.

Velikovsky discovered that the Hindu records from before the second millennium B.C. spoke of four visible planets, not five, omitting Venus. The Babylonians, who were also meticulous in their observations, likewise made no mention of Venus in their tables of planets. In Greek mythology, Venus was the goddess Pallas Athene, unique among the deities in being born during the time of human history and not present, like all the other gods, from the beginning. The hymn dedicated to her by Homer describes Pallas Athene as being born from the head of Zeus, i.e., Jupiter. And once again mythologies of other peoples, too, carry accounts of the birth of their deity that corresponds to Venus, but not Jupiter, Saturn, Mars, Mercury, or any of the other gods.

In Greek legend, Athene was attacked by a monster, Pallas-Typhon, whom she fought and killed. Likewise, the newborn

Egyptian Horus battled with the serpent-monster, Seth, as did the Hindu Vishnu, also a newcomer to the celestial family, born of the many-armed Shiva. Horus was originally the Egyptian name for Jupiter, apparently transferred to the new object that became supreme in the sky—possibly due to some initial confusion as to which was which. The same thing happened in the Babylonian version, where Ishtar was originally Jupiter and became Venus, Jupiter being renamed Marduk.

Many ancient traditions divide the history of the world into a series of ages each ending in calamity, the birth of the new age being attended by altered appearances of the heavens. Early astronomers diligently recorded the motions of celestial bodies, looking for changes that might signal coming destruction and the end of the current age. The times following the above happenings saw repeated allusions to the motion of the Sun and the stars being reversed, and north and south changing place. Both the Ipuwer and the Ermitage papyruses speak of the land turning upside down and south becoming north. Herodotus, in his visit to Egypt in the second half of the fifth century B.C., was told by priests about a former era when the Sun rose where it now sets and set where it now rises. Plato and Seneca wrote about the same thing. The architect of Hatshepsut's tomb included a stone panel from an earlier age showing the celestial constellations upside down. Similar accounts are found in the Hebrew Talmud and the Islamic Koran; with the Chinese, whose zodiac signs also have the strange property of proceeding in a retrograde direction; and in the written or oral myths of Greeks, Syrians, Aztec, Maya, Mexican Indians, Greenland Eskimos, and tribes of western Brazil and the Indian Ocean Andaman Islands, to name a few.

Velikovsky's conclusion, then, was that Venus is not billions of years old as believed according to orthodox theory, but a young object ejected from Jupiter within the span of recorded human history. In the course of evolving into the planet that we see today it had passed close enough to bring death, terror, and destruction on an immense scale, and disturbed the motion of the Earth itself. This carried the impertinent suggestion that the ancients might not have been so facile as to spend lifetimes inventing fairytales and building imposing monuments to them, but might actually have known what they were talking about and had something important to say; that the "mythologies" dismissed by the authorities of today as fanciful fictions could in fact have been attempts by nontechnical people to describe events that they actually witnessed. This would mean, of course, that the comforting picture of a safe and secure Solar System acting out its predictable cycles with minor variations, arrived at by projecting back today's quiescent conditions, was wrong; the Solar System could be a very violent and unpredictable place indeed. But Velikovsky had already shown from his historical revisions what he thought of conventionally accepted pictures of things if what appeared to be the facts indicated otherwise.

What first suggested a cosmic connection was a passage that Velikovsky came across in the Book of Joshua, describing what sounded like an intense meteorite shower causing widespread destruction before the famous incident where the Sun "stood still." (The meteorites killed more of the enemy than Joshua's soldiers did.) This led to the discovery of the wider pattern of cataclysms associated with Venus and suggested the possibility that the events at the time of the Exodus, fifty-two years previously, might have been an early instance of the same thing. Velikovsky's eventual conclusion was that Venus had come close to Earth on both occasions, although the second encounter was farther away and less violent. Maya records also tell of a time of destruction coming fifty years after an earlier, greater catastrophe. Interestingly, their account talks about the night being abnormally long.

Thereafter, priests and astronomers everywhere followed the movements of Venus relentlessly for signs of its returning again. Whole temples and cults were devoted to worshiping and appeasing the deity that it was taken to be, invariably regarded as violent and wrathful. A fifty-year cycle between times of hardship and destruction is recounted in the traditions and records of cultures the world over. The natives of pre-Columbian Mexico observed a ceremony of congregating every fifty-two years to await a catastrophe, fearful that the Sun would fail to rise again. They watched for the appearance of Venus, and when the world didn't end, celebrated with bonfires and sacrifices the new period of grace that had been granted. The Israelite festival of the Jubilee was proclaimed every fifty years as a time for leaving the land fallow, releasing slaves, and returning land to the original owners as a sign of repentance in preparation for the Day of Atonement.

THE UNIVERSAL WAR GOD: MARS

This pattern continued for something like seven centuries. Then a striking change took place in the order of precedence the ancients gave to their celestial gods: Venus ceased being the most feared object in the heavens, the destroyer and bringer of chaos, and was replaced in this role by Mars, universally acclaimed as the war god.

Mars had not figured as a significant figure in the celestial pantheon before the eighth century B.C. It was known, of course, and its motions tabled, but it seems generally to have been considered a minor player. Then, suddenly, it achieved prominence. This was not a period shrouded in the distant past, but a time when observations and written records had become more refined and extensive. Mythologies abound with accounts of battles between Venus and Mars, one of the most well known being Homer's *Iliad*, in which heavenly deities influenced the fortunes of the combatants in the ten-year siege of Troy, Athene siding with the Greeks, while the Trojans were backed by Ares, the Greek name for Mars. Interestingly, this practically mirrors the situation on the other side of the world in the wars between the Aztecs and the Toltecs, where Mars rooted for the former, and Venus, the latter. (Once again this questions conventional chronology, making the American civilizations much older than is generally held. Of which, more later.)

Following these encounters, Mars continued to menace Earth periodically for about ninety years, bringing earthquakes, floods, and times of desolation, though never with a ferocity rivaling the first two visits of Venus. This was the age of prophets, who developed reputations for knowing when hard times were ahead; it could also be the source of the astrological belief in celestial events portending disasters and affecting lives down on Earth—it would be a peculiar notion to arise today, with the planets being insignificant pinpoints. The prophet Amos predicted destruction that arrived in 747 B.C., but didn't live to see it because he seized the opportunity to link the event to morality and warn people to mend their ways, so they killed him. Amos's cue might have been an encounter that conceivably took place in 776 B.C., the year the Olympic games were founded—possibly in commemoration of it.

Isaiah, Joel, and Micah all had their turns until 687 B.C., which marked the final Mars approach. This was the year in which the army of Sennacherib was "smote" in the night, while preparing to attack Jerusalem, by something usually translated as "blast" that left 185,000 dead in the morning. Velikovsky guesses at an interplanetary electrical discharge. The Hebrew Talmud and Midrash date this event as the first night of the Passover, which would make it March 23. Chinese sources ascribed to Confucius, and also Chinese annals referring to the tenth year of the Wu Dynasty under Emperor Kwei pinpoint this date as a time when "the five planets went out of their courses. In the night, stars fell like rain. The Earth shook." [92]

Before this time, the calendars of the Chinese, Greeks, Egyptians, Persians, Hindus, Chaldeans, Assyrians, and Hebrews, as well as the Incas of Peru and the Mayas of the Yucatan had all shown a year of 360 days. The modern year of 365 1/4 days was introduced subsequently. Following this final event, Mars and Venus retreated to take up their stations as we know them today. And the gods, their anger, and their caprices faded from being a vivid and terrifying reality in human affairs, to a realm regarded these days as imaginative fancy and superstition.

WORLDS IN COLLISION

THE END OF EVERYTHING YOU THOUGHT YOU KNEW

After something like ten years of research into the subject, Velikovsky's account was published as *Worlds in Collision*, which appeared in 1950. Its essential thesis can now be summarized in modern terms as follows.

Some time before the middle of the second millennium B.C., a white-hot, fiery object was ejected from Jupiter. For an indeterminate period, possibly centuries, it moved as a giant comet on a highly elongated orbit that passed close around the Sun and intersected the orbit of the Earth. Eventually, around 1450 B.C., it emerged from perihelion—the point of closest approach to the Sun—on a path that brought it to an encounter with Earth.

Approaching tail-first, it engulfed the Earth in the outer regions of its millions-of-miles-long coma, from which a rain of caustic, asphyxiating dust filtered down through the atmosphere, turning red the landscape everywhere, and choking rivers and lakes with dead fish. As the Earth moved deeper into the tail, this intensified into rains of red-hot gravel and meteorites, destroying crops, livestock, and towns, and laying waste whole regions. Hydrocarbon gases torn from Jupiter's atmosphere, unable to ignite in the oxygen-free space environment, mixed with Earth's atmosphere to form explosive mixtures that fell as flaming naphtha, causing fires that burned for years and smoke that darkened the entire surface. Unburned petroleum sank into the ground in enormous quantities forming broad swathes across the planet.

As the two bodies closed under their mutual gravitational grip, volcanoes, earthquakes, tectonic upheavals, and hurricane-force winds rent the Earth's surface, while the oceans piled up into huge tides that surged across continents. Through the pall of dust and smoke, the comet loomed with the appearance of a monstrous dragon spitting fire in the form of electrical discharges between its head and writhing coma arms of charged plasma, and then down upon the surface of the Earth itself as the magnetospheres of the two bodies met. The forces of mutual gyration eventually tore the intruder away to retreat back toward the outer Solar System, in the process of which the Earth turned over to emerge with inverted poles, and its orbit and spin perturbed. Velikovsky speculated that given the electrically active condition of the ionized plasma enveloping and still forming much of the bulk of the incandescent proto-planet, electromagnetic forces probably played a significant part in this.

Having thus interacted, the Earth and Venus moved in a resonant pattern that brought them into proximity again every fifty years or so, though with the closeness of the encounters reducing. This continued for about seven hundred years until Venus's still-eccentric orbit brought it close to Mars, which in those days was nearer to Earth. Here, Mars and Venus exchanged roles. Venus receded to become no-longer threatening, while Mars was diverted into an Earth-encounter that changed Earth's motion again and commenced another series of destructive interactions until Mars finally settled into the orbit it describes today. The close approaches of Earth and Mars every fifteen years, the similar tilts of their axes, and the almost identical lengths of their days could, Velikovsky suggests, be remnants of the period of repeated interaction between them.

If such events indeed happened, they would be expected to

have left evidence discernible today. Velikovsky offered a number of suggestions for findings that would support his theory, many of them going against the prevailing scientific beliefs of the times. One was that close encounters between the Earth and bodies the size of Venus and Mars would also have major effects on the Moon. (The lunar deity is also involved in the mythological scenarios of all cultures, usually in some kind of amorous entanglement or rivalry with the other gods.) Hence, the Moon's craters and other surface features should be relatively young—in the order of thousands of years, not billions. It should show evidence of recent heating, possibly with some remnant volcanic activity still detectable, and exhibit magnetic effects impressed into its rocks.

Similarly with Mars. Mars has a mass of around a tenth that of the Earth and a radius slightly over a half, whereas Venus is only slightly smaller than Earth. Tidal effects of a larger body upon a smaller one will be immensely greater than those of a small body on a larger one. Therefore Mars would be a devastated planet, its surface scarred by rifts and fissures. This suggestion was put forward at a time when the possibility of life on Mars was still being vigorously debated by many scientists, and some believed that the "canals" might be the legacy of a lost civilization. It also seemed probable that a small body like Mars would lose a portion of its atmosphere in encounters with Earth. Since oxygen and water vapor are not present in the Martian atmosphere, Velikovsky reasoned that some other elements of the terrestrial atmosphere should be found there. He urged that a search be made for argon and neon.[93]

As for Venus itself, the mainstream view propounded in 1950 held it to be an Earthlike sister planet, probably somewhat warmer than Earth on account of its closer position to the Sun. Some astronomers predicted that its clouds would turn out to be water vapor and its surface covered by oceans. This was despite infrared and spectroscopic data available at that time that indicated a higher temperature and complete absence of water, but which were largely discounted because the current theory had no explanation for them. Further, although indications were that Venus's rotation about its axis was very slow, there was no difference between the radiated temperatures of the dark and light sides, which seemed anomalous. For Velikovsky there was no contradiction. Because of its violent expulsion from Jupiter and recent history as an incandescent object, it would be innately very hot, swamping any day-night effect due to the Sun.

Velikovsky also reasoned that the bulk of the Venusian cometary tail would have been derived from the atmosphere of Jupiter and hence have contained large amounts of hydrocarbons, much of which fell upon the Earth. Hydrocarbons and other carbon derivatives should therefore be abundant in Venus's atmosphere today and contribute to its high reflective brightness. If oxygen exists in any significant amount, conceivably obtained via gas exchange with the Earth, hydrocarbon fires could still be burning on the surface.

Since petroleum hydrocarbons were universally attributed to organic origins, Velikovsky speculated that life might exist on Jupiter, and that its transportation in some form that could survive might account for the "vermin" that came with the other Egyptian plagues. While acknowledging that the heat and general conditions were in themselves sufficient to produce proliferations of things like frogs and locusts, he thought it possible that the plague of flies could have come as larvae, known to be capable of surviving extremes of temperature and the absence of oxygen. The suggestion of life first arriving here in some preserved larval or microbial form has been put forward since from other quarters too. [94] (Personally, I think that the rivers full of dead fish, along with all the animal and human corpses from everything else that was going on provide a ready explanation for flies and the like.)

Jupiter's Great Red Spot, Velikovsky suggested, would be a structural scar marking the place where Venus erupted, still giving rise to atmospheric perturbations. And in a lecture at Princeton in 1953 he proposed that contrary to the prevailing view of Jupiter's being cold and dead, it should be emitting nonthermal radio energy. His reason for supposing this was that if electrical forces played a role in planetary dynamics, and the Solar System as a whole was neutral, the Sun and planets would have opposite charges. Jupiter would have the largest planetary charge, and its rapid rotation should radiate electromagnetically. He had asked Einstein, with whom he maintained friendship, to use his influence to have a radio survey performed to look for such an effect. In the same talk, Velikovsky suggested that while the Earth's magnetic field was known to decrease with distance at lower altitudes, it could be stronger beyond the ionosphere and extend at least as far as the Moon— again violating currently held opinions.

Science in Convulsion: The Reactions

I always think it's pathetic when writers resort to phrases like "Words cannot describe . . ." It's the writer's job, after all, to find words that do describe. But the reaction of the scientific community to *Worlds in Collision* came pretty close. "Vituperative," "vitriolic," "hysterical," "irrational" jostle for consideration. Critics vied with each other in the shrillness of their denunciations.

Word of the impending release by the Macmillan Company had circulated in the publishing trade, and a preview article entitled "The Day the Sun Stood Still" appeared in the in January 1950 issue of *Harpers*, which sold out in a few days. The following month, *Readers Digest* featured a popularization that interpreted Velikovsky as proving the assertions of the Old Testament scientifically. Velikovsky had also contracted with *Collier's Magazine* to produce what he understood would be a three-part serialization, but the manuscripts that he received for approval were condensations, and so sensationalized without examination of the scholarship behind the work that he threatened public disavowal unless they were severely revised. Eventually the first two appeared; the third was abandoned.

On the strength of these articles, the storm from the academic and scientific camp, and the media who sought their opinions, began. The Dallas *News* thought *Worlds In Collision* was a Russian propaganda ploy. The Communist press saw it as a sure sign of the dying of bourgeois society. One British intellectual felt it was a move by U.S. warmongers to soften the world up for the atomic war they were preparing to launch. Any suggestion that there could anything worthwhile to learn from prescientific texts that talked about gods and dragons was an anathema, never mind—horror of horrors— quoting the *Bible*! (even though Velikovsky used it purely as a historical record, and then only when it was corroborated by other sources). The work, the chorus insisted, was spurious, uninformed, and utterly without scientific merit.

Harlow Shapley, director of the Harvard College Observatory, wrote twice to Macmillan, expressing astonishment that they would consider venturing into the "Black Arts," threatening to cut of all relations with the company (Macmillan owned a substantial and profitable textbook division), and insinuating that their reputation might be severely damaged if they went ahead. The February 25 issue of *Science News Letter*, a publication directed by Shapley, printed a condemnation of *Worlds in Collision* by authorities in the fields of archeology, oriental studies, anthropology, and geology, as well as astronomy—the last topic spoken for by Shapley himself. The book was only then going to press, so not one of the critics had actually seen it. Somewhat taken aback, the president of the Macmillan Company submitted the manuscript to three independent arbiters and decided to abide by their recommendation. Their vote was to go ahead with publication, and the book was released on schedule in April. Although the names of the arbiters were never officially disclosed, one of them later identified himself as the chairman of the Department of Physics at New York University and confirmed that he had voted in favor.

Meanwhile, the attacks had intensified, spurred by an article in the *Reporter* written by Shapley's associate at Harvard, Cecilia Payne-Gaposchkin, based on the January *Harpers* article and circulated to scientists, science editors, and publishers. It insisted, essentially, that electromagnetic phenomena can have no effect in space, where processes are purely mechanical, and the events described in *Worlds in Collision* were impossible. The gist of this was cited in the March 25 issue of *Science News Letter* as a "Retort to Velikovsky," who as yet had not been heard from.

Gordon Atwater, curator of the Hayden Planetarium and chairman of the Department of Astronomy of the American Museum of Natural History, had read the manuscript and recommended publication before the original Macmillan contract was signed. When he received a letter from Otto Struve, director of the Yerkes Observatory, requesting that he change his position, he failed to appreciate the situation and replied that while he didn't accept all of Velikovsky's claims, he felt the work had merit. Accordingly, he was preparing a favorable review of the book for *This Week* magazine and planning a program at the planetarium depicting the events that it described. A week later, Atwater was summarily fired from both his positions and instructed to vacate his office immediately. Attempts were also made to suppress his review in the April 2 issue of *This Week*, but failed. However, the credentials that appeared alongside his name, above an article pleading for open-mindedness in evaluating the new theory, were already history.

An intended review in the New York *Herald Tribune*, also scheduled for April 2, was pulled, and instead readers found a denunciation by Struve with a reference to Payne-Gaposchkin stating that observations of Venus extended back at least five hundred years before the Exodus, "thus refuting the absurd idea that a comet had turned into a planet." But Velikovsky had given no date for the ejection of Venus by Jupiter, saying only that it had occurred at some earlier time. And as Velikovsky had pointed out in his book, the Babylonian tablets cited by Gaposchkin ("Venus Tables of Ammizaduga") describe Venus as exhibiting erratic motions that have baffled translators and astronomical commentators ever since their discovery. So even if the tablets do date from early in the second millennium B.C., what they show is that Venus was moving enigmatically at that time, in a way quite unlike a planet. This was a preview of the kind of distortion that was to become typical. The *New York Times Book Review*, again April 2, followed Gaposchkin in accusing Velikovsky of ignoring or suppressing the Ammizaduga tablets completely. But they couldn't have reviewed it very carefully. Velikovsky devotes over four pages to the tablets, quoting the complete texts for observations from five successive years and discussing the opinions of seven orientalists and astronomers who had studied them. [95]

In the following months, astronomers descended from their telescopes in droves to put down the heresy. Newspapers across the country were bombarded with abusive letters, frequently syndicated to achieve better coverage. Ignoring Velikovsky's suggestion that tilting the axis of a rotating body could produce the visual effect of an arrested or even retrogressing Sun, the director of one observatory castigated him for not being bothered by "the elementary fact that if the earth were stopped, inertia would cause Joshua and his companions to fly off into space at a speed of nine hundred miles an hour" (also brought up by Gaposchkin). But the argument is disingenuous. Even if Velikovsky is read as conceding that the Earth stopped, he makes no mention of the rate at which it decelerated. If the Earth under present conditions were to halt its rotation totally in six hours, the deceleration experienced at the equator would be the same as a car traveling at sixty miles per hour taking twenty minutes to stop. Stopping the car in an easy span of thirty seconds would be equivalent to halting the Earth in a cool 8.7 minutes—not enough to strain a seat belt, never mind throw people off the planet.

Nevertheless, many writers and reviewers were enthusiastic, as, evidently, was the general public, for *Worlds in Collision* topped the bestsellers list for twenty successive weeks. But letters continued to come in to Macmillan from scientists demanding that they cease publishing the book, and some large institutions were refusing to see Macmillan salesmen. One astronomer dismissed the book as nothing but lies, on the same page declaring that he had not read and never would read it. Macmillan backed down and persuaded Velikovsky to accept a deal they had worked out to transfer the rights to Doubleday, who had no textbook division and were immune to pressure and blackmail in that direction. All remaining copies of the Macmillan edition were burned, and the editor who had accepted the book was fired after twenty-five years with the company.

The campaign continued. Gaposchkin attacked Velikovsky again in the June 1950 issue of *Popular Astronomy*, the essence of the argument being that his claims couldn't be true because they violated undemonstrable dogmatisms that antedated him and therefore took precedence. In an article in *Isis* that was widely reproduced and circulated, Professor Otto Neugebauer of Brown University, a specialist in Babylonian and Greek astronomy, accused Velikovsky of altering quoted source material to suit his case—specifically, that he had changed a figure of 3° 13' to 33° 13'. When Velikovsky protested to the editor that his figure was correct and that the 33° 13' figure was Neugebauer's substitution, not his, the professor dismissed the incident as "simply a misprint of no concern." [96]

But it didn't change his fundamental position, which was that since Babylonian astronomical tables from before the seventh century B.C. cannot be reconciled with the celestial motions seen today, they must have been compiled in disregard for actual observations. In other words, the people who not only understood the number systems and astronomical procedures that we still use today, but who developed them, couldn't have seen what they say they saw because it contradicts what boils down to faith in a dogma.

There were some sympathetic voices, to be sure, such as Walter Adams, director of the Mount Wilson and Palomar Observatories, who complimented Velikovsky on the accuracy of his astronomical material although not agreeing with all of it; Professor Lloyd Motz, astronomer at Columbia University, who was interested in the new proposals for celestial mechanics; and S. K. Vsekhsviatsky, director of Kiev University, who corresponded extensively and cited Velikovsky in support of his own views. But in the main the general pattern continued of critics repeating the same worn fallacies, citing misquotes of their own making, and academic journals publishing attacks on Velikovsky's person but not his arguments, and then refusing him space to respond. This systematic disinformation left the majority of scientists with the impression that Velikovsky had been demolished by those who knew better, and that no answers existed to the only version of the debate that they were permitted to hear.

As noted earlier, the first volume of Velikovsky's revisions to ancient history, *Ages in Chaos*, followed in 1952, this time producing what the *Herald Tribune* described as "howls of anguish" among historians. The scientific press did not devote as much space to analyzing this work, but a measure of the criticism and its quality can be gained from one example, where the only fault that one professor could allege was that Velikovsky had mistaken the cuneiform plural sign *mesh* for the name of the Moabite king, Mesha. However, Velikovsky twice calls attention to the fact that in several instances the normal reading cannot apply, since the grammatical construction definitely alludes to an individual. Further commentators repeated the professor's erroneous claim, inviting the suspicion that they had read the critics but not the actual work that they purported to review.

One person who did take notice of Velikovsky's theories was Einstein. According to his secretary, Helen Dukas, just before his death in 1955 he intended writing a letter to the curator of the Egyptology Department of the Metropolitan Museum of Art to request carbon-14 dating tests to check some of the theses presented in *Ages in Chaos*. Velikovsky had been trying for years to persuade the British Museum and other institutions to test relics from the New Kingdom and late period, which in conventional chronology spans some twelve hundred years. Generally, such items tended to be omitted from testing programs because they were notorious for being "contaminated" and yielding unacceptably low ages. When Einstein died, a copy of *Worlds in Collision* was found open on his desk.

TESTIMONY FROM THE ROCKS: EARTH IN UPHEAVAL

A line that some critics of *Worlds in Collision* had been harping on was that if events as violent as those Velikovsky described had really happened in recent times, they would have left unmistakable signs all over the surface of the Earth. Either the critics hadn't heard of Cuvier, or they had forgotten him. In November 1955, Velikovsky obliged them with the publication of *Earth in Upheaval*, a testimony drawn not from myth or anything created by the minds of Man, but written into the rocks of the planet itself. In it, he examined the then-unquestioned principle of Lyellian gradualism, and contrasted its tenets with what is actually found the world over, testifying to immense cataclysms that changed the face of the Earth.

THE FOSSIL GRAVEYARDS

From Alaska to Florida, Europe to Far Eastern Asia, huge graveyards are found, containing the remains of millions of animals, many types abundant and well adapted until recent times, but now extinct. They didn't die out gradually but were overwhelmed suddenly and violently across whole regions, along with entire forests that were uprooted and splintered. The fast-frozen mammoths with pieces of their last meal still preserved between their teeth that most people today have heard about represent just a tiny part of the picture. Off the north coasts of Siberia are islands hundreds of feet high that consist of practically nothing but heaped up bones and tusks of mammoths, elephants, rhinoceroses, and smashed trees. Fissures, caves, and excavations across the British Isles, France, Switzerland, and Gibraltar yield elephants, rhinoceroses, hippopotami, lions, tigers, bears, wolves, hyenas, and others that the perplexed archeologists of earlier times could only guess had been brought by the Romans. But the numbers were too vast for that to be credible. In many instances the types were already extinct by the time of the Romans; others were later found spread across parts of Europe that they were just as foreign to, but which the Romans had never occupied. Whales somehow found their way to lodgements 500 feet above sea level in Michigan, Vermont, and Quebec.

The scale and nature of the devastation is consistent with a gigantic tidal surge away from the equator, being stopped at barriers such as the Himalaya chain and the Alps, but elsewhere funneling through the northern Atlantic and Pacific inlets to the Arctic Basin and then rebounding in a backwash rolling southward across the Asian and North American continents. In many places the animal and plant debris are of all types from all regions, marine and land forms, from tropical and temperate climates, all jumbled and heaped up together. The Siwalik Hills on the southern edge of the Himalayas consist of sedimentary deposits 2,000 to 3,000 feet high and extending for several hundred miles, abounding with fossil beds of so many and so varied species that the animal world of today looks impoverished by comparison. Thirteen hundred miles away, in central Burma, the deposits cut by the Irrawaddy river reach 10,000 feet and contain a comparable variety, along with hundreds of thousands of entire trunks of silicified trees. Yet, as also happens in other places, the beds are separated by huge thicknesses of sediment—4,000 feet in the case of the Irrawaddy— that contain no fossils or trace of any organic material at all, suggesting the sudden halting of colossal volumes of water.

EARTHMOVING AND EXCAVATION

Rapidly moving water can move amazingly heavy objects. Erratic rocks and boulders found hundreds of miles from their places of origin have usually been attributed to transportation by glaciers or ice sheets. But they occur widely across parts of Siberia where there are no high grounds to impart motion to ice, and in places that were never covered by ice.

The evidence Velikovsky presents is of precisely the kind that the events proposed in *Worlds in Collision* would be expected to leave, such as of meteorite storms, pole shifts, abrupt climate changes, alterations of sea level, and increased tectonic activity. Mountain uplifts and other formations show indications of being younger than conventional geology maintains. The Columbia Plateau consists of solidified lava sheets covering two hundred thousand square miles of Washington, Oregon, and Idaho. The Snake River at Seven Devils Canyon has cut more than three thousand feet deep and not reached the bottom of them. Tens of thousands of elliptical craters, many now flooded to form lakes, occur all along the coastal areas from New Jersey to northeast

Florida, but especially in the Carolinas. They all exhibit a parallel alignment from northwest to southeast, and many have raised rims at the southern end, suggestive of scars from an intense meteorite shower coming down at a grazing angle. Similar patterns occur at other parts of both hemispheres. Volcanic and earthquake activity has declined significantly even since Roman times. In the Andes, ruins of fishing villages and ports are found 12,000 feet above sea level. What were once cultivated agricultural terraces today disappear under the snow line.

Of course, much of this clashes with the orthodox dating system. In his usual fashion, Velikovsky cares little for theory and sides with the evidence, questioning the assumptions that the conventional dating system rests on. It was more a product of materialism's fight with religion than an empirical construct, he contends, manufactured to provide the long time scales that Lyell and Darwin needed. Paralleling much of what we said earlier in this book, he was skeptical that natural selection had the ability to do what was claimed of it and offered evidence that biological change occurred in sudden epochs of repopulation by radically new designs, triggered by the occurrence of global-scale catastrophes. Needless to say, this didn't earn him many friends in that department either.

ORTHODOXY IN CONFUSION

EMBARRASSING CONFIRMATIONS

The reactions after release of *Earth in Upheaval* were more restrained, possibly because some were beginning to feel that things had gone too far for the good of the professional image the first time. Others no doubt hoped that if they ignored Velikovsky he might just go away. But a big part of the reason could have been that an embarrassing number of his predictions were beginning to be shown as correct.

When *Worlds in Collision* was published, four Yale University professors had collaborated in preparing a rebuttal in the *American Journal of Science*, where one of them ridiculed the suggestion that the Mesoamerican civilization appeared to be much older than conventional history allowed. Five years later, the National

Geographical Society announced: "Atomic science has proved the ancient civilizations of Mexico to be some 1,000 years older than had been believed." [97] The chief of the Bureau of American Ethnology at the Smithsonian Institution declared this to be the most important archeological discovery in recent history.

Another of the Yale critics scorned Velikovsky's suggestion that petroleum might have a cosmic origin. Two years later, in 1952, P. V. Smith reported in *Science* (October 24) the "surprising fact" that oil from recently deposited sediments along the Gulf of Mexico could be only thousands of years old. Hydrocarbons were subsequently found in the composition of some types of meteorites. A smallish carbonaceous chondrite asteroid—say, around ten kilometers in diameter—is estimated to contain a trillion tons of them. [98] In 1960, Professor A. T. Wilson of Victoria University in Wellington, New Zealand, produced high-molecular-weight hydrocarbons by electric discharges in Jupiter-like gases and suggested that terrestrial petroleum might have come from elsewhere—a theme that others have taken up since. [99] Both he and Professor W. Libby, chemist at the University of California, speculated that oil might exist on the Moon. By the early 1960s, neon and argon were repeatedly being found in meteorites, too.

In April of the same year as *Earth in Upheaval* was published, 1955, scientists from the Carnegie Institution startled their audience at a meeting of the American Astronomical Society by announcing the chance detection of unexpected radio emanations from Jupiter, which they had recorded for several weeks before identifying the source. When a Doubleday editor wrote, calling attention to Velikovsky's anticipating just such a finding, one of them replied that even Velikovsky was entitled to a "near miss once in a while." The full extent of the radiation belt encompassing Jupiter, a hundred trillion times more powerful than Earth's, was established in 1960.

Dr. Harry Hess, head of the Department of Geology at Princeton University, who had always been sympathetic toward Velikovsky's theories, submitted a memorandum to the U.S. National Committee in December 1956, proposing as part of the planned agenda for the International Geophysical Year a search for the extended region of terrestrial magnetic influence as Velikovsky had suggested. The Van Allen Belts were discovered in 1958 and featured as one of the high points of the program. In 1960 the *Pioneer V* space probe was launched, and after it had been in solar orbit for six weeks NASA called a press conference to announce that "In one exciting week, man has learned more about the near reaches of space that surround the earth than the sum of his knowledge over the last 50 years. . . . [A] fantastic amount of cosmic traffic (hot gaseous clouds, deadly rays, bands of electricity) rushes by at high speed, circles, crisscrosses, and collides."[100] The tail of the Earth's magnetosphere was later measured as extending beyond the orbit of the Moon.

There was also news from Venus. As late as 1959, many astronomers still maintained that because of the great reflectivity of its cloud cover its surface temperature would be little different from Earth's, despite its closer orbit to the Sun. However, in April 1961, radio astronomers announced that the figure had to be at least 600°F. In 1963, after analysis of data from the *Mariner 2* probe, the measured value turned out to be 800°F. At about the same time, radiometric measurements by the U.S. Naval Observatory and the Goldstone Tracking Station in California showed Venus to have a very slow retrograde rotation, making it unique among the planets and suggesting something unusual about its history. Some astronomers wondered if it might have been created separately from the others.

Further results from *Mariner 2* were interpreted as indicating atmospheric condensation and polymerization into heavy molecules at temperatures around 200°F, leading to the conclusion that Venus's atmosphere must contain heavy hydrocarbons and possibly more complex organic compounds. Lloyd Motz of Columbia, who had supported Velikovsky before, along with Princeton physicist V. Bargmann, wrote a joint letter to *Science* drawing attention to Velikovsky's priority in predicting these seemingly unrelated facts about the Solar System and urged that his whole thesis be objectively reexamined. When the letter was published, Velikovsky submitted a paper showing that the points brought out in the letter were just a few of many his books raised, that had been supported by independent research. The paper was returned unread. Instead, *Science* published a facetious letter from a reader stating that "the accidental presence of one or two good apples does not redeem a spoiled barrelful." Or a barrelful of sour grapes, maybe?

MORE ELECTRICAL HERESIES: CHARGES AND COUNTER-CHARGES

The theoretical front was seeing some interesting developments also. One of Velikovsky's suggestions that had been greeted with derision was that electromagnetic forces might play a part in celestial dynamics as well as gravity, and that astronomical bodies could be affected by acquiring electrical charge during their encounters. At a meeting of the American Philosophical Society in 1952, Cecilia Payne-Gaposchkin presented a paper taking Velikovsky to task on selected biblical quotations, but which was itself riddled with misrepresentations. [101] Velikovsky, who was in the audience, came forward to give a rebuttal and was warmly received. But when he requested that his remarks be reproduced along with Gaposchkin's in the society's *Proceedings*, he was refused.

Appended to Gaposchkin's paper, however, was a "quantitative refutation of Velikovsky's wild hypotheses" by Donald H. Menzel, also of Harvard. To show how preposterous Velikovsky's hypothesis was, Menzel demonstrated that to contribute ten percent of its gravitational attraction on the Earth, the Sun would need a charge of 10^{19} volts, whereas he calculated it was incapable or retaining anything greater than 1800 volts. (He also showed that the sudden acquisition of such a charge would involve a supply of more energy than the Sun radiates in a thousand years, which was neither here nor there since Velikovsky had said nothing about its being acquired suddenly.)

Then in 1960, Professor V. A. Bailey, professor of physics at the University of Sydney, Australia, who was not familiar with Velikovsky's work, announced that the magnitudes of five different known astronomical phenomena could be explained by the single hypothesis that a star like the Sun carries a net negative charge. Bailey's figures for making this work gave a surface potential of 10^{19} volts—precisely that which Menzel had used to show how wacky Velikovsky was. Menzel wrote to Bailey pointing out what he perceived as an error and asked that Bailey revoke his theory since it wasn't helping the American scientists' campaign to discredit Velikovsky. Bailey took exception to the suggestion and in turn uncovered an arithmetical slip in Menzel's calculations that invalidated Menzel's whole argument. Menzel duly published a correction, but without acknowledging that it demolished his widely publicized anti-Velikovsky claim.

With regard to the radio emissions from Jupiter, Menzel wrote that since scientists generally didn't accept the theory of *Worlds in Collision*, "any seeming verification of Velikovsky's predictions is pure chance." [102] He dismissed the prediction of the high temperature of Venus on the grounds that Velikovsky hadn't supplied a figure but said only that it would be hot, which was a relative term—liquid air, for example, being "hot" relative to liquid helium.

Velikovsky's suggestion of electrical interaction as an agency for arresting the motion of the Earth and circularizing the orbit of Venus had been scoffed at by the eminences because they insisted that the bodies of the Solar System were not charged and the space between them electromagnetically inert. Both these assertions had been shown to be wrong. 1960 was also the year when Professor André Danjon, director of the Paris Observatory, reported to l'Académie des Sciences that following an unusually large solar flare, the length of the day suddenly increased by 0.85 milliseconds, which he ascribed to electromagnetic forces induced by the flare. Thereafter, as the charge acquired by the Earth leaked away into the conductive medium afforded by the recently discovered solar wind, the Earth's rotation recovered at the rate of 3.7 microseconds every 24 hours. [103]

We saw earlier how fiercely the entrenched priesthood resisted Hans Alfvén's theories about space being an electrically active medium—from one of the club, who later received a Nobel Prize for his work in celestial electrodynamics. It isn't difficult to imagine how they must have felt about being upstaged by a scholar in ancient history and classical languages, who was not only asking questions that they themselves should have been asking long before, but moving in on the turf and coming up with some good answers.

A NEW VIEW OF PLANETS: VIOLENT ORIGINS; RAPID CHANGE

Needless to say, the proposal of Venus erupting out of Jupiter, and that the Greeks hadn't imagined it or made it all up, sent the Establishment into a frenzy. Everybody knew that all the planets had been formed at the same time billions of years ago. The two prevalent mechanisms doing the rounds in the fifties were the tidal theory, going back to Laplace, in which the planets had condensed from a blob pulled off the Sun by a close-passing star, and the more recent model of accretion from a contracting nebular disk.

However, in 1960 the president of the Royal Astronomical Society in Britain, W. H. McCrea, rocked the applecart with a theoretical analysis showing that neither of these models would work, since planetary formation within the orbit of Jupiter by either process would be disrupted by its tidal effects. [104] The following year, the British cosmologist Raymond. A. Lyttleton concluded from a fluid-dynamic study of Jupiter's core that an object of its size and estimated accretion rate, rotating at such a speed, would periodically become unstable and assume the form of an ovoid rotating about its short axis. The ovoid would elongate into an asymmetrical dumbbell and eventually fission to shed excess mass. Most of this ejected amount—up to 10 percent the mass of the original body—would be expelled from the Solar System. But lesser drops torn out in the process could be captured by the Sun and have formed the inner planets. Thus the only primordial members of the planetary system would be the gas giants. [105] And as we saw previously, Alfvén also concluded (in 1963 [106]) from considerations of angular momentum that the gas giants must have been formed before the terrestrial planets. A doctoral thesis presented in 1969 doubted if planets could form beyond the orbit of Saturn and suggested that the planets now out there had been propelled by encounters with others. [107]

These days, the shortcomings of the accretion theory are more widely acknowledged, and it is permissible to propose alternatives. Conference papers discussing the origination of planets and other objects through fission from larger ones are commonplace and receive due consideration. Impact theories are in vogue following identification of the Cretaceous event believed to have caused the extinctions that included the dinosaurs, the most recent proposal for the formation of the Moon attributing it to ejection from the Earth following a strike by a possibly Mars-size body. But no citation ever acknowledges Velikovsky as the first whose ideas had departed from the idealized, endlessly repeating Laplacian machine. [108]

The Earth itself had also departed from the picture of gradual, nonthreatening change that had persisted since the days of Lyell and Darwin. It had been argued that pole shifts and crustal movements of the magnitude that Velikovsky described would have left no stalactites or stalagmites unbroken in caves, yet it was known—according to accepted theory—that such structures were far older than the dates he talked about. But in 1962, in the Gnome Cavern, New Mexico, to the astonishment of geologists, stalactites had grown within one year of the nuclear test explosion there. A newspaper dispatch reported, "All nature's processes have been speeded up a billionfold." (Within five years of the 1980 Mount St. Helens eruption in Washington, strata deposited in new-formed canyons had hardened into rock. With the presence of a fine-grained ingredient to act as a binder, the process resembles the setting of cement and can occur very rapidly.)

The modern picture of plate tectonics—laughed at in the 1920s when Alfred Wegener first put forward his ideas that continents moved—was coming together in the mid fifties, with new evidence appearing in the journals just about every month for magnetic reversals, shifting poles, ice sheets covering what had once been tropics, mountain tops that had been seabeds, and slabs of crust rifting, separating, and colliding like grease patches on cold soup. Velikovsky's sympathizer, Harry Hess, was one of the leading figures in these developments. (Current theory still assumes millions-of-years time scales, arrived at by extrapolating backward the rates of plate movement observed today. My own guess is that these will turn out to be the cooled-down remnant of processes that once operated much faster.)

Cores from the ocean bottoms were read as testifying to prodigious falls of meteorites, dust, and ash over enormous areas. Claude Schaeffer of College de France, unaware at the time of Velikovsky's work, concluded in a study of archeological strata that the ancient East, as documented for every excavation from Troy to the Caucasus, Persia, Palestine, and Syria, underwent immense natural paroxysms unknown in the modern experience of seismology. Five times between the third and first millennia B.C., cultures disappeared, empires collapsed, cities were buried, climates altered. [109]

REJECTED CALL FOR REAPPRAISAL

Eric Larrabee, whose original preview article in *Harpers* in 1950 of *Worlds in Collision* could be said to have started the whole thing off, wrote again thirteen years later, in the August 1963 issue of the same magazine, a piece called "Scientists in Collision," citing the new discoveries in astronomy, space science, geology, and geophysics that supported Velikovsky's case and calling for the establishment to reappraise its position.

"Science itself," he wrote, "even while most scientists have considered his case to be closed, has been heading in Velikovsky's direction. Proposals which seemed so shocking when he made them are now commonplace. . . . There is scarcely one of Velikovsky's central ideas—as long as it was taken separately and devoid of its implications—which has not since been propounded in all seriousness by a scientist of repute."

The responses were fast and ireful, but for the most part repeated all the old fallacies. On the subject of conducting plasmas and magnetic fields in interplanetary space, the tune changed to "we knew all that before Velikovsky" (maybe because of publication of Alfvén's work?). The debate carried on through the August, October, December 1963, and January 1964 issues of *Harpers*. Larrabee's performance in taking it upon himself to answer the opposition was described by one commentator as "a classic example of the demolition of a scientist's arguments by a non-scientist." The "scientific" side was reduced to arguing that since nonscientists did not understand scientific issues and the scientific method, they should be restrained from debating in a public forum. [110]

In the same period, Velikovsky, feeling optimistic that the new findings might have earned him a more considered hearing by now, prepared an article entitled "Venus, a Youthful Planet," which Harry Hess agreed to recommend to the American Philosophical Society for publishing—the same organization whose publications committee in 1952 had rejected Velikovsky's corrections of Cecilia Payne Gapschkin's misquotations in its *Proceedings*. This time the committee was split into two belligerent camps who argued for something like six months. In January 1964, the decision was taken not to publish Velikovsky's paper.

An article entitled "The Politics of Science and Dr. Velikovsky," documenting the scientific community's treatment of the whole affair and accusing it of conspiracy and suppression, appeared in the September 1963 issue of *American Behavioral Scientist*, requiring a second printing even though the initial run had been unusually large in anticipation. The response of the readership, composed mainly of specialists in fields that Velikovsky's work hadn't touched upon, was predominantly favorable. A number of sociologists felt the *ABS* account should be required reading in social science courses. Professor G. A. Lundberg of the University of Washington wrote, "[T]he A.A.A.S., not to mention individual scientists and groups, must now prepare a detailed answer. What is really at issue are the mores governing the reception of new scientific ideas on the part of the established spokesmen for science." [111]

Since the issue was essentially one of scientific ethics, the seemingly natural choice for a vehicle to pursue the matter in was the *Bulletin of the Atomic Scientists*, which prided itself on being a medium for expression of such issues. In a later letter to Harry Hess, the editor of the *Bulletin,* Eugene Rabinowitch, acknowledged the reawakening of interest in Velikovsky's theories and alluded to the situation as requiring "remedial action," i.e., rallying to the defense of the threatened citadels. The ensuing piece, "Velikovsky Rides Again" (*Bulletin*, April 1964), was jeering and uncivil, employing all the devices seen when the earlier outcry was raised, of unfounded charges, misrepresentation, and dogmatically presenting received opinion as established fact. The writer given the assignment was unfamiliar with the fields of ancient languages and Egyptology in which he chose to attack Velikovsky—and even, apparently, with the elementary French needed to read one of Velikovsky's sources. But these were areas that typical readers of a journal like the *Bulletin* would have to take on trust, and the tone met with satisfied and often eager approval.

One protector of the faith sent a copy of the *Bulletin* article to Moses Hadas, Jay Professor of Greek at Columbia University, who had remarked in an earlier review that Velikovsky appeared to be approaching vindication. Doubtless to illuminate him as to the error of his ways, Hadas was told that he should find the piece "of interest and perhaps amusing." But the ploy backfired. Hadas replied that he had no opinion about Velikovsky's astronomical theories "but I know that he is not dishonest. What bothered me was the violence of the attack on him: if his theories were absurd, would they not have been exposed as such in time without a campaign of vilification? One after another the reviews misquoted him and then attacked the misquotation.... [Regarding the *Bulletin* article] It is his critic, not Velikovsky, who is uninformed and rash." [112]

Eric Larrabee was promised an opportunity to reply in the *Bulletin,* but on meeting the stated deadline he was informed that space was not available. When challenged, Rabinowitch affirmed that the matter should be resolved in the "spirit of scientific argumentation" and agreed that since the *Bulletin*'s article had made claims involving Hebrew and Egyptian paleographic and philological evidence, it should devote space to material disputing them. Velikovsky, however, would not consent to entering into such a debate, since in his view the author of the piece had amply demonstrated incompetence in those subjects. Instead, he proposed publication of "Venus, a Youthful Planet," which Hess had again agreed to submit. This was turned down on the grounds that the *Bulletin* was "not a magazine for *scientific* controversies." But wasn't that the reason why it had been chosen as a forum in the first place? The article was returned unread with a letter from Rabinowitch stating that he wasn't qualified and didn't have the time to study Velikovsky's books. But he knew enough about the absence of dogmatism in modern science to trust the pronouncements of qualified experts. As Epictetus observed almost two thousand years go, "A man cannot begin to learn that which he thinks he already knows."

The summer of 1965 saw the release by Delta of paperback editions of *Worlds in Collision* and *Earth in Upheaval*, provoking another round of reactions along the same general lines that had been seen before. One reviewer, ridiculing the former book, flaunted his own ignorance of the content of the latter by declaring blithely that the alleged events couldn't have happened since "animal life went through the fateful year of 1500 B.C. without any disturbance." *Science* and *Scientific American* both refused to accept advertisements for the Delta editions.

THE PLANETS SPEAK, REGARDLESS

An interesting twist to the suppression or ignoring of inconvenient facts was added by *Sky & Telescope*, a journal for amateur astronomers published by Harvard Observatory. Their report on the findings of *Mariner 2*, a summary from the book *Mariner, Mission to Venus* (1963), by the staff of Jet Propulsion Laboratory, deleted references to (a) Venus's retrograde motion; (b) an interpretation of the clouds as consisting of condensed hydrocarbons held in oily suspension; (c) absence of water and the possibility of small lakes of molten metal; and (d) the paltriness of sunlight, if any, finding its way down through the fifteen-mile-thick cloud blanket (effectively demolishing the notion of a "runaway greenhouse effect" that had been cobbled together in an attempt to explain the temperature). It could, of course, have been coincidence that these were precisely the points that lent the most support to Velikovsky's contentions. As Larrabee had commented in his 1963 *Harpers* piece, science itself continued to unfold at its own pace regardless of what some scientists tried to make of it.

Theoretical studies showed that the tidal pumping effect of a large, plastic, plasma object orbiting in a strong gravitational field would convert orbital to thermal energy and was consistent with the rapid circularization of Venus's orbit. [113] (Einstein was of the opinion that Velikovskian orbits could arise through purely gravitational influence, although it would require some fortuitous coincidences.) It had also been shown that a combination of electromagnetic and gravitational forces on the scale envisioned for a Venus encounter was quite capable of producing an arrest of apparent celestial motions as seen from Earth without violent deceleration by tilting the Earth's axis and producing a temporary transfer of momentum from axial spin to a precessional wobble. [114]

From Jupiter: In April 1964, radio astronomers measured a sudden change in the rotation rate, speculated as caused by interaction of its intense electromagnetic field with fields permeating the Solar System.

From the Moon: The *Explorer 18* satellite measured a lunar magnetosphere extending at least 68,000 miles. Unexpected volcanic and seismic activity was detected on the Moon—supposedly a tectonically dead body for billions of years. Dome structures were identified all over the surface that seemed to be bubbles of once-molten magma that had failed to burst—raising the question of how many other crater formations might be the marks of bubbles that had. The first tests of lunar rock brought back by the Apollo astronauts yielded unexpected amounts of neon and argon. The solar wind was excluded as a source, yet the elements had to have come from the outside, since the concentration was found to be proportional to the area of the soil grains, not the volume. Hydrocarbons were also found. The *Apollo 11* crew observed peculiar glazed regions where the surface appeared to have been molten too recently for erosion of the reflective surface by meteorite and

James P. Hogan

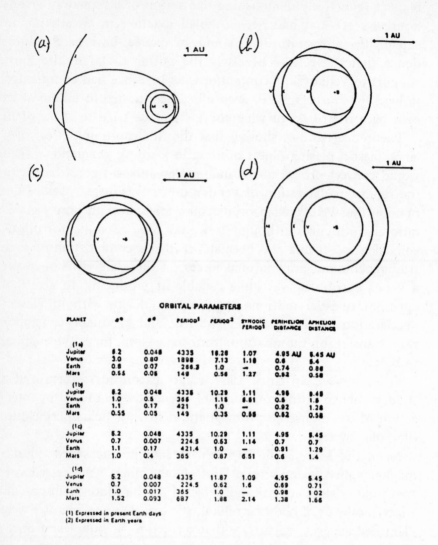

ORBITAL PARAMETERS

PLANET	a°	e°	PERIOD[1]	PERIOD[2]	SYNODIC PERIOD[1]	PERIHELION DISTANCE	APHELION DISTANCE
(1a)							
Jupiter	5.2	0.048	4335	16.26	1.07	4.95 AU	5.45 AU
Venus	3.0	0.80	1898	7.13	1.18	0.6	5.4
Earth	0.8	0.07	266.3	1.0	—	0.74	0.86
Mars	0.55	0.05	149	0.56	1.27	0.52	0.58
(1b)							
Jupiter	5.2	0.048	4335	10.29	1.11	4.96	5.45
Venus	1.0	0.5	366	1.15	8.51	0.5	1.5
Earth	1.1	0.17	421	1.0	—	0.92	1.28
Mars	0.55	0.05	149	0.35	0.55	0.52	0.58
(1c)							
Jupiter	5.2	0.048	4335	10.29	1.11	4.95	5.45
Venus	0.7	0.007	224.5	0.63	1.14	0.7	0.7
Earth	1.1	0.17	421.4	1.0	—	0.91	1.29
Mars	1.0	0.4	365	0.87	6.51	0.6	1.4
(1d)							
Jupiter	5.2	0.048	4335	11.87	1.09	4.95	5.45
Venus	0.7	0.007	224.5	0.62	1.6	0.69	0.71
Earth	1.0	0.017	365	1.0	—	0.98	1.02
Mars	1.52	0.093	687	1.88	2.14	1.38	1.66

(1) Expressed in present Earth days
(2) Expressed in Earth years

A sequence of Velikovskian orbits satisfying the requirements of conservation of angular momentum and energy. From Ransom & Hoffee, 1972

dust infall. Experiments performed by the *Apollo 15* team measured a temperature gradient in the surface layers indicating heat flow from the interior, which surprised scientists.

From Mars: In 1965 *Mariner 4* had shocked scientists by finding Mars to be more Moon-like than Earth-like. By the early seventies, pictures from *Mariner 9* were showing large surface tracts of lava flows crossed by faults and fissures, as well as apparently recent water channels and runoff patterns covering huge areas. The motion of Mars exhibited peculiarities that could be explained by its path being disturbed at some time. From studies of the distribution of mass and angular momentum across the Solar System, it appeared that Mars had lost much of its spin momentum, rotating in slightly over twenty-four hours against the eight hours that calculation said it should exhibit, but had gained far more in orbital momentum.

And from the Earth itself: A paper in *Nature* in 1971 [115] suggested interaction between Earth and an external body as the cause of magnetic pole reversals and claimed that tektites—a type of small, glass stone—were deposited on Earth at the time of the last reversal. This had previously been believed to have occurred 700,000 years ago, but later studies of ancient hearthstones and pottery brought it down first to 12,500 years ago, and then to the eighth century B.C.

Velikovsky had been trying for over a decade to have dating tests performed to check his theories of Egyptian chronology but met evasion and obstruction. Eventually, the radiocarbon laboratory at the University of Pennsylvania determined dates for samples of wood from the tomb of Tutenkhamen as being 200 to 300 years younger than the fourteenth century B.C. that accepted chronology assigns. Velikovsky had placed Tutenkhamen in the ninth century. The reported dating fell midway between the two, but it doesn't present a problem for Velikovsky's revised chronology because the objects that the samples were taken from could have been fashioned from wood that was older. On the other hand, they could hardly have been made from trees that grew centuries later, which means that the conventional system can only admit a discrepancy.

There are other reasons why wood can yield incorrectly high radiocarbon dates. Shorter-lived items should be more reliable. In a 1964 letter to Dr. Elizabeth Ralph at the University of

Pennsylvania, Velikovsky had stated that he expected short-lived items from Tutenkhamen's tomb would give figures around 840 B.C. The British Museum finally reported tests on reed and palm nut kernels as giving 846 B.C. and 899 B.C. respectively (designated by the Museum as BM 642A and BM 642B). Despite an assurance that these results would be published "shortly," they weren't. But they were discussed in the May 1972 issue of the journal *Pensée*. A Dr. Van Oosterhout of the Department of Chemistry and Chemical Engineering at the University of Delft, the Netherlands, wrote to *Pensée* in 1973, saying that he could find no details in the published radiocarbon data from the British Museum and asking for additional information. After follow-up and questioning, an official of the British Museum admitted that results deviating substantially from the expected values were often discarded without being published. Another letter from the Museum to Van Oosterhout denied that tests on materials from the tomb had ever been performed at all. [116]

SLAYING THE MONSTER: THE AAAS VELIKOVSKY SYMPOSIUM, 1974

Through all of this, two traits stand out in the treatment of Velikovsky by his detractors. One is repeated admissions, frequently boasts, by his most vehement critics that they hadn't read the material they castigated—as if the touch of it might be somehow unclean and defiling. They just "knew" that he *couldn't* be right, and that was sufficient. The other was that after solemnly reciting commitment to such scholarly principles as scientific objectivity, fairness, and civility of discourse, they would then go on to immediately violate every one of them. Organized science had tried every tactic of distortion, evasion, misrepresentation, intimidation, vilification, and suppression of evidence to slay the monster that threatened the entire foundation of the collective uniformitarian worldview and mind-set. But after twenty years, interest in Velikovsky's theories was not only getting stronger with the apparent vindication from all quarters that was getting past the censorship and receiving coverage, but Velikovsky was no longer

virtually alone. Scientists from many disciplines were beginning
to organize in his defense, bringing the message to a new generation
of readers and students. The topic became included in university
courses, and Velikovsky symposia and invitations for Velikovsky
to speak on university campuses multiplied. The list of venues from
1970 to 1974 included Harvard; SUNY-Buffalo, Notre Dame, and
North Carolina Universities, as well as McMasters and Lethbridge
in Canada; NASA Ames Research Center; Lewis and Clark College,
Portland; the IBM Research Center; and a conference in Switzerland devoted to his work. In 1971 the editors of *Pensée* decided
to publish a special issue on the purely scientific aspects of
Velikovsky's ideas, but the amount of material available was by then
so vast that it became a ten-issue series—later compiled into book
form as *Velikovsky Reconsidered* (1976)—which attracted widespread
attention.

It couldn't be allowed to go on. The occasion for exorcizing
Velikovsy and his heresies from the land and reaffirming the true
faith was selected to be the 1974 meeting of the American Association for the Advancement of Science (AAAS), which that year
was scheduled to be held in San Francisco. [117]

A GLIMPSE OF THE GROUND RULES

In the summer of 1972, a past president of the AAAS, astronomer and atmospheric scientist Walter Orr Roberts, had written to
Stephen L. Talbott, the editor of *Pensée*, suggesting that a symposium be held on Velikovsky's work. It seems that Roberts's
motives were fair and aimed at an honest reappraisal. The following
year an announcement appeared in *Science*, inviting suggestions
for the 1974 AAAS meeting agenda. Dr. C. J. Ransom, a plasma
physicist, AAAS member, and Velikovsky supporter, proposed the
topic of "Venus—A Youthful Planet," offering himself as conference organizer and proposing several more names as speakers. This
was rejected without explanation, but less than a month later a
similar proposal was accepted from the AAAS Astronomy Committee, the salient difference being that it was to be organized by
noted critics of Velikovsky: Ivan King, astronomer at U.C. Berkeley;
Donald Goldsmith, assistant professor of astronomy at the
State University of New York, Stony Brook; and Professor Owen
Gingerich, historian of science at Harvard. Because of time

limitations, it was decided that the symposium should concentrate on the nature and motions of the planets, with particular regard to Venus and Jupiter.

It soon became clear that the intention was not to stage an impartial debate but a court of inquisition, where the verdict already had been determined. The aim was not to give Velikovsky a hearing but to discredit him in the eyes of the press and the public, and banish his ideas from the forum of acceptable scientific discourse. In this it was resoundingly successful and for the most part remains so to the present time.

The agreement had been that there would be six panelists, three pro- and three anti-Velikovsky, and that Velikovsky would be allotted excess time since he would be presenting his own paper as well as answering his opponents. The promises were promptly broken. The two others that Velikovsky nominated to make up his side were Ransom, cited above, and Professor Lynn E. Rose, a specialist in the history, philosophy, and method of science, who had also taught ancient history and classical languages. These would have made up a formidable team indeed, fully conversant with Velikovsky's theories and between them amply informed to speak on all of the important issues. That was probably why the rules were hastily changed to exclude them. Rose was disqualified on the grounds that he was not from the "hard sciences"—although nothing about such had been said up to this point. Ransom obviously fitted this stipulation, but it suddenly became necessary to be an "academician," whereas he was at the time employed in corporate research. Velikovsky was unwilling to go away and come back with further names when the ones he'd said he wanted were turned down, which later resulted in his being blamed for the blatant inequality that he was to face.

However, the AAAS committee dropped its criteria when it came to selecting their own speakers: Norman Storer, a professor of the hard science of sociology at Baruch College, part of the City University of New York; Peter Huber, professor of mathematical statistics at the Swiss Federal Institute of Technology, whose qualification was what he described as his "hobby" of cuneiform writing; J. Derral Mullholland, professor of astronomy at the University of Texas, Austin; and, doubtless to secure the popular vote, the scientific celebrity figure Carl Sagan, from the laboratory for planetary studies at Cornell University. A further speaker, not listed on either side of the panel since he gave his position as neutral, was Dr. Irving Michelson, professor of mechanical and aerospace engineering at the Illinois Institute of Technology.

Originally the deal had been for equal time for both sides of the panel. This was now reinterpreted to mean equal time for each *speaker*. So, for every half hour that Velikovsky was given, every one of his opponents would receive a half hour too. The flagrant bias was hardly allayed by a statement from King to *Pensée* stating that "What disturbs the scientists is persistence of these views, in spite of all the efforts the scientists have spent on educating the public" and "This is not a debate on the correctness of Velikovsky's view of the planetary system; none of us in the scientific community believes that such a debate would be remotely justified at a serious scientific meeting." [118]

So much for the promised impartiality. It apparently followed that the considerable number of specialists who evidently *did* believe that such a debate would be justified were by definition not among "us" of the scientific community.

Velikovsky's hope that the flood of evidence and rekindled interest in his ideas might finally have won him a fair hearing had clearly been misplaced. Many of his supporters advised him to pull out right there rather than accept a pitch that had already been tilted seismically against him. The bind, of course, was that this would immediately have been seized upon as showing that he had no answers. Lynn Rose has since speculated that Velikovsky knew exactly what he was doing, and accepted the inevitability of short-term defeat, given the climate of the times, in return for an even stronger verdict in his favor that history would one day pronounce.

So it came about that on February 25, 1974, in the Grand Ballroom of the St. Francis Hotel, Velikovsky, then in his seventy-ninth year, watched by a press corps that had been appropriately primed and apparently saw nothing amiss with the arrangements, mounted the dais to take on four hostile opponents all around half his age in an ordeal that would last until 1:00 A.M. and continue the following day. The final low trick was that the only paper he was permitted to see in advance was Storer's, which didn't deal with Velikovsky's scientific issues. The others were withheld until the day itself, forcing Velikovsky to muster what defense he could in the time he could find—a practice that would be illegal in any law court not rigged by a totalitarian state. At the end of the first session, which went on for five and a half hours, one reporter, seeing that Velikovsky looked tired, remarked that he was not his own best spokesman. Not one of the press representatives mentioned that at the end of it all, he had acquitted himself well enough to receive a standing ovation.

Echoing the tone of his memorandum to *Pensée*, King's opening statement included the words, "No one who is involved in the organization of this symposium believes that Dr. Velikovsky's ideas are correct. Yet millions of people have read his books and after more than twenty years of condemnation by the scientific establishment he still has a large and often devoted following. . . . It is in this spirit that we present this morning's symposium." In other words, this isn't to debate a scientific theory. The purpose is to investigate the persistence of views that we know are wrong. We're here to stamp out heresy.

The first speaker was Storer, who talked about the norms of science and the ideals of method and behavior that it seeks to live up to. Acknowledging that the scientific community had violated these standards in its treatment of Velikovsky back in the fifties, he reminded the audience that this had been a period when science and indeed the whole intellectual enterprise was under attack. The Cold War had been at its chilliest, with loyalty oaths being demanded, blacklists drawn up, and Senator Joseph McCarthy waiting to pounce at the first hint of deviancy or Communist connection. Simply being a scientist was to be a potential traitor, and it was perhaps understandable that they had reacted defensively and failed to welcome with open arms another apparent attempt to discredit established scientific knowledge—and in particular by an outsider.

If that were the case, then we would expect a different reception to be accorded to insiders presenting revolutionary ideas at times of lesser political tension, not gripped by corresponding extremes of paranoia. But as we already saw in the case of Halton Arp and the cosmologists, and will meet again when we look at Peter Duesberg's reception by the AIDS establishment, it turns out not to be so. One could as well argue that the political stresses of the Reformation excused the Catholic Church's suppression of Galileo and others. In all cases the real crime was the challenging of established authority.

ONLY THE DATA THAT'S FIT TO PRINT: THE VENUS TABLETS

Peter Huber's profession and hobby were inverted both in the official program, which described him as a "professor of ancient history" speaking on "ancient historical records," and King's introduction as one who "has made a study of the ancient archaeological records relating to astronomy. He also, incidentally, has a second specialty in statistics . . ." [119]

The essence of Huber's paper was that ancient Babylonian records show Venus to have been where it is today, orbiting as it does today, long before the events that Velikovsky claims, and therefore those events could not have happened. This was a rehash of the same line that Payne-Gaposchkin had used twenty years before, and which Velikovsky had answered. The opposition either hadn't read the earlier exchanges or didn't care, since it would all be new anyway to the public who were to be "educated."

Huber maintained that "Velikovsky draws on historical and archeological evidence to support his hypothesis, but unfortunately his arguments are mainly based on late and secondary sources, in part on obsolete and erroneous translations, and therefore lack force." A devastating indictment, by the sound of it, from one listed and presented as an authority on the subject. It is acknowledged that discrepancies exist between old translations and modern ones, and then asserted that the modern ones contain the truth, whereas the older ones do not. A better way to phrase it, however, would be that the older ones say what the original records said, whereas the modern ones are "corrected" to reflect what proponents of today's approved theory think they should have said. This couldn't have been better demonstrated than by the procedure that Huber himself followed. It would have been far more "unfortunate" for Huber if Lynn Rose, who was in the audience, had been allowed on the panel as Velikovsky requested. Rose made some pointed observations during the questions session afterward, and later, working with Raymond C. Vaughan, wrote a detailed rebuttal showing just how far the evidence has to be twisted to make it conform to current preconceptions. The title, "Just Plainly Wrong," speaks for itself. [120]

Huber's first claim boiled down to stating that records from Uruk, in Mesopotamia, show Venus to have existed in the early third millennium B.C., before Velikovsky's Venus encounter occurred.

But Velikovsky had never denied that Venus *existed* before then and was visible. His answer at the symposium was, "That Venus was observed before it came into conflict with Earth is clear from what I wrote. It did not come from Jupiter just on the eve of that collision. It came thousands of years before. It could be seen." And what Velikovsky had said all along could have been seen since 1950.

From the floor, Lynn Rose made the point that the symbols for Venus in these very sources that Huber cited, along with representations of Inanna, the goddess associated with Venus, all take the form of a compact body attached to a long, spreading and sometimes curving fan shape, distinctly suggestive of a comet. Huber's defense amounted to saying that sometimes they don't. This part of his paper was omitted from the version that appeared in the final book form of the proceedings two and a half years later, entitled, aptly enough, *Scientists Confront Velikovsky* (1977). [121]

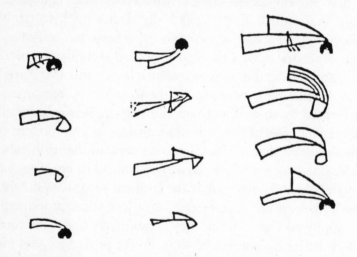

Variants of the Innana symbol. From Rose, 1977

Huber's second claim drew upon the Ammizaduga tablets, mentioned earlier, which were introduced with something of an air of revelation, as if Velikovsky had avoided them because they would damage his case. In fact, Velikovsky cites them extensively for doing just the opposite—provided they're allowed to be taken as meaning what they say.

Since some doubts have been expressed about their conventional assignment to the time of Ammizaduga, Rose refers to them as the

"Ninsianna" (Venus) document. They record the appearances and disappearances of Venus as it moves close to the Sun and it is swamped by the solar glare, causing it to be seen first at sunset to one side of the solar disk, and then, following a period of invisibility, at dawn on the other. Today, on its inner orbit, Venus is seen for about 260 days as the "Evening Star," disappears behind the Sun for 63 to 70 days, reappears on the other side as the "Morning Star" for about another 260 days, and after vanishing in front of the Sun for around 8 days becomes the Evening Star again. (It took many ancient cultures some time to figure out that it was the same object.) Note that there's no conflict in the suggestion of a comet on an eccentric orbit spending part of its period inside the Earth's orbit, and hence disappearing periodically behind the Sun. During the time it spent outside the Earth's orbit it would at times appear overhead at night, which could never happen with Venus in today's circumstances. Older translations, however (the ones dismissed as obsolete by Huber), clearly state it as appearing at *zenith*.

Huber's contention was that when properly understood, the ancient observations match the orbits of Venus and Earth that are seen today, and so the orbits haven't changed. To make this work, a period given in the cuneiform records as 5 months, 16 days had to be changed to 2 months, 6 days. Several of the names of the months had to be changed. Places where the texts read "west" had to be changed to "east," and places where they said "east" were changed to "west." Intercalary months—inserted between the regular months of a calendar to correct the cumulative error that builds up from years not being exact multiples of days—were taken out from where they had been put in and inserted where the modern translators thought they should go. Huber justified such alterations as being necessary to amend "scribal errors" in the originals. All in all, under further questioning, he admitted changing thirty percent of his data in this way. So presumably a culture that is noted for astronomical records whose accuracy in some areas was not rivaled until the nineteenth century employed scribes who couldn't tell east from west, didn't know what month it was, and who bungled their figures thirty percent of the time. But that wasn't the end of it. In his later, more thorough analysis, "Just Plainly Wrong," Rose found the actual count of errors and fudged data to be closer to seventy-five percent. And even after that amount of abuse, they still don't fit today's orbits.

The press and the custodians of truth who had taken it upon themselves to educate the public were evidently satisfied that the interests of the public were in good hands. The following month, Owen Gingerich, one of the organizers, was quoted in *Science* (March 14, 1974), in an interview by Robert Gillette, as saying that "He [Huber] demolished Velikovsky" and "There was no point in continuing after that." As with the Egyptian dating figures that we talked about earlier, whatever didn't fit the assumptions was thrown out, and what remained was pointed to as proving the assumptions. The logic is totally circular. Or anything else if you like. On this basis you could pick four points from a circle, alter the rest to suit, and show that it's a square. Small wonder that modern translations fit the approved theory better.

A final argument by Huber was again one that had been used before, namely that dates of eclipses retrocalculated from modern observations match records from before the events that should have made them invalid. Velikovsky responded that none of the instances he was aware of proved much at all, since the locations and dates are not specified, the year alone typically being named or inferred indirectly. One of Huber's examples, taken from the Chinese *Spring and Autumn Annals,* was given as occurring in the eighth century B.C. In his later study, however, Rose points out that the furthest back this document can be traced is 500 to 600 years after that time. So the question arises of whether the eclipse was actually observed, or was it inferred through retrocalculation by the compilers of the *Annals* a half a millennium later?—known to be a not-unusual practice. In support of his cautioning against relying too much on such sources, Rose cites a work entitled *Science Awakening II: The Birth of Astronomy*, by Bartel L. Van der Waerden, where Chapter 4 contains the statement, "Very often it is difficult to decide whether text data were observed or calculated. We know from the diaries of later times that missing observations were filled in by calculation sometimes without explicit indication of the fact." [122]

A contributor to the book, who in his Preface Van der Waerden says wrote considerable parts of Chapters 3 and 4—was Peter Huber.

PRONOUNCEMENTS FROM THE CELESTIAL HEIGHTS

Derral Mullholland was introduced by King as "a celestial mechanician whose name is almost synonymous with high precision." The open snub to Velikovsky, whose ideas, the gathering had shortly before been informed, "No one who is involved in the organization of this symposium believes . . . are correct," was difficult to miss; as were the implied directions to those interpreting the event for the public as to how they should apportion their impartial evaluation.

Mulholland opened: "Before I am asked the question, I would like to point out that I first read Dr. Velikovsky's work in *Collier's* magazine, when I was sixteen years old, and have read that same work three times since, the most recent yet this year. I found it entertaining when I was sixteen, incidentally, and I still do." [123] The celestial mechanician whose name was almost synonymous with high precision, having given his source as a popular magazine, then began with a synopsis of Velikovsky's planetary theory that read: "Within the folk memory of man, Venus and Mars erupted into the sky and rushed close to the Earth and each other several times. . . . Finally, the two giant comets settle down into their present harmless orbits and became peaceable planets."

Whether he had in mind this invented scenario or the one that Velikovsky actually described, Mulholland repeated the usual insistence that gravitational dynamics provides the most clear-cut contradiction to its being possible. Well, without repeating all that was said earlier, suffice it to say that Einstein didn't think so. The critique then went on to question the validity of accounts of abnormally long days and nights from various parts of the world, when the durations given by people said to possess clocks of high accuracy varied from three to ten days. The lowest form of wit notwithstanding, it's difficult to restrain an impulse toward sarcasm at a suggestion that people in terror, beset by earthquakes, hurricanes, totally enveloping darkness, and torrents of meteorites should be faulted for losing track of time and failing to check with their sundials and water clocks. Mulholland also stated that the myths Velikovsky quotes "do not seem to satisfy the simple requirement" that abnormally long day in one hemisphere ought to be accompanied by abnormally long night in the other. Perhaps the myths Velikovsky quotes that do say precisely this were not among the excerpts condensed in *Collier's*.

In *Worlds in Collision*, Velikovsky discusses various ancient sundials and water clocks that read incorrectly for the locations that they are found at, and offers this as evidence of changes in the Earth's motion in space. Mulholland's rejoinder was to doubt the accuracy of such old artifacts and question whether they were constructed at the sites where they are found. No independent evidence is cited of such inaccuracies, or that any relocation of the instruments in question actually took place. The assumptions are made ad hoc, to conform to a preconceived theory that the lengths of days, months, and years *must* have been the same as they are today. Therefore ancient peoples were unable to measure the time of day. In fact, Babylonian water clocks were accurate enough to be used for astronomical observations and measuring the distances between stars in arc degrees. [124] Moving sundials to another location would make no sense, as anyone capable of designing them would know. A water clock would function correctly at a different latitude if it told only constant hours, but not if it measured different hours in summer and winter. Some water clocks divided day into twelve hours and night into twelve hours, which vary with latitude and with the seasons. Again, it's difficult to imagine designers who were aware of these differences not having the competence to set them up correctly.

The other objection was that according to Velikovsky's account of the errors involved, if they were due to repositioning of the Earth, Babylon would seem to have moved southward 250 kilometers, Faijum in Egypt also southward but by an unspecified amount, while Thebes moved 1,000 kilometers north. The assumption here is that they all moved during the same time period, while Velikovsky says nothing of the kind. Indeed, historians assign the shadow clock at Faijum that Velikovsky refers to, and the water clock at Thebes, to two widely spaced dynasties. [125]

In any case, Mulholland maintained, if the spins and orbits of the bodies Velikovsky talks about were seriously disturbed, they would depart from the smooth progression showing angular momentum as a function of mass across the bodies of the Solar System. But he admitted that Mercury, Venus, the Moon, and Mars didn't fit the relationship. Ransom and Rose later showed that the function line misses Mercury, Venus, Earth, Mars, Neptune, and the Sun. Too bad they weren't up on the panel.

It would not be out of place to mention here that the pictures of Mars returned by *Mariners* 6 and 7 in 1969 had shown a system of surface cracks ("lineaments") running more or less straight over extended distances and aligned with the rotational axis, indicating a violent deceleration and change in angular momentum at some time, stressing the crust. Comparable structures are seen also on the Moon and on Earth.

During the question session after Storer's talk earlier, Mulholland had given anomalous mass concentrations on the Moon and the unexpected internal heat of the Moon as examples of scientists' readiness to accept new concepts when they were justified. Velikovsky asked if he knew who had been the first person to claim that the Moon would be found to have internal heat, and if there was any explanation for the mass concentrations other than an encounter with other celestial bodies. Mulholland had no suggestion regarding the second, and admitted that he didn't know the answer to the first, apparently not realizing that the person had been Velikovsky himself.

Irving Michelson's talk was in the evening session and went back to the notion of electrical forces playing a role in celestial dynamics. Mulholland rejected the suggestion that they played any role, and when Velikovsky cited Danjon's report of a temporary slowing of the Earth's rotation by electrical influences following a large solar flare, Mulholland denied that Danjon's data had shown any such effect.

Toward the end of his paper, Michelson mentioned a "curious but tantalizing" finding of his: that the energy required to turn the Earth's rotational axis through 180° corresponded closely to estimates of a single moderately strong geomagnetic storm that could be triggered by a solar flare—in the way the energy of a bomb is triggered by the small energy release of a detonator. Evidently missing the point, Mulholland scoffed at the idea, pointing out that since 10^8 times as much energy is emitted by a solar flare as is intercepted by the Earth, Michelson's result was in error by that amount. When Michelson responded wearily, "I'll let that go," his remark was widely misinterpreted as meaning that he had no answer. A stormy exchange of correspondence resulted subsequently with the editorial department of *Science*, who tried to suppress a letter from Michelson straightening out the error.

Dr. Robert Bass, who had been a keen observer of the whole affair for some years, wrote a concise reply to a number of the points that Mulholland had raised in the day and requested time to present them at the same evening session, which was supposedly open to all. He was told that this wouldn't be allowed since the public might become confused if a noted authority disagreed with the expert chosen by the committee.

Well, at least we can be comforted that the organizers hadn't forgotten their commitment to education.

CARL SAGAN: THE STAR BILLING

And then there was Dr. Carl Sagan. . . . How to begin here?

Professor Lynn Rose records that in January 1974, when arrangements for the symposium were being finalized, he commented in a letter to Stephen Talbott at *Pensée* that Sagan delivered errors and untruths at a rate faster than it would be possible to *list* in the time Velikovsky was being given, let alone be able to refute them. In a tape of a lecture by Sagan at Cornell in March 1973 entitled "Venus and Velikovsky," Rose timed them at three or four per minute, giving a grand total of several score. His review of them appeared some years later in the journal *The Velikovskian*, edited by Charles Ginenthal. [126]

Sagan's perspective on the subject can perhaps be judged from his statement in *Broca's Brain*, published five years after the symposium: "Catastrophism began largely in the minds of those geologists who accepted a literal interpretation of the Book of Genesis, and in particular, the account of the Noahic flood." [127] Even after the time that had been given to reflect, as far as Sagan was concerned all questioning of accepted theory originated in the *minds* of the—implicitly—deluded, to justify religious convictions. No possibility exists that it could have originated in the form of real events in the real universe before anything at all was written. On page 126 he goes on, "Velikovsky attempts to rescue not only religion but also astrology."

Hence, the question of a scientific debate never arose. The presumption of fighting an evangelical crusade was written into the ground rules from the beginning, and when saving souls from heresy is at stake, winning is the only thing that counts, at whatever cost and by any means. Robert Anton Wilson writes:

"Sagan likes to quote a 'distinguished professor of Semitics' who told him no Semitic scholars take Dr. Velikovsky very seriously. . . .

[T]his 'distinguished professor' remains anonymous, and thus Sagan's hearsay about him would get thrown out of any civilized court. Three distinguished professors of Semitic studies, however, have all shown cordial support for Dr. Velikovsky: Prof. Claude F. A. Schaeffer, Prof. Etienne Droiton, and Prof. Robert Pfeiffer. Look them up in any *Who's Who* of Semitic studies, archeology and Egyptology. They have a lot more prestige in those fields than Sagan's Prof. Anonymous, who doesn't have a single entry under his name anywhere . . ." [128]

At the San Francisco symposium, Sagan presented ten problems, which he referred to as "plagues," with Velikovsky's proposals. Ginenthal's book (1995) that I cited near the beginning is a compilation and rebuttal of the errors, evasions, denials of evidence, and self-contradictions that took the author eight years of research and occupies 447 pages. I will touch on all of them, elaborating on just a few.

SAGAN ON ASTRONOMY

Problem 1. The Ejection of Venus by Jupiter

Sagan stated that "Velikovsky's hypothesis begins with an event that has never been observed by astronomers and that is inconsistent with much that we know about planetary and cometary physics, namely the ejection of an object of planetary dimensions from Jupiter."

One wonders who, exactly, the "we" in the authoritarian "we know" is, since the literature makes it clear that the scientific community didn't pretend to know, and nothing much in that respect has changed since. As related above, grave doubts had been cast on the fashionable tidal and accretion theories of Solar System formation, and such figures as McCrea and Lyttleton couldn't have been among the "we" who "knew," since the fission theory that their work (among others) pointed to emerged as an alternative that *was* consistent with planetary physics. And the reason for their conclusions? Gravitational theory—precisely what Velikovsky was accused of not understanding or ignoring. But he was fully conversant with Lyttleton's work, which he had cited in "Venus—A Youthful Planet" seven years previously. Sagan also produced figures for energy and heat generation showing that a volcanic eruption on Jupiter couldn't have ejected an object resembling Venus, which was all neither here nor there because Velikovsky never said that a volcanic eruption had.

Sagan went on: "From the fact that the apehelia (greatest distances from the Sun) of the orbits of short-period comets have a statistical tendency to lie near Jupiter, Laplace and other early astronomers hypothesized that Jupiter was the source of such comets. This is an unnecessary hypothesis because we now know [again] that long-period comets may be transferred to short-period trajectories by the perturbations of Jupiter."

Later in the same year that Sagan said this, the International Astronomical Union held its twenty-fifth colloquium at Greenbelt, Maryland. In the *Proceedings*, a paper by Edgar Everhart entitled "The Evolution of Cometary Orbits" states that: "*Although it is possible for an orbit of short-period to be the result after a parabolic comet makes a single close encounter with Jupiter, this mechanism does not explain the existence of the short-period comets.* This was shown by H. A. Newton (1893). Not wanting to believe his results, and being a little dubious about Newton's procedures, I redid the problem as a numerical experiment and came to exactly the same conclusion." [Emphasis in the original] [129]

So ever since 1893 there had been people who not only didn't "know," but found such a transfer model unsupported by the evidence. The main problem is that it would only happen very rarely that a comet entering the Solar System would pass close enough to Jupiter to be pulled into an elliptical orbit that returns it periodically to near Jupiter's distance from the Sun. S. K. Vsekhsviatsky estimates 1 in 100,000, whereas the observed ratio is about 1 in 25. About 70 comets are known in the Jupiter family, and their lifetime is estimated to be not more than 4,000 years before repeated passes by the Sun evaporate all their volatiles and cause them to break up. Capturing this number from parabolic comets entering from afar would require seven million comets entering the Solar System over the last 4,000 years, which works out at five per day. Since a comet would remain in the System for a few years, the night sky should contain somewhere around 9,000 of them. It doesn't. A further difficulty is that all the Jovian comets orbit the Sun in the same direction, but since incoming trajectories should show no preference, according to the capture model about half should be retrograde. As a final embarrassment, the perturbation of comets by planets can work to eject them from the Solar System too, and this in fact turns out to be a more likely and effective mechanism, resulting in the number of short-period comets as a whole being in the order of one hundred times too large.

On the other hand, all of these observations are consistent with the suggestion of many such objects being created recently inside the Solar System. (Accounts from the Roman period indicate significantly more comets occurring then than are seen today.) And no elaborate and implausible construction is needed to explain why they should appear to have originated from the vicinity of Jupiter, for the simple reason that they did.

The conventional way of preserving the short-term-capture principle is the "Oort Cloud," postulated to contain millions of cometary bodies and extend halfway to the nearest stars, which once in a while is disturbed by a passing star to send showers of comets into the Solar System. However, studies of the distribution of comet trajectories and energies show the long-term comets to be quite distinct from shorter-period ones. Arrivals from such a remote source should exhibit preponderantly hyperbolic orbits incapable of being converted to short-term ones. To explain the short-term comets, a new cloud termed the "Kuiper Belt" is then proposed, existing in deep space near the planetary plane. Finally, a belt of "dark matter," the invisible astronomical duct tape that fixes anything, is introduced to induce the Kuiper Belt comets to approach the Solar System. None of this has ever been "observed by astronomers" either. It's invented to enable what the theory requires.

Plenty of people, on the other hand, did claim to have observed the event that Sagan denies, and they left precise descriptions of it. But since Babylonians, Assyrians, Greeks, Maya, and the like aren't figured among the exalted "we," they don't count as astronomers.

Problem 2. Repeated Collisions Among the Earth, Venus, And Mars

Sagan produces a mathematical proof that the probability of five or six near collisions occurring between a comet and a planet are in the order of a "trillion quadrillion" (10^{27}) to one against. The trouble with it is that it treats each near-collision as an independent event unrelated to the others, which in effect ignores gravity. It's a simple consequence of Newton's laws that two celestial bodies, once they have interacted gravitationally, will continue to approach one another periodically. The astronomer Robert Bass wrote that this was "so disingenuous that I do not hesitate to label it a deliberate fraud on the public or else a manifestation of unbelievable incompetence or hastiness combined with desperation." [130] On the other hand, Sagan has no hesitation in accepting that "most short-period comets may have achieved their orbits by multiple encounters with Jupiter, or even by multiple encounters with more distant planets and eventually Jupiter itself"—a process calculated to require hundreds of repeated near-collisions.

In his own book *Comet* (1985) Sagan states (p. 266) that a collision with an Earth-crossing asteroid kilometers across, which he believes to be extinct comets, would represent "a major catastrophe, of a sort that must have happened from time to time during the history of the Earth. It is a statistical inevitability." Enough said.

Problem 3. The Earth's Rotation

Sagan's question here is how, if the Earth slowed down in its rotation, could it get speeded up again? The Earth couldn't do it by itself, he insisted, because of the law of conservation of angular momentum. In 1960, as we've already seen, Danjon measured precisely this happening and attributed it to electrical effects. Conceivably Sagan, like Mulholland, simply refused to believe it. But in 1972 it had happened again, this time even more impressively. On August 7–8, after a week of frenzied solar activity, Stephen Plagemann and John Gribbin measured a 10-millisecond lengthening of the day, once more followed by a gradual return to normal. [131]

This is in accord with electrical fundamentals, whereby adding charge to a rotating flywheel constitutes a current that increases the polar moment of inertia, which by the conservation of angular momentum must be accompanied by a decrease in angular velocity, i.e., the flywheel slows down. When the wheel is grounded, dissipating the charge, then by the same principle of conservation— the very law that Sagan invokes—the wheel, still storing the same mechanical energy but with no electrical force to overcome, will speed up again. The application of this to planetary dynamics is discussed by Ralph Juergens. [132]

Sagan goes on to another mathematical proof, this time showing that the energy released by the Earth's stopping would be enough to boil all the oceans and generate enough heat to end all advanced life forms. But once again, it isn't necessary for the Earth to halt to produce the visual effect of the Sun's motion being arrested or even reversed. Ginenthal points out that with proto-Venus approaching from the sunward direction, the Earth would be pulled first inward and then outward from its normal orbit, the differences in distance being sufficient on their own to make the Sun appear to move more slowly, without appreciable change in the Earth's rotation at all. He refers anyone skeptical of such a possibility to the well-known astronomer Carl Sagan, who later wrote:

"There is another strange thing about Mercury. It has a highly elliptical orbit. That is, there is a commensurate relation between how long the planet takes to turn once around its axis and how long it takes to go around the Sun. . . . Suppose you stood at one particular place on the equator of Mercury. During the course of the day there you would observe the following. You would see it rising . . . moving toward the zenith . . . Then one degree past the zenith it stops, reverses its motion in the sky, stops again, then continues its original motion. . . ." [133]

That was in 1975. I can only wonder what might have prompted the inspiration.

SAGAN ON TERRESTRIAL AND LUNAR GEOLOGY

Problem 4. Terrestrial Geology And Lunar Craters

Sagan repeats the assertion that there ought to be ample geological and archeological evidence of such catastrophes if they happened, but he was unable to find records of any. One can only suggest visiting the library on that one—as Velikovsky did, and found enough to fill a whole book.

Sagan was aware of Velikovsky's contention that major mountain uplifts had attended these recent events, but stated that this was belied by geological evidence that put them at tens of millions of years old or more. It's true that the evidence Sagan cites is generally interpreted that way. But we've already seen how sufficient prior belief in a theory can influence interpretation of the evidence by uncritically accepting whatever conforms to it and rejecting anything that doesn't. Much of Velikovsky's evidence was of a kind that doesn't lend itself to a wide range of interpretation—for example, of human presence in the Alps and Andes at heights that are uninhabitable today. It's difficult to read this in any other way than that within the time of human history the land was a lot lower, or else the climate at high altitudes was a lot milder. The second alternative has trouble on other counts, for instance that in the historical period usually assigned to these cultures, glacial cover was more extensive.

But once a theory is "known" to be true, the determination of the believers in making the evidence fit knows no bounds. Ginenthal cites an example where investigators of Lake Titicaca in Peru and the ancient fortress city of Tiahuanacu on its shores, thirteen thousand feet above sea level, faced with clear indications that the region must have been at sea level during the times of human habitation, were driven to conclude that the remains of the cities must be millions of years old since the uplift couldn't be anything less.

With regard to Velikovsky's claim that the Moon should show signs of recent disturbances and melting, Sagan responds that the samples returned by the Apollo missions show no melting of rock more than a few hundred million years ago. We've already seen some examples of how strong expectations of what the results ought to be can lead to circular reasoning in dating procedures. And lunar dating is no exception. When it was believed early on that lunar rocks would provide a direct measure of the age of the Moon and hence the Earth, the results subsequently released with confidence and which found their way into textbooks cited 4.5 billion years, which agreed exactly with the predictions of the most widely accepted theory. Later, the actual data were found to cover the range 2 billion years to 28 billion, in other words from less than half of what was expected to 8 billion years before the universe was supposed to have existed.

But aside from that, Velikovsky had suggested in a letter to the *New York Times* in 1971 that tests be performed on lunar material by the dating method of thermoluminescence, which many authorities consider to be more reliable than radioisotope testing. NASA did in fact have such tests performed, at the Washington University, St. Louis. The results on samples from six inches or so beneath the surface—below recently deposited dust and mixing of micrometeorites—showed them to have been molten less than ten thousand years ago. Sagan should surely have been aware of this. It's also worthy of mention that the darker "maria" features of the lunar surface, which consist of vast solidified lava sheets, occur not haphazardly but cover a broad swathe following a great circle across one hemisphere—consistent with tidal melting induced by a close-passing massive object.

And speaking of the great lunar plains, what happened to all the dust that ought to be covering them? According to estimates of the rate of infalling meteorite dust and other debris on Earth— including some made by Sagan himself—if the lunar surface has been exposed for over four billion years, it ought to have accumulated dust to a depth of more than fifty feet. An early concern of the space program had been that the landers would sink into the dust or become too bogged down in it to take off again. But all that was found was about an eighth of an inch. On the other hand, such features as rills, rifts, and crater walls that should, by those same figures, have been eroded away and disappeared long ago seemed sharp and fresh—dare one say "young"? The features that should have been gone were still there, while the dust that should have worn them down and buried them was not. And even of the dust that does exist, only 1 to 2 percent turns out to be meteoritic. The rest comes from "gardening" (after remelting?) of the moon rock itself.

Exposed lunar rock is a natural particle counter. Fast-moving particles of cosmic dust produce tiny, glass-lined microcraters, and if the exposure age is known—which solar-flare particle tracks in the glass linings should indicate—a count of the crater density will give a measure of the rate at which the rock was bombarded. Studies of a large *Apollo 16* sample showed exposure on the lunar surface for abut eighty thousand years, but with the rate of particle bombardment going up during the last ten thousand years. Nuclear tracks on interplanetary dust particles collected in the Earth's stratosphere also indicate an age no greater than ten thousand years. [134]

SAGAN ON PLANETARY BIOLOGY AND CHEMISTRY

Problem 5. Chemistry and Biology of the Terrestrial Planets

According to Sagan, "Velikovsky's thesis has some peculiar biological and chemical consequences, which are compounded by some straightforward confusion of simple matters. He seems not to know (p. 16) that oxygen is produced by green-plant photosynthesis on the Earth."

What Velikovsky says on p. 16 of *Worlds in Collision* is that under the conditions envisaged by the tidal and nebular theories of planet formation, the iron of the globe should have oxidized and combined with all the available oxygen. Thus there would be no oxygen to form the abundance found in the modern atmosphere. Sagan says it comes from photosynthesis. But plants are also composed partly of oxygen, and hence need it to form before they can start making it. And before it existed in any significant amount, there would be no ozone in the upper atmosphere to block harmful bands of ultraviolet that would stop biological molecules forming. Moving the process under water as some theorists have tried to do doesn't help much, since water is about as damaging and corrosive as oxygen and UV for organic chemistry without complex biological defenses to protect it. So it's not clear how the earliest plants got started.

This is a well-known problem that has been widely acknowledged among scientists, including Sagan himself in *Broca's Brain*. The usual assumption is that the plants got started somehow on trace amounts of oxygen, and once it was in production, bootstrapped themselves from there. The snag with this is that while the beginnings of life are conventionally put at around a billion years ago, the existence of massive "red beds" of rock rich in oxidized iron testify to the existence of not traces but large amounts of available oxygen a billion years earlier. So where did that come from? That's what Velikovsky was saying. Answering that "the green plants did it" doesn't solve the problem. It doesn't sound to me as if it was Velikovsky who was confused here.

Worlds in Collision has petroleum liquids falling to Earth at the time of the meteorite storm as Earth moves into the comet's tail, before the time of intense darkness to which smoke from the widespread fires contributed. In a later section of the book, entitled "Ambrosia," Velikovsky speculates that the "manna from heaven" that saved the Israelites when no other food was to be had could have been carbohydrates formed from hydrocarbon vapors reacting with oxygen under the influence of sunlight in the upper atmosphere. (The difference between them is that carbohydrates, such as sugars, contain oxygen whereas hydrocarbons don't.) Interestingly, traditions from as far removed as Iceland, the Maoris of the Pacific, Greece, India, Egypt, and Finland all tell of a time when a sweet, sticky, milky or honey-like substance precipitated from the skies. Sagan's reading of this is that Velikovsky claimed there were carbohydrates on Jupiter and Venus; that he displayed a sustained confusion of carbohydrates and hydrocarbons; and "seems to imagine that the Israelites were eating motor oil rather than divine nutriment . . ." The irony is that all of Sagan's errors here can be explained by his showing precisely that confusion himself.

If Venus came from Jupiter and was a comet carrying hydrocarbons, then presumably it brought those hydrocarbons from Jupiter. Sagan asks (1) Are hydrocarbons found on Jupiter? (2) Do comets contain hydrocarbons? (3) Is there a process that converts hydrocarbons to carbohydrates? which questions, he says, pose "grave difficulties" for Velikovsky.

In answer to (1), Ginenthal cites the well-known astronomer Carl Sagan, who at a NASA conference, after describing the Jovian atmosphere, relates a series of experiments that he and his associates performed on comparable mixtures, producing a high yield of a brownish colored substance. Analysis showed it to be " . . . a very complex mixture of organic molecules, that is carbon-based molecules, some of very high complexity. Most of them were of the kind called straight chain hydrocarbons." [135]

This information was also available from the *Encyclopedia Britannica* by 1972, which in Vol.13, p.142 for that year states that "the upper atmosphere of Jupiter is a giant organic factory producing complex organic molecules that include many of biological importance."

In answer to (2), yes, "in large amounts," according to the same well-known astronomer, in his book *Comet* (p.153).

And to (3), again yes. Ginenthal mentions six reaction pathways and confirms that the products can be edible. (Animal foods were being manufactured from hydrocarbons by 1974.) Ginenthal also lists instances of other occasions through into modern times where substances similar to those that Velikovsky describes were seen to fall or were found on the ground; they were eaten by animals, sometimes gathered and baked into bread, or used as resins and waxes.

Next, we move to Mars. Sagan cites Velikovsky as saying that the Martian polar caps are "made of manna, which are described ambiguously as 'probably in the nature of carbon.'" Actually, it's Sagan's inversion of the text that loses clarity. Velikovsky states that the white precipitate masses are "probably of the nature of carbon," having been derived from Venus, and later refers to this substance as "manna"—using the double quotes—when speculating that the differences from terrestrial conditions prevent it from being permanently dissolved by sunlight.

There seem to be two ingredients to the Martian polar caps. One disappears during the summer and is thought to be solid carbon dioxide that sublimates, while the nature of the other, which remains, is still "unsettled"—the word Sagan uses in his book *The Cosmic Connection* (1973), published the year before the symposium. Since then, others have concluded that it contains carbon, hydrogen, and oxygen, the elements needed for carbohydrates— and enough ultraviolet exists there to produce them.

Before *Mariner 4*, scientists had felt confident that Mars would turn out to be generally flattish, at most with a gently undulating surface. The craters, uplifts, and planetwide system of canyons and fractures that they saw in the pictures came as a shock. Sagan seems to have forgotten this when he assures us that the features observed are fully compatible with an ancient surface shaped hundreds of millions of years ago than a planet recently devastated by catastrophic events. But the fact that these features can be seen at all belies this. Thin as it may be, the atmosphere of Mars creates high-velocity dust storms for seasons that last from three to six months and at times blanket the entire planet. The erosion from this process should long ago have worn down any features of prominence, and things like cracks, river beds, flood plains, and runoff channels would be completely obliterated by the volume of sand produced. We even have some indication of the rates that would be involved from the following, which appeared in *Aviation Week and Space Technology*, January 29, 1973—a year before the symposium.

> Using *Mariner 9* wind data, Dr. Carl Sagan of Cornell
> University calculated erosion rates, assuming a dust storm
> peak wind of 100 mph blowing ten percent of the time.
> This would mean erosion of 10 km (6.2 miles) of sur-
> face in 100 million years. . . . there is no way to reconcile
> this picture with a view of the planet.

The enormous amounts of water that evidently existed on Mars at one time could only add to the process of erasing the ancient surface and reworking it. Where all the water went and why is another mystery, along with the atmosphere that must have existed to be compatible with liquid oceans. Observers have commented repeatedly on the sharpness and definition of the surface formations, and found themselves at a loss to explain how they could have the appearance of being so new. That the obvious answer never seemed to occur to anyone, or was repressed as taboo, perhaps testifies to the power of professional indoctrination and the pressures to conform.

Problem 6. Manna

Yes, I know we already covered this, but Sagan evidently couldn't let it go. Here, he concedes that "comet tails" contain hydrocarbons "but no aldehydes—the building blocks of carbohydrates." However, in his book *Comet* (p. 134) he shows how, in the Earth's atmosphere, water vapor, methane, and ammonia, all of them constituents of comets (pp.149–150) "are broken into pieces . . . by ultraviolet light from the Sun or electrical discharges. These molecules recombine to form, among other molecules . . . formaldehyde." Which, in case the connection isn't clear, is an aldehyde.

It's okay for Sagan to quote the Bible, incidentally. "In Exodus, Chapter 16, Verse 20," he states, "we find that manna left overnight was infested with worms in the morning—an event possible with carbohydrates but extremely unlikely with hydrocarbons." True, Carl, but check *Worlds in Collision* one more time. It clearly states, Chapter 2, page 53, under the heading "Naphtha," also referred to in the text as "oil" and "petroleum," "The tails of comets are composed mainly of carbon and hydrogen gases. Lacking oxygen, they do not burn in flight." And Chapter 6, page 134, under the heading "Ambrosia," "Has any testimony been preserved that during the many years of gloom *carbohydrates* precipitated?" (emphasis added) You've read them the wrong way around again.

But that's beside the point because "it is now known that comets contain *large quantities* of simple nitriles—in particular, hydrogen cyanide and methyl cyanide. These are poisons, and it is not immediately obvious that comets are good to eat." (emphasis added)

Sagan also deals with the question of cyanide in comets in his book *Comet*. Here, however, he ridicules people in the past for imagining that the amounts were anything to worry about. For example, with regard to the passage of Halley's comet relatively close to the Earth in 1910 (pp. 143–144): "People imagined themselves choking, gasping, and dying in millions, asphyxiated by the poison gas. The global pandemonium ... was sadly fueled by a few *astronomers who should have known better.*" (emphasis added) "The cyanogen gas is in turn a minor constituent in the tails of comets. Even if the Earth had passed through the tail in 1910 and the molecules in the tail had been mixed thoroughly down to the surface of the Earth, there would have been only one molecule of cyanogen in every trillion molecules of air."

Problem 7. The Clouds of Venus

The layer of bright clouds covering Venus is perhaps its most immediately striking characteristic, making it one of the brightest objects in the skies. What these clouds are composed of has long been a topic of debate and study. The atmosphere of Earth consists mostly of nitrogen and oxygen, but the clouds that form in it are water vapor.

Sagan was long of the opinion that Venus's clouds were water vapor, too—the subject formed a large part of his research as a graduate student. This could perhaps have been partly why he clung to the conviction long after others, including Velikovsky, had noted that it wasn't compatible with the *Mariner 2* findings from 1963. *Intelligent Life in the Universe* (1966), coauthored by Sagan and I. S. Shklovskii, states (p. 323), "From a variety of observations ... it has recently been established that the clouds of Venus are indeed made of water [ice crystals at the top and droplets at the bottom]." In 1968 his published paper "The Case for Ice Clouds on Venus" appeared in the *Journal of Geophysical Research* (Vol. 73, No. 18, September 15).

Velikovsky had predicted that the atmosphere of Venus would contain "petroleum [hydrocarbon] gases," which perhaps explains the somewhat peevish tone when Sagan tells us that "Velikovsky's prognostication that the clouds of Venus were made of carbohydrates has many times been hailed as an example of a successful scientific prediction." (No, Carl. The carbohydrates were produced in the atmosphere of *Earth*. The one that's got "ate" in it is the one that you "eat." Try remembering it that way.)

By 1974 Sagan had decided that "the question of the composition of the Venus clouds—a major enigma for centuries—has recently been solved (Young and Young, 1973; Sill 1972; Young 1973; Pollack *et. al.*, 1974). The clouds of Venus are composed of an approximately 75 percent solution of sulfuric acid." [136]

However, in the following year Andrew T. Young, one of the sources whom Sagan cites as an architect of that theory, was to caution in a NASA report that "none of the currently popular interpretations of cloud phenomenon on Venus is consistent with all the data. Either a considerable fraction of the observational evidence is faulty or has been misinterpreted, or the clouds of Venus are much more complex than the current simplistic models." [137] The enigma still did not seem generally to be considered solved by the 1980s, and several of the models being proposed then made no mention of sulfuric acid.

But it had been reported back in 1963, following the *Mariner 2* flyby in December of 1962, that the clouds of Venus contained hydrocarbons. At the symposium Sagan dismissed this as an instance of journalists seizing on a scientist's personal conjecture and reporting it as fact. Velikovsky disagreed, having established that the person who originated the statement, Professor L. D. Kaplan of the Jet Propulsion Laboratory (JPL), had arrived at his conclusion after careful consideration of the data and had repeated it in several papers and memoranda. Sagan's assertion that JPL revoked the statement was also untrue. JPL's report *Mission to Venus (Mariner II)*, published in 1963, states that "At their base, the clouds are about 200°F and probably are comprised of condensed hydrocarbons."

Having evidently done his homework, Velikovsky had also ascertained that in a later letter to a colleague at the Institute of Advanced Study at Princeton, Kaplan's identifying of "hydrocarbons" caused a violent reaction among astronomers—at that time Kaplan was seemingly unaware of just why. In a later version he amended the offending term to "organic compounds."

The tenor of the astronomers who reacted violently might perhaps be gauged from a later item in *Popular Science* (April 1979) reporting that the head of the mass spectrometer team for *Pioneer Venus 2* stunned colleagues by reporting that the atmosphere of Venus contains 300 to 500 times as much argon as Earth. He then went on to say there were indications that the lower atmosphere may be rich in methane—the simplest hydrocarbon, and also a constituent of Jupiter's atmosphere. A follow-up article in *Science News* (September 1992) describes the researchers as being so surprised by the findings of methane that they were loathe to publish them. The explanation concocted was that the probe must have just happened to come down over a volcanic eruption of a size which, to produce the amount of methane indicated, would occur about once in a hundred million years.

As an amusing footnote, if it turns out that Sagan was indeed correct in his insistence on sulfuric-acid clouds (we left the jury as still being out), then it would seem to rule out the possibility of Venus being 4 billion years old, since sulfuric acid would decompose under solar ultraviolet radiation. People who have done the calculations give sulfuric acid a lifetime in the upper atmosphere of ten thousand years at most. The hydrogen resulting from its dissociation would escape into space, as would hydrogen released by the dissociation of water released through volcanic outgassing. What's missing is all the oxygen that this ought to produce. Similar considerations apply to the abundance of carbon dioxide, CO_2, which splits into O and CO (carbon monoxide) under ultraviolet, and the two do not readily recombine. Once again, where is all the oxygen that ought to be there?

In considering Earth, earlier, we touched on the puzzle of abundant oxygen combining with iron (also identified on Venus) in early times, a billion years before life is supposed to have emerged, and asked where it came from. So everything is consistent with the suggestion that when looking at Venus now, we're watching a new Earth in the making.

SAGAN ON PLANETARY PHYSICS AND SURFACES

Problem 8. The Temperature of Venus

The conventional view before results from *Mariner 2* showed, in early 1963, the surface temperature of Venus to be 800°F had been that it would be slightly warmer than Earth. By the time of the symposium Sagan's recollection had become, in effect, that "we knew it all along." In fact, the only person—apart from Velikovsky—who had predicted a high temperature was a Dr. Rupert Wildt, whose work was based on a greenhouse mechanism and not generally accepted. (By 1979 Sagan's memory had evidently suffered a further lapse, for in *Broca's Brain* he states [p. 153], "One now fashionable suggestion I first proposed in 1960 is that the high temperatures on the surface of Venus are due to a runaway greenhouse effect.") When the conventional view was shown to be spectacularly wrong (one is tempted to say "catastrophically"),

Wildt's proposal was hastily resurrected in an attempt to explain why, while preserving the doctrine of a long-established planet and slow, uniformitarian change.

But it doesn't really wash. Contrary to current media fictions, the main agent responsible for Earth's greenhouse effect (a natural phenomenon, without which we'd be around 33°F cooler) isn't carbon dioxide but water vapor, which contributes over 90 percent. Back in the days when Venus's atmosphere was believed to contain a considerable amount of water, the suggestion of an enhanced greenhouse effect yielding temperatures considerably higher than those generally proposed wasn't unreasonable. But it just doesn't work as a plausible mechanism for sustaining the huge temperature gradient that exists down through Venus's atmosphere. Especially when it turns out that the heat source is at the bottom, not the top.

Besides an efficient medium for absorbing and reradiating incoming radiation, an effective greenhouse also needs adequate penetration of the medium by sunlight to utilize the available mass. With Venus, for a start, only about twenty percent of the incoming sunlight gets past the cloud tops forty to forty-five miles above the surface, the rest being reflected back into space—which is why Venus is so bright. The surface pressure on Venus is around ninety times that of Earth's, which translates into something like seventy-five times the mass of gases, giving it more the optical characteristics of a sea—in fact, corresponding to a depth of about three thousand feet. Virtually all the sunlight entering the oceans is absorbed within the top three hundred feet. Likewise, any greenhouse mechanism on Venus would be confined to the top fifteen percent of the atmosphere. These objections were well known. In 1968 the British astronomer V. A. Firshoff, in *The Interior Planets*, put it like this:

> The greenhouse effect cannot be magnified *ad lib*.
> Doubling the [glass] thickness may enhance its thermal
> insulation, so raising its temperature, but it will cut down
> the transmitted sunshine, so reducing its heat. In the end
> the process becomes self-defeating. . . . The sea is a perfect
> "greenhouse" of this kind—none of the obscure heat
> from the bottom can escape into space. But it is not
> boiling; in fact it is not much above freezing point.
> Sagan's deep atmosphere would behave in exactly the

same way. . . . An adiabatic atmosphere of a mass
envisaged by Sagan is possible only if it is heated from
below. In other words, the surface of Venus would have
to be kept at a high temperature by internal sources.

By the time the official version of the proceedings was published over two years later as *Scientists Confront Velikovsky*, Sagan
had embellished his argument by reference to the Soviet *Venera*
9 and *10* landings in October 1975. (True to the spirit of the
whole affair, while Sagan was permitted to add a revised appendix
of new points, Velikovsky was denied space to respond to them.)
The Soviet craft, Sagan claimed, were able to obtain clear pictures
in sunlight of surface rocks, showing Velikovsky wrong in saying
that light does not penetrate the cloud cover. This doesn't seem
to appreciate the fact that the Soviet landers were equipped with
floodlights. Further, as reported by Professor Lewis Greenberg,[138]
the *Venera* instruments detected nothing but gloom and darkness after descending through the clouds, until a glow appeared
and grew brighter as they neared the surface. The atmosphere
at the surface was much brighter than had been expected. V. A.
Avduevsky, deputy director of the Soviet Space Flight Control
Center, described the terrain as showing distinct, dark shadows
that persisted even when the floodlights were turned off, which
was unanticipated since sunlight from the clouds would be diffuse. He and his colleagues agreed that it indicated a direct light
source on the surface but they could not guess what it was.
Velikovsky had proposed that there could still be hydrocarbons
burning on the extremely hot surface.

If Sagan is permitted to draw on information from after the
symposium, then so shall we. In *Scientists Confront Velikovsky* and
also in *Broca's Brain*, Sagan charges that the reflected spectrum from
Venus is entirely consistent with the infrared cloud temperature
of 240°K, in other words the temperature is what would be
expected for the amount of sunlight, and this negates Velikovsky's
prediction of Venus giving off more heat than it receives from the
Sun. That is to say, Venus is in thermal equilibrium with its surroundings, whereas Velikovsky says it shouldn't be. Well, in an
article headed "The Mystery of Venus' Internal Heat," the U.K.
journal *New Scientist* reported in 1980 (November 13) that data
from the *Pioneer Venus* orbiter showed Venus to be radiating fifteen percent more energy than is received from the Sun (later

figures put it at twenty percent). This would mean that Venus is producing ten thousand times more heat than the Earth—stated as being "inconceivable, according to present theories of planetary formation."

It was so inconceivable, in fact, that the scientists resorted to "correcting" the data that clearly pointed to it. Calculation of thermal balance is quite sensitive to the figure used for albedo, the fraction of sunlight that's reflected. Ground-based measurements (examples: 0.878, Muller, 1893; 0.815, Danjon, 1949; 0.815, Knuckles, Sinton and Sinton, 1961; 0.80, Travis, 1975) and measurements from space probes (0.80, Tomasko et al., 1980), allowing for the better accuracy of modern instruments, show a clustering around 0.8, which would normally be averaged to give what would be taken as a good indication of the actual figure. [139] But for Venus to be in thermal balance, while at the same time having an internal heat comparable to Earth's, the figure should be about 0.76—more sunlight being absorbed to account for the temperature. The procedure followed, therefore, was that both these conditions were *assumed*, and the error ranges of the instruments recalculated to allow the observed data—all the presumed errors being biased in the desired direction. And lo and behold, the final massaged figure comes out at 0.76 +/- 0.01—entirely consistent with expectations. So why bother sending anything at all?

It doesn't end there. Albedo corrections deal only with the situation at the cloud tops. For Venus to be in thermal equilibrium, a balance between emitted and incoming energy should apply all the way down. If Venus is the predominant source of heat, the imbalance should become greater closer to the surface. And this was what *all* the American and the Soviet landers found. The four *Pioneer Venus* probes entered at locations varying from 30° south to 60° north, both in daylight and night, and each one found more energy being radiated up from below than was coming down as sunlight. To complicate things further, the upward energy flux varied from place to place by a factor of two, which is difficult to reconcile with any greenhouse model but fits perfectly well with some areas being hotter than others on the young and still primarily volcanic surface of a recently incandescent planet. The *Pioneer* data indicated a progressive increase in thermal imbalance from twenty percent at the cloud tops to fifty percent at around seven miles altitude, where all inputs terminated. The Soviet *Venera* landers showed the trend accelerating all the way to the surface, where the emitted infrared flux was *forty times* more than that coming from overhead.

None of which was acceptable, of course. Accordingly, the investigators again searched for instrument errors, and having found one that they considered could have increased the *Pioneer Venus* readings, adjusted the figures for the low-level data to what they considered to be "reasonable values." But with *Venera*, there was no saving the situation. So as with the scribes who cut the Babylonian tablets, and the dating of reed and nut samples from Egyptian tombs, the story of what they say they saw was dismissed.

As a final word on Venus's temperature, Dr. George Talbott, whose field is thermodynamics, particularly with regard to space application, wrote in the pro-Velikovskian journal *Kronos* that the thermal calculations presented in *Scientists Confront Velikovsky* were irrelevant, and developed a cooling curve for an incandescent body the size and mass of Venus. It showed that in the course of thirty-five hundred years the surface temperature would fall to 750°K— just about the observed value. [140] My understanding is that Talbott's paper was not well received in establishment circles.

Problem 9. The Craters of Venus

Sagan turns to Venus's topography to show that it must be as ancient as the Earth. He tells us that radar observations reveal enormous linear mountain ranges, ringed, basins, a great rift valley and abundant cratering, maybe with areas saturated like parts of the Moon. Such tectonic or impact features couldn't be supported by the thin and fragile crust that Velikovsky's theory requires.

Well, whatever the earlier interpretations of the radar images may have been, many of these features seemed to have disappeared in later years. Studies of the *Pioneer-Venus* radar mappings were described in various journals in 1980. *Science*, July 4, reported (p. 103) that "plate tectonics is also absent"; *Scientific American*, August, (p. 65) concluded "the motion of large plates appears not to have played a dominant role"; while the *Journal of Geophysical Research*, December 30, found a pattern "indicative of global tectonism has not been identified" (p. 8232). Rick Gore wrote in *National Geographic*, January, 1985 (p. 36), "Until the orbiter's cloud penetrating radar began, crudely mapping the Venusian surface, we knew relatively nothing about the planet's terrain. . . . [until a surge of new imaging revealed] Venus as a volcanic cauldron . . . with shapes suspiciously like lava flows across the planet."

So maybe that accounts for the elevated formations that Sagan knew were mountain chains and continents—which couldn't have been produced through tectonic processes since there weren't any. Thick plates and a supporting mantle like those the Earth possesses wouldn't have had time to cool and form on a young planet. Gore's article goes on to say, "Stunning images from the Soviet Union's *Venera 15* and *16* orbiters not only revealed abundant evidence of volcanism, but also far fewer ancient meteoric impact craters than on the Moon or Mars."

By then Sagan had stopped seeing areas saturated with craters like parts of the Moon. His book *Comet* of the same year, coauthored with Ann Druyan, tells us (p. 258) "[T]he sparseness of craters on Venus shows that the surface is continually being modified—probably by volcanism."

Problem 10. The Circularization of the Orbit of Venus

This was a continuation of the insistence that had been heard since 1950 that electromagnetic forces play no part in celestial dynamics. However, Einstein, since the outset, had been of the opinion that given some unlikely coincidences they didn't have to, and since Sagan himself conceded that the odds against a Velikovskian scenario were "not overwhelming," it wasn't essential that they be brought up. Velikovsky had introduced the suggestion as a possibility, and as mentioned earlier various candidates for contributory mechanisms have been investigated, such as proto-Venus being in a charged plasma state, and tidal effects on a plastic body acting to pull it toward a lower-energy, hence more circular orbit, converting orbital momentum into heat. And let's bear in mind that electrical conditions across the Solar System following an event like the ejection of Venus from Jupiter could well be vastly different from the relatively quiescent conditions that we observe today. The debate is still going on, and while nothing put forward so far has been sufficient to convince everybody, the subject is far from closed.

And then there's the unthinkable question: Is conventional gravitational theory really on such solid ground as is almost universally supposed? Sagan assures us that literally millions of experiments testify to its validity. Yet, those reports keep coming in from what would seem to be reputable sources of pendulums doing things they're not supposed to under certain conditions of electrical charge and during solar eclipses, when the Sun is obscured. [141] Sagan reminds us of the accuracy achieved in injecting *Venera 8*, and *Voyager 1* precisely into their designated orbits, and getting within one hundred kilometers with the *Viking* orbiters, using Newtonian mechanics alone.... Well, yes; but they did employ course-corrections in flight. And *Mariner 2* missed its target area by twelve thousand miles. And in the last year or so we've been hearing that probes now in the outer Solar System are deviating from their expected trajectories and nobody is sure why.

Appealing though Newton's gravitation law may be in its simplicity, the only tests actually performed so far have been very close by in our own backyard. Everything beyond that is based on faith that it continues to apply over unlimited distances because the formula says so. But what if, as in many relationships of physics, this turns out to be an approximation to a more complex function whose deviation becomes more significant as distance increases? The only observational evidence we have of how gravity operates over distances much larger than those found in the Solar System are from the courses of stars within the disks of faraway galaxies, thousands of light-years across. And these are so much in violation of expectations that all kinds of exotic unseen matter are invented to explain them. Could the whole exercise, I can't help wondering, turn out one day to be another case of self-deception arising from a refusal to accept the most simple explanation— that the evidence means what it says—because "we know" it can't be possible.

AFTER THE INQUISITION: THE PARALLEL UNIVERSE

Velikovsky died in 1979. From working essentially alone through most of the first twenty years of his research, supported by a few who, while receptive to his ideas and prepared to defend them, in the main tended not to be active contributors, he saw the emergence of a vigorous new generation of participating researchers from archeology, history, philosophy, as well as practically all of the physical sciences.

The journal *Pensée*, was founded by Stephen and David Talbott in 1971, and that gave way in 1976 to *Kronos*, under the editorship of Lewis Greenberg, stimulating the growth in North America of what has become something of a parallel universe of catastrophism existing alongside the traditional mainstream disciplines. In Britain, the Society for Interdisciplinary Studies was founded under the impetus of Howard Tresman and puts out the journal *Chronology and Catastrophism Review*, besides hosting a regular program of workshops and conferences. In 1989 the journal *Aeon* appeared, edited by David Talbott, Dwardu Cardona, and Ev Cochrane, and since 1993 Charles Ginenthal has been publishing *The Velikovskian*, usually running at four issues of 120 pages or so each per year.

Establishment science, on the other hand—in its official stance, anyway—seems still to be ruled by its own propaganda from twenty-five years ago. The notion of catastrophic events figuring in the Earth's history has become commonplace, sure enough—but only if they are kept comfortably in the remote past and involve impacts by minor objects occurring in essentially the Solar System as it exists today. But any thought of major instabilities and encounters between the planets themselves is still off-limits, let alone the possibility of their happening recently. It would mean opening minds to accepting that it could happen again, and maybe unconsciously that's simply too much to face.

Electromagnetic influences far from Earth are a familiar part of the picture revealed by the space program; conferences are held regularly to present papers on such topics as ancient cometary encounters, revisions to history, mass extinctions, sudden climatic changes, and the fission of minor planets from the gas giants. It's hard to find one of Velikovsky's ideas that wasn't once derided and rejected with ill grace, only to be quietly wheeled in through the back door of "respectable" science later. That would be forgivable to a degree if the originator of the ideas were acknowledged and given credit as such in the references. But in what are considered the mainstream journals, he never is. Any mention of Velikovsky is a fast ticket to rejection by the review committees, academic ostracism, and probable oblivion. It would be too clear an admission of how the system works to preserve the Establishment monopoly on funding, tenure, journal access, and influence on policymaking.

But fiction writers are free to follow their inclinations, and so I gave Velikovsky's work the dedication for *Cradle of Saturn*—a tribute to a person I consider to have been one of the most original and innovative thinkers of our time. I'm sure he didn't get everything right, and his supporters remain divided over many issues. But Velikovsky's true genius, I would submit, lies in recognizing the possibility that ancient myths and legends might represent cosmic events that actually happened, and asking why planets that most people today would be unable even to find in the sky should have dominated human life to the degree that they did, and been seen universally as objects of awe and terror.

Copernicus didn't have all the details right either—he got the Sun in the center but thought the planets moved on circles rather than ellipses—but that doesn't diminish what we refer to today as the Copernican revolution. For that to get past the Aristotlean professors of the day and catch on generally took about a hundred years. Of the names that took part in the Inquisition hearing in San Francisco in 1974, I wonder which will be known, say, two centuries from now.

Section Notes

87 Ginenthal, 1995
88 Ransom, 1976, p. 46
89 Velikovsky, 1952
90 All descriptions taken from Velikovsky, 1950
91 Velikovsky, 1950, p. 63
92 Velikovsky, 1950, p. 235
93 First suggested by Velikovsky in a lecture entitled "Neon and Argon in the Atmosphere of Mars," copyrighted in 1945.
94 For example Hoyle, 1983
95 Velikovsky, 1950, pp. 198–202
96 De Grazia, Juergens, and Stecchinni, 1966, p. 27
97 Juergens, 1966, p. 28
98 Savage, 1992, p. 270
99 For example, Gold and Soter, 1980
100 *Newsweek*, May 9, 1960
101 See De Grazia, Juergens, and Stecchini, 1966, Appendix 2 for some examples of the alleged quotes and the originals side by side
102 Juergens, 1966, p. 53
103 Velikovsky, 1966, p. 234
104 McCrea, 1960
105 Lyttleton, 1961
106 Alfvén, H., *Astro Physical Journal*, pp. 137, 981
107 J. G. Hills, Ph.D. thesis, Michigan University, Ann Arbor, 1969
108 An exception is the Velikovsky-Angiras theory, which proposes Venus as having been ejected from Jupiter as a plasma rebound following a major impact. See Angiras 1999 and 2000
109 Velikovsky, 1966, p. 243
110 De Grazia, Juergens, and Stecchini, 1966
111 Juergens, 1966(a), p. 61
112 Juergens, 1966(a), p.64
113 Sherrerd, 1972; See also Van Flandern, 1993, pp. 148–153
114 Sherrerd, 1973
115 S. A. Durrani and H. A. Khan, *Nature*, 1971, pp. 232, 320
116 Full story in Ransom, 1976, pp. 164–174
117 The summary of the 1974 AAAS Symposium that follows is taken primarily from the accounts given in Ransom, 1976; Greenberg, 1977; Rose, 1996; Ginenthal, 1996

118 Rose, 1996, p. 157

119 Rose, 1996, p.177

120 Rose, 1977. See also Rose and Vaughan, 1976

121 Goldsmith, 1977. See also *Scientists Confront Scientists Who Confront Velikovsky*, Greenberg, 1978

122 Rose, 1978

123 Ginenthal, 1996, p. 93

124 Pannekoek, 1989, p. 51

125 Ginenthal, 1996, p. 100

126 Rose, 1993. Originally written for inclusion in a book, *The Sins of the Sons: A Critique of Velikovsky's A.A.A.S. Critics*, by Velikovsky and Rose, which was never published.

127 Sagan, 1979, p. 84

128 Wilson, R. A., 1995, p. 196

129 Ginenthal, 1995, p. 110

130 Ginenthal, 1996, p. 125

131 Summarized by Gribbin in *New Scientist*, May 10, 1975, p. 339

132 Juergens, 1977

133 Ginenthal, 1996, p.127, quoting from Sagan's *Man and Cosmos*, 1975 (p. 80)

134 Ginenthal, 1995, p. 178

135 Ginenthal, 1995, p. 240 ff.

136 Goldsmith, 1977, p. 75

137 Ginenthal, 1995, p. 289

138 Ginenthal, 1995, p. 303

139 From Ginenthal 1995, p. 313

140 Ginenthal, 1995, p. 321; Talbott 1993

141 Ginenthal, 1995, p. 346 ff. gives some examples

FIVE

ENVIRONMENTALIST FANTASIES
Politics and Ideology
Masquerading As Science

Every age has its peculiar folly: some scheme, project, or phantasy into which it plunges, spurred on by the love of gain, the necessity of excitement, or the mere force of imitation.
—Charles Mackay, *Extraordinary Popular Delusions and the Madness of Crowds*, 1841

Nothing is more predictable than the media's parroting of its own fictions and the terror of each competitor that it will be scooped by others, whether or not the story is true. . . . In the news game these days we don't have the staff, time, interest, energy, literacy or minimal sense of responsibility to check our facts by any means except calling up whatever has been written by other hacks on the same subject and repeating it as gospel.
— John le Carré, from *The Tailor of Panama*

I mentioned in the Introduction that one of the things that first turned me from being an eager apologist for anything pronounced in the name of Science to taking a more skeptical view was the discrepancy between what the world was being told about such things as pesticides and holes in the ozone layer, and the accounts that I heard from people I talked to directly, who specialized in such fields. Once again we have a massive body of evidently wrong information being delivered to the public, endorsed by an authoritative stamp of science. The difference here, however, was that for the main part the working scientists in these areas seemed to have a reliable picture of the way things were in the real world. But nobody was hearing from them. The lurid accounts of a despoiled and poisoned planet accelerating in a headlong rush to doom were coming from popularizers and activists with other agendas, or from institutional administrations with an eye on political visibility and funding. So I've grouped the selection of topics that this applies to into one section. (It also makes organizing the references easier.)This is a highly politicized area in today's world. Compared to the long-established and prestigious institutions that we've talked about so far, the environmental sciences are new arrivals to the scene of experiencing constant public awareness and exercising a voice in the running of society's affairs. Departments which thirty years ago consisted of a few dedicated specialists running on a pittance, whose subjects and terminology few on the outside had heard of, today wallow in lavish federal funding, send delegates to internationally reported conferences, and provide headlines for the evening's news. This makes them a target for invasion and takeover by the kind of opportunism that thrives wherever the limelight shines and the reward system beckons. In such circumstances the integrity of preserving truth is quick to suffer, since the object of the game was never to discover and report truth for its own sake in the first place, but to mold the beliefs that affect what is construed as success.

Environmentalist issues are also the kind of thing that can easily lead scientists feeling a need to "make a difference" to allow ideology to bias their professional judgment. Of course, scientists have as much right to an opinion on these matters as anyone else. The danger comes when authority earned in some totally unrelated field is accepted—by themselves as much as anyone, in some cases— as qualification to speak for "science" on matters in which their information is really no different from anyone else's, being drawn from the same sources.

If being an environmentalist means preferring to eat wholesome food, drink clean water, and not be poisoned by the air one breathes, then surely we're all environmentalists. But in many of its manifestations the term these days has come to mask an ideological campaign rooted in disenchantment with technology and hostility toward the Western style of capitalist industrialized civilization. At its extreme, this assumes the form of a neo-Malthusian world view that sees us heading inexorably toward a disaster of overpopulation and diminishing resources, making such pursuits as abundant wealth and cheap energy foolish delusions that would simply produce too many people and hasten the day when everything runs out. I happen to disagree, but these are perfectly valid concerns to hold.

New technologies create new resources. And when breakthroughs occur such as harnessing a qualitatively new realm of energy density, they do so on a scale dwarfing anything that went before, opening up possibilities that were inconceivable within the limits of earlier paradigms. Powered flying machines were impossible by the sciences known to the Greeks and the Romans, and spacecraft unattainable by the engineering of the nineteenth century. The average Englishman today lives a life style that commands more accessibility to energy, travel, communication, and variety than was available to Queen Victoria.

A resource isn't a resource until the means and the knowledge exist to make use of it. Oil was of no use to anyone until the industries had come into being to extract and refine it, and produce devices capable of applying it to useful purposes. Oil is nothing more than hydrogen and carbon configured into molecules that lock up a lot of energy. Both elements are plentiful, and it seems far more likely to me that human ingenuity and a sufficiently concentrated energy source will produce cheaper, more convenient alternatives long before the last barrel of the stuff we're squabbling about today is pumped out of the ground. A suitably concentrated source would be nuclear, when the world gets over its present phobia, and the disincentives that arise from the commitment to the current worldwide commercial and political infrastructure lessen. This is one of the reasons why nuclear technology—not just in energy generation, but for eventually obsoleting today's methods in such industries as metals extraction, refining, and processing; chemicals manufacture; desalination, all forms of waste disposal, to name a few—represents a breakthrough into the next qualitatively distinct realm, while the so-called alternatives, do not. [142]

In earlier societies that existed before the days of life insurance, retirement pensions, social services, and the like, children were an economic asset. They contributed to a family's productivity, and having a couple of strong sons to run the farm provided the security in later years. But since half the family on average would be girls, not all the sons might be fit and healthy, and with untold perils lying in wait along the road from infancy to adulthood, it was better start out with a dozen or so to give two strong sons reasonably good chances of making it. In today's modern state, by contrast, children are an expense to raise, to educate, and to prepare for life; families are correspondingly smaller—and raising families in the traditional way ceases to be the automatic choice of a great number of people, in any case. The result is that as wealth and living standards improve, new factors come into play that cause populations to become self-limiting in numbers in ways that Thomas Malthus never dreamed of. And neither, it seems, do his ideological descendants today, who apply results taken from the population dynamics of animals, who consume resources and create nothing, to humans. No big noise is made about it, but the populations of all the advanced industrial nations are now reproducing at below the minimum replacement rate—to the point that some European states are offering cash incentives for couples to have larger families. (Malthus was obsessed by the geometric growth rate of population, compared to what he assumed could only be an arithmetic growth for food supplies. But once a decline sets in, the collapse is geometric too.)

But for populations where traditional values and customs still exist alongside the increased longevity and reduced mortality that come with the shift to industrialization, *of course*, for a while, the population is going to increase as numbers adjust to come into balance with the new conditions. It's a sign of things getting better, not worse.[143] The increases happening in the Third World today are following the same pattern that occurred in Europe in the eighteenth century and in America in the ninteenth. But since the 1950s, the UN projections for the future global population have consistently been revised downward, meaning that the curve is already leveling out again.

No one is questioning that the world today is experiencing social and political problems that are perhaps going to call for some radical reappraisals of long-held attitudes and cultural values to solve. But abandoning the gains we have achieved in improving the quality of life as far as material comfort and security goes would be an irrational reaction and contribute nothing to the solving them, besides being a travesty in throwing away unquestionable triumphs of the human intellect. Some would argue that our material gains have been taken too far, and that's the largest part of the problem. Maybe so. But the point I would contend is that our material problems are effectively solved. We have the knowledge and the ability to ensure that every child born on the planet can grow up with a healthy and well-fed body, an educated mind, and the opportunity to make of themselves as much as they are able. The real problems that confront us are social and political—deciding who gets what share, and who gets the power and authority to make such decisions.

But they should be acknowledged as social and political issues and dealt with openly as such, not hidden behind a facade of phony science. The main victim in the end can only be real science and its credibility. That's what this section is all about.

GARBAGE IN, GOSPEL OUT:
COMPUTER GAMES AND GLOBAL WARMING

Hain't we got all the fools in town on our side? and ain't that a
big enough majority in any town?
— Mark Twain, *Adventures of Huckleberry Finn*

Out of all the environmentalist alarms that were raised from
around the early seventies onward, global warming emerged as
the banner issue that all the cohorts rallied behind. It was the
perfect formula for everyone with stakes in the man-made-
disaster business: scenes of polar meltdown, drowning cities, and
dried-up farmlands providing lurid graphics for the media; a
threat of global dimensions that demanded global action for
political crusaders and the would-be abolitionists of sovereign
nation-states; and all of the usual suspects to blame for opponents of industrialism and the Western world in general.

The picture the world was given is sufficiently well known not
to require much elaboration here. "Greenhouse gases" produced by
industry, automobiles, and human agricultural practices, notably
carbon dioxide (CO_2), nitrous oxides, methane, and chlorofluorocarbons (CFCs), are building up in the atmosphere. They trap heat
from the Sun like an enormous hothouse, which will melt the icecaps
and glaciers, raising raise sea levels hundreds of feet, and turn productive land into deserts, which will lead to famine, epidemics, riots,
wars over dwindling resources, and the end of the world as we know
it. The only solution is to end the world as we know it by other
means, specifically by taking immediate and draconian political
action to shut down or cut back offending economic activities of
the industrialized Western nations—but curiously not those of the
Third World, which are less effectively controlled and growing
faster—and setting up an international apparatus for planning and
policing future growth. The side less publicized was that the tril-
lions-of-dollars cost, when you got down to taking a close look at
what was really being talked about, would have the effect of cutting the world's economy to the level of being able to support only
a drastically reduced population, with the remainder reduced for
the most part to serving a global controlling elite and their bureaucratic administrators and advisors. The Soviet nomenklatura

reinstated on a world scale. It seems to me that the world would want to check its facts very carefully before letting itself be sold a deal like that.

A COMFORTABLE NATURAL GREENHOUSE

The first thing to be said is that the "greenhouse effect" isn't something new, brought about by human activities. It's a natural phenomenon that has existed for as long as the Earth has had an atmosphere. All objects above zero degrees Kelvin radiate heat. As an object gets hotter, the peak of the frequency band that it radiates (where most of the radiated energy is emitted) shifts toward shorter wavelengths. Thus, a warm hotplate on a stove radiates mainly in the infrared band, which while invisible can still be felt as heat. As the hotplate is heated more, its radiation peak moves up into the visible region to red and then orange. The Sun radiates a lot of energy at ultraviolet wavelengths, shorter than the visible. The atmosphere is transparent to certain bands of this, which reach the Earth's surface and are absorbed. But since the Earth is a lot cooler than the Sun, this energy is reradiated not at ultraviolet wavelengths but at the much longer infrared, to which the atmosphere is not as transparent. Atmospheric gas molecules that consist of three or more atoms typically absorb energy at characteristic wavelengths within the infrared band, which heats them up, and consequently the atmosphere. Note that this excludes the diatomic gases N_2 and O_2 that form the bulk of the atmosphere (78 and 20 percent respectively), and also the monatomic traces, argon and neon.

This, then, defines the notorious "greenhouse gases" that are going to stifle the planet. The one that gets all the publicity is carbon dioxide, which human activities generate in five main ways: making cement (CO_2 being driven out of the limestone used in the process); breathing; rearing animals; using wood (which once harvested, eventually decomposes one way or another); and burning fossil fuels. This translates into the release of about 3 million liters on average of CO_2 per human per year, for a grand yearly total of 1.6×10^{16} liters, or 30 billion tonnes. [144] (1 tonne = a "metric ton" = 1,000 kilograms = 0.984 ton.) The other gases, while present in smaller amounts, have a greater relative absorptive capacity that ranges from fifty-eight times that of CO_2 in the case of methane to several thousand for CFCs, and the amounts of them have been increasing.

This all sounds like something that should indeed be a cause for concern, until it's realized that the atmosphere contains something like 1,800 billion tonnes of carbon dioxide already from such sources as volcanoes, the outgassing of oceans, and the natural functioning of the biosphere. In other words, all of human activity adds less than two percent to the gases that nature puts out anyway. And then it turns out that all of these gases put together add up to a minor player, for the greatest contributor by far is water vapor. Although the exact figure varies from place to place and season to season, water vapor is typically present at ten times the concentration of carbon dioxide; further, it is active across the whole infrared range, whereas heat absorption by CO_2 is confined to two narrow bands. Without this natural greenhouse mechanism, the Earth would be about 33°C cooler than it is, which would mean permanent ice at the equator. Estimates of the contribution of water vapor vary from 95 to 99 percent, thereby accounting for somewhere around 32°C of this. The remaining one degree is due to other gases. The effects of all of human activity are in the order of two percent of this latter figure. But, of course, you can't put a tax on water vapor or lambaste your favorite industrial villains for producing it, and so water vapor never gets mentioned in the polemics. Even professionals uncritically buy the publicized line. An astronomer reports that in an impromptu survey, six out of ten of her fellow astronomers replied "carbon dioxide" when asked what was the major greenhouse gas. [145]

TWIDDLING WITH MODELS

So where does the idea come from that humans are upsetting the climate in ways that are already visible and about to spiral out of control? Just about exclusively from computer models. And despite the awe that many hold for anything that comes out of a computer, these are not yet models that can demonstrate realism or reliability to any great degree. They were created as research tools to investigate their usefulness in climatic simulation, and while such application no doubt has potential, that still closely describes the situation that exists today. The physics of planetary water vapor and the effect of clouds is not well understood, and so the models are unable to correctly represent the largest part of reality. Known phenomena such as the ocean transport of heat from the tropics to the polar latitudes are ignored, and the computational units used to simulate the dynamics across the Earth's surface might be as coarse as squares 500 miles on a side. But given the sheer complexity of the interactions taking place, this is to a large degree unavoidable even with the most advanced computers and methods available today. Sallie Baliunas, an astrophysicist at the Harvard-Smithsonian Center for Astrophysics and deputy director of the Mount Wilson Observatory, points out that to reliably simulate a climatic change over several decades, an ideal computer model would need to track 5 million parameters and apply ten million trillion degrees of freedom.[146] Nevertheless, the outputs from programs that do exist—which can only be extrapolations of the assumptions built into them—are treated as authentic predictions.

Thus, focusing on CO_2 effects, models being used in 1990 postulating a doubling in concentration by the year 2100 showed a global warming typically in the order of 4°C. When the effects of concomitant increases in other gases were factored in, this became 6.5°C. On top of this, some theorists proposed that "biogeochemical" feedback could double that figure yet again to the range 12°C–14°C, with the warming in the polar regions twice the average or more, rivaling the 33°C natural greenhouse effect.[147] However, as the models became more sophisticated, the base temperature rise being predicted as due to CO_2 in 2100 had reduced progressively to 3°C by 1992 and 2°C by 1996.

One TV production brought it all vividly to life by portraying a 2050 in which it had all happened, with the world ruled by a "Planetary Management Authority" that invades South America to redistribute that land; beef so heavily taxed that the staple diet is "cactus potatoes," genetically engineered to grow in the desert that was once America's grain lands; and Florida slipping away beneath the waves.[148] This wouldn't have been so bad had it been portrayed as a piece of doomsday science-fiction entertainment, but it was advertised as if it were a science documentary.

MEANWHILE, IN THE REAL WORLD . . .

Predictions of what will happen decades in the future or at the end of the century can't be tested, of course. But what can be tested are results from the same models of what temperatures ought to be today, given the known changes in the atmosphere that have taken place in years gone by. And when this is done, the models are found not to do too well.

Accurate measurements of carbon dioxide concentrations through the last century are available. There's no dispute that it has risen from the region of 280 parts per million (ppm) at the end of the nineteenth century to 350 ppm by the close of the twentieth, an increase of 25 percent, attributed mainly to the burning of fossil fuels. When the "carbon-dioxide equivalent" of other gases is factored in, the effective figure comes closer to 50 percent. Depending on whose model one takes, this should have resulted in a temperature rise of 1°C to 2°C. Of this 0.5°C should have occurred during the period 1979–2001.

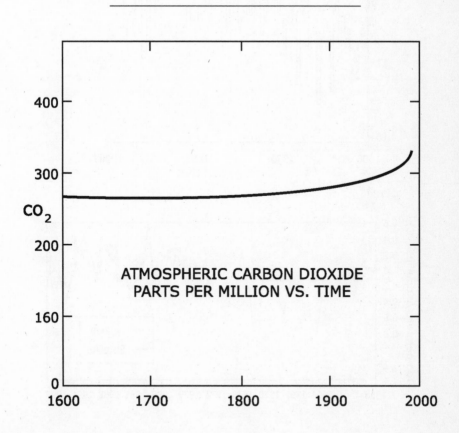

Atmospheric carbon dioxide over the last four hundred years.

The most precise measurements available for comparison over that period are from the *Tiros-N* satellites, which yield a figure of 0.08°C—a sixfold discrepancy.[149] Other analyses of satellite- and balloon-based measurements show no increase at all. Ocean measurements tend to be sparse and scattered, but a joint study of thousands of ships' logs by MIT and the British Meteorological Office indicate no change in sea-surface or marine-air temperature

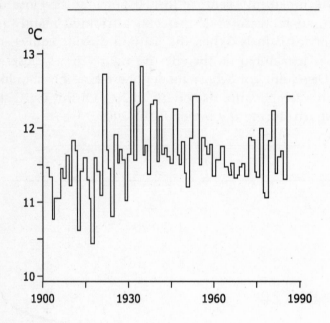

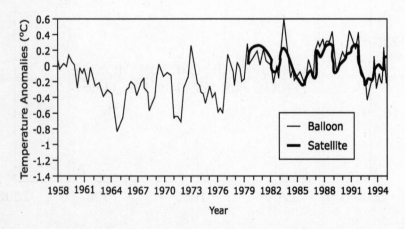

Temperatures as measured for the United States, (upper), and globally, (lower). From Robinson, 1997

in the 130 years since 1856.[150] Land-based measurements do show some increase. However, meteorological stations tend to be located at places like airports and on urban rooftops that become centers of local hot spots created by expansion and development going on around them over the years. When allowance is made for such "heat island" effects, the figure that emerges as a genuine global temperature rise through the twentieth century is of the order of 0.5°C.

Even if off from the predictions by 400 percent, this 0.5°C rise is seized upon by the global warming lobby as being due to the CO_2 increase, hence proving the theory. And as is inevitably the case when the aim is to advance an agenda in the eyes of the public, anything that appears to fit is embellished with visibility and publicity, while equally irrelevant counter-examples are ignored. Thus, the hot summer of 1988, when the Mississippi was unusually low, was blamed on global warming, as was the record Mississippi high in 1993. Then the unusually mild 1998 winter in the Eastern United States was singled out as the long-awaited global warming "fingerprint," while the winter of 1996, when New York City froze under an all-time record of 75.6 inches of snow, was forgotten. Hot years through the eighties and nineties were singled out, but not the all-time lows in Alaska and subzero conditions across Scandinavia and in Moscow. Nor was it mentioned that North America's high was reached on July 10, 1913, when Death Valley hit 134°F, Africa's in 1922, Asia's in 1942, Australia's in 1889, and South America in 1905.

A huge fuss was made in early 2002, when the Larsen B ice shelf in Antarctica broke up into a mosaic of icebergs; but nothing about it's being part of a peninsula that projects into open water that isn't even inside the Antarctic Circle—where such an event is inevitable and had been expected—or that the remaining 98 percent of the continent had been steadily cooling and accumulating ice. In October 1998 an iceberg the size of Delaware—92 miles long and 30 miles wide—broke off from Antarctica and was described by the U.S. National Oceanic and Atmospheric Administration as "a possible indicator of global warming." But *The American Navigator*, a prestigious naval text updated annually since 1799, reports in 1854 a crescent-shaped iceberg in the South Atlantic with horns 40 and 60 miles long, and 40 miles separating the tips; in 1927, a berg 100 miles long by 100 miles wide. In 1956 a U.S. Navy icebreaker reported one 60 miles wide by 208 miles long—more than twice the size of Connecticut. A federal agency was unable to ascertain this? Or was its public-relations policy driven by politically correct ideology?

But the biggest fact that refutes the whole thing is that the 0.5°C warming that occurred over the twentieth century took place before 1940, while 80 percent of the increase in CO_2 didn't happen until *afterward*, with the rapid industrialization worldwide that followed World War II. Not even by environmentalist logic can an effect come before the cause that was supposed to have produced it. The complete lack of correlation is clear. In fact, from 1940 to the mid seventies, when the buildup in CO_2 was accelerating, global temperatures actually fell. The dire warnings that were being dispensed then, couched in virtually the same language that we hear today, were that the Earth was facing an imminent ice age. *Science*, March 1, 1975, announced that the Earth had better prepare for "a full-blown, 10,000-year ice age." *Newsweek*, April 28, declared that "the Earth's climate seems to be cooling down [which would] reduce agricultural production for the rest of the century." *International Wildlife* in July of the same year agreed that "A new ice age must stand alongside nuclear war as a likely source of wholesale death and misery." The cause? Industry, of course, by releasing smoke and other particulates into the atmosphere, cutting down incoming solar radiation. The cure? Drastic restrictions enforced through international action, more controls, higher taxes to pay for it all. Sounds familiar, doesn't it?

And then from about 1970 to the present we've seen a rise back to less than 0.1°C above 1940. Just when the predicted increase should have been greatest according to the CO_2 models, temperatures since around 1980 have actually declined.

BUT THE 0.5°C NET RISE IS STILL THERE: IF THE CO_2 INCREASE DIDN'T DO IT, WHAT DID?

Well, one of the most compelling correlations with the temperature rise of 0.5°C from 1890 to 1940, the fall of 0.2°C to 1970, the recovery to 1990, and a leveling since then turns out to be with the length of the nominally eleven-year sunspot cycle. When the Sun is more active the Earth is warmer, and vice versa. The tail end of a decreasing curve from around 1870 to 1890 also matches, but before then the data become imprecise. Overall, in

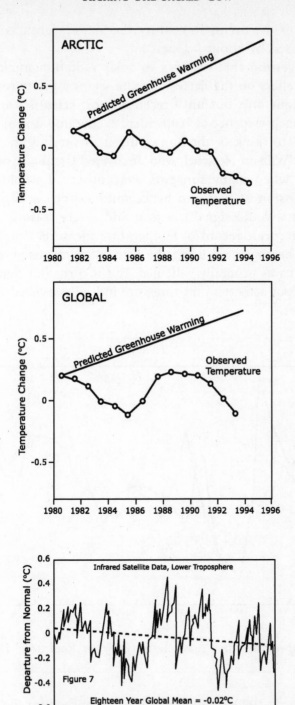

Prediction versus the actuality since 1980. From Robinson, 1997

the course of the twentieth century the Sun's brightness seems to have increased by about 0.1 percent.

The suggestion that changes in solar radiation might have a significant effect on the Earth's climate seems a pretty reasonable, if not obvious one, but until recently most scientists apparently dismissed such evidence as "coincidences" because it simply wasn't fashionable to think of the Sun's output as varying. In 1801, the astronomer William Herschel, who discovered Uranus, hypothesized that times when many sunspots were observed would mean a greater emission of heat and hence mild seasons, while times of few sunspots would signal less heat and severe seasons. Since he lacked an accurate record of temperature measurements to check his theory he suggested using the price of wheat as an indicator instead, but was generally ridiculed. But it turns out that periods of low sunspot activity in his times are indeed associated with high wheat prices.

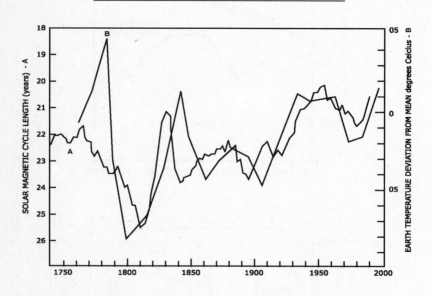

Global temperature and solar activity. From Robinson, 1997

By the early 1990s enough had been published for the primacy of the solar-climate connection to be gaining general acceptance, or at least, serious consideration (outside the world of global warming advocacy, that is). The way the mechanism seems to work is that sunspots are produced during periods of high solar magnetic activity, which is carried outward by the solar wind enveloping the Earth. This solar field acts as a shield to deflect incoming cosmic rays (primarily high-energy protons and helium nuclei) from reaching the Earth's surface. (The curves of sunspot activity and neutron counts from upper-atmosphere cosmic ray collisions show a close inverse correlation on a cycle that varies around eleven years.) The ionizing effects of cosmic rays has a great influence on cloud formation—again the curves match almost perfectly—meaning that at times of solar maximum, cloud cover diminishes and the Earth becomes warmer.

Reconstructions of earlier times show the pattern as extending back to long before any human industrial activity existed.[151] The net 0.1 percent solar brightening and 0.5°C mean temperature rise that took place through the twentieth century was the last phase of a general warming that has been going on since early in the eighteenth century, a time known as the Little Ice Age, when the Thames river in England froze regularly in winter with ice thick enough for fairs to be held on it. This was also the period that astronomers refer to as the "Maunder Minimum" of solar activity, with sunspots virtually disappearing. R. D. Blackmore's novel *Lorna Doone* tells that in the winter of 1683–4, trees in Somerset could be heard bursting from the cold.

The cooling that reached its low point in the Little Ice Age had begun around 1300. Before then there had been a warm period of several centuries centered around 1100, known as the "medieval climate optimum." This was a time when Greenland was indeed green, and the Vikings established farms and settlements there. (There's evidence that they explored into North America as well. Markers that they used to denote their day's travel have been found mapping a trail southward from Hudson Bay into Minnesota.) This in turn is revealed as being part of an approximately 2,500-year-long cycle of greater temperature swings. It reached a low just before 3,000 years ago, and before that peaked between 4,000 and 5,000 years ago, being as high above today's global mean as the Little Ice Age was below it. This was when forests and herd animals numbering millions thrived across what today are barren Siberian tundra, the Sahara was green and traversed by rivers, and the plains of Europe and North America resembled safari parks. None of this was due

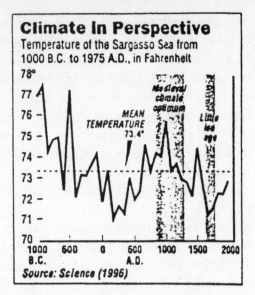

*Sea surface temperature variations as inferred from isotope studies
of marine organism remains in sediments.* [152]

---

to fossil-fuel power plants or refrigeration industries operated
by the Vikings or Paleolithic village dwellers.

This longer-term variation could have had something to do with
several distinct cycles that have been identified with respect to the
relationship between the Sun and the Earth, primarily from the
work of Miliutin Milankovitch (1920). The ones he studied were
first, the 26,000-year precession of the equinoxes, resulting from
the slow wobble of the Earth's axis; a 40,000-year variation in the
tilt of the axis; and a 90,000 to 100,000 change in the eccentricity
of the orbit. When the ascending portions of these cycles fall into
phase, as is claimed to be the case at present, their effects add.
Although this line of explanation has been challenged by catastrophist interpretations that reject such long-term constancy, [153] the
general basis is agreed for cosmic events outside the Earth being
the prime determinants of climatic changes.

And yes, the global warmers are correct in their insistence on a
connection between temperature and carbon dioxide levels. The
records from ice cores, isotope ratios in the shells of marine fossils, growth ring patterns in trees, and so forth show that at times
when temperatures were high, carbon dioxide levels were high, and
vice versa. But they get the order the wrong way around. Detailed

analysis of the timings shows consistently that the temperature changes come *first*, with the CO_2 increases following after a lag of typically forty to fifty years—just as has happened recently. [154] Although in the latter instance the CO_2 rise is conventionally attributed to human activities, before accepting it as the final word or the whole explanation, let's be aware that the Earth possesses enormous reservoirs of carbon in various forms that would find ready release into the atmosphere given even a mild rise in atmospheric and ocean temperature. The frozen soil and permafrost of the polar regions contain carbonates and organic matter that will be reemitted as carbon dioxide upon thawing and melting. Peat, the great Irish fossil-fuel contribution, occurs in a huge belt around the Arctic, passing through Greenland and Labrador, across Canada and Alaska, through Siberia and Scandinavia to the British Isles. It can reach thirty or forty feet in depth, and two million tons of dried fuel can be extracted from a square mile, almost three quarters of it carbon. The oxygenation of this material as air permeated downward after the thawing of a overlying permafrost layer would produce more CO_2.

A final source worth mentioning are methyl hydrate deposits, estimated at 2,000 billion tons contained in tundra and as much as 100,000 billion tons in ocean sediments. [155] Raising the ocean temperature just a few degrees would cause this source to release methane at the rate of 8 billion tons per year—a greenhouse gas 50 times more effective than CO_2. This is equivalent to eight times all the fossil fuel burned in the hundred years from 1850 to 1950.

GLOBAL GREENING

All this suggests that in the warmer epochs that have occurred in the past, CO_2 levels must have been a lot higher than those that are causing the hysteria today. And so they were. The concentration 100 million years ago is estimated to have been 3,000–5,000 ppm against today's paltry 350. [156] And the biosphere thrived. Carbon dioxide is the most basic of plant foods, after all; and it's the plants that we and everything else depend on. Most of the plants on this planet can't survive below CO_2 concentrations in the range 50–100 ppm. During the coldest part of the last ice age the content of the atmosphere fell to around 180 ppm—perilously close to the extinction threshold for practically everything above microbes. Outside the make-believe world of computer models, there's actually more evidence over the longer term for cooling rather than warming, and as a number of scientists have remarked, the warm periods between glacials seem to last about 11,000 years, and we're 10,800 years into the current one. Sherwood B. Idso, a research physicist at the Water Conservation Laboratory of the U.S. Department of Agriculture, argues that flooding the atmosphere with CO_2 could be just about the best thing we could do right now—our "one good deed for the other life forms with which we share the planet." [157]

Given the conditions that prevailed in past epochs, plants ought to be better adapted to higher concentrations of atmospheric CO_2 than the level that exists today. And this turns out to be exceedingly true. Field and laboratory experiments show that a simple doubling of the air's CO_2 content increases plant yield by about a third, at the same time reducing evaporation and doubling the efficiency of water use. Sour orange trees planted as seedlings in open-top enclosures supplied with an extra 300 ppm CO_2 almost tripled in biomass compared to untreated controls. Hence, biologists refer to the process as "enrichment," and commercial agriculturalists, who apply the technique routinely in growing houses, as "aerial fertilization." (This didn't stop a member of the Canadian House of Commons from speaking of it as a poison gas. [158] Which about sums up the scientific literacy of the captains we entrust the ship to.)

But that's only the beginning of the good news, for the rate of improvement continues itself improving all the way out to CO_2 concentrations of 1,000 ppm or more. And unlike the signs of warming that the doomsday advocates seek desperately to tease out of spiky thickets of data points, or see in every above-average month of heat or below-average month of rainfall, there could already be very clear fingerprints of a different kind telling of the CO_2 increase that we are unquestionably experiencing. Standing timber in the United States has increased by 30 percent since 1950, and tree-ring studies confirm a spectacular increase in growth rates. Mature Amazon rain forests are increasing in biomass by about two tons per acre per year. [159]

The transformation this could bring to our partly frozen, largely desertified planet could be stupefying. It would mean a return of forests and grasslands to vast areas that are currently wastes, with all the concomitant benefits of cycling greater amounts of organic matter back to the soil, increased populations of microorganisms, deeper rooting systems capable of mining nutrients from greater depths, greater penetration, purifying, and circulation of water, all leading toward greater size and diversity of the animal populations that the system supports—in short, a proliferation of the kind of ecological richness that we associate with rain forests. It is quite conceivable that such "bootstrapping" of the biosphere could result in a tenfold increase in the totality of Earth's bioprocesses.

THE BANDWAGON ROLLS REGARDLESS

But little of this finds its way to the public through the agencies that are generally considered to be entrusted with informing the public. What the public hears is a litany of repetitions that scientists are in agreement on the imminence of a global calamity, accompanied by the spectacle of a political circus bent on foisting the canon that any delay beyond taking drastic action now could be too late. With the exception of the *Wall Street Journal*, none of the mass media mentioned the Heidelberg Appeal, signed initially by 218 leading scientists including 27 Nobel Prize winners in April 1992, after the "Earth Summit" in Rio, as a condemnation of irrational ideologies opposed to scientific and industrial progress. By the fall of that year the number of signatories had grown to 500 scientists, including 62 Nobel Prize winners, and by 1997, S. Fred Singer, who heads the Science and Environmental Policy Project in Washington D.C., reported the figures as 4,000 and 70 respectively.[160] Nor do the media publicize the Leipzig Declaration, based on an international symposium held in Germany in November 1995, which contains the statements "there does not exist today a general scientific consensus about the importance of greenhouse warming" and "we cannot subscribe to the politically inspired worldview that envisages climate catastrophes and calls for hasty actions." This was reissued in 1997 prior to the climate treaty conference due to be held in Kyoto in December, signed by almost a hundred atmospheric specialists, and carried the caveat "we consider the drastic emission control policies likely to be endorsed by the Kyoto conference—lacking credible support from the underlying science—to be ill-advised and premature."[161]

Instead, the world was told there was a virtually unanimous

scientific consensus on the existence of a clear and present danger. On July 24, 1997, President Clinton held a press conference at which he announced that the catastrophic effects of man's use of fossil fuels was now an accepted scientific fact, not a theory. To underline this, he produced a list stated as being of 2,500 scientists who had approved the 1996 Intergovernmental Panel on Climate Change (IPCC) report preparing the ground for Kyoto. That sounded conclusive, and most of the world at large accepted it as such.

However, upon further delving, things turn out to be not quite that simple. For a start, by far the majority of the signers were not climate scientists but political representatives from their respective countries, ranging all the way from Albania to Zimbabwe, with degrees in the social sciences. Their listing as "contributors" meant, for example, that they might have been given a part of the report and asked to express an opinion, and even if the opinion was a negative one they were still listed as "reviewers."[162] Only seventy-eight of the attendees were involved in producing the document. Even then, to give it even a hint of supporting the global warming position, the executive summary, written by a small IPCC steering group, was purged of all politically incorrect skepticism and modified—*after* the scientists had signed it!—which caused an uproar of indignation from the qualified atmospheric specialists who participated. [163]

Fred Singer later produced a paper entitled "The Road from Rio to Kyoto: How Climatic Science was Distorted to Support Ideological Objectives," which couldn't have put it much more clearly.[164] The IPCC report stated the twentieth century to have been the warmest in six hundred years of climate history. Although correct, this avoided any mention of the Little Ice Age that the twentieth century was a recovery from, while going back just a little further would have brought in the "medieval optimum," which was warmer than today. Another part of the report told that increases in carbon dioxide in the geological past were "associated with" increases in temperature. This is disingenuous in that it obviously aims at giving the impression that the CO_2 increases caused the temperature rises, whereas, as we've seen, the temperature rises came first. If any causation was involved, there are stronger reasons for supposing it to have been in the opposite direction.

These are just two of twelve distortions that Singer's paper discusses, but they give the general flavor. Two phrases edited out of the IPCC report were, "None of the studies cited above has shown clear evidence that we can attribute the observed [climate] changes to the specific cause of increases in greenhouse gases" and "When will an anthropogenic effect on climate be identified? . . . [T]he best answer is, 'we do not know.'"

Frederick Seitz, former head of the National Academy of Sciences and Chairman of the George C. Marshall Institute, wrote (*Wall Street Journal*, June 12, 1996), "But this report is not what it appears to be—it is not the version that was approved by the contributing scientists listed on the title page. . . . I have never witnessed a more disturbing corruption of the peer-review process than the events that led to this IPCC report." Yet a year later it was being cited as proof of a consensus by the scientific community.

HOW THE REAL SCIENTISTS FEEL

So how did atmospheric physicists, climatic specialists, and others with scientific credentials feel about the issue? To find out, Dr. Arthur Robinson, president and research professor of the Oregon Institute of Science and Medicine, also publisher of the newsletter *Access to Energy*, in February 1998, conducted a survey of the professional field by circulating a petition calling for the government to reject the Kyoto agreement of December 1997, on the grounds that it would harm the environment, hinder science, and damage human health and welfare; that there was no scientific evidence that greenhouse gases were or were likely to cause disruption of the climate; and on the contrary there was substantial evidence that such release would in fact be beneficial.[165] After six months the petition had collected over seventeen thousand signatures.

At about the same time the German Meteorologisches Institut Universitat Hamburg and Forschungszentium, in a survey of specialists from various branches of the climate sciences, found that 67 percent of Canadian scientists rejected the notion that any warming due to human activity is occurring, while in Germany the figure was 87 percent, and in the US, 97 percent.[166] Some consensus for Kyoto!

After all the vivid depictions of drowning coastlines, devastated landscapes, and hunger-crazed mobs fighting amid the ruins of derelict cities, I can't think of a better contrasting note to finish on than the words of Arthur Robinson and his son, Zachary, from the piece cited ealier:

> What mankind is doing is moving hydrocarbons from below the ground and turning them into living things. We are living in an increasingly lush environment of plants and animals as a result of the carbon dioxide increase. Our children will enjoy an Earth with twice as much plant and animal life as that with which we are now blessed. This is a wonderful and unexpected gift from the industrial revolution.

HOLES IN THE OZONE LOGIC— BUT TIMELY FOR SOME

— *Cui Bono?* (Who Benefits?)

The early 1990s saw the coming to a crescendo of the panic over alleged depletion of the ozone layer being caused by CFCs. The following is based on an article of mine that appeared in *Omni* magazine in June 1993. It's reproduced here with a few minor changes.

Man-made chlorofluorocarbons, or CFCs, we're told, are eating away the ozone layer that shields us from ultraviolet radiation, and if we don't stop using them now, deaths from skin cancer in the United States alone will rise by hundreds of thousands in the next half century. As a result, over eighty nations are about to railroad through legislation to ban one of most beneficial substances ever discovered, at a cost that the public doesn't seem to comprehend, but which will be staggering. It could mean having to replace virtually all of today's refrigeration and air-conditioning equipment with more expensive types running on substitutes that are toxic, corrosive, flammable if sparked, less efficient, and generally reminiscent of the things that people heaved sighs of relief to get rid of in the 1930s.

And the domestic side will be only a small part. The food

industry that we take for granted depends on refrigerated warehouses, trains, trucks, and ships. So do supplies of drugs, medicines, and blood from hospitals. Whole regions of the sunbelt states have prospered during the last forty years because of the better living and working environments made possible by air conditioning. And to developing nations that rely totally on modern food-preservation methods to support their populations, the effects will be devastating.

Now, I'd have to agree that the alternative of seeing the planet seared by lethal levels of radiation would make a pretty good justification for whatever drastic action is necessary to prevent it. But when you ask the people who do have the competence to know: scientists who have specialized in the study of atmosphere and climate for years, a very different story emerges. What they point out, essentially, is that the whole notion of the ozone layer as something fixed and finite, to be eroded away at a faster or slower rate like shoe leather, is all wrong to begin with—it's simply not a depletable resource; that even if it were, the process by which CFCs are supposed to deplete it is highly speculative and has never actually been observed to take place; and even if it did, the effect would be trivial compared to what happens naturally. In short, there's no good reason for believing that human activity is having any significant effect at all.

OZONE BASICS

To see why, let's start with the basics and take seashores as an analogy. Waves breaking along the coastline continually generate a belt of surf. The surf decomposes again, back into the ocean from where it came. The two processes are linked: Big waves on stormy days create more surf; the more surf there is to decay, the higher the rate at which it does so. The result is a balance between the rates of creation and destruction. Calmer days will see a general thinning of the surfline, and possibly "holes" in the more sheltered spots—but obviously the surf isn't something that can run out. Its supply is inexhaustible for as long as oceans and shores exist.

In the same kind of way, ozone is all the time being created in the upper atmosphere, by sunshine, out of oxygen. A normal molecule of oxygen gas consists of two oxygen atoms joined together. High-energy ultraviolet radiation, known as UV-C, can split one of these molecules apart—a process known as "photo-dissociation"— into two free oxygen atoms. These can then attach to another oxygen molecule to form a three-atom species, which is ozone. It's produced mainly in the tropics above 30 kilometers altitude, where the ultraviolet flux is strongest. The ozone sinks and moves poleward to accumulate in lower-level reservoirs extending from 17 to 30 kilometers altitude—the so-called ozone "layer."

Ozone is destroyed by chemical recombination back into normal oxygen in several ways: by reaction with nitrogen dioxide (produced by high-altitude cosmic rays); through ultraviolet dissociation by the same UV-C that creates ozone; and also by a less energetic band known as UV-B, which is not absorbed in the higher regions. Every dissociation of an oxygen or ozone molecule absorbs an incoming UV photon, and that is what gives this part of the atmosphere its ultraviolet screening ability.

The height and thickness of the ozone reservoir region are not constant, but adjust to accommodate variations in the incoming ultraviolet flux. When UV is stronger, it penetrates deeper before being absorbed; when weaker, UV penetration is less. Even if all the ozone were to suddenly vanish, there would still be 17 to 30 kilometers of hitherto untouched, oxygen-rich atmosphere below, that would become available as a resource for new ozone creation, and the entire screening mechanism would promptly regenerate. As Robert Pease, professor emeritus of physical climatology at the University of California, Riverside, says, "Ozone in the atmosphere is not in finite supply."[167] In other words, as in the case of surf with oceans and shores, it is inexhaustible for as long as sunshine and air continue to exist.

THE DEPLETION CONTROVERSY

Even though the physics makes it difficult to see how, the notion of something man-made destroying the ozone layer has always fascinated an apocalyptic few, who have been seeking possible candidates for over forty years. According to Hugh Ellsaesser, retired and now guest scientist at the Atmospheric and Geophysical Sciences Division of the Lawrence Livermore National Laboratory, "There has been a small but concerted program to build the possibility of man destroying the ozone layer into a dire threat requiring governmental controls since the time of CIAP." [169] (Climatic Impact Assessment Program on the supersonic transport, conducted in the early seventies.)

In the 1950s it was A-bomb testing, in the sixties the SST, in the seventies spacecraft launches and various chemicals from pesticides to fertilizers. All of these claims were later discredited, and for a while the controversy died out. [170] Then, in 1985–1986, banner headlines blared that a huge ozone hole had been discovered in the Antarctic. This, it was proclaimed, at last confirmed the depletion threat, the latest version of which had been around for just under a decade.

In 1974, two chemists at the University of California, Irvine, Sherwood Rowland and Mario Molina, hypothesized that ozone might be attacked by CFCs—which had come into widespread use during the previous twenty years. [171] Basically, they suggested that the same chemical inertness that makes CFCs noncorrosive, nontoxic, and ideal as a refrigerant would enable them to diffuse intact to the upper atmosphere. There, they would be dissociated by high-energy ultraviolet and release free atoms of chlorine. Chlorine will combine with one of the three oxygen atoms of an ozone molecule to produce chlorine monoxide and a normal two-atom oxygen, thereby destroying the ozone molecule. The model becomes more insidious by postulating an additional chain of catalytic reactions via which the chlorine monoxide can be recycled back into free chlorine, hence evoking the specter of a single chlorine atom running amok in the stratosphere, gobbling up ozone molecules like Pac Man. Scary, vivid, sensational: perfect for activists seeking a cause, politicians in need of visibility, and the media, always hungry for anything sensational. But it doesn't fit with a few vital facts.

First, CFCs don't rise in significant amounts to where they need to be for UV-C photons to break them up. Because ozone absorbs heat directly from the sun's rays, the stratosphere exhibits a reverse temperature structure, or thermal "inversion"—it gets warmer with altitude, rather than cooler. As Robert Pease points out, "This barrier greatly inhibits vertical air movements and the interchange of gases across the tropopause [the boundary between the lower atmosphere and the stratosphere], including CFCs. In the stratosphere, CFC gases decline rapidly and drop to only 2 percent of surface values by 30 kilometers of altitude. At the same time, less than 2 percent of the UV-C penetrates this deeply."[172] Hence the number of CFC splittings is vastly lower than the original hypothesis assumes, for same reason that there aren't many marriages between Eskimos and Australian aborigines: the partners that need to come together don't mix very much.

For the UV photons that do make it, there are 136 million oxygen molecules for them to collide with for every CFC—and every such reaction will *create* ozone, not destroy it. So even if we allow the big CFC molecule three times the chance of a small oxygen molecule of being hit, then 45 million ozone molecules will still be created for every CFC molecule that's broken up. Hardly a convincing disaster scenario, is it?

Ah, but what about the catalytic effect, whereby one chlorine atom can eat up thousands of ozone molecules? Doesn't that change the picture?

Not really. The catalysis argument depends on encounters between chlorine monoxide and free oxygen atoms. But the chances are much higher that a wandering free oxygen atom will find a molecule of normal oxygen rather than one of chlorine monoxide. So once again, probability favors ozone creation over ozone destruction.

At least 192 chemical reactions occur between substances in the upper stratosphere, along with 48 different, identifiable photochemical processes, all linked through complex feedback mechanisms that are only partly understood.[173] Selecting a few reactions brought about in a laboratory and claiming that this is what happens in the stratosphere (where it has never been measured) might be a way of getting to a predetermined conclusion. But it isn't the end of the world.

But surely it's been demonstrated! Hasn't one thousand times more chlorine been measured over the Antarctic than models say ought to be there?

Yes. High concentrations of *chlorine*—or to be exact, chlorine monoxide. But all chlorine atoms are identical. There is nothing to link the chlorine found over the Antarctic with CFCs from the other end of the world. It might also be mentioned that the measuring station at McMurdo Sound is located 15 kilometers downwind from Mount Erebus, an active volcano currently venting 100 to 200 tons of chlorine every day, and which in 1983 averaged 1,000 tons per day. Mightn't that have more to do with it than refrigerators in New York or air conditioners in Atlanta?

World CFC production is currently about 1.1 million tons annually, 750,000 tons of which is chlorine. Twenty times as much comes from the passive outgassing of volcanoes. This can rise by a factor of ten with a single large eruption—for example that of Tambora in 1815, which pumped a *minimum* of 211 million tons straight into the atmosphere. Where are the records of all the cataclysmic effects that should presumably have followed from the consequent ozone depletion?

And on an even greater scale, 300 million tons of chlorine are contained in spray blown off the oceans every year. A single thunderstorm in the Amazon region can transport 200 million tons of air per hour into the stratosphere, containing 3 million tons of water vapor. On average, 44,000 thunderstorms occur daily, mostly in the tropics.[174] Even if we concede to the depletion theory and allow this mechanism to transport CFCs also, compared to what gets there naturally the whiff of chlorine produced by all of human industry (and we're only talking about the *leakage* from it, when all's said and done) is a snowflake in a blizzard.

Despite all that, isn't it still true that a hole has appeared in the last ten years and is getting bigger? What about that, then?

In 1985 a sharp, unpredicted decline was reported in the mean depth of ozone over Halley Bay, Antarctica. Although the phenomenon was limited to altitudes between 12 and 23 kilometers, and the interior of a seasonal circulation of the polar jet stream known as the "polar vortex," it was all that the ozone-doomsday pushers needed. Without waiting for any scientific evaluation or consensus, they decided that this was the confirmation that the Rowland-Molina conjecture had been waiting for. The ominous term "ozone hole" was coined by a media machine well rehearsed in

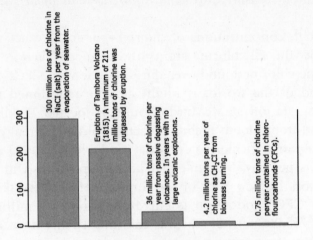

CHLORINE EMITTED BY NATURAL PROCESSES
VS. ANNUAL PRODUCTION OF CHLORINE IN CFCS

The miniscule amount of chlorine from CFCs compared to the chlorine
from natural processes leaves a big hole in the ozone hole theory.

*Chlorine in the atmosphere from natural processes compared to that
contained in CFCs.*

---

environmentalist politics, and anything that the scientific community had to say has been drowned out in the furor that has been going on ever since.

Missing from the press and TV accounts, for instance, is that an unexpectedly low value in the Antarctic winter-spring ozone level was reported by the British scientist Gordon Dobson in 1956—when CFCs were barely in use. In a forty-year history of ozone research written in 1968, he notes: "One of the most interesting results . . . which came out of the IGY [International Geophysical Year] was the discovery of the peculiar annual variation of ozone at Halley Bay."[175] His first thought was that the result might have been due to faulty equipment or operator error. But when such possibilities had been eliminated, and the same thing happened the following year, he concluded: "It was clear that the winter vortex over the South Pole was maintained late into the spring and that this kept the ozone values low. When it suddenly broke up in November both the ozone values and the stratosphere temperatures suddenly rose."

A year after that, in 1958, a similar drop was reported by French scientists at the Antarctic observatory at Dumont d'Urville—larger than that causing all the hysteria today. [176]

These measurements were on the edge of observational capability, especially in an environment such as the Antarctic, and most scientists regarded them with caution. After the 1985 "discovery," NASA reanalyzed their satellite data and found that they had been routinely throwing out low Antarctic ozone readings as "unreliable."

The real cause of the variation is slowly being unraveled, and while some correlation is evident with volcanic eruptions and sunspot cycles, the dominant factor appears to be the extreme Antarctic winter conditions, as Dobson originally suspected. The poleward transportation of ozone from its primary creation zones over the tropics does not penetrate into the winter vortex, where chemical depletion can't be replaced because of the lack of sunshine. Note that this is a localized minimum relative to the surrounding high-latitude reservoir regions, where global ozone is thickest. As Hugh Ellsaesser observes, "The ozone hole . . . leads only to spring values of ultraviolet flux over Antarctica a factor of two less than those experienced every summer in North Dakota." [177]

But isn't it getting bigger every year? And aren't the latest readings showing ozone depletion elsewhere too?

In April 1991, EPA Administrator William Reilly announced that the ozone layer over North America was thinning twice as fast as expected, and produced the figures for soaring deaths from skin cancer. [178] This was based on readings from NASA's *Nimbus-7* satellite. I talked to Dr. S. Fred Singer of the Washington-based Science and Environmental Policy Project, who developed the principle of UV backscatter that the ozone monitoring instrument aboard *Nimbus-7* employs. "You simply cannot tell from one sunspot cycle," was his comment. "The data are too noisy. Scientists need at least one more cycle of satellite observations before they can establish a trend." In other words, the trend exists in the eye of the determined beholder, not in any facts that he beholds.

February this year (1992) saw a repeat performance when a NASA research aircraft detected high values of chlorine monoxide in the northern stratosphere. Not of CFCs; nor was there any evidence that ozone itself was actually being depleted. Nor any mention that the Pinatubo volcano was active at the time. Yet almost as if on cue, the U.S. Senate passed an amendment only two days later calling for an accelerated phaseout of CFCs. It just so happened that NASA's budget was coming up for review at the time. After getting their funding increase they have since conceded that perhaps the fears were premature, and the Great American Ultraviolet Catastrophe isn't going to happen after all.

CREATING CATASTROPHE: THE WIZARDS OF OZONE

But apart from all that, yes, world mean total ozone declined about five percent from 1979 to 1986. So what? From 1962 to 1979 it increased by five and a half percent. And since 1986 it has been increasing again—although that part is left out of the story that the public gets. On shorter timescales it changes naturally all the time and from place to place, and hence surface ultraviolet intensity is not constant and never was. It varies with latitude, i.e., how far north or south from the equator you are, with the seasons, and with solar activity. And it does so in amounts that are far greater than those causing all the fuss.

The whole doomsday case boils down to claiming that if something isn't done to curb CFCs, ultraviolet radiation will increase by 10 percent over the next twenty years. But from the poles to the equator it increases naturally by a whopping factor of fifty, or 5,000 percent, anyway!—equivalent to 1 percent for every six miles. A family moving house from New York to Philadelphia would experience the same increase as is predicted by the worst-case depletion scenarios. Alternatively, they could live 1,500 feet higher in elevation—say, by moving to their summer cabin in the Catskills.

Superposed on this is a minimum 25 percent swing from summer to winter, and on top of that a ten- to twelve-year pattern that follows the sunspot cycle. Finally there are irregular fluctuations caused by the effects of volcanic eruptions, electrical storms, and the like on atmospheric chemistry. Expecting to find some "natural" level, that shouldn't be deviated from, all this is like trying to define sea level in a typhoon.

Skin cancer is increasing, nevertheless. Something must be causing it.

An increasing rate of UV-induced skin cancers means that more people are receiving more exposure than they ought to. It doesn't follow that the intensity of ultraviolet is increasing, as it would

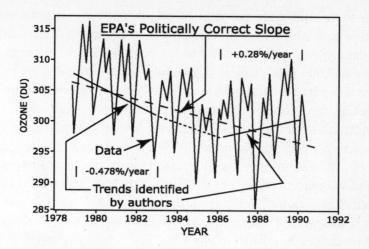

EPA's depletion trend as sold to the public, compared to what actually happens. The extrapolation ignores the obvious reversal following the solar minimum in 1985. Source of original data: "Global average ozone change from November 1978 to May 1990," J. R. Herman et al, Journal of Geophysical Research.

---

if ozone were being depleted (in fact it's decreasing. Other considerations explain the facts better, such as that sun worship has become a fad among light-skinned people only in the last couple of generations; or the migrations in comparatively recent times of peoples into habitats for which they are not adapted, for instance the white population of Australia. (Native Australians have experienced no skin cancer increase.)

Deaths from drowning increase as you get nearer the equator—not because the water becomes more lethal, but because human behavior changes: not many people go swimming in the Arctic. Nevertheless, when it comes to skin cancer the National Academy of Sciences has decided that only variation of UV matters, and from the measured ozone thinning from poles to equator, and the change in zenith angle of the Sun, determined that a 1 percent decrease in ozone equates to a 2 percent rise in skin cancer. [179]

How you make a disaster scenario out of this is to ignore the decline in surface UV actually measured over the last fifteen years, ignore the reversal that shows ozone to have been increasing again since 1986, and extend the 1979–86 downward slope as if it were going to continue for the next forty years. Then, take the above formula as established fact and apply it to the entire United States population. Witness: According to the NAS report (1975), approximately 600,000 new cases of skin cancer occur annually. So, by the above, a 1 percent ozone decrease gives 12,000 more skin cancers. Projecting the 5 percent ozone swing from the early eighties through the next four decades gives 25 percent, hence a 50 percent rise in skin cancer, which works out at 300,000 new cases in the year 2030 A.D., or 7.5 million over the full period. Since the mortality rate is around 2.5 percent, this gives the EPA's "200,000 extra deaths in the United States alone." *Voilà*: instant catastrophe.

As if this weren't flaky enough, it is known that the lethal variety of skin cancer has little to do with UV exposure, anyway. The cancers that *are* caused by radiation are recognizable by their correlation with latitude and length of exposure to the Sun, and are relatively easily treated. The malignant melanoma form, which does kill, affects places like the soles of the feet and underarm as well as exposed areas, and there is more of it in Sweden than in Spain. It is increasing significantly, and as far as I'm aware the reasons why are not known.

A FEW COINCIDENCES

So, what's going on? What are publicly funded institutions that claim to be speaking science doing, waving readings known to be worthless, faking data, pushing a cancer scare that contradicts fact, and force-feeding the public a line that basic physics says doesn't make sense? The only thing that comes through at all clearly is a determination to eliminate CFCs at any cost, whatever the facts, regardless of what scientists have to say.

Would it come as a complete surprise to learn that some very influential concerns stand to make a lot of money out of this? The patents on CFCs have recently run out, so anybody can now manufacture them without having to pay royalties. Sixty percent of the world market is controlled by four companies—DuPont Chemical and Allied Chemical in the United States, Imperial Chemical Industries in Britain, and Atochem in France, who are already losing revenues and market share to rapidly growing chemicals industries in the Third World, notably Brazil, South Korea, and Taiwan, which threatens their entire pricing structure.

They also hold the patents in a sharing arrangement on the only substitutes in sight, which will restore monopoly privileges once again if CFCs are outlawed.

Ultraviolet light has many beneficial effects as well as detrimental. For all anyone knows, an increase such as the one that's being talked about could result in more overall good than harm. But research proposals to explore that side of things are turned down, while doomsayers line up for grants running into hundreds of millions. United Nations departments that nobody ever heard of and activists with social-engineering ambitions could end up wielding the power of global police. The race is on between chemicals manufacturers to come up with a better CFC substitute, while equipment suppliers will be busy for years. Politicians are posturing as champions to save the world, and the media are having a ball. Bob Holzknecht, who runs an automobile air-conditioning company in Florida, and who has been involved with the CFC industry for over twenty years observed when I talked to him, "Nobody's interested in reality. Everyone who knows anything stands to gain. The public will end up paying through the nose, as always. But the public is unorganized and uninformed."

Good science will be the victim too, of course. For a while, anyway. But truth has a way of winning in the end. Today's superstitions can spread a million times faster than anything dreamed of by the doom prophets in days of old. But the same technologies which make that possible can prove equally effective in putting them speedily to rest, too.

Well, that's the way I wrote it originally. Nowadays I'm not so sure about the "equally effectively" in that last sentence. It can take a long time. Yet I still find grounds for optimism in the long term. Wrecking is so much easier than building. But machines and cities are constructed; works of art and thought are accomplished. Overall, the human propensity to create seems vastly to outweigh the destructiveness.

To round things off, the following is taken from "Fact-Free Science," which appeared two years later, in *Analog Science Fiction and Fact*, April 1995.

The bottom-line test, after all the modeling and arguments over atmospheric chemistry are said and done with, is the amount of ultraviolet light reaching the Earth's surface. If stratospheric ozone were under relentless chemical attack in the way that we're told, the measured UV ought to be increasing. People who have measured it say it isn't.

In 1988, Joseph Scotto of the National Cancer Institute published data from eight U.S. ground stations showing that UV-B (the wavelength band affected by ozone) decreased by amounts ranging from 2 to 7 percent during the period 1974–1985. [180] A similar politically wrong trend was recorded over fifteen years by the Fraunhofer Institute of Atmospheric Sciences in Bavaria, Germany. [181]

The response? Scotto's study was ignored by the international news media. He was denied funding to attend international conferences to present his findings, and the ground stations were closed down. The costs of accepting the depletion theory as true will run into billions of dollars, but apparently we can't afford a few thousand to collect the data most fundamental to testing it. In Washington, D.C., scientists who objected were attacked by environmentalist pressure groups, and former Princeton physics professor William Happer, who opposed the (1995) administration and wanted to set up an extended instrumentation network, was dismissed from his post as research director at the Department of Energy. The retiring head of the German program was replaced by a depletionist who refused to publish the institute's accumulated data and terminated further measurements, apparently on the grounds that future policy would be to rely on computer models instead. [182]

Critics jeered, and the depletion lobby was not happy. Then, after a lengthy silence, a paper appeared in *Science,* claiming that upward trends in UV-B had been shown to be linked to ozone depletion. [183] So, suddenly, all of the foregoing was wrong. The party line had been right all along. Depletion was real after all.

The study showed plots of ozone above Toronto declining steadily through 1989–1993, and UV increasing in step over the same period. But Dr. Arthur Robinson, the same whom we met before in the discussion on Global Warming, noticed something curious: Although the whole point was supposed to be the discovery of a correlation between decreasing ozone and increasing UV-B, nowhere in the study was there a graph relating these two quantities one to the other. [184] Neither were there any numbers that would enable such a graph to be constructed. Robinson enlarged the published plots and performed his own analysis. And the reason why no consequential trend line was shown, he discovered, was that there was no trend.

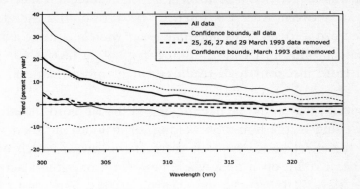

Changes in radiation flux. The heavy solid curve claims an increase over five years reaching 20 percent per year at 300 nm, compiled from 312 data points. The long-dashed curve shows the result of removing just four anomalous points resulting from short-lived, abnormal atmospheric chemistry. The remainder reveal no significant change.

For the first four years, the ozone and UV-B rose and fell together: completely opposite to what the paper claimed to show. The result wouldn't have surprised depletion skeptics, however, who never accepted that UV has to go up as ozone goes down, in the first place. Rather, since UV creates ozone out of oxygen in the upper atmosphere, more UV getting through means a high UV flux, and so more ozone is being made up there. Hence, all else being equal, both quantities should change together with the seasonal variations and fluctuations of the sun. And the 1989–1992 pattern shows just that.

But all else isn't always equal. Ozone worldwide fell through the second half of 1992 to reach an extraordinarily low level in 1993. Satellite maps for this period show the diffusion through the stratosphere of huge plumes of sulfur dioxide from the Mount Pinatubo volcano eruption in 1991. This would extend to global dimensions the depletion chemistry usually restricted to polar ice clouds and responsible for the notorious Antarctic "hole" (replacement can't occur in the winter months because there's no sun).

So the low 1993 ozone was not caused by unusually low solar

activity. Solar activity was normal, which would be expected to result in above-normal UV intensity because of the chemically thinned ozone cover. This *one-time event* was then stretched out to create an illusory trend beginning in 1989. In fact, it was produced from just four high readings out of more than 300 data points. [185]

Logically, this would be like proving to the landlord that there's damp rising in the house by waiting for a flood and then averaging the effect back over four years. If the lawyers catch on to this one, it could open up a whole new world of liability actions.

The May 27, 1994, issue of *Science* carried a letter from Professors Patrick J. Michaels, Office of Climatology of the University of Virginia, and S. Fred Singer, director of the Science and Environmental Policy Project, Maryland, and research associate Paul C. Knappenberger, also from the University of Virginia, stating that the study was "So flawed as to require a formal withdrawal from the Scientific Literature."

SAVING THE MOSQUITOES: THE WAR ON DDT

When all its work is done the lie shall rot;
The truth is great, and shall prevail,
When none cares whether it prevails or not.
— Coventry Patmore, from the poem "Magna est Veritas"

The DDT controversy takes us back over thirty years and might have slipped from the memories of some. Others may never have been cognizant of it in the first place. And that's a good reason for selecting it for inclusion, for it constitutes the original, model environmental catastrophe scenario and protest movement, setting the pattern for just about all of the major issues that have become news since.

SOME BACKGROUND INTELLIGENCE: MALARIA

The biggest single killer of human beings through history has been malaria. Before the 1940s, 300 million new cases were contracted annually worldwide, and of those stricken, 3 million died.

6 to 7 million cases occurred every year in the United States, primarily in the South and parts of California.

Malaria is caused by a genus of protozoan—the simplest, single-cell animal form—called *Plasmodium*, which comes in four species. In the human bloodstream they take a form known as merozoites, which burrow into the red blood cells and reproduce asexually, each one producing 6 to 26 new individuals which burst out to infect new blood cells on a cycle that repeats every forty-eight hours. When the number of merozoites exceeds about 50 per cubic milliliter of blood (a typical drop), the victim suffers a malaria attack every forty-eight hours. In a heavily infected person, the number of plasmodia present can be as high as 2 million per milliliter.

The severity of the symptoms depends on the species involved, but a typical attack consists of severe frontal headache and pain in the neck, lower back, and limbs, dizziness and general malaise, accompanied by waves of chill and seizures alternating with fever temperatures of up to 104°F and profuse sweating, acute thirst and vomiting being not uncommon. The falciparum variety can kill up to 40 percent of those affected. Deaths occur mainly among children under five years old. For those who survive, the pattern continues for several months, and then gives way to symptom-free periods punctuated by relapses that occur over anywhere from a year to ten years. The effects can be sufficiently debilitating to incapacitate 80 percent of a workforce, with such consequences as preventing harvesting of a food crop, thus rendering a population vulnerable to all of the opportunistic threats that come with malnutrition and an impaired immune system, such as hepatitis, tuberculosis, dysentery, and typhoid fever. Transmission from person to person takes place through the ingestion of blood by females of the *Anopheles* mosquito, and re-injection of *Plasmodium* into a new victim via the saliva after undergoing another part of its life cycle within the mosquito's stomach.

Since, through most of history, eliminating the mosquito was never feasible, attempts at checking the spread of the disease were directed at destruction of the breeding grounds. The two main methods were draining of swamps and marshy areas, which dates back to the Romans, and the flooding of lakes and open areas of water with oil from early spring to fall, to prevent the mosquito larvae from breathing. Where irrigation channels were needed for agriculture, a common practice was to introduce the "mosquito fish" *Gambusia*, a typically arduous and expensive undertaking, since it was usually necessary to first eradicate such predatory types as catfish, which were partial to *Gambusia*. These measures were partially successful at best, and confined to the more developed countries. Only Italy achieved what seemed to be eradication, after a fifteen-year program of intensive effort under Mussolini, but the victory turned out to be temporary.

Then, in 1939, Paul Mueller, a chemist working for J. R. Geigy S.S. in Switzerland, developed a compound, ichloro-diphenyl-trichloroethane—DDT—by combining chlorals with hydrocarbons and phenols that was cheap, easy to produce and use, nontoxic to mammals and plants, but extremely toxic on contact to insects and various other arthropods. The Allies quickly recognized its value for wartime use and found it 100 percent effective as a fumigant against the ticks and body lice that transmit typhus, which in World War I had killed millions of soldiers and civilians in Europe. In early 1944 an incipient typhus epidemic in Naples was halted with no adverse side effects apart from a few cases of very minor skin irritation, after efforts with more conventional agents achieved only limited results. A plague epidemic in Dakar, West Africa, was stopped by using DDT to eliminate the carrier fleas, and it was mobilized with great success against malaria in the Pacific theater, Southeast Asia, and Africa. After the war, DDT became widely available not only for the reduction of insect-transmitted human diseases but also of a wide range of agricultural, timber, and animal pests. The results from around the world seemed to bear out its promise as the perfect insecticide.

For combating malaria, it was sufficient to spray the walls and ceiling of dwellings once or twice a year. Malaria mosquitoes rested in these places when inactive, and the DDT penetrated via their feet. Incidence in India in the 1940s was over 100 million cases annually, of which 2.5 million died. By 1962 these numbers were down to 5 million and 150,000, while life expectancy had risen from thirty-two to forty-seven.[186] A 1.5-ounce shot glass of DDT solution covered twelve by twelve feet of wall. The cost per human life saved worked out at about twenty cents per year. In the same period, India's wheat production increased from less than 25 million tons to over 100 million tons per year due to a combination of pest reduction and a healthier workforce. Ceylon—now Sri Lanka—

reduced its malaria figures from 3 million cases and 12,000 deaths per year in the early fifties to 31 cases total in 1962, and 17 cases the year after, with zero deaths. Pakistan reported 7 million cases of malaria in 1961, which after the introduction of an aggressive spraying program had fallen to 9,500 by 1967. [187]

In Africa, in what is considered to be its second most important medical benefit after reducing malaria, DDT proved effective in a program to control the bloodsucking tsetse fly, which transmits the protozoan responsible for deadly sleeping sickness and also fatal cattle diseases. According to the World Health Organization, 40 million square miles of land that had been rendered uninhabitable for humans because of tsetse fly infestation became available.

Another serious menace in parts of Africa and Central American is the blackfly that transmits roundworms causing "river blindness" in humans. Before DDT was introduced, more than 20,000 victims of this affliction in Africa were blind, with incidences as high as 30 percent of the populations of some villages. The larvae of the flies live in fast-flowing streams and had proved impossible to control until the occurrence of a fortunate accident in the 1950s in the Volta River basin, when a mule carrying DDT powder to a spraying project slipped while fording a stream and spilled its load into the water. Blackfly larvae were killed for a mile downstream without ill effects on other forms of aquatic life, and a river treatment program was implemented subsequently, greatly reducing the number of river-blindness sufferers. No masks or protective clothing were required for the operatives. In this entire period no instance of DDT-induced illness was reported among the estimated 130,000 spraying personnel employed, or the millions of people whose dwellings were treated. S. W. Simmons, chief of the technology branch of the Communicable Disease Center of the U.S. Public Health Service, said in 1959:

> The total value of DDT to mankind is inestimable. Most of the peoples of the globe have received benefit from it either directly by protection from infectious diseases and pestiferous insects, or indirectly by better nutrition, cleaner food, and increased disease resistance. The discovery of DDT will always remain an historic event in the fields of public health and agriculture. [188]

Such being the perversity of human nature, it could only be a

matter of time before people started finding reasons why something as good as that couldn't be allowed to continue.

OPENING ASSAULT: SILENT SPRING

Throughout history there have been those who opposed, or who
were simply left not especially impressed by, the furthering of
technology and its application to ends traditionally considered
indicative of human progress toward better things. Their motives
vary from sincere conviction as to the folly of playing God and
the likely outcomes of meddling with nature, through simple
disenchantment with the results, political opportunism, publicity
and status seeking, to resentment at society's building itself around
values that they feel exclude them. In some ages they have been
lonely minorities, largely ignored and at odds with the fashion of
the times; at others, particularly when change has been rapid or
heightened social conflict results in yearnings for stability or a
return to the imagined tranquility of an earlier age, their influence has been significant in shaping the flow of events.

The 1960s was a time when all these currents converged. A new
generation separated from roots in the past by the disruptions of
World War II was manifesting an awakening social conscience
through such channels as the civil rights movement and challenges
to all forms of traditional authority. The destructiveness of the war,
particularly its climaxing in the atomic devastation of two Japanese cities, followed by the specter of general nuclear annihilation
promulgated through the Cold War with the Soviet Union, made
for a climate of distrust in "Big Science" wedded to "Big Politics,"
with widespread questioning of whether all the effort and upheaval
had brought any worthwhile benefits at all. And waves of radical
technological change coming in such forms as mass automobile
and jet travel, computing and electronics, nuclear energy, the space
program, coupled with social revolutions sweeping away the old
political and economic order across three quarters of the world
had left people everywhere reeling in bewilderment and the social
organism in need of respite to collect itself back together and regain
cohesion.

In 1962, naturalist and writer Rachel Carson published a book
called *Silent Spring* that touched a sympathetic note in just about
every one of the simmering discontents and nagging apprehensions

waiting to be released. But for once, the dangers were straight-forward and comprehensible, the villains of the piece identifiable, and rising frustrations saw the prospect of relief through a chance to take action that could make a difference. Carson's work was an eloquent and passionate indictment of what many had come to regard as man's reckless chemical assault in the name of misplaced humanitarianism and the pursuit of profits on the natural environment. Its major target was DDT. The general tenor can perhaps be assessed from the following, taken from the first chapter, "Fable for Tomorrow," which in execution and effect must be described as brilliant.

"There was once a town in the heart of America where all life seemed to live in harmony with its surroundings. The town lay in the midst of a checkerboard of prosperous farms, with fields of grain and hillsides of orchards where, in spring, white clouds of bloom drifted above the green fields." The idyllic picture is developed at some length and concludes, "So it had been from the days many years ago when the first settlers raised their houses, sank their wells, and built their barns."

There continues (pp. 13–14):

> Then a strange blight crept over the area and everything began to change. Some evil spell had settled on the com-munity: mysterious maladies swept the flocks of chickens; the cattle and sheep sickened and died. Everywhere was a shadow of death. The farmers spoke of much illness among their families. In the town the doctors had be-come more and more puzzled by new kinds of sicknesses appearing among their patients. . . .
>
> There was a strange stillness. The birds, for example—where had they gone? . . . The few birds seen anywhere were moribund; they trembled violently and could not fly. It was a spring without voices. On the morning that had once throbbed with the dawn chorus . . . only silence lay over the fields and woods and marsh. . . .
>
> The roadsides, once so attractive, were now lined with browned and withered vegetation as though swept by fire. These, too, were silent, deserted by all living things. Even the streams were now lifeless. Anglers no longer visited them, for all the fish had died.
>
> In the gutters under the eaves and between the shingles

of the roofs, a white granular powder still showed a few patches; some weeks before it had fallen like snow upon the roofs and the lawns, the fields and streams.

No witchcraft, no enemy action had silenced the rebirth of new life in this stricken world. The people had done it themselves.

J. Gordon Edwards is a professor emeritus of entomology at San Jose State University in California, having taught biology and entomology there for over forty years, and a lifetime fellow of the California Academy of Sciences. He is also a long-term member of both the Audubon Society and the Sierra Club, the latter of which published his book *Climbers' Guide to Glacier National Park*. Such a person should certainly qualify as a sincere lover of nature and knowledgeable scientist with concerns for protecting living things. In 1992 he wrote of *Silent Spring*:

" . . . I was delighted. I belonged to several environmental-type organizations, had no feelings of respect for industry or big business, had one of my own books published by the Sierra Club, and I had written articles for *The Indiana Waltonian*, *Audubon Magazine*, and other environmental magazines. . . . I eagerly read the condensed version of *Silent Spring* in the *New Yorker* magazine and bought a copy of the book as soon as I could find it in the stores." [189] The enthusiasm carried him onward for a while. "As I read the first several chapters, I noticed many statements that I realized were false; however, one can overlook such things when they are produced by one's cohorts, and I did just that."

But by the middle of the book, his feeling had grown that "Rachel Carson was really playing loose with the facts and deliberately wording many sentences in such a way as to make them imply certain things without actually saying them." Upon checking the references that were cited, Edwards found that they did *not* support the book's contentions about harm being caused by pesticides. He concluded, "When leading scientists began to publish harsh criticisms of her methods and her allegations, it slowly dawned on me that Rachel Carson was not interested in the truth about these topics, and that I really was being duped, along with millions of other Americans."

Millions of other Americans, however, did not possess the background knowledge of somebody like Edwards or read the journals in which leading scientists published their criticisms. What they did see was a media and journalistic frenzy of sensationalism, nascent action groups discovering a moral crusade of fund-raising potential that was without precedent, and politicians vying for public visibility as champions of the cause. Leading environmentalist organizations found they had become big business and campaigned to expand the operation. In July 1969 the National Audubon Society distributed seventeen thousand leaflets to its members urging them to support the position that DDT should be banned throughout the United States and its export prohibited. In February 1971 the director of the Sierra Club declared , "The Sierra Club wants a ban, not a curb, on pesticides, even in the tropical countries where DDT has kept malaria under control." [190]

THE OFFENSIVE DEVELOPS

The attack against DDT was based, essentially, on three broad allegations: (1) that it interfered with bird reproduction, causing mass die-offs among the population; (2) that it persisted in the environment and its concentration was magnified at higher levels of the food chain, and (3) that it caused cancer. While all of these claims continued to draw vigorous opposition within the scientific community, the popular imagery depicted a heroic grass-roots battle affecting everyone.

The imagery and attendant political pressures had their effects overseas, too. Many of the countries that had joined energetically in the war on malaria cut back or abandoned their programs. In 1967 the World Health Organization (WHO) changed its official goal from worldwide "eradication" to "control of the disease, where possible." In India, where health officials at one point had believed malaria on the point of being eradicated, the number of cases returned to a million in 1972, to quadruple by 1974. Ceylon, which in 1963 had brought its incidence down to just 17 cases with no deaths, halted its program on the strength of the claims and public opposition in the West. The number of cases went back up to 308 in 1965; 3,466 in 1967; 17,000 in January 1968; 42,000 in February, and thereafter, millions. [191]

A new phenomenon in the midst of all the stirred-up passions was the emergence of groups of scientists taking openly partisan positions on controversial issues. Hence, in addition to receiving a one-sided treatment from large sections of the press, the public was also exposed to statements from positions accepted as carrying scientific authority, but which represented advocacy rather than the impartial exposition that was expected. The situation was exacerbated by the tendency for professional disapproval of such practices to be expressed in limited-circulation, specialized journals rather than the popular media where the original slanted material appeared.

In 1967 the Environmental Defense Fund (EDF) was founded by Victor Yannacone, a New York attorney; Charles Wurster, then assistant professor of biology at the State University of New York, Stony Brook; George Woodwell, a plant physiologist at the Brookhaven National Laboratories on Long Island, and several other scientists with environmental concerns. The stated aim was "to create, through litigation, a body of legal interpretations for natural resource conservation and abatement of ecologically perilous situations." The law courts, then, would be made the forum for the environmental debate. This meant that procedures followed in legal hearings, where each side presents only those points that best support its case, would be applied to deciding what were essentially scientific issues—even if the consequences had significant social implications. But a scientific debate can only be properly decided after consideration of all the pertinent data and all of the available evidence. The truth value of a scientific statement is not affected by debating skill or the persuasive powers of a trained advocate.

In the late sixties the EDF initiated a number of legal actions challenging local practices in various areas, an example being 1967, where it filed suit in western Michigan to restrain nine municipalities from using DDT to spray trees against Dutch elm disease. While in the main these cases lost in court, they were successful nevertheless in gaining publicity and attracting broadbased support through a process of education-by-headlines. Scientists heady with the new feeling of celebrity status took to the laboratories and produced results backing their claims, for example two studies published in 1969 purporting to show that DDT caused cancer in mice.[192] When public interest waned, they called journalists to organize press conferences.

In 1971 a group of environmentalist organizations led by the EDF brought suit against the recently formed (1970) Environmental Protection Agency, which had taken over from the Department of Agriculture the regulation of pesticide registration and use, for the sale and use of DDT to be banned. In response to an appeal by the Montrose Chemical Company, the sole remaining manufacturer of DDT in the United States, and the Department of Agriculture in conjunction with about thirty suppliers of products containing DDT, the EPA appointed a scientific advisory committee to investigate and report on the situation. The hearings began in August 1971.

THE 1971 EPA HEARINGS

WELL-DESIGNED, WELL-EXECUTED EXPERIMENTS: DDT AS A CARCINOGEN

One of the major causes of public concern was the claim that even small amounts of DDT residues could accumulate in the body tissues over time and cause cancers. Samuel Epstein, a principal witness for the EDF, testified that DDT had been shown to be carcinogenic in well-designed experiments, and that in his opinion there was no safe exposure level. [193] This was immediately picked up and echoed widely by the popular press, and also cited in the "Point of View" column in *Science* (175: 610). None of the press, however, gave space to the testimonies of several other experts, among them Jesse Steinfield, the U.S. Surgeon General, and John Higginson, director of the International Agency for Research on Cancer, that DDT is not a human carcinogen. Neither did *Science* condescend to publish a letter from W. H. Butler of the British Medical Research Council, who also testified at the hearing, opposing the view expressed by Epstein. So, regardless of the hyped phrases and the font sizes in which the headlines were set, what can be made of the facts?

Repeated incessantly by the media, and still heard today, was the mantra that a single molecule of a carcinogen is capable of initiating a tumor, and hence no level of exposure is safe. All one can say here is that this goes against the long-established principle of toxicology that recognizes a threshold of dose below which adverse effects become undetectable—and hence to assert their reality becomes a matter of faith, not science. This was acknowledged as far back as the sixteenth century by Paracelsus, who noted that "The dose makes the poison." Were it not so, it is doubtful whether any individual could ever survive to maturity and perpetuate the species, for in sufficient doses and under suitable conditions just about anything can be made to induce cancers, examples being honey, egg yolk, plain table salt, and even water. Of course, anyone is free to disagree. But when such a view is presented in such a way that it is likely to be taken as representative of expert opinion, the result is clearly misleading. In the words of Claus and Bolander (p. 324):

> [F]or although [Epstein's] right to hold his own opinions
> and make dissenting evaluations cannot be questioned,
> his views cease to be mere private judgments when he
> either claims or implies the agreement of his scientific
> colleagues and speaks for them in a public forum. It then
> becomes a matter for public argument whether he rep-
> resents properly what is in the literature and whether
> he describes accurately the consensus among scientists.

Now let's return to the well-designed experiments that showed DDT to be a carcinogen.

Extensive human and animal studies to assess the toxicity of DDT had been conducted ever since its introduction. In 1956, a group of human volunteers ingesting DDT for periods of from twelve to eighteen months at 1,750 times the average amount for the United States population showed no adverse effects either at the conclusion of the trial or in follow-up studies five years later. A 1964 study of the incidence of different forms of cancer from all areas of the U.S. from 1927 to the early 1960s showed no correlation with the use patterns of DDT, nor with its presence in food or human body tissues. Similar results were reported from studies of industrial workers exposed for years to 600 to 900 times the intake of the general population, inhabitants of tropical countries who had been liberally dusted with DDT, and the work crews employed in applying it as spray and powder. The FDA had conducted prolonged investigations of fifteen groups of heavily exposed persons, each group consisting of one hundred individuals matched with controls, that looked especially for gradual or delayed effects but found none. One paper of a different kind described an experiment in the therapeutic use of DDT, where administration of a daily dose 7,500 times greater than the average produced no ill effects but was highly effective as a treatment for congenital jaundice. [194]

Epstein's response was to dismiss all of these studies as "irrelevant" or "a travesty of the scientific data."[195] The irrelevance seemed to follow from his emphatic statement that there were no data to be found anywhere in the literature on chronic inhalation studies, which was a significant mode of human exposure. Claus and Bolander offer a list of references to precisely such studies covering the period 1945 to 1969 that were right there, in the literature. A direct contradiction. What more can be said? The latter comment is apparently to be taken as meaning that it's a travesty of the data to find a substance safe simply because no carcinogenic effects can be found among heavily exposed humans after many years.

This attrition left just seven papers presumably judged to be relevant, separated into two categories: (1) three that were considered "highly suggestive" but flawed in method or statistical analysis, and (2) the remaining four, "conclusive." One of the first group dealt with rainbow trout (exceptionally sensitive to DDT) reported as developing liver cancers. However, the doses involved, over a period of twenty months, were up to 27,000 times what other researchers had found to be lethal, which makes it difficult to see how any of the fish could have lived at all, let alone develop tumors of any kind, and so results can only be suspect. The second group included two WHO studies that were in progress at the time, one being conducted in France, the other in Italy. Since they were as yet incomplete, the appellation "conclusive" is hardly justified. What, then, of the four papers that this leaves?

First, the two group (1) cases. In 1969, Tarján and Kemény, in Hungary, feeding low dosages to successive generations of a strain of inbred mice, reported a higher tumor incidence among the experimental animals than the controls, becoming statistically significant in the third and fourth generations.[196] But there were puzzling features. For one thing, tumors were lower in the controls than in the breeding stock, indicating some factor in the experiment that was not accounted for. Further, while the strain used was supposed to be leukemia-free, leukemia in fact occurred in both the experimental and control groups. Finally, nothing comparable—nor any cancer of any type—had been found by other researchers working with similar dose levels. A subsequent WHO investigation showed that all of the oddities could be explained by suspected contamination of the feed with aflatoxins—among the most potent of naturally occurring carcinogens. So one can agree with Epstein's assessment of the study's being defective in method or analysis. But of "highly suggestive"? Hardly.

The remaining paper in this category described an earlier series of several experiments with rats.[197] Evaluation of the results was complicated by the fact that more than two-thirds of the test animals were lost for one reason or another over the two-year period. Of the 75 from 228 that survived, 4 developed liver tumors compared to 1 percent of the controls. Whether this is statistically significant is debatable, since the four came from different test groups, and no relationship was indicated between dose and effect. On the contrary, some of the rats that showed no liver cell necrosis had reportedly existed for twelve weeks on doses that other workers had found to be 100 percent lethal. Subsequent attempts to duplicate the reported results failed. The British pathologist, Sir Gordon Roy Cameron, who conducted one of these endeavors, a fellow of the Royal College of Pathologists, later knighted for his contributions to the field, observed that the 1947 study had employed formalin as a fixative agent for the tissues, which is not suitable for cytological studies on account of its tendency to produce artifacts of precisely the kind that had been identified as hyperplasia nodules. The inference could therefore be made that the results were "highly suggestive" of wrongly fixed tissue.[198]

This leaves us with two studies qualifying as well-designed and well-executed. In this connection Epstein sprang something of a surprise on the defense by introducing data from an in-house FDA experiment performed between 1964 and 1969 that nobody else had heard of, describing it as an excellent piece of work and expressing puzzlement that its findings had never been published.[199] The experiment involved two compounds, DDT and methoxychlor, fed to two strains of inbred mice. Epstein disregarded all the results for the strain-A mice, which experienced high mortality from a bacterial infection. This was not mentioned in the actual report but came to light in a memorandum from one of the researchers later, which included a terse comment that its effect on the study as a whole had not been determined. A second possible contributory factor was found in the sixty-seventh week with the discovery that the strain-A had been fed three times the intended dose for an undetermined period of time. Whether this had also been the case with the strain-B mice was not known. Well, one can only speculate that a good reason for refraining from publication and saving further expenditure of funds and effort might be found right there.

Anyway, delving deeper regardless we find that taking both strains together there were actually more tumors among the controls (males 66, females 82) than among the experimental animals (males 63, females 73). For strain-B alone, a slight increase occurs for DDT-fed (males 42, females 50) versus controls (males 39, females 49). However, this applied to *benign* tumors only. If it is permissible to select just one subgroup from the entire study to make a point, then we could by the same token select just the strain-B females that developed malignant tumors, where the numbers were controls 10, DDT-fed 3. Hence, by a far larger margin, the same study could be shown as equally "conclusively" demonstrating DDT to be an *anti*carcinogen.

The final paper, however, was the one presented as *the* proof, the main source that media articles ever since have cited in branding DDT as a carcinogen: the 1969 Bionetics Report, sometimes referred to as the Innes paper, after the first-named of its thirteen authors.[200] The work was part of an ambitious study performed by Bionetics Laboratories, a subsidiary of Litton Industries, under contract to the National Cancer Institute, on the effects of 123 chemical compounds in bioassays on 20,000 mice covering periods of up to eighty-four weeks. Epstein's confidence notwithstanding, the methods and findings have been widely criticized in the professional literature.

One objection was that the researchers did not assure random distribution of the litters. Genetic disposition counts heavily in tumor occurrences among mice. Subjecting litter mates to the same compound runs the risk that genetic factors can mask the results, making any ensuing statistics worthless. Others were that the study failed to distinguish between malignant tumors and benign nodules, the significance of what was being measured being further obscured by relying on a single figure of "maximum tolerated dose" in lieu of providing more orthodox dose-effect relationships—at levels 100,000 times higher than those of residues typically encountered in food.

But perhaps the greatest oddity, pointed out by Claus and Bolander (p. 351) was that whereas the authors of the paper lumped all five control groups together on the grounds that there was no significant variation between them, the actual data showed there to be large differences. For strain-X, as an example, the percentage of mice developing tumors varied from 0 to 41.2 percent for the males and 0 to 16.3 percent for the females. Applying regular statistical procedures reveals that for the group showing the highest tumor incidence—strain-X males at 41.4 percent—with the above degree of variation present in the controls, the maximum part of this that could be attributed to DDT is 5.5 percent, which no amount of manipulation could make significant. Following the same procedure with the strain-Y mice yields higher tumor percentages among the controls than among the DDT-fed groups.

Their skepticism highly aroused by this time, the authors of *Ecological Sanity* then turned their attention to the report's listing where the tested substances were classified as "tumorigenic," "doubtfully tumorigenic," or "not tumor-producing," i.e., safe. And again, a raft of inconsistencies was found. Substances widely agreed upon as being carcinogenic received a clean score. Others considered to be innocuous—one, in fact, used for the treatment of alcoholics—did not. Compounds with similar molecular structures and chemical behavior received very different ratings. And piperonyl butoxide, which was tested twice, managed to end up on both the "doubtful" and the "safe" lists.

Claus and Bolander point out that a program of this magnitude would involve the preparation of about 48 million tissue sections placed on 2,400,000 microscope slides, requiring 60,000 boxes. Making what appear to be reasonable estimates of the likely workforce, rate of working through such a phenomenal task, and the time available, they doubt that meaningful results would even be possible. They ask (p. 362): "What kind of an expert panel is it that can not only so warmly endorse this ambitious but dismally sloppy study and dignify it with the name of the NCI but also provide rationalizations for its obvious weaknesses?"

A PLAGUE OF BIRDS

One of the most serious ravages that can befall woodlands is infestation by the gypsy moth. The larvae devour *all* the foliage of trees, especially oaks, and in large numbers can strip bare entire areas, forcing other life left without food or habitat to either perish or migrate. This can be unpleasant and even dangerous, as inhabitants of northern New Jersey discovered in the seventies when large numbers of rattlesnakes and copperheads invaded suburban areas there. In 1961, the year before *Silent Spring* was published, large areas of Pennsylvania were sprayed with DDT to eradicate this pest. The Scranton Bird Club kept careful records but didn't report a single case of bird poisoning. Officials of the National Audubon Society were satisfied that no harm was done to bird life, including nesting birds.

Yet *Silent Spring* was to state (p. 118) that the robin was on the verge of extinction, as was the eagle; (p. 111) "Swallows have been hard hit. . . . Our sky overhead was full of them only four years ago. Now we seldom see any." Here we have another instance of assertion being flatly contradicted by the facts, for the very next year ornithologist Roger Tory Peterson described the robin as "probably North America's number one bird" in terms of numbers.[201] The Audubon Society's figures for annual bird counts bore him out, reporting 8.41 robins per observer in 1941 (pre-DDT) and 104.01 for 1960, representing a more-than twelve-fold increase during the years when DDT use was at its highest. The corresponding figures for the eagle and swallow were increases by factors of 2.57 (counts per observer 3.18, 8.17) and 1.25 (0.08, 0.10) respectively.[202] This pattern was general for most of the species listed, showing 21 times more cowbirds, 38 times more blackbirds, and no less than 131 times more grackles, the average total count per observer being 1,480 in 1941 and 5,860 in 1960. Gulls became so abundant on the East Coast that the Audubon Society itself obtained permission to poison 30,000 of them on Tern Island, Massachusetts, in 1971. Wild turkeys increased from their rare status of the pre-DDT years to such numbers that hunters were bagging 130,000 annually. Of the few species that did decrease, some, such as swans, geese, and ducks, are hunted, while bluebirds are known to be susceptible to cold winters.

Ironically, some of the areas where birds seemed to thrive best were those of heaviest DDT use, such as in marshes sprayed to control mosquitos. Part of the reason seems to be that DDT is also effective in reducing insects that transmit bird diseases and which compete with birds for seeds and fruit. But perhaps even more important, DDT triggers the induction of liver enzymes that detoxify potent carcinogens such as aflatoxins that abound in the natural diets of birds

None of this prevented any real or imagined decline in bird

population from being immediately attributed to pesticides.[203] A severe reduction in eastern ospreys turned out to be due to high levels of mercury in the fish upon which they fed and to pole traps set around fish hatcheries—blamed on DDT even though reported as early as 1942. Alaska ospreys continued to do well despite high DDT residues. California brown pelicans increased almost three-fold during the heavy DDT years but experienced a sharp decline at the beginning of the seventies—two months after an oil spill at Santa Barbara surrounded their breeding island of Anacapa (not mentioned in the reports of the state and federal wildlife agencies). In 1969 the colony had been severely afflicted by an epidemic of Newcastle disease transmitted from pelican grounds along the Mexican coast of the Gulf of California (also not mentioned). It was later established that helicopter-borne government investigators collected 72 percent (!) of the intact eggs on Anacapa for analysis and shotgunned incubating pelicans in their nests.[204] DDT was also implied as being connected with the reduction of the Texas pelican, even though the decline had been noted in 1939 and attributed to fishermen and hunters.

The great eastern decline in the peregrine falcon was to a large degree due to the zealousness of egg collectors who have been known to rob hundreds of nests year after year, and then attribute the ensuing population collapse to the encroachments of civilization. In 1969, "biologists" studying peregrines in Colville, Alaska, collected fully one-third of the eggs from the colony and then dutifully reported that only two-thirds of the expected number of falcons subsequently hatched. [205]

CRACKING OPEN THE EGGSHELL CLAIMS

But by the time of the 1971 hearings, the main allegation, still perpetuating the fiction that a catastrophic fall in bird populations was taking place, had become that DDT was the cause not as a result of immediate toxicity, but indirectly through disruption of the reproductive cycle by the thinning of eggshells. This again goes back to *Silent Spring*, which states (p. 120), "For example, quail into whose diet DDT was introduced throughout the breeding season survived and even produced normal numbers of fertile eggs. But few of the eggs hatched." This was a reference to experiments performed by James DeWitt of the U.S. Fish and

Wildlife Service, published in the *Journal of Agricultural Food and Chemistry* in 1956 (4: 10 pp. 853–66). The quail were fed 3,000 times the concentration typically encountered in the wild. 80 percent of the eggs from the treated group hatched, compared to 83.9 percent of the untreated controls, so the claim of a "few" was clearly false, and the difference in results hardly significant. Moreover, 92.8 percent of the eggs from the DDT-fed birds were fertile, compared to 89 percent from the controls, which reverses the impression created by the quoted text. Also omitted was that DeWitt's study was actually conducted on quail and pheasant. Of the pheasants, 80 percent of the eggs from the treated birds hatched compared to 57.4 percent for the controls, and 100 percent of the DDT birds survived against 94.8 percent of the control group.

A number of later studies were cited at the EPA hearings, purporting to account for an effect (major decline in bird populations) that wasn't happening. All of them are examined in *Ecological*

EFFECTS OF DDT ON REPRODUCTION OF QUAIL AND PHEASANT

| Level in diet | | Number of birds | Mortality % | Egg/hen Average | Hatch % | % Chicks surviving at end of | |
In winter (ppm)	During reproduction (ppm)					2 weeks	6 weeks
Quail							
0 (control)	0 (control)	32	6.25	52	83.9	88.9	83.3
100	0	8	0	61	75.7	86.2	64.3
100	100	12	25.0	65	75.3	67.7	7.1
0	200	12	25.0	55	80.0	32.3	12.9
Pheasants							
0 (control)	0 (control)	28	0	48	57.4	94.8	89.7
0	50	10	0	31	58.6	100	86.0
50	50	10	0	18	80.6	100	93.3
0	100	10	0	19	52.0	100	82.4

Source: James DeWitt, *Journal of Agricultural and Food Chemistry*, 1958.

The complete results of the DeWitt study, 1956. From Edwards, 1992

Sanity—with more care and thoroughness, it would appear, than by the witnesses who built their cases on them.

A 1969 experiment (Heath et al.) on mallard ducks, performed at the Patuxent Wildlife Center at Laurel, Maryland, reported that birds fed DDT and DDE (the major metabolic residue from DDT breakdown) suffered a mortality among embryos and hatchlings of from 30 to 50 percent. The first thing that struck Claus and Bolander upon reviewing the paper was an enormous range of variation with the control groups that nobody else had apparently objected to. For instance, the number of eggs laid per hen in one control group was 39.2, whereas in another it was 16.8. This difference alone was far greater than any of the differences said to be "significant" among the experimental birds. The difference in live fourteen-day-old hatchlings in the same groups was 16.1 versus 6.0, which again was greater (69 percent) than the 50 percent deficit in ducklings per hen reported for the birds fed the highest DDT diet. When the variations among the controls are greater than the variations between the control and experimental animals, it should be obvious that some factor other than the test variable is operating (a bacterial infection, for example), which affects both groups. Claus and Bolander conclude (p. 406):

> On the basis of these absurd differences . . . the entire study becomes meaningless, and all of the conclusions presented by the authors have to be discarded." And (p.408) "How this paper could have been passed for publication in *Nature* is unfathomable, for even rapid scanning of the tables presented in the article should have made it immediately evident to the referees that the data for the two series of control birds invalidated the whole experiment.

But published in *Nature* it was (227: 47–48), and it remains virtually unchallenged as one of the most frequently cited references in support of the contention that sublethal concentrations of DDT can be held responsible for declines in wildlife populations.

The same issue of *Nature* (was there some editorial decision to convey a message here?) carried another paper cited at the hearings, this time by Dr. Joel Bitman and coworkers, describing experiments on Japanese quail. It concluded from direct measurements that DDT and related compounds induce a decrease in eggshell calcium and produce thinner eggshells. How were these conclusions arrived at?

The quantities of test compound fed to the experimental birds were of the order of 100 times that found in the natural environment. As if this were not enough, the experimenters also introduced "calcium stress" in the form of a diet (given both to the control and two experimental groups) reduced from the normal level of around 3 percent calcium content to 0.56 percent. The question that the results needed to answer was, "Did the feeding of DDT add to any calcium depletion caused by the calcium stress conditions? The authors of the experiment claimed that it did.

Their results, however, showed no significant differences in the calcium content of the blood or the bones that were analyzed from the three groups. It seems odd that if the calcium reserves of the parent birds showed no reduction, there should be a significant difference in the eggshells they produce. The significance reported was 0.07 percent, arising from 2.03 percent calcium content measured in the shells from the controls, versus 1.95 and 1.96 for the test groups. While mathematically the claim of significance is correct, it turns out that the method followed was to analyze the shell for the weight of calcium, which was then expressed as a percentage of the fresh weight of the entire egg. The weights of the shells themselves were not given, leaving wide open the possibility that eggs smaller and presumably lighter in total weight could nevertheless have possessed shells that were heavier. Hence, it's not possible to tell from the presented data whether the percentage of eggshell calcium was reduced or not, which was the whole point of the exercise.

It gets even more interesting when we look at the measuring of eggshell thickness. This was done with a mechanical screw-type micrometer after the shell membranes were removed. An average reduction is reported of 69.5×10^{-4} inches for the controls to 66.7×10^{-4} in. and 65.6×10^{-4} in. for the eggs of two groups of test birds, and is described as "highly significant." Well, let's look at it.

Converting these figures to metric at the same accuracy as that given—namely of three significant figures—yields figures for reduction in thickness of 0.00711 and 0.00991 millimeters. The last two digits of each are below the resolving power of a light microscope, and eliminating them leaves reported thinnings of 7 and 10 microns. (1 micron = 0.001 mm—about half the size of a well-developed bacterium.) Screw micrometers available at the time were not considered to resolve differences below 50 microns reliably. More recent devices graduated to 10 microns are useful for gauging thicknesses of materials like metal foil, but for compressible samples such as paper—or eggshells—the determination of "end point" is a subjective quantity based on feel, typically resulting in variations of 10 to 30 microns. To borrow the phrase so beloved of textbook writers, it is left as an exercise for the reader to judge if such methods could have given results justifiably acclaimed as being highly significant.

Everywhere, and Indestructible

The final allegation was that DDT persisted virtually indefinitely, accumulating in the environment, which again traced back to *Silent Spring* and had been faithfully repeated ever since by the media. In response to one of these widely circulated claims, J. Gordon Edwards sent to dozens of radio and TV stations, and newspapers a list of over 150 scientific articles documenting the breakdown of DDT by living things. Not one of them ever made any reference to that material or modified the false impression that they had helped convey to the public.

One of the witnesses who testified at the hearings to the persistence of DDT claimed, under questioning, not to be aware of the work of his own research colleagues at Gulf Breeze, Florida, who had demonstrated in 1969 that 92 percent of all DDT, DDD, and DDE broke down in seawater within thirty-two days. [206]

Dr. George Woodwell, who in 1967 had coauthored a paper with EDF founder Charles Wurster on DDT residues measured at a salt marsh on the shore of Long Island, admitted that the figure published had been 13 times too high because the spot they had selected for taking soil samples just happened to be at the place where the spray trucks cleaned out their tanks. When asked if he had ever published a retraction, Woodwell replied (Hearings, p. 7238) "I never felt that this was necessary." In fact, he had published work that showed the earlier results to have been grossly exaggerated, but EDF lawyers had advised him not to mention it. [207]

Wurster himself did also testify, with regard to experiments he had performed in 1968 at the Woods Hole Oceanographic Institution into the effects of DDT on marine algae, which showed a marked reduction in photosynthetic activity—to three-quarters of normal and less. He had commented at the time that all animal life on Earth ultimately depends on this process, and speculated that changes in growth patterns at this level could have repercussions throughout the entire food chain. This caused tremendous agitation among environmental alarmists, resulting in wild media stories about an imminent disruption of the Earth's oxygen manufacturing ability that were repeated by the secretary general of the United Nations, U Thant.

Strangely, however, Wurster's group had never measured the amount of DDT actually taken into the organisms, but simply assumed it to be the case, that assumption carrying with it the further one that the observed reduction in photosynthesis was a result of biochemical action on the algal metabolism. But a simpler interpretation of the data suggests it to have been a purely physical effect caused by DDT particles adsorbing to the outside surfaces of the algae and cutting down the light supply.[208] This was reinforced by the work of others (e.g., Mendel et al., 1970), showing that the effect does not occur with filtered solutions of the compound, indicating that the DDT needs to be present in the form of large (hence filterable) flakes. Inhibition of algal growth, although also widely aired in the public forum, had been mentioned by Wurster only speculatively and was not confirmed experimentally. Despite all the furore, therefore, all these experiments really proved was that photosynthesis works better in clearer water.

The further two broad issues concerning the persistence of DDT were that it was ubiquitous, showing up everywhere from Asian jungles to the Antarctic, and that once taken up into the animal food chain its concentration was progressively magnified through successively higher trophic levels, such as algae—fish—predator fish—fish-eating bird—predator bird.

The examples cited to illustrate the first turned out invariably to be artifacts of the measuring techniques used, or results of misidentification. One of the principal instruments used in pesticide analysis, introduced in the early sixties, was the gas chromatograph, in which the sample being tested is vaporized into a stream of carrier gas that is passed through a column of porous material. The various constituents, having different molecular weights, separate out into distinct bands which can be identified by their emergence after a characteristic propagation time to be registered, usually as a "peak" of signal voltage, at a detector. (The process is analogous to the way in which water from a plumbing leak spreads out across a ceiling tile and dries to leave a ring pattern of successively colored haloes—hence the name.)

Although highly sensitive, it is a fact with this technique that totally different substances with similar mobilities can have similar "signatures," making skilled interpretation an imperative. The much-publicized finding of "DDT" in the Antarctic, for example, turned out to be due to contamination by molecules from the connecting tubing of the apparatus. Soil samples sealed in glass jars since 1911 gave results that were interpreted as five kinds of pesticides that didn't exist until thirty years later. A similar story applies to a gibbon from Burma, preserved since 1935. [209]

The examples given to "prove" the hypothesis of magnification along the food chain were based on selected data. Figures were taken for DDT concentrations found in hawk brains, where they are highest, fish muscle, where it is lowest, and duck fat, which is intermediate. Comparison of figures for *muscle* tissue from crustaceans, fish, duck, hawk shows no magnification. [210]

THE SCIENTISTS' FINDINGS AND THE ADMINISTRATOR'S RULING

The hearings went on for seven months, during which 125 witnesses were heard and 9,362 pages of testimony recorded. The EPA's hearing examiner, Judge Edmund Sweeney, was even-handed in his dealings, which seemed to infuriate environmentalists and drew criticism from the *New York Times* and *Science*, neither of which sent reporters to cover the proceedings. The scientific advisors had also followed the testimony and were unanimous in their eighty-page recommendation that the claims were unsubstantiated and there was no reason for DDT to be banned. Sweeney issued his conclusions on April 25, 1972.[211] They included the following:

♦ DDT is not a carcinogenic hazard to man...

♦ DDT is not a mutagenic or teratogenic hazard to man....

♦ The uses of DDT under the registrations involved here do not have a deleterious effect on freshwater fish, estuarine organisms, wild birds, or other wildlife....

♦ The adverse effect on beneficial animals from the use of DDT under the registration involved here is not unreasonable on balance with its benefit.... There is a present need for the continued use of DDT for the essential uses defined in this case.

This was in line with the professional scientific and medical scientific pleas that had been made worldwide. During the EPA hearings the World Health Organization issued a statement that included:

Improvement in health occasioned by antimalarial campaigns has broken the vicious cycle of poverty and disease in many areas by preventing incapacity and death .... [N]o economic alternative to DDT is available

> and the . . . consequences of the withdrawal of DDT
> would be very grave. . . . [T]he safety record of DDT for
> man is truly remarkable.

Six weeks after Sweeney's findings, on June 2, 1972, the EPA Administrator, William Ruckleshaus, reversed the decision, rejected the scientific evidence, and ordered a ban on the sale and production of DDT. Ruckleshaus had not attended any of the sessions during the seven-month hearing and admitted that he had not read the transcript. The decision, he stated, was taken for political reasons. Environmentalist groups have campaigned vigorously ever since for a full ban on all use, by all nations.

Today, more than 2 billion people—40 percent of the world's population—live in malarious countries. Around 300 million are infected, and something like 100 million cases are estimated to occur each year along with millions of deaths, most of them children. Africa is one of the worst sufferers, with nearly 85 percent of the world's cases. More than 30 percent of childhood deaths there are caused by malaria.

Perhaps the most charitable interpretation of the 1972 decision would be that it was intended as a demonstration by a fledgling federal agency, in its first major test, that it was genuinely a disinterested arm of the national executive and not a lackey to financial or private corporate interests. One can only say here that if public perceptions are to take precedence over fact in the formulation of policy, it's a sad day for science. Critics have seen the ruling as part of a deliberate policy of population control, in a period when global overpopulation has been widely promoted as one of the greatest problems that the world faces.

In the foregoing, I have leaned heavily on the book *Ecological Sanity*, by George Claus and Karen Bolander, which devotes almost six hundred pages to the subject of which I have managed to address only a few selected details briefly. The authors are meticulous in their treatment. They obviously read and studied the materials which in many cases expert witnesses who testified at the EPA hearing appeared not to have understood. In a number of instances they redid calculations and replotted graphs, showing data to indicate the reverse of what the authors of the papers maintained. In other words, as a source reference for anyone wanting seriously to grasp the issues at stake and how they were handled, I would recommend it as invaluable. It is, however, out of print. After reading a review, I managed to track a copy down in a used bookstore in New Jersey.

Silent Spring can be found in mass-market editions at any bookstore, and is reprinted regularly.

"VITAMIN R": RADIATION GOOD FOR YOUR HEALTH [212]

It is very difficult, and perhaps entirely impossible, to combat the effects of brainwashing by argument.
— Paul Feyerabend

RADIATION PHOBIA

It seems that the public is at last coming around to accepting that a nuclear power-generation plant cannot explode like a bomb. The majority that I talk to appear to concede, also, that the Chernobyl accident that occurred in the Soviet Union in 1986 was a result of practices and policy very different from the West's, and that there are other methods of bomb-making that are easier, quicker, cheaper, and safer than fooling around with used power-plant fuel. This leaves fear of radiation as probably the only effective weapon for carrying on the crusade against nuclear energy, as well as justifying what has become a lucrative and no-doubt for some, morally gratifying, cleanup industry. The key credo that keeps both sides of the act in business, re-aired periodically lest we forget, is that "no level of radiation is safe." In other words, any exposure to ionizing radiation, however small, is damaging to health. Yet despite the colossal cost to society in terms of a stalled energy policy, the waste of funds and effort on windmills and solar toys, and millions of tax dollars diverted into hauling away dirt and burying it in holes in the ground, the belief rests on a theoretical construct that has never been substantiated by evidence. In fact, what evidence there is tends to disprove it.

At levels encountered ordinarily—i.e., excluding bomb victims and patients subjected to massive medical doses, usually as a last resort in terminal situations—no measurable results of low-level radiation doses are actually observed at all. Low-level effects are *inferred* by taking a known high-level point where the effect is measurable, and assuming that it connects to the zero-point (zero dose, therefore zero effect) as a straight line. From this presumed relationship it is possible to read off as an act of faith the pro-rata effects that small doses ought to have, if one accepts the straight-line assumption. In the early days of radiation physics, when comparatively little was known, this was about as good a relationship as any to use when attempting to set safety standards for researchers and workers. By the same token, since little was known about the natural ability of biological systems to repair radiation damage, it was assumed that the effects would accrue cumulatively with dose—a bit like equating a shot of whiskey every night for a month with a full bottle straight down. If this over-stated the risk, then so much the better, for in the absence of firm knowledge one would obviously prefer to err toward the safe side.

However, somewhere along the line what started out as a sensible precaution came to be perceived as reality. The invisible but assumed effects then took on substance with the introduction of the curious practice of extrapolating them across the whole of an exposed population to derive a total figure for persons X dose, from which effects were deduced statistically. This would be like saying that since a temperature of 1000°C is lethal, 1 degree kills 1/1000th of a person. Therefore raising the temperatures of classrooms in schools containing a million children by two degrees will kill two thousand children. Yet this is the kind of model that the figures the media are so fond of repeating are based on. Research that has been known to the health and radiation physics community for many years indicates, however, that it is wrong.

"THE DOSE MAKES THE POISON": HORMESIS

Trying to emulate the labors of Hercules would cause most of us to drop dead from exhaustion. Nevertheless, jogging a few miles a week makes lots of people feel good and keeps them in shape. A dip in the boilers of an ocean liner would be decidedly damaging to one's health, but soaking in a hot tub is relaxing. Things that get lethal when taken to extremes are often beneficial in small quantities.

This has long been acknowledged for chemical and biological

toxins. Trace amounts of germicides can *increase* fermentation of bacteria. Too-small doses of antibiotics will stimulate growth of dormant bacteria that they are supposed to kill. A moderate amount of stress keeps the immune system fit and in good tone, no less than muscles. The phenomenon is known as "hormesis," from the Greek *hormo,* meaning "to stimulate." For around two decades, evidence has been mounting that hormesis holds true also for ionizing radiation. Not that sunbathing during a nuclear strike is good for you; but low levels aren't as bad as many would have us believe.

In the early eighties, Professor T. D. Luckey, a biochemist at the University of Missouri, published a study[213] of over twelve hundred experiments dating back to the turn of the century on the effects of low-level radiation on biota ranging from viruses, bacteria, and fungi through various plants and animals up to vertebrates. He found that, by all the criteria that biologists use to judge the well-being of living things, modest increases above the natural radiation background make life better: living things grow bigger and faster; they live longer; they get sick less often and recover sooner; they produce more offspring, more of which survive.

And the same appears to be true also of humans. The state that the EPA found as having the highest average level of radon in the home, Iowa, also has below-average cancer incidence.[214] The mountain states, with double the radiation background of the U.S. as a whole (cosmic rays are stronger at higher altitudes, and the rocks in those states have a high radioactive content), show a cancer rate way below Iowa's. The negative correlation— more radiation, less cancer—holds for the U.S. in general and extends worldwide.[215] The waters of such European spas as Lourdes, Bath, and Bad Gastein, known for their beneficial health effects since Roman times, are all found to have high radioactivity levels. British data on over ten thousand U.K. Atomic Energy Authority workers show cancer mortality to be 22 percent below the national average, while for Canada the figure is 33 percent.[216] Imagine the hysteria we'd be seeing if those numbers were the other way around.

This kind of relationship is represented not by a straight line, but by a *J*-shaped curve sloping upward to the right. Dose increases to the right; the damage that results is measured vertically. The leftmost tip of the *J* represents the point of no dose/no effect. ("No

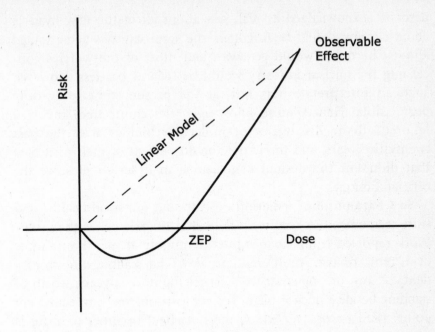

Shape of dose-response relationship showing hormesis

dose" means nothing above background. There's some natural background everywhere. You can't get away from it.) At first the curve goes down, meaning that the "damage" is negative, which is what we've been saying. It reaches an optimum at the bottom, and then turns upward—we're still better off than with no dose at all, but the beneficial effect is lessening. The beneficial effect disappears where the curve crosses its starting level again (the "zero-equivalent point), and beyond that we experience progressively greater discomfort, distress, and, eventually, death.

This has all been known for a long time, of course, to the authorities that set limits and standards. The sorry state of today's institutionalized science was brought home at a conference I attended some time ago now, in San Diego. Several of the speakers had been involved in the procedures that are followed for setting standards and guides for low-level ionizing radiation. The conventional model, upon which international limits and regulations are based, remains the Linear, Non-Threshold (LNT) version. Yet *all* the accumulated evidence contradicts it. According to the speakers, the reality of hormesis is absolutely conclusive. Were it to be acknowledged as real, just about all of the EPA hysteria about cleanups could be forgotten, the scare-statistics being touted about Chernobyl would go away, and most of the worries concerning the nuclear industry would be seen as baseless. However, such an interpretation is not, at the present time, politically permissible. Hence, quite knowingly, the committees involved ignored all the discoveries of molecular biology over the past twenty-five years, and threw out the 80 percent of their own data that didn't fit the desired conclusions in order to preserve the official fiction.

So what optimum radiation dose should our local health-food store recommend to keep us in the better-off area below the x-axis? Work reported from Japan[217] puts it roughly at two-thousandths of a "rem," or two "millirems," per day. That's about a tenth of a dental X ray, or one coast-to-coast jet flight, or a year's worth of standing beside a nuclear plant. For comparison, the "zero equivalent point" (ZEP) crossover where the net effect becomes harmful is at around two rems per day; fifty (note, we're talking rems now, not millirems) causes chronic radiation sickness, and a hundred is lethal.

On this basis, if regulatory authorities set their exposure limits too low, i.e., to the left of where the J bottoms out, then reducing levels to comply with them can actually make things worse. In a study of homes across 1,729 U.S. counties, Bernard Cohen, professor of physics and radiation health at the University of Pittsburgh, has found a correlation between radon levels and lung cancer mortality almost as high as that for cigarette smoking. Except, it's in the opposite direction: As radon goes up, cancer goes down. [218]

Perhaps radioactive tablets for those who don't get enough regular exposure wouldn't be a bad idea. Or a good use for radioactive waste might be to bury it underneath radon-deficient homes. And perhaps cereal manufacturers should be required to state on their boxes the percentage of the daily dietary requirement that a portion of their product contributes. After all, if radiation is essential for health in minimum, regular amounts, it meets the accepted definition of a vitamin.

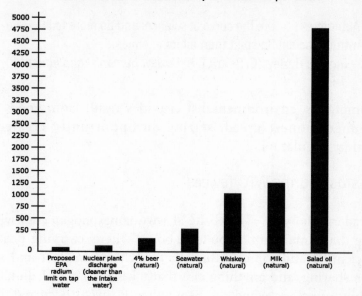

Concentration of Radioactivity in Picocuries per Liter

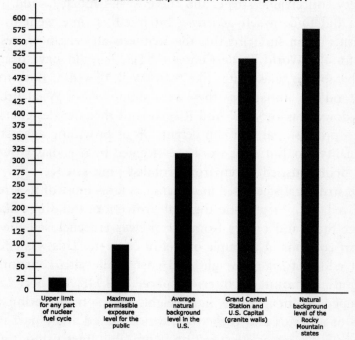

Full-Body Radiation Exposure in Millirems per Year:

Some comparisons to put things in perspective

Rip-Out Rip-Off: The Asbestos Racket

Authorities . . . are the curse of science; and do more to interfere
with the scientific spirit than all its enemies.
— Thomas Huxley, (C. Bibby: *T. H. Huxley: Humanist and Educator*)

Sometimes, environmentalist crusades result from good, old-
fashioned, honest greed, seizing an opportunity created by
fanatical regulators.

Asbestos and the WTC Towers

Readers who visit my website at www.jamesphogan.com will be
aware that I maintain a "bulletin board" there, carrying postings
on scientific and topical issues that catch my interest and seem
worth sharing, and anything else that takes my fancy. I didn't put
anything up there when the September 11 event occurred, since
it seemed that everyone in the world was already airing opinions
of every conceivable stripe, and there wasn't much to add. However, I did find myself getting a bit irked as time went by, and
criticisms began surfacing that the architects and engineers responsible for the World Trade Center (WTC) "should have designed
it to be able to take things like that." Well, they did. Both towers
withstood the impacts as they were supposed to. What brought
them down was the fire. And it turns out that the designers had
done a professional and competent job of providing against that
eventuality too, but their work was negated by over-hasty bureau-
cracy being pushed by environmentalist junk science.

The structural steel used in skyscrapers loses most of its strength
when red hot. To provide thermal protection, buildings like the
Empire State and others from the prewar era enclosed the steel
support columns in a couple of feet of concrete. This was effective
but it added a lot of weight and cost, while also consuming a
substantial amount of interior space. In 1948, Herbert Levine
developed an inexpensive, lightweight, spray-on insulation composed of asbestos and rock wool, which played a key part in the
postwar office-tower construction boom. Buildings using it would
tolerate a major fire for four hours before structural failure, allowing time for evacuation of the building below the fire and airlift

by helicopters from the roof for people trapped above. By 1971, when the two WTC towers were being built, the country was being beset by various environmentalist scare campaigns, one of which was the demonization of asbestos. When the use of asbestos was banned, Levine's insulation had already been installed in the first sixty-four floors. The newer lightweight construction didn't permit using the traditional heavy concrete insulation for the remaining fifty-four floors, and so a non-asbestos substitute was jury-rigged to complete the buildings. On studying the arrangement, Levine said, "If a fire breaks out above the sixty-fourth floor, that building will fall down." He was right.

I finally put an item up on the bulletin board in May, 2002, giving the gist of the above and also commenting that it was all a result of baseless hysteria, and there had never been a shred of evidence that insulating buildings with asbestos was harmful to health. A number of readers wrote to say that they hadn't been aware that the whole things was a scam, and asked for more details. I posted a follow-up piece accordingly, and since it seems relevant to the subject matter of this part of the book, I thought I'd include it here too.

INSULATED FROM REALITY

In the late 1960s, Dr. Irving Selikoff of the Mount Sinai Hospital, New York, published a study of lung cancers among insulation workers.[219] Although the figures indicted cigarette smoking as the primary culprit by far, media accounts played up the asbestos connection and hyped the "one-fiber-can-kill" mantra that was being repeated widely at the time—essentially the same false notion that we came across with low-level radiation. By 1978 the ensuing misrepresentations and exaggerations formed the basis of an OSHA report that predicted 58,000 to 73,000 cancer deaths each year from asbestos, on the basis of which the government upped its estimate of industry-related cancers from 2 percent to 40 percent.[220] A full-blown epidemic had become reality, and the witch-hunt was on. Mining in the U.S. Southwest ceased. Over a dozen companies were forced into bankruptcy by tens of thousands of tort cases, clogging the courts and costing thousands of jobs. An Emergency Response Act was passed by Congress mandating removal from over 700,000 schools and other buildings, worded such as to levy the cost on the school system, diverting tens of billions of dollars away from education. Many private and parochial schools were forced to close.

Yet ten years later the forecast of 58,000–73,000 deaths had been reduced to 13–15 (yes, a dozen-odd, not thousands), which the New Orleans-based Fifth U.S. Circuit Court of Appeals threw out in November 1988, because the EPA was unable to their satisfaction to substantiate even that figure. But by then a lucrative legal and removal industry worth an estimated $150–200 billion had come into being that many interests were not about to let go away. So the country continued to witness such absurdities as space-suited OSHA workers conducting tests of air samples among unprotected children in school buildings where the fiber content of the air was lower than in the street outside. After walls were torn down and the insulation removed, levels of airborne asbestos measured up to forty thousand times higher than it had been before—remaining so for months afterward.

But the whole nonsense, it turns out, traces back to phobia of a word. "Asbestos" is a generic name for a family of several types of related but distinct materials. And as with mushrooms, the particular type one is dealing with makes the world of a difference.

Ninety-five percent of the asbestos ever used in the U.S. and Canada, and 100 percent of that mined there, is the "chrysotile," or "white" form, well suited to building insulation, auto brake linings, cement, and the like on account of its strength and fire resistance. It consists of a tubular fiber that is dissolved and expelled by the lungs, and represents a negligible cancer hazard—21,500 times less than cigarettes, according to a Harvard study. [221] Exposure over many years to the high concentrations that existed in the unregulated workplace in times gone by can, it is true, lead to the lung condition known as asbestosis, where the tissue becomes fibrous and ceases functioning. But similar problems exist with heavy concentrations of coal or silica dust, baking flour, or any other dusty environment, whatever the material. No excess cancers above the population average have been found from exposure to the chrysotile variety of asbestos.

The other significant form is crocidolite, also known as "blue asbestos," a hard, needlelike fiber that lodges in the tissues and is deadly. As little as three months of exposure can result in fatal cancers not only of the lungs but also the body cavities. It is mined only in South Africa, and was used during the 1930s and '40s in such demanding areas as warship construction, causing cancers among shipyard workers that became apparent only in later years. So the true problem, while real, is one of the past.

But the EPA legislators ignored this distinction and classified *all* asbestos equally as a carcinogen, despite being told of these differences in scientific reports submitted in 1978, 1979, and 1984, and severe criticism from *Science* and *The Lancet*. Sir Richard Doll, the Oxford epidemiologist who proved the causal link between cigarette smoking and lung cancer, wrote of their decision, "No arguments based even loosely on [these estimates] should be taken seriously. It seems likely that whoever wrote the OSHA paper did so for political rather than scientific reasons."[222] Quite perspicacious, possibly. In the late 1980s, the EPA director involved became president of one of the largest asbestos abatement companies in the United States.

A statistician who helped produce the original OSHA paper later lamented of the fiasco, "We did what scientists so often do, which was to use . . . estimates without questioning them."[223] Wrong. It's what regulators bent on advancing a political ideology do, not scientists interested in facts.

In this connection, it should also be recalled that the O-ring failure that was finally pinpointed as the cause of the *Challenger* shuttle disaster occurred with the first use of a replacement for the original sealant putty, well suited to the task, that had been used safely in all prior shuttle missions and seventy-seven successful *Titan III* rocket launches. So why was it replaced? Under EPA regulations it had to be phased out because it contained asbestos— as if astronauts are going to climb out of a spacecraft and start snorting it.

MAKERS AND TAKERS

So bureaucrats and sloppy legislators prosper, while people who actually produce something useful are thrown out of work, schools are closed or robbed of their funding, and competently designed structures and systems are sabotaged by incompetents. I hadn't followed the asbestos story after the eighties, until my attention was drawn to its connection with the WTC tragedy. Since the press seemed to have gotten the facts straight finally, I had naively

assumed that the matter was effectively ended, the damage consigned
to the endless catalog of past silliness. And then I came across an
article by Arthur Robinson in the November 2002 issue of his
newsletter, *Access to Energy*, entitled "Goodbye to Union Carbide."
The extracts below need no comment.

> Union Carbide, now a division of Dow Chemical, has
> many plants that provide numerous useful plastics and
> other essential synthetic materials to American industry
> and individuals. My father designed and supervised the
> construction of some of these Union Carbide plants.
>
> "Dow Chemical Held Responsible In Asbestos Cases"
> by Susan Warren in *The Wall Street* Journal, October 25,
> 2002, p. A6, reports, however, that the scourge of asbestos
> litigation has now hit Union Carbide. A Charleston, West
> Virginia, jury has ruled in favor of no less than 2,000
> 'plaintiffs' in finding that Union Carbide operated unsafe
> facilities from 1945 to 1980.
>
> Regardless of Dow's best legal efforts, this is the
> beginning of the end for another American corporation.
> Asbestos, useful and safe, was used throughout Ameri-
> can industry for more than a century. It was also used
> in nearly every research laboratory in the United States
> for everything from lab benches to fume hoods. We
> suppose that when these leeches are finished with
> American industry, they will go after the endowments
> of our universities too. . . .
>
> Why conduct military operations against terrorists
> abroad when we are allowing people with no better prin-
> ciples to destroy our country in American courts? The
> "asbestos lawyers" are doing more damage to the United
> States than all the terrorists on Earth will ever do. . . .
> If, however, the legal profession continues to refuse to
> police itself, this problem will continue to worsen.
>
> It will be no pleasure to watch my father's life's work
> along with that of the tens of thousands of productive
> men and women who built Union Carbide ruined by
> these reprehensible thieves who have perverted and are
> destroying America's legal system as well.

Section Notes

142 Explored in greater detail in "Know Nukes," Hogan, 1988

143 See Simon 1981 and 1990 for a view of population and its implications that presents an alternate picture to the standard fare of doom and gloom

144 Elmsley, 1992

145 Tomkin, 1993

146 Baliunas, 2002

147 Idso, 1992

148 *After the Warming*. PBS, 1990. Ironically, this was paid for by PBS after they rejected the British documentary *The Greenhouse Conspiracy*, which challenged the global warming theory, as being too one-sided. The *Financial Times* of London judged *The Greenhouse Conspiracy* as being "quite possibly the best science documentary of the year."

149 Environment and Climate News, May 2000, p. 8

150 Stevenson, 1996

151 For example Weber, 1990; Ellsaesser, 1992; Robinson, 1997

152 Kegwin, L. D., *Science*, 1997, pp. 274, 1504–1508

153 For example Ginenthal 1997, p.178 ff.

154 Baliunas, 1994

155 Ginenthal, 1997, pp. 178 ff

156 Smith and Schultz, 1992

157 Idso, 1992, p. 424

158 See Hayden, 2002

159 Robinson and Robinson, 1997

160 Singer, 1997(a)

161 Further details available from the Science and Environmental Policy Project, Fairfax, VA

162 Singer, 1997

163 Accounts in *The Energy Advocate*, Vol. 2, No. 4, November 1997, and *Access to Energy*, Vol. 25, No. 7, March 1998

164 Singer, 1999

165 Full text in Access to Energy, February, 1998. Also on the web, with a list of signatories, at http://www.oism.org/pproject/

166 *eco-logic*, November/December 1997, p. 21. From 1229 Broadway, #313, Bangor, ME 04401

167 Pease, 1989

168 Maduro and Schaurhammer, 1992

169 Ellsaesser, 1991

170 Ellsaesser, 1978 and 1978(a)

171 Molina and Rowland, 1974

172 Pease, 1990; also personal communications

173 Maduro, 1989

174 Maduro and Schaurhammer, 1992, p. 11 ff.

175 Dobson, 1968

176 Ellsaesser, 1991, p. 5

177 Ellsaesser, 1991, p. 7

178 Address to the St. Paul, Minnesota, Rotary Club, April 14

179 *Access to Energy*, May, 1991 and July, 1991

180 Scotto et al., 1988

181 Penkett, 1989

182 Maduro and Schaurhammer, 1992, p. 159

183 Kerr and McElroy, 1993

184 Robinson, 1994

185 Singer, 1994

186 Pike, 1979; Edwards, 1993, p.c23

187 Pike, 1979

188 Jukes, 1994, p.47

189 Edwards, 1992, p. 41

190 McCloskey, M., news release, February 25

191 Edwards, 1993, p.23

192 Described in Claus & Bolander, 1977, p. 303

193 Claus and Bolander, 1977, p. 323

194 Details of all these in Claus and Bolander, 1977, p. 328 ff.

195 Epstein, 1971

196 Claus and Bolander, 1977, p. 335

197 Fitzhugh and Nelson, 1947, described in Claus and Bolander, 1977, p. 336

198 Cameron and Cheng, 1951. See Claus and Bolander, 1977, p. 338

199 Hansen et al, 1969; see Claus and Bolander, 1977, p. 342

200 Claus & Bolander, 1977, p.346 ff.

201 *The Birds*, Life Magazine Nature Library, New York, 1963

202 "42nd Christmas Bird Count," *Audubon Magazine*, 1942; "61st Christmas Bird Count," *Audubon Field Notes 15*, 1961

203 Edwards, 1985, p. 195 ff.

204 Edwards, 1995, p. 197

205 Pike, 1979, p. 66

206 Pike, 1979, p. 66

207 *Ibid.*

208 Claus and Bolander, 1977, p. 384–385

209 Examples from Edwards, 1985, p. 207

210 *Doctors for Disaster Preparedness* newsletter, Vol. XVI, No.6, November, 1999, p. 2. Tucson, AZ

211 Edmund M. Sweeney, 1972, *Hearing Examiner's Recommended Findings, Conclusions, and Orders* (40 CFR 164.32)

212 This is also taken from "Fact Free Science," which appeared in *Analog*, April 1995

213 Luckey, 1980

214 EPA statement October 15, 1989, reported in Access to Energy, December

215 Luckey, 1992

216 *Nuclear Issues*, Vol. 12, 1993, pp. 2–3, British Nuclear Fuels

217 K. Sakamoto, *Health Physics Society Newsletter*, May 1991

218 *Health Physics*, Vol. 57, 1989, p. 897

219 Bennett, 1991

220 Bennett, 1993

221 Reported in *New York Post*, February 12, 1999: "The Great Asbestos Ripoff"

222 Bennett, 1993

223 Schneiderman, Journ. *Nat. Cancer Inst.*, April 1992. Quoted in Bennett, 1993(a)

SIX
CLOSING RANKS

AIDS Heresy In The Viricentric Universe

Sometimes a deception cannot be prevented from running its course, even at terrible cost, until eventually it collides with reality.
— Phillip Johnson

Maybe someday AIDS experts will be as well informed as they are well funded.
— Christine Maggiore, director, Alive and Well

Science is supposed to be concerned with objective truth—the way things are, that lie beyond the power of human action or desires to influence. Facts determine what is believed, and the consequences, good or bad, fall where they may. Politics is concerned with those things that are within human ability to change, and in the realm of politics, beliefs are encouraged that advance political agendas. All too often in this case, truth is left to fall where it may.

When the hysteria over AIDS broke out in the early eighties, I was living in the mother lode country in the Sierra Nevada foothills of northern California. Since I had long dismissed the mass media as a credible source of information on anything that mattered, I didn't take a lot of notice. A close friend and drinking buddy of mine at that time was a former Air Force physicist who helped with several books that I worked on there. Out of curiosity we checked the actual figures from official sources such as various city and state health departments. The number of cases for the whole of California turned out to be somewhere between 1,100 and 1,200, and these were confined pretty much totally to a couple of well-defined parts of San Francisco and Los Angeles associated with drugs and other ways of life that I wasn't into. So was this the great "epidemic" that we'd been hearing about? Ah, but we didn't understand, people told us. It was caused by a new virus that was 100 percent lethal and about to explode out into the population at large. You could catch it from sex, toilet seats, your dentist, from breathing the air, and once you did there was no defense. "One in five heterosexuals could be dead from AIDS at the end of the next three years."[224] Our species could be staring at extinction.

But I didn't buy that line either. I can't really offer a rationally packaged explanation of why. Part of it was that although AIDS had been around for some years, it was still clearly confined overwhelmingly to the original risk groups to which the term had first been applied. If it was going to "explode" out into the general population, there should have been unmistakable signs of its happening by then. There weren't. And another large part, I suppose, was that scaring the public had become such a lucrative and politically fruitful industry that the more horrific the situation was made to sound, the more skeptically I reacted. All the claims contradicted what my own eyes and ears told me. Nobody that I knew had it. Nobody that I knew knew anybody who had it. But "everybody knew" it was everywhere. Now, I don't doubt that when the Black Death hit Europe, or when smallpox reached the Americas, people *knew* they had an epidemic. When you need a billion-dollar propaganda industry to tell you there's a problem, you don't have a major problem.

So I got on with life and largely forgot about the issue until I visited the University of California, Berkeley, to meet Peter Duesberg, a professor of molecular and cell biology, whom a mutual friend had urged me to contact. Talking to Duesberg and some of his colleagues, both then and on later occasions, left me stupefied and led to my taking a new interest in the subject. This has persisted over the years since and involved contacts with others not only across the U.S., but as far removed as England, Ireland, Germany, Russia, Australia, and South Africa. We like to think that the days of the Inquisition are over. Well, here's what can happen to politically incorrect science when it gets in the way of a band-wagon being propelled by *lots* of money—and to a scientist who ignores it and attempts simply to point at what the facts seem to be trying to say.

An Industry Out of Work

The first popular misunderstanding to clear up is that "AIDS" is not something new that appeared suddenly around 1980. It's a collection of old diseases that have been around for as long as medical history, that began showing up in clusters at greater than the average incidence.[225] An example was *Pneumocystis carinnii*, a rare type of pneumonia caused by a normally benign microbe that inhabits the lungs of just about every human being on the planet; it becomes pathogenic (disease-causing) typically in cancer patients whose immune systems are suppressed by chemotherapy. And, indeed, the presence of other opportunistic infections such as esophagal yeast infections confirmed immunosuppression in all of these early cases. Many of them also suffered from a hitherto rare blood-vessel tumor known as Kaposi's sarcoma. All this came as a surprise to medical authorities, since the cases were concentrated among males aged twenty to forty, usually considered a healthy age group, and led the conditions being classified together as a syndrome presumed to have some single underlying cause. The victims were almost exclusively homosexuals, which led to a suspicion of an infectious agent, with sexual practices as the main mode of transmission. This seemed to be confirmed when other diseases associated with immune deficiency, such as TB among drug abusers, and various infections experienced by hemophiliacs and transfusion recipients, were included in the same general category too, which by this time was officially designated Acquired Immune Deficiency Syndrome, or "AIDS."

Subsequently, the agent responsible was stated to be a newly discovered virus of the kind known as "retroviruses," later given the name Human Immunodeficiency Virus, or HIV. The AIDS diseases were opportunistic infections that struck following infection by HIV, which was said to destroy "T-helper cells," a subset of white blood cells which respond to the presence of invading microbes and stimulate other cells into producing the appropriate antibodies against them. This incapacitated the immune system and left the victim vulnerable.

And there you have the basic paradigm that still pretty much describes the official line today. This virus that nobody had heard of before—the technology to detect it didn't exist until the eighties—could lurk anywhere, and no vaccine existed to protect against it. Then it was found in association with various other kinds of sickness in Africa, giving rise to speculations that it might have originated there, and the media gloried in depictions of a global pandemic sweeping across continents out of control. Once smitten there was no cure, and progression to exceptionally unpleasant forms of physical devastation and eventual death was inevitable and irreversible.

While bad news for some, this came at a propitious time for a huge, overfunded and largely out-of-work army within the biomedical establishment, which, it just so happened, had been set up, equipped, trained, and on the lookout for exactly such an emergency. [226] Following the elimination of polio in the fifties and early sixties, the medical schools had been churning out virologists eager for more Nobel Prizes. New federal departments to monitor and report on infectious diseases stood waiting to be utilized. But the war on cancer had failed to find a viral cause, and all these forces in need of an epidemic converged in a crusade to unravel the workings of the deadly new virus and produce a vaccine against it. No other virus was ever so intensively studied. Published papers soon numbered thousands, and jobs were secure as federal expenditures grew to billions of dollars annually. Neither was the largess confined to just the medical-scientific community and its controlling bureaucracies. As HIV came to be automatically equated with AIDS, anyone testing positive qualified as a disaster victim eligible for treatment at public expense, which meant lucrative consultation and testing fees, and treatment with some of the most profitable drugs that the pharmaceuticals industry has ever marketed.

And beyond that, with no vaccine available, the sole means of prevention lay in checking the spread of HIV. This meant funding for another growth sector of promotional agencies, advisory centers, educational campaigns, as well as support groups and counselors to minister to afflicted victims and their families. While many were meeting harrowing ends, others had never had it so good. Researchers who would otherwise have spent their lives peering through microscopes and cleaning Petri dishes became millionaires setting up companies to produce HIV kits and drawing royalties for the tests performed. Former dropouts were achieving political visibility and living comfortably as organizers of programs financed by government grants and drug-company handouts. It was a time for action, not thought; spreading the word, not asking questions. Besides, who would want to mess with this golden goose?

STORM-CLOUD OVER THE PARADE

And then in the late eighties, Peter Duesberg began arguing that AIDS might not be caused by HIV at all—nor by any other virus, come to that. In fact, he didn't even think that "AIDS" was infectious! This was not coming from any lightweight on the periphery of the field. Generally acknowledged as one of the world's leading authorities on retroviruses, the first person to fully sequence a retroviral genome, Duesberg had played a major role in exploring the possibility of viruses as the cause of cancers. In fact it was mainly his work in the sixties that showed this conclusively not to be the case, which had not exactly ingratiated him to many when that lavishly funded line of research was brought to a close. But this didn't prevent his being tipped as being in line for a Nobel Prize, named California Scientist of the Year in 1971, awarded an Outstanding Investigator Grant by the National Institutes for Health in 1985, and inducted to the prestigious National Academy of Sciences in 1986.

What Duesberg saw was different groups of people getting sick in different ways for different reasons that had to do with the particular risks that those groups had always faced. No common cause tying them all together had ever been convincingly demonstrated; indeed, why such conditions as dementia and wasting disease should have been considered at all was something of a mystery, since they are not results of immunosuppression. Drug users were ruining their immune systems with the substances they were putting into their bodies, getting TB and pneumonia from unsterile needles and street drugs, and wasting as a consequence of the insomnia and malnutrition that typically go with the lifestyle; homosexuals were getting sarcomas from the practically universal use of nitrite inhalants, and yeast infections from the suppression of protective bacteria by overdosing on antibiotics used prophylactically; hemophiliacs were immune-suppressed by the repeated infusion of foreign protein contained in the plasmas of the unpurified clotting factors they had been given up to that time; blood recipients were already sick for varying reasons; people being treated with the "antiviral" drug AZT were being poisoned; Africans were suffering from totally different diseases long characteristic of poverty in tropical environments; and a few individuals were left who got sick for reasons that would never be explained. The only difference in recent years was that some of those groups had gotten bigger. The increases matched closely the epidemic in drug use that had grown since the late sixties and early seventies, and Duesberg proposed drugs as the primary cause of the rises that were being seen. [227]

Although Duesberg is highly qualified in this field, the observations that he was making really didn't demand doctorate knowledge or rarefied heights of intellect to understand. For a start, years after their appearances, the various "AIDS" diseases remained obstinately confined to the original risk groups, and the victims were still over 90 percent male. This isn't the pattern of an infectious disease, which spreads and affects everybody, male and female alike. For a new disease loose in a defenseless population, the spread would be exponential. And this was what had been predicted in the early days, but it just hadn't happened. While the media continued to terrify the public with a world of their own creation, planet Earth was getting along okay. Heterosexuals who didn't use drugs weren't getting AIDS; for the U.S., subtracting the known risk groups left about five hundred per year—fewer than the fatalities from contaminated tap water. The spouses and partners of AIDS victims weren't catching it. Prostitutes who didn't do drugs weren't getting it, and customers of prostitutes weren't getting it. In short, these had all the characteristics of textbook non-infectious diseases.

It is an elementary principle of science and medicine that correlation alone is no proof of cause. If A is reported as generally occurring with B, there are four possible explanations: (1) A causes B; (2) B causes A; (3) something else causes both A and B; (4) the correlation is just coincidence or has been artificially exaggerated, e.g., by biased collecting of data. There's no justification in jumping to a conclusion like (1) until the other three have been rigorously eliminated.

In the haste to find an infectious agent, Duesberg maintained, the role of HIV had been interpreted the wrong way around. Far from being a common cause of the various conditions called "AIDS," HIV itself was an opportunistic infection that made itself known in the final stages of immune-system deterioration brought about in other ways. In a sense, AIDS caused HIV. Hence, HIV acted as a "marker" of high-risk groups, but was not in itself responsible for the health problems that those groups were experiencing. The high correlation between HIV and AIDS that was constantly being alluded to was an artifact of the way in which AIDS was defined:

HIV + indicator disease = AIDS
Indicator disease without HIV = Indicator disease.

So if you've got all the symptoms of TB, and you test positive for HIV, you've got AIDS. But if you have a condition that's clinically indistinguishable and don't test positive for HIV, you've got TB.

And that, of course, would have made the problem scientifically and medically trivial.

ANATOMY OF AN EPIDEMIC

When a scientific theory fails in its predictions, it is either modified or abandoned. Science welcomes informed criticism and is always ready to reexamine its conclusions in the light of new evidence or an alternative argument. The object, after all, is to find out what's true. But it seems that what was going on here wasn't science. Duesberg was met by a chorus of outrage and ridicule, delivered with a level of vehemence that is seldom seen within professional circles. Instead of willingness to reconsider, he was met by stratagems designed to conceal or deny that the predictions were failing. This is the kind of reaction typical of politics, not science, usually referred to euphemistically as "damage control."

For example, statistics for new AIDS cases were always quoted as cumulative figures that could only get bigger, contrasting with the normal practice with other diseases of reporting annual figures, where any decline is clear at a glance. And despite the media's ongoing stridency about an epidemic out of control, the actual figures from the Centers for Disease Control (CDC), for every category, *were* declining, and had been since a peak around 1988. This was masked by repeated redefinitions to cover more diseases, so that what wasn't AIDS one day became AIDS the next, causing more cases to be diagnosed. This happened five times from 1982 to 1993, with the result that the first nine months of 1993 showed as an overall rise of 5 percent what would otherwise—i.e., by the 1992 definition—have been a 33 percent drop. [228]

Currently (January 2003) the number of indicator diseases is twenty-nine. One of the newer categories added in 1993 was cervical cancer. (Militant femininists had been protesting that men received too much of the relief appropriations for AIDS victims.) Nobody was catching anything new, but suddenly in one group of the population what hadn't been AIDS one day became AIDS the next, and we had the headlines loudly proclaiming that heterosexual women were the fastest-growing AIDS group.

A similar deception is practiced with percentages, as illustrated by figures publicized in Canada, whose population is around 40 million. In 1995, a total of 1,410 adult AIDS cases were reported, 1,295 (91.8%) males and 115 (8.2%) females. The year 1996 showed a startling decrease in new cases to 792, consisting of 707 males (89.2%) and 85 females (10.8%). So the number of adult female

AIDS cases actually decreased by 26% from 1995 to 1996. Yet, even though the actual number decreased, because the percentage of the total represented by women increased from 8.2% in 1995 to 10.8% in 1996, the Quarterly Surveillance Report (August 1997) from the Bureau of HIV/AIDS and STD at the Canadian Laboratory Centre for Disease Control issued the ominous warning that AIDS cases among Canadian women had dramatically increased. [229]

Meanwhile, a concerted campaign across the schools and campuses was doing its part to terrorize young people over the ravages of teenage AIDS. Again, actual figures tell a different story. The number of cases in New York City reported by the CDC for ages 13–19 from 1981 to the end of June 1992 were 872. When homosexuals, intravenous drug users, and hemophiliacs are eliminated, the number left not involving these risks (or not admitting to them) reduces to a grand total of 16 in an eleven-year period. (Yes, 16. You did read that right.) [230]

The correlation between HIV and AIDS that was repeatedly cited as proving cause was maintained by denying the violations of it. Obviously if HIV is the cause, the disease can't exist without it. (You don't catch flu without having the flu virus.) At a conference in Amsterdam in 1992, Duesberg, who had long been maintaining that dozens of known instances of AIDS patients testing negative for HIV had been suppressed, produced 4,621 cases that he had found in the literature. The response was to define them as a new condition designated Idiopathic CD4+ Lymphocytopenia, or ICL, which is obscurese for "unexplained AIDS symptoms." The figures subsequently disappeared from official AIDS-counting statistics. [231]

QUESTIONING THE INFECTIOUS THEORY

Viral diseases strike typically after an incubation period of days or weeks, which is the time in which the virus can replicate before the body develops an immunity. When this didn't happen for AIDS, the notion of a "slow" virus was introduced, which would delay the onset of symptoms for months. When a year passed with no sign of an epidemic, the number was upped to five years; when nothing happened then either, to ten. Now we're being told ten to fifteen. Inventions to explain failed predictions are invariably a sign of a theory in trouble. (Note: This is not the same as a virus going dormant, as can happen with some types of herpes, and reactivating later, such as in times of stress. In these cases, the most pronounced disease symptoms occur at the time of primary infection, before immunity is established. Subsequent outbreaks are less severe—immunity is present, but reduced—and when they do occur, the virus is abundant and active. This does not describe AIDS. A long delay before any appearance of sickness is characteristic of the cumulative buildup of a toxic cause, like lung cancer from smoking or liver cirrhosis from alcohol excess.)

So against all this, on what grounds was AIDS said to be infectious in the first place? Just about the only argument, when you strip it down, seems to be the correlation—that AIDS occurs in geographic and risk-related clusters. This is not exactly compelling. Victims of airplane crashes and Montezuma's revenge are found in clusters too, but nobody takes that as evidence that they catch their condition from each other. It all becomes even more curious when you examine the credentials of the postulated transmitting agent, HIV.

One of the major advances in medicine during the nineteenth century was the formulation of scientific procedures to determine if a particular disease is infectious—carried by some microbe that's being passed around—and if so, to identify the microbe; or else a result of some factor in the environment, such as a dietary deficiency, a local genetic trait, a toxin. The prime criteria for making this distinction are known as Koch's Postulates, from a paper by the German medical doctor Robert Koch published in 1884 following years of investigation into such conditions as anthrax, wound infections, and TB. It's ironic to note that one of problems Koch was trying to find answers to was the tendency of medical professionals, excited by the recent discoveries of bacteria, to rush into finding infectious causes for everything, even where there were none, and their failure to distinguish between harmless "passenger" microbes and the pathogens actually responsible for illness.

There are four postulates, and when all are met, the case is considered proved beyond reasonable doubt that the disease is infectious and caused by the suspected agent. HIV as the cause of AIDS fails every one. [232]

(1) The microbe must be found in all cases of the disease.

By the CDC's own statistics, for 25 percent of the cases diagnosed in the U.S. the presence of HIV has been inferred presumptively, without actual testing. And anyway, by 1993, over four thousand cases of people dying of AIDS diseases were admitted to be HIV-free. The redefinition of the criteria for AIDS introduced during that year included a category in which AIDS can be diagnosed without a positive test for HIV. (How this can be so while at the same time HIV is insisted to be the cause of AIDS is a good question. The required logic is beyond my abilities.) The World Health Organization's clinical case-definition for AIDS in Africa is not based on an HIV test but on certain clinical symptoms, none of which are new or uncommon on the African continent. Subsequent testing of sample groups diagnosed as having AIDS has given negative result in the order of 50 percent. Why diseases totally different from those listed in America and Europe, now not even required to show any HIV status, should be called the same thing is another good question.

*(2) The microbe must be isolated from the host
and grown in a pure culture.*

This is to ensure that the disease was caused by the suspect germ and not by something unidentified in a mixture of substances. The tissues and body fluids of a patient with a genuine viral disease will have so many viruses pouring out of infected cells that it is a straightforward matter—standard undergraduate exercise—to separate a pure sample and compare the result with known cataloged types. There have been numerous claims of isolating HIV, but closer examination shows them to be based on liberal stretchings of what the word has always been understood to mean. For example, using chemical stimulants to shock a fragment of defective RNA to express itself in a cell culture removed from any active immune system is a very different thing from demonstrating active viral infection.[233] In short, no isolation of HIV has been achieved which meets the standards that virology normally requires. More on this later.

(3) The microbe must be capable of reproducing the original disease when introduced into a susceptible host.

This asks to see that the disease can be reproduced by injecting the allegedly causative microbe into an uninfected, otherwise healthy host. It does not mean that the microbe must cause the disease every time (otherwise everyone would be sick all the time).

Two ways in which this condition can be tested are injection into laboratory animals, and accidental infection of humans. (Deliberate infection of humans would be unethical). Chimpanzees have been injected since 1983 and developed antibodies, showing that the virus "takes," but none has developed AIDS symptoms. There have been a few vaguely described claims of health workers catching AIDS from needle sticks and other HIV exposure, but nothing conclusively documented. For comparison, the figure for hepatitis infections is fifteen hundred per year. Hence, even if the case for AIDS were proved, hepatitis is hundreds of times more virulent. Yet we don't have a panic about it.

(4) The microbe must be found present in the host so infected.

This is irrelevant in the case of AIDS, since (3) has never been met.

The typical response to this violating of a basic principle that has served well for a century is either to ignore it or say that HIV is so complex that it renders Koch's Postulates obsolete. But Koch's Postulates are simply a formalization of commonsense logic, not a statement about microbes per se. The laws of logic don't become obsolete, any more than mathematics. And if the established criteria for infectiousness are thrown away, then by what alternative standard is HIV supposed to be judged infectious? Just clusterings of like symptoms? Simple correlations with no proof of any cause-effect relationship? That's called superstition, not science. It puts medicine back two hundred years.

SCIENCE BY PRESS CONFERENCE

So how did HIV come to be singled out as the cause to begin with? The answer seems to be, at a press conference. In April 1984, the Secretary of Health and Human Services, Margaret Heckler, sponsored a huge event and introduced the NIH researcher Robert

Gallo to the press corps as the discoverer of the (then called HTLV-III) virus, which was declared to be the probable cause of AIDS. This came before publication of any papers in the scientific journals, violating the normal protocol of giving other scientists an opportunity to review such findings before they were made public. No doubt coincidentally, the American claim to fame came just in time to preempt the French researcher Luc Montagnier of the Pasteur Institute in Paris, who had already published in the literature his discovery of what later turned out to be the same virus. From that point on, official policy was set in stone. All investigation of alternatives was dropped, and federal funding went only to research that reflected the approved line. This did not make for an atmosphere of dissent among career-minded scientists, who, had they been politically free to do so, might have pointed out that even if the cause of AIDS were indeed a virus, the hypothesis of its being HIV raised some distinctly problematical questions.

Proponents of the HIV dogma assert repeatedly that "the evidence for HIV is overwhelming." When they are asked to produce it or cite some reference, the usual response is ridicule or some ad hominem attack imputing motives. But never a simple statement of facts. Nobody, to my knowledge, has ever provided a definitive answer to the simple question "Where is the study that proves HIV causes AIDS?" It's just something that "everybody knows" is true. Yet despite the tens of thousands of papers written, nobody can produce one that says why.

Reference is sometimes made to several papers that Gallo published in *Science* after the press conference, deemed to have settled the issue before any outside scientists had seen them. [234] But even if the methods described are accepted as demonstrating true viral isolation as claimed, which as we've seen has been strongly disputed, they show a presence of HIV in less than half of the patients with opportunistic infections, and less than a third with Kaposi's sarcoma—the two most characteristic AIDS diseases. This is "overwhelming" evidence? It falls short of the standards that would normally be expected of a term-end dissertation, never mind mobilizing the federal resources of the United States and shutting down all investigation of alternatives.

And the case gets even shakier than that.

Biology's Answer to Dark Matter? The Virus that Isn't There

Viruses make you sick by killing cells. When viruses are actively replicating at a rate sufficient to cause disease, either because immunity hasn't developed yet or because the immune system is too defective to contain them, there's no difficulty in isolating them from the affected tissues. With influenza, a third of the lung cells are infected; with hepatitis, just about all of the liver cells. In the case of AIDS, typically one in one thousand T-cells shows any sign of HIV, even for terminally ill cases—and even then, no distinction is made of inactive or defective viruses, or totally nonfunctional viral fragments. But even if every one were a lethally infected cell, the body's replacement rate is thirty times higher. This simply doesn't add up to damage on a scale capable of causing disease. [235]

Retroviruses, the class to which HIV belongs, survive by encoding their RNA sequences into the chromosomal DNA of the host cell (the reverse of the normal direction of information flow in cell replication, which is DNA to RNA to protein, hence the name). When that part of the host chromosome comes to be transcribed, the cell's protein-manufacturing machinery makes a new retrovirus, which leaves by budding off through the cell membrane. The retrovirus therefore leaves the cell intact and functioning, and survives by slipping a copy of itself from time to time into the cell's normal production run. This strategy is completely different from that of the more prevalent "lytic" viruses, which take over the cell machinery totally to mass-produce themselves until the cell is exhausted, at which point they rupture the membrane, killing the cell, and move on, much in the style of locusts. This is what gives the immune system problems, and in the process causes colds, flu, polio, rabies, measles, mumps, yellow fever, and so on.

But a retrovirus produces so few copies of itself that it's easy meat for an immune system battle-trained at dealing with lytic viruses. For this reason, the main mode of transmission for a retrovirus is from mother to child, meaning that the host organism needs to live to reproductive maturity. [236] A retrovirus that killed its host wouldn't be reproductively viable. Many human retroviruses have been studied, and all are harmless. (Some rare animal cancers arise from specific genes inserted retrovirally into the host DNA. But in these cases tumors form rapidly and predictably soon after infection—completely unlike the situation with AIDS. And a cancer is due to cells proliferating wildly—just the opposite of killing them.)

HIV conforms to the retroviral pattern and is genetically unremarkable. It doesn't kill T-cells, even in cultures raised away from a body ("in vitro"), with no immune system to suppress it. Indeed, HIV for research is propagated in immortal lines of the very cell which, to cause AIDS, HIV is supposed to kill!—and in concentrations far higher than have ever been observed in any human, with or without AIDS. Separated from its host environment it promptly falls to pieces.

Most people carry traces of just about every microbe found in their normal habitat around with them all the time. The reason they're not sick all the time is that their immune system keeps the microbes inactive or down to numbers that can't cause damage. An immune system that has become dysfunctional to the point where it can't even keep HIV in check is in trouble. On their way downhill, depending on the kind of risk they're exposed to, every AIDS group has its own way of accumulating a cocktail of just about everything that's going around—unsterile street drugs; shared needles; promiscuity; accumulated serum from multiple blood donors. By the time HIV starts to register too, as well as everything else, you're right down in the lowest 5% grade. And those are the people who typically get AIDS. Hence, HIV's role as a marker of a risk group that collects microbes. Far from being the ferocious cell-killer painted by the media, HIV turns out to be a dud.

Some researchers, looking skeptically at the assortment of RNA fragments, bits of protein, and other debris from which the existence of HIV is inferred go even further and question if there is really any such entity at all. (*Question:* If so, then what's replicating in those culture dishes? *Answer:* It has never been shown conclusively that anything introduced from the outside is replicating. Artificially stimulating "something" into expressing itself—it could be a strip of "provirus" code carried in the culture-cell's DNA—is a long way from demonstrating an active, pathogenic virus from a human body.)

A research group in Perth, Western Australia, headed by Eleni Papadopulos-Eleopulos, finds that *every one* of the proteins that the orthodox theory interprets as components of a viral antibody can be expressed by the DNA of any cell in the human body

KICKING THE SACRED COW

subjected to sufficient levels of oxidative stress—without any infectious agent from another individual being present at all. [237]

Is it not significant that chemical stimulation of precisely this nature is needed to induce "HIV replication" in cultures? Immuno-suppressive oxidative stress, as a consequence either of environment or behavior, is also a common denominator across all of the recognized AIDS risk groups. If this explanation is correct, it implies that immune systems under stress from such causes as toxic drug assault or overload by foreign proteins frequently begin manufacturing proteins that parts of the rich mixture of antibodies usually found in such circumstances react to. Finding out precisely what these proteins do and why they are produced would perhaps be a better use for the billions of dollars so far spent futilely on conventional AIDS research. (My own suspicion is that they are part of a mechanism for updating the genome with new survival information, thus violating the dogma of evolutionary biology that says mutations are unaffected by the environment. But that's another story.)

Detection of activity of the enzyme reverse transcriptase is still cited as proof of the existence of a retrovirus. Although this was believed—somewhat rashly, it would seem—at one time, the enzyme has been shown to be present in all living matter, with no particular connection to retroviruses per se.

A key step in demonstrating the existence of a new virus has always been the production of a micrograph showing the purified virus, exhibiting the expected structural and morphological features. Despite repeated demands by skeptics, no example was published until 1997. It turned out to be a mishmash of cellular debris, in which what had been identified as viruses turned out to be assorted fragments of material being similar only in having the size and general appearance of viruses, long familiar to virologists and known as "viral-like particles." According to Dr. Etienne de Harven, emeritus professor of pathology, University of Toronto, who worked on the electron microscopy of retroviral structures for twenty-five years at the Sloan Kettering Institution in New York, "Neither electron microscopy nor molecular markers have so far permitted a scientifically sound demonstration of retrovirus isolation directly from AIDS patients." [238]

The German virologist Stefan Lanka puts it more bluntly:

The dispute over who discovered HIV was a distraction

from the question of whether the virus actually exists
at all. The public was impressed that if a President and
a Prime Minister had to meet to resolve attribution, then
the thing they were negotiating about had to be real. [239]

Well, the royalties on antibody testing were certainly real.

AN EPIDEMIC OF AIDS TESTING

If HIV is virtually undetectable even in its alleged terminal
victims, how do you test for it? You don't; you test for the antibody. What this means in principle is that a culture containing
"antigens"—foreign proteins that provoke an immune response,
in this case proteins allegedly from the HIV virus—are exposed
to a sample of the patient's blood. If the blood plasma contains
antibodies to that antigen, they will bind to it in a reaction that
can be made visible by suitable means.

Wait a minute. . . . Aren't antibodies part of the body's own
defense equipment—that you either acquired from your mother,
learned to make yourself at some time in life when you encountered the virus, or were tricked into making by a vaccine? If you
have no symptoms of an illness and no detectable virus, but your
system is supplying itself with antibodies, isn't this a pretty good
description of immunity?

Yes—for any other disease, and if we were dealing with ratio-
nality. But this is the land of AIDS. The usual reason for antibody
testing is as a check to see if somebody needs to renew their shots.
Also, there are situations where testing for the antibody to a
pathogen suspected of causing a condition can make sense, given
the right circumstances. *If* a person is showing clinical symptoms
that are *known* to be caused by that pathogen, (perhaps by satisfying Koch's postulates), *and* a test has been shown *independently*
to identify an antibody specific to that pathogen, *then* testing for
the antibody can be a convenient way of confirming the suspected
disease without going through the rigmarole of isolation.

But none of this is true of HIV. It has never been shown to cause
anything, nor has a likely explanation even been advanced as to
how it could. And the only way of showing that an antibody test
is specific to a virus is to compare its results with a "gold standard" test, one that has been shown to measure the virus and
nothing else. Establishing such a standard requires isolating the

virus from clinical patients in the true, traditional sense, and for HIV that has never been done. What, then, if anything, does the "HIV test" mean?

A genuinely useful antibody test can confirm that an *observed sickness* is due to the microbe thought to be the culprit. A positive HIV result from somebody who is completely symptom-free, on the other hand, means either that the antibody has been carried from birth without the virus ever having been encountered, or that the virus has been successfully neutralized to the point of invisibility. So in this context, "HIV positive" means HIV-immune. Interpreting it as a prediction that somebody will die years hence from some unspecifiable disease makes about as much sense as diagnosing smallpox in a healthy person from the presence of antibodies acquired through childhood vaccination.

TESTING FOR WHAT?

The test can mean a lot of other things too. The most common, known as ELISA (Enzyme-Linked Immuno-Sorbent Assay, for those who love quoting these things at cocktail parties), was developed in 1984 for blood screening. Now, when you're looking for contaminated blood, you *want* a test that's oversensitive—where anything suspect will ding the bell. If the positive is false, after all, you merely throw away a pint of blood; but if a false negative gets through, the consequences could be catastrophic. (Whether or not what you're screening for is a real hazard isn't the issue here.) But the same test started being used for diagnosis. And when people are being told that a positive result means certainty of developing a disease that's inevitably fatal, that's a very different thing indeed.

Here are some of the other things that can give a positive result, which even some doctors that I've talked to weren't aware of: prior pregnancy; alcoholism; certain cancers; malaria antibodies; leprosy antibodies; flu vaccination; heating of blood sample; prolonged storage of the sample; numerous other viruses; various parasitic diseases; hepatitis B antibodies; rheumatoid arthritis. In fact, almost seventy other causes have been shown to be capable of causing a positive reaction that have nothing to do with AIDS conditions.[240] In a mass screening in Russia in 1991, the WHO performed thirty million tests over a two-year period and found

30,000 positive results. Attempts to confirm these yielded around 300, of which 66 were actual AIDS cases. [241]

In addition to the tests being uncertain in that precisely what they measure has never been defined, and nonspecific in that many other factors can give the same result, they are not standardized. This means that no nationally or internationally accepted criteria exist for deciding what constitutes a positive result. What people take as a death sentence on the basis of the things they've been told varies from one country to another, and even from one testing authority to another within the same country. The U.S. practice is to require a repeated positive result to an ELISA "search" test, to be "confirmed" by a test known as the HIV Western Blot (WB), which is supposed to be more accurate—although the United Kingdom won't use it because of the risk of misinterpretation due to cross-reactions.

However, despite the reassuringly suggestive terminology, the WB remains as nonspecific, since it tests for the same antigen proteins as ELISA (but separated out into bands, so it's possible to see which ones are causing the reaction) and has likewise never been verified against any gold standard. [242] In fact, some authorities cite it as the "standard" for assessing ELISA. This is a bit like using one clock to check the accuracy of another, when neither has been verified to be correct in the first place. According to the WB interpretations handed down in different places, an HIV positive African would not be positive in Australia; a positive from the U.S. Multicenter AIDS Cohort Study 1983–1992 would not be positive anywhere else in the world, including Africa. [243] The pamphlet supplied with the ELISA test kit from Abbot Laboratories states: "At present there is no recognized standard for establishing the presence or absence of antibodies to HIV-1 and HIV-2 in human blood."

BIOTECHNOLOGY'S XEROX MACHINE

A new diagnostic definition, introduced with several others in 1993, now makes it possible to have AIDS simply on the basis of a low CD4 cell count, without the presence of HIV being established at all. However, this amendment was not followed in Canada. Since 1995, more than half the new AIDS cases diagnosed in the U.S. have been in persons with no overt symptoms of AIDS illness, but who exhibited a "bad" cell count. All of those people, it seems, could be cured immediately by simply by heading northward and crossing the 49th parallel. It would certainly be a lot cheaper than going on medication of dubious benefit—and with the certainty of suffering no side effects.

The latest diagnostic disease indicator, "viral load," is an indirect measure divorced from any actual symptoms at all, which means that the efficacy of a drug is judged according to the observed change in a number deemed to be a "surrogate marker," and whether you're actually better, worse, or felt fine to begin with has got nothing to do with it. It's based on the "polymerase chain reaction" (PCR) method of amplifying formerly undetectable amounts of molecular genetic material—in this case, fragments of RNA that are said to be from HIV—by copying them in enormous numbers. *Forbes* magazine called it biotechnology's version of the Xerox machine. But errors are amplified too, by the same amount. The PCR process will indiscriminately copy dud HIVs that have been neutralized by antibodies, defectives that never formed properly in the first place, scraps of free-floating RNA, all of which end up being counted. And incredibly, these counts are presented as if they represented active viruses detected in the patient and not creations of the PCR process itself.[244] The Australian mathematician Mark Craddock has shown the mathematical basis of the model to be fatally flawed and based on wrong assumptions about what the number of RNA fragments says about the number of free viruses.[245] The inventor of the PCR method, Nobel Prize winner Kary Mullis, holds "quantitative PCR" to be a self-contradiction and dismisses its application in this way as worthless. The whole point is that if HIV were present and active in the body in the way that the viral load advocates claim, regardless of the foregoing, it should be readily amenable to standard virus-counting techniques. It shouldn't be necessary to use extra-high-sensitivity film to get an image if there's plenty of sunlight.

THE EXPORT INDUSTRY: AFRICA AND ASIA

"Everybody knows," from the flow of government and U.N. agency handouts uncritically passed on by the media that Africa is being devastated by an AIDS epidemic running out of control, with cases counted in tens of millions. What they probably don't realize is that the figures are estimates arrived at by basing very questionable statistical manipulations on what are often ludicrously small numbers, for example leftover blood samples in a village prenatal clinic. So when UNAIDS announces that 14 million Africans are AIDS victims, it doesn't mean that 14 million bodies have been counted, but that computers in Geneva have run a model with an assumed relationship between positive test results and AIDS deaths, and extrapolated the results to the population of the entire continent.[246] Thus in 1987 the WHO reported 1 million cases of "HIV disease" in Uganda. Yet ten years later, the *cumulative* number of AIDS cases actually reported was 55,000.[247] Nobody knew what had happened to the other 945,000. There are strong financial and other pressures that encourage the reporting as AIDS of old diseases that have been endemic on the African continent throughout history. According to Dr. Harvey Bialy, an American with long experience in Africa, because of the international funds poured into AIDS and HIV work, "It has become a joke in Uganda that you are not allowed to die of anything but AIDS. . . . A friend has just been run over by a truck; doctors put it down as AIDS-related suicide"[248]

Unlike the cases in New York and San Francisco, the conditions that are reported as AIDS in Africa affect both sexes equally, which should be an immediate indicator that what's being talked about in the two instances are not the same thing. This is hardly surprising, since "AIDS" in Africa is accorded a different definition. The unifying factor that makes all of the 30-odd disparate indicator diseases "AIDS" in the West is testing positive for antibodies claimed to be specific to HIV. But in Africa no such test is necessary.[249]

Virus hunters armed with antibody test kits began descending on the continent in the mid eighties because of three pointers possibly linking it to AIDS: a now-discredited theory that HIV might have originated there; the presence in Africa of an AIDS-related sarcoma (although it had existed in Africa since ancient times); and the presence of a small number of native Africans among AIDS cases reported in Western countries.[250] And sure enough, they began finding people who reacted positive. Furthermore, the numbers were distributed equally between the sexes— just what was needed to demonstrate that AIDS was indeed an infectious condition, which statistics in the West refused, obstinately, to confirm. However, in 1985 a different, "clinical" definition was adopted, whereby "AIDS" was inferred from the presence of prolonged fever (a month or more), weight loss of 10 percent or greater, and prolonged diarrhea.

The problem, of course, is that attributing these symptoms to a sexually transmitted virus invites—indeed, makes inevitable—the reclassifying of conditions like cholera, dysentery, malaria, TB, typhus, long known to be products of poverty and tropical environments. More insidious, funds and resources are withdrawn from the support of low-cost but effective traditional clinics and the provision of basic nutrition, clean drinking water, and sanitation, and directed instead on ruinously expensive programs to contain a virus that exists for the most part in WHO statisticians' computers.[251] Since it's decreed that "AIDS is caused by HIV," cases diagnosed according to the above definition are attributed to HIV presumptively. But studies where actual tests have been conducted show up to a third as testing negatively[252]—making "AIDS" a catch-all that arises from the loosely interpreted antibody testing.

For as we've seen, many factors that are common in most African regions, such as malaria, leprosy, parasitical infections, TB, can also test positive. This is a particular problem in Africa, where the population carries a naturally high assortment of antibodies, increasing the probability of cross-reactions to the point of making any results worthless. A study in central Africa found that 70 percent of the reported HIV positives were false.[253] Nevertheless, the official reports attribute all positives to HIV, making every instance automatically an AIDS statistic. Of the resulting numbers, every case not known to be a homosexual or drug abuser is presumed to have been acquired through heterosexual transmission, resurrecting tendencies to sexual stereotyping that go back to Victorian racial fantasies. Given the incentives of limitless funding, a glamorous crusader image, and political visibility, it isn't difficult to discern an epidemic in such circumstances. People in desperate need of better nutrition and sanitation, basic health care and education, energy-intensive industrial technologies, and productive capital investment are instead lectured on their morals and distributed condoms.

With the hysteria in the West now largely abated (although at the time of writing—early 2003—a campaign seems to be gathering momentum, targeting blacks), the bandwagon has moved on to embrace other parts of the Third World too. This follows a pattern that was set in Thailand, where an AIDS epidemic was said to be raging in the early nineties. Now, it so happens that over 90 percent of the inhabitants of Southeast Asia carry the hepatitis B antibody. The figure for actual disease cases in this region populated by tens of millions was around 700 in 1991, and by 1993 it had grown to 1,500 or so. Perhaps what the reports meant was an epidemic of AIDS testing. Just like the inquisitors of old, the more assiduously the witch hunters apply their techniques and their instruments, sure enough they find more witches.

"SIDE EFFECTS" JUST LIKE AIDS: THE MIRACLE DRUGS

LIQUID PLUMBER: AZT

In the cuckoo land of HIV "science" anything becomes possible. To combat the effects of an agent declared soon after its discovery as being inevitably lethal after a dormancy of ten to fifteen years (now, how could that be known?), HIV positives, sick and symptom-free alike, were put on the drug AZT, which was billed as "antiviral." AZT was developed in the 1960s as a chemotherapy for leukemia but never released because of its toxicity. It's known as a "nucleoside analog" drug, or DNA chain terminator, which means it stops the molecule from copying. It kills cells that try to reproduce. The idea for cancer treatment is that a short, shock program of maybe two or three weeks will kill the tumor while only half-killing the patient, and then you get him off it as quickly as possible. You *can't* take something like that four times a day indefinitely and expect to live. (Although some people don't metabolize it but pass it straight through; hence the few long-term AZT survivors that are pointed at to show how benign it is).

Chemotherapies are notoriously immunosuppressive. The "side effects" look just like AIDS. Officially acknowledged effects of nucleoside analog drugs include diarrhea, dementia, lymphoma (cancer), muscle wasting, and T-cell depletion, which are also

AZT advertised in the Lancet for administration to children

"Helping keep HIV disease at bay in children. Generally well tolerated; Improved cognitive function; Survival rates similar to adults; Improvements in growth and well being. RETROVIR. A world of antiretroviral experience."

Label on bottles of AZT for experimental administration to primates and rodents

"Toxic by inhalation, in contact with skin and if swallowed. Target organs(s): Blood Bone marrow. If you feel unwell, seek medical advice (show the label where possible). Wear suitable protective clothing."

The two faces of AZT. The label below has appeared on bottles containing as little as 25 milligrams. Patients have been prescribed daily doses 0f 500 to 1,500 milligrams.

AIDS-defining conditions. Christine Maggiore, director of the West Coast-based organization Alive & Well, who, after being given a positive diagnosis and sternly delivered death-sentence that turned out to be false, went on to research the entire subject exhaustively and became an activist to share her findings. In her highly informative book, *What If Everything You Thought You Knew About AIDS Was Wrong?* (2000) she describes these medications superbly as "AIDS by Prescription."

Yet this is the treatment of choice. Nobody says it actually cures or stops AIDS, but the recipients have been told that they're due to die anyway—which could possibly be one of the most ghastly

self-fulfilling prophecies in modern medical history. The claim
is that it brings some temporary respite, based on results of a
few trials in which the augurs of biochemistry saw signs of short-
term improvement—although bad data were knowingly included,
and other commentators have dismissed the trials as worthless.[254]
In any case, it is known that a body subjected to this kind of
toxic assault can mobilize last-ditch emergency defenses for a
while, even when terminal. A sick chicken might run around the
yard for a few seconds when you cut its head off, but that isn't
a sign that the treatment has done it any good.

In the fifteen years or so up to the late eighties, the life expectancy of hemophiliacs doubled. This was because improved clotting
factor—the substance they can't make for themselves—meant
fewer transfusions. The cumulative burden of constantly infused
foreign proteins eventually wears down an immune system and
opens the way for infections. Many also acquired HIV, but the
death rates of those testing positive and negative were about the
same. Then, from around the late eighties, the mortality of the
HIV positives from conditions diagnosed as AIDS rose significantly, and a widely publicized study cited this as proof that their
AIDS was due to HIV.[255] What it didn't take into account, however, was that only the HIV positives were put on AZT. Nobody
was giving AZT to the HIV negatives. Peter Duesberg believes
that AZT and other "antivirals" are responsible for over half the
AIDS being reported today.

PROTEASE INHIBITORS—HYPE UNINHIBITED

The AZT story of hastily rushing into print to claim miracle
cures based on selective anecdotal reporting and uncompleted
trials performed without controls seems to have been repeated
with the new drug "cocktails" based on protease inhibitors (PIs).
The theory that's proclaimed is similar to that of nucleoside
analogs in that the aim is to disrupt the replication of HIV, but
this time by inhibiting the protease enzyme crucial to assembling
the virus. However, despite their "antiviral" labeling, these drugs
have no way of distinguishing between HIV protease and the
human proteases that are essential to the digestive process,
resulting in a list of ill effects every bit as daunting as that

pertaining to AZT, including kidney and liver failure, strokes, heart attacks, and gross deformities. [256]

Researchers who have worked with PIs all their professional lives state flatly that they are incapable of doing what the highly publicized claims say they do. [257] The efficacy of the drugs is assessed by measuring the reduction of the number designated "viral load," which has never been shown to correspond to anything defining sickness in the real, physical world. As a "control," the viral load of those given cocktails is compared with the former level when they received AZT. A decrease in the number is taken as meaning that the cocktails have reduced sickness. To me this sounds a bit like saying that beer cures hangovers because the headache you wake up with isn't as bad as the one you get from whiskey.

One thing the cocktail drugs can be credited with without doubt is the resurgence to even greater heights of extravaganza of drug-company advertising, following a growing disenchantment with AZT. PIs are hyped as working the "miracle" of reducing AIDS mortality by 50 percent as reflected in the figures reported since the mid nineties. A closer look at them, however, shows the story not to be quite that straightforward. The greatest reductions occurred in 1995, which was before PIs had been approved for general use, and in 1996, by which time somewhere between 10 and 20 percent of HIV positive cases had been issued prescriptions for them. As mentioned above, in 1993 the definition of AIDS was expanded by the Centers for Disease Control, causing a large increase in the number of people qualifying as AIDS patients. One of the new diagnostic conditions was having a CD4 T-cell count of 200 or less at some point during a given year, no HIV positive condition being necessary. From 1993 forward, the majority of declared new AIDS cases were individuals with no clinical illness. When the size of a population hitherto consisting for the most part of people who are sick in one way or another is suddenly increased by the addition of large numbers of people who are illness-free, this must result in an increased survival rate for the overall population. It has to do with the restructuring and labeling of statistical groups, not with the effects of any treatment.

A VIRUS FIXATION

Although not a lot is said publicly, a growing number of scientific and medical professionals are becoming skeptical of the received dogma but tend, especially in times of uncertainty over careers and funding, to keep a low profile. When you see what happened to Duesberg, you can see why. Maybe after his derailing of the previous gravy train by showing cancers were not virally induced, nobody was going to let him loose on this one. He was subjected to ridicule and vilification, abused at conferences, and his funding cut off to the point that by the end of the eighties he could no longer afford a secretary. In two years, he had seventeen applications for funding for research on alternative AIDS hypotheses turned down. Graduate students were advised to shun his classes or risk adverse consequences to their careers. Publication in the mainstream scientific literature was denied—even the right of reply to personal attacks carried in the journal *Nature*, violating the most fundamental of scientific ethical traditions. His scheduled appearances on talk shows were repeatedly canceled at the last moment upon intervention by officials from the NIH and CDC.

Duesberg has been accused of irresponsibility on the grounds that his views threaten confidence in public health-care programs based on the HIV dogma. But scientific truth doesn't depend on perceived consequences. Public policy should follow science. Attempting to impose the reverse becomes Lysenkoism. And in any case, what have those programs achieved that should command any confidence? After all these years they have failed to save a life or produce a vaccine. (And if they did, to whom would it be given? The function of a vaccine is to stimulate the production of antibodies. By definition, HIV-positive individuals have them already. If they are given the HIV negatives and they work, then everyone will presumably become an AIDS case. So, finally, the prediction of a global pandemic will have come true.) No believable mechanism has been put forward as to how HIV kills T-cells. And billions of dollars continue to be spent every year on trying to unravel the mysteries of how HIV can make you sick without being present, and how an antibody can neutralize the virus but not suppress the disease. Scientific principles that have stood well for a hundred years are arbitrarily discarded to enable what's offered as logic to hang together at all, and the best that can be done at the end of it all is to prescribe a treatment that's lethal even if the disease is not. Yet no looking into alternatives is permitted; all dissenting views are repressed. This is not the way of science, but of a fanatical religion putting down heresy.

The real victim, perhaps not terminally ill but looking somewhat jaded at the moment, is intellectual honesty and scientific rigor. Maybe in its growth from infancy, science too has to learn how to make antibodies to protect itself from opportunistic infection and dogmatism. There was a time when any questioning of Ptolemy's geocentric model of the cosmos was greeted with the same outrage and fury. Perhaps one day Peter Duesberg will be celebrated as the biological Copernicus who challenged late-twentieth-century medical science's viricentered model of the universe. Just take viruses away from being the center around which everyone is trying to make everything revolve, let the other parts fall naturally into place, and suddenly the whole picture makes sense.

Section Notes

224 *Oprah Winfrey Show*, February 18, 1987

225 Duesberg, 1996, p. 210

226 Duesberg, 1996, Chapters 4, 5

227 See Duesberg, 1992 for a full account of the theory

228 Root-Bernstein, 1993

229 Maggiore, 2000, p. 46

230 Thomas, 1993

231 Thomas et al., 1994

232 Duesberg, 1996, pp. 174–186

233 Papudopulos et al, 1993

234 *Science* 224: pp. 497–500; 503–505; 506–508

235 Duesberg, 1992, p. 210

236 *Ibid.*, p. 222

237 Papudopulos et al., 1996; Lanka, 1995

238 De Harven, 1998

239 Lanka, 1995

240 Ransom and Day, 2000, p. 71; Maggiore, 2000, p. 11

241 Shenton, 1998, p. 164

242 Papadopulos-Eluopulos et al., 1993

243 Turner and McIntire, 1999

244 Philpott and Johnson, 1996

245 Craddock, 1995 and 1996

246 See Malan, 2002, for the story of a journalist true-believer who became an apostate.

247 Geshekter, 1998

248 Quoted in Hodgkinson, 1993

249 Papadopulos-Eluopulos et al., 1995

250 Johnson, 2001

251 Johnson, 1994, cites health care costs in Nigeria falling from $10–20 per person in 1974 to 3 cents in 1994

252 Shenton, 1998

253 Geshekter, 1998

254 For example, Lauritsen, 1990

255 Darby et al., 1989

256 Maggiore, 2000, p. 34

257 Rasnick, 1996

AFTERWORD

Gothic Cathedrals And The Stars

The fact is, most 'scientists' are technicians. . . . Because their noses are often buried in the bark of a particular tree, it is difficult to speak meaningfully to them of forests.
— Gary Zukav

Radio has no future. Heavier-than-air flying machines are impossible. X-rays will prove to be a hoax.
—William Thomson, Lord Kelvin, English scientist, 1899

If science is the quest to find out what's true regardless of how we might feel about the answers, then a sign of genuine science is a readiness to change a belief if the evidence seems to call for it. The topics we've covered represent a fair sampling of subjects on which I've held very different views in times gone by—see some of my earlier militant defending of Darwinism, for example. The exceptions would be mainly on environmental issues, where I never found the alarmist accounts very persuasive. Science as the ideal that exists in textbooks and the rhetoric of its popularizers would appear to be a very fine thing. But as is so often the case with this messy, distinctly non-Platonic real world that we inhabit, the actuality often turns out to be a different matter. The same disposition to healthy skepticism would appear to be in order when receiving pronouncements made in the name of "science" as when evaluating the patter on a used-car lot or the story-of-my-life as related in a singles-bar pitch. People have ways of making reality fit their own aims, needs, and agendas.

Every human society possesses its own cultural myths that help hold it together. Darwinian fixations on competition notwithstanding, humans are at heart a cooperative animal, and a commonly shared structure of belief in fundamental truths provides the social glue that binds a culture. The beliefs don't have to be true to be effective. Every culture believes itself to be unique in that its own beliefs *are* true, of course, and it appears that ours is little different. Well, yes, we do claim to be different in that we attempt to check what we believe against reality. But as we've seen, it turns out to be all-too-easy to proclaim the verdict as being what we "know" it ought to be, or would have it be, rather than what reality actually says, laying the idealized scientific paradigm open to the charge that some cynics have made of Christianity and socialism: A good idea; somebody should try it sometime.

The reasons are varied, and as we've seen, go no deeper than human nature. Sometimes a theory is simply too elegant or perfect in its intellectual appeal to be wrong, and any degree of mental contortion to avoid seeing the implication of a result can seemingly become possible. Similarly again, enlistment to social causes or defense of a moral high ground can set off emotional chords (which I would back against intellect and reason every time) that easily drown out any protest from impartiality and rigor. It's difficult to accept negation of a conviction when one's preferred way of life is perceived to be at stake, or even the existence of the world as we know it. And by no means least is the active discouragement of any willingness to question by the system we have in place today of scientific education and training.

In his book, *Disciplined Minds*,[258] Jeff Schmidt, a physicist and editor at *Physics Today* (until he was fired for writing it), argues that the political constraints and demands for conformity imposed by the academic training and selection process, and the priorities of today's workplace suppress independent thought and inclinations toward free creativity.

> Our society features a single, thoroughly integrated system of education and employment," he said when interviewed. "The education component is hierarchical and competitive because it is a sorting machine for employers, a gate-keeper for the corporations and academic institutions. Learning doesn't require credentialing, ranking, grading, high-stakes testing, groveling for letters of recommendation and so on. Good teachers don't need—or want—the power to crush their students socially.[259]

Berkeley law professor Phillip Johnson comments: "As science is brought more under centralized control, researchers must concentrate more on the agenda set by paradigm; see what they have been trained to see."[260]

An illusion of democratic freedoms is maintained by the forum of debates that take place over details, so long as the core belief system is not challenged—examples that come to mind here being those we looked at of AIDS and Evolution. As with the priesthoods of old, serious consideration of possibilities beyond the permissible limits becomes literally inconceivable.

The history of science reveals strikingly that it has been predominantly *outsiders*, not trained to think within the mental walls of the assumptions governing a given discipline, who have contributed the most to having genuinely new insights and making real break-throughs, such as formulating basic laws of physics and chemistry, founding entire new disciplines, and making innumerable original inventions and discoveries. A few examples:

Leonardo da Vinci (1452–1519), trained as a painter, otherwise for the most part self-taught. A total polymath of original concepts in architecture, hydraulics, mechanics, astronomy, geology, anatomy, military and naval engineering, mapmaking, design of harbors and other works.

Antony van Leeuwenhoeck (1632–1723), haberdasher and chamberlain for the sheriffs of Delft, Holland. Ground lenses as a hobby and invented the microscope.

Gottfried Leibnitz (1646–1716), Newton's mathematical rival, trained as a librarian and diplomat.

Joseph Priestley (1733–1804), Unitarian minister banned from English universities, stimulated by science after meeting Benjamin Franklin (by trade, a printer). Proposed an inverse square law for electrical charge, and credited with being the first to prepare oxygen, nitric oxide, and gaseous ammonia.

William Herschel (1738–1832), joined a regimental band in Hanover, Germany, at fourteen and went to England to work as a musician. Self-taught in mathematics and astronomy, built his own reflecting telescopes, pioneered the study of binary stars and nebulae, discoverer of Uranus, infrared solar rays, and the basic form of the Milky Way.

Thomas Young (1773–1879), general medical physician, mostly self-taught, who pioneered discoveries concerning interferometry and the wave theory of light, as well as in fluids and solids, theory of kinetic energy.

Michael Faraday (1791–1867), prolific experimenter in chemistry and physics, especially of electrical phenomena, apprenticed to a bookbinder.

Nicolas Leonard Carnot (1796–1832), army engineer of fortifications, pioneered work on mathematics and heat engines as a hobby, effective founder of the science of thermodynamics.

John Dunlop (1840–1921), Scottish vet, invented the pneumatic tire to help his son win a bicycle race. Went on to found a company that sold for three million pounds in 1896, after five years trading.

George Westinghouse (1846–1914), ran away as a schoolboy to

fight in the Civil War, prolific inventor and electrical pioneer who later secured the services of Nikola Tesla.

George Eastman (1854–1932), self-educated, worked as a bank clerk. Patented first practicable photographic roll film and perfected the Kodak camera.

Albert Einstein (1879–1955), patents clerk with no academic qualifications in theoretical physics. [261]

The conventional image of academic research pushing back an ever-widening horizon of pure knowledge, which is formulated into new theories to be applied through technology is tidy and attractive, but doesn't describe the way the real world works. Overwhelmingly, it turns out to be the people with an insatiable need to know that comes from somewhere inside and can't be channeled or trained, or with a practical bent and incentive to roll their sleeves up and find out, who break the new ground. From steam engines and telescopes, through seed improvement and screw propellers, to jet aircraft, rocketry, and electronics, the academic theories to explain what was going on came afterward. While most research today depends ultimately on government funding, either directly through grants or indirectly through support of the participating institutions, history shows that bureaucratic stifling and an inherent commitment to linear thinking makes officially inaugurated programs the least productive in terms of true creativity. [262] Much the same could be said about research commissioned and directed by commercial interests.

Although lip service is paid to the virtues of truth and integrity, the social dynamic that rules is a reflection of the value system of society at large, where the rewards are in material compensation, power, and prestige. Acceptance to an honored elite can be the greatest source of self-esteem, with excommunication and ostracism the ultimate unthinkable. Pointing to successful applications of technology such as computers and the space telescope as vindicating any theory of "science," as if they were all products of the same method, is to claim false credentials. Notions on such issues as how life originated or the nature of the cosmos face no comparable reality checks that can't be evaded. The Halton Arps and Immanuel Velikovskys, for whom the inner need to *know*, and a compulsion to speak out, outweigh effects on personal life, career advancement, and all else, are rare. Very rare.

I remember a lunch with Peter Duesberg and others on one

occasion, when his funding had been cut off, his laboratory effectively shut down, his marriage had broken up partly as a consequence, and the department had snubbed him by giving him as his only official appointment that year the chairing of its picnic committee. Somebody asked him if it was worth the destruction of his professional and personal life; wouldn't he have been better off just forgetting the whole thing and going with the mainstream Establishment? Duesberg blinked, frowned, and thought for a moment as if trying to make sense of the question. Finally, he replied, "But it wouldn't alter what is true."

Corruption of society's primary institution of faith accelerated the decline of the medieval order. When Martin Luther nailed his accusations up on the church door, a new era began. I see faith in what has been presented as the primary vehicle for revealing truth in our order eroding too. Science is losing its popular constituency as the rewards and the accolades are seen more blatantly to flow not in recognition of contribution to human knowledge, but of efficacy in contributing to profit-making or military capability. The way toward truth that was to be unique in the human experience, a model of impartiality and integrity, turns out to be as open to the serving of vested interests and as subject to all the familiar human propensities toward self-delusion and wilful deception. Small wonder, then, that we arrive at an age where lying and the packaging of things and people as other than what they are become richly rewarded professions, classes are offered in the faking of résumés, and the arts of what used to be statecraft are reduced to coaching in how to look good on TV.

Will there be a new Reformation and Renaissance, and if so, what will drive them? My answers would be first, yes, because in the long run the human animal is incapable of giving in, and second, I don't know. But it will have to be something larger than an individual life, something that will give meaning to a life to have been a part of, and which will last long after the individual has gone; something that will provide the kind of vision and spiritual force that motivated whole Gothic communities to embark on projects to build the towering cathedrals that inspire awe in us today, in which the work was completed by the grandchildren of the initiators.

Presumably such an age would be founded on a different value system than buying and selling, shopkeeper economics, petty promotions, and emphasis on Darwinian rivalries, that produce alienated societies in which everyone becomes a threat or an opportunity to be exploited for some kind of gain. If the romance with materialism has taught anything, it's surely that the foundation has to rest on solid, culturally instilled human qualities that no amount of gimmickry or slick talk from self-help bestsellers can substitute for. Such old-fashioned words as truth, justice, honor, integrity, compassion come to mind, among which technology has its place in securing the material aspects of life, without dominating life or becoming a substitute for it, and education means being taught how to think, not drilled in what to say. Imagine what a difference it would make if businesses saw their foremost function in society as the providing of employment and the supplying of needs, and departments of government existed to actually serve its citizens. And where truth is valued for its own sake, without having to be conscripted to politics or economics, real science flourishes naturally.

And here we come to a great irony. For it could be that the system of values needed to make real science, the new world view that was to replace religion, work, turns out to be just what all the world's true religions—the original models, as opposed to the counterfeits they were turned into later to serve power structures—have been trying to say all along. The first discipline to be mastered for truth to be apprehended clearly is control of passions, delusions, and material distractions; in other words, the cultivation of true objectivity: the ability, honestly, to have no preconception or emotional investment in what the answers turn out to be. For unmastered passions enslave us to those who control what we imagine will satisfy them.

Like a lot of the other ideals that we've touched upon, it's probably unrealizable. But that doesn't mean that it's impossible to get closer to. I think that those philosophers who wonder if the world is perfectible, and then, on arriving after maybe years of agonizing at the answer that should have been obvious, "No, its not," get depressed even to the point of suicide, ask the wrong question. They should be asking instead, "Is the world improvable?" Since nothing could be plainer that a resounding "Yes!" they could then live content in the knowledge that contributing even a nickel's worth to leaving things better than they found them would make an existence worthwhile.

Meanwhile, of course, we have some wonderful themes to be explored in science fiction—which after all is the genre of asking "what if?" questions about the future and creating pictures of possible answers. Submarines, flying machines, space ships, computers, and wrist TVs aren't science fiction anymore. At least not real science fiction, in the sense that stretches the imagination. But we can still paint visions of an age, possibly, in which confidence and a sharing of the simple fact of being human replace fear and suspicion, the experience of living life is the greatest reward to be had from it, and the ships of the new Gothic builders launch outward to explore the universe for no better reason than that it's out there.

And who knows? Maybe one day those dreams of science fiction will come true too.

Section Notes

258 Schmidt, 2000
259 Schmidt, 2001
260 Johnson, 1991, p. 121
261 A sample from Newgrosh, 2000
262 Kealey, 199

REFERENCES & FURTHER READING

ONE

HUMANISTIC RELIGION—The Rush to Embrace Darwinism

Behe, Michael J., 1996, *Darwin's Black Box,* Free Press, NY

Borel, Emile, 1962, *Probabilities and Life*, Dover, NY

Cook, N. D., 1977, "The Case for Reverse Translation," *Journal of Theoretical Biology*, Vol. 64, pp. 113–35

Darwin, Charles, 1859, *The Origin of Species by Means of Natural Selection or the Preservation of Favoured Races in the Struggle for Life*

Dawkins, Richard, 1976, *The Selfish Gene*, Oxford Univ. Press, NY

Dawkins, Richard, 1986, *The Blind Watchmaker*, Norton, NY; Longmans; Penguin edition, 1988

Dawkins, Richard, 1996, *Climbing Mount Improbable*, Norton, NY

Dawkins, Richard, 1997, "Is Science a Religion?" *The Humanist*, Vol. 57, Jan-Feb, p. 26

Dembski, William A., 1998, *The Design Inference: Eliminating Chance Through Small Probabilities*, Cambridge Univ. Press, NY

Dembski, William A., 1999, *Intelligent Design*, Intervarsity Press, Downers Grove, IL

Dembski, William A., 2002, *No Free Lunch*, Rowman & Littlefield, NY

Dennett, Daniel C., 1995, *Darwin's Dangerous Idea*, Simon & Schuster, NY

Denton, Michael, 1985, *Evolution: A Theory in Crisis* (1986 edition). Adler & Adler, Bethesda, MD

Gish, Duane T., 1995, *Evolution: The Fossils Still Say No!*, ICR, El Cajon, CA

Hall, Barry G., 1982, "Evolution in a Petri dish: the evolved β-galactosidase system as a model for studying acquisitive evolution in a laboratory," *Evolutionary Biology*, Vol. 15, pp. 85–150

Himmelfarb, Gertrude, 1962, *Darwin and the Darwinian Revolution*, W.W. Norton, NY

Ho, M-W, and P. T. Saunders, 1979, "Beyond Darwinism: An epigenetic approach to evolution," *Journal of Theoretical Biology*, Vol. 78, pp. 573–591

Hogan, James P., 1977, *Inherit the Stars*, Ballantine Del Rey, NY

Hogan, James P., 1988, "The Revealed Word of God," *Minds, Machines, & Evolution* (Baen edition, 1999), Bantam, NY, pp.147–153

Hoyle, Fred, 1983, *The Intelligent Universe*, Michael Joseph, London

Johnson, Phillip, 1991, *Darwin on Trial*, Regnery, Washington, D.C.

Johnson, Phillip, 1997, *Defeating Darwinism by Opening Minds*, InterVarsity Press, Downers Grove, IL

Judson, Horace Freeland, 1979, *The Eighth Day of Creation: The Makers of the Revolution in Biology*, Simon & Schuster, NY

Macbeth, Norman, 1971, *Darwin Retried*, Dell, Boston

Milton, Richard, 1992, *Shattering the Myths of Darwinism* (Park Street Press, Rochester, VT, 1997)

Raup, David M., 1991, *Extinction: Bad Genes or Bad Luck?* W. W. Norton, NY

Rosen, Donn E., and Donald G. Buth, 1980, "Empirical Evolutionary Research versus Neo-Darwinian Speculation," *Systematic Zoology*, Vol. 29, pp. 300–308

Simpson, George Gaylord, 1951, *Horses*, Oxford University Press, NY

Slusher, Harold S., and Francisco Ramirez, 1984, *The Motion of Mercury's Perihelion*, ICR, El Cajon, CA

Sober, Elliott, 1993, *Philosophy of Biology*, Westview Press, Boulder, CO

Spetner, Lee, 1997, *Not By Chance!* Judaica Press, NY

Stanley, S, 1979, *Macroevolution*, W. H. Freeman & Co., San Francisco, CA

Sunderland, Luther, 1989, *Darwin's Enigma: Ebbing the Tide of Naturalism*, Master Books, Green Forest, AZ

Vardiman, Larry, 1990, *The Age of the Earth's Atmosphere*, ICR, El Cajon, CA

Vardiman, Larry, 1993, *Ice Cords and the Age of the Earth*, ICR, El Cajon, CA

Wells, Jonathan, 2000, *Icons of Evolution*, Regnery, Washington, D.C.

Woodmorappe, John, 1999, *The Mythology of Modern Dating Methods*, ICR, El Cajon, CA

TWO

OF BANGS AND BRAIDS: Cosmology's Mathematical Abstractions

Arp, Halton, 1987, *Quasars, Redshifts, and Controversies*, Interstellar Media, Berkeley, CA

Arp, Halton, 1998, *Seeing Red: Redshifts, Cosmology, and Academic Science*, Apieron, Montreal, Quebec, Canada

Assis, André Koch Torres, Cesar Marcos, and Danhoni Neves, 1995, "History of 2.7 K Temperature Prior to Penzias and Wilson," *Apeiron*, Vol. 2, No. 3, July, pp. 79–84.

Dicke, R. H., P. J. E. Peebles, P. G. Roll, and D. T. Wilkinson, 1965, *Astrophysical Journal*, 142, pp. 414–19

Gamow, George, 1947, *One, Two, Three Infinity* (Bantam, NY, 1972)

Lerner, Eric J., 1986, "Magnetic Self-Compression in Laboratory Plasma, Quasars and Radio Galaxies," *Laser and Particle Beams*, Vol. 4, pp.193–222

Lerner, Eric J., 1988, "The Big Bang Never Happened," *Discover*, June, pp. 70–80

Lerner, Eric J., 1991, *The Big Bang Never Happened* (Simon & Schuster, London 1992)

Marmet, Paul, 1990, *Big Bang Cosmology Meets an Astronomical Death*, 21st Century, Science Associates, Leesburg, VA

Marmet, Paul, 2000, "Discovery of H$_2$ in Space Explains Dark Matter and Redshift," *21st Century*, Spring

Peratt, Anthony, 1983, "Are Black Holes Necessary?" *Sky and Telescope*, July

Peratt, Anthony, and James Green, 1983, "On the Evolution of Interacting Magnetized Galactic Plasmas," *Astrophysics and Space Science*, Vol. 91, pp. 19–33

Slusher, Harold S., 1978, *The Origin of the Universe*, ICR, El Cajon, CA

Valentijn, E. A., and P. P. van der Werf, 1999, "First Extragalactic Direct Detection of Large-Scale Molecular Hydrogen," *Astrophysical Journal Letters*, Vol. 552, No.1, Sept. 1, pp. L29–35

THREE

DRIFTING IN THE ETHER. Did Relativity Take A Wrong Turn?

Assis, A. K. T., 1992, "Deriving gravitation from electromagnetism," *Canadian Journal of Physics*, Vol. 70, pp. 330–40

Assis, A. K. T., 1995, "Gravitation as a Fourth Order Electromagnetic Effect," *Advanced Electromagnetism—Foundations, Theory, and Applications*, Editors T.W. Barrett and D.M. Grimes, World Scientific, Singapore, pp. 314–31.

Beckmann, Petr, 1987, *Einstein Plus Two*, Golem Press, Boulder, CO

Chang, Hasok, 1993, "A Misunderstood Rebellion," *Stud. Hist. Phil. Sci.* Vol. 24, No. 5, pp. 741–90, Elsevier Science, Ltd., London.

Dingle, Herbert, 1972, *Science at the Crossroads*, Martin Brian & O'Keeffe, London

Dinowitz, Steven, 1996, "Field Distortion Theory," *Physics Essays*, Vol. 9, No. 3, pp. 393–417

Einstein, Albert, 1961, *Relativity*, Crown, NY

Graneau, Peter and Neal Graneau, 1993, *Newton Versus Einstein*, Carlton Press, NY

Graneau, Peter and Neal Graneau, 1996, *Newtonian Electrodynamics*, World Scientific, Singapore

Hafele, J. C., and R. E. Keating, 1972, "Around-the-world atomic clock: predicted relativistic time gains" and "Measured relativistic time gains," both in *Science* 177, pp. 166–170

Hatch, Ronald R., 1999, *Escape from Einstein*, Kneat Kompany, Wilmington CA

Hatch, Ronald R., 2000, "A Modified Lorentz Ether Theory." Available at http://www.egtphysics.net

Hayden, Howard, 1990, "Light Speed as a Function of Gravitational Potential," *Galilean Electrodynamics* Vol.1, No. 2, March/April, pp. 15–17

Hayden, Howard, 1991, "Yes, Moving Clocks Run Slowly, Is Time Dilated?" *Galilean Electrodynamics*, Vol. 2, No. 4, July/Aug, pp. 63–66

Hayden, Howard, 1993, "Stellar Aberration," *Galilean Electrodynamics*, Sep/Oct, pp. 89–92

Lewis, Gilbert N., 1908, "A Revision of the Fundamental Laws of Matter and Energy," *The London, Edinburgh, and Dublin Philosophical Magazine and Journal of Science*, November

McCausland, Ian, 1999, "Anomalies in the History of Relativity," *Journal of Scientific Exploration*, Vol. 13, No. 2, pp. 271–90

Michelson, A. A., 1913, "Effects of reflection from a moving mirror on the velocity of light," *Astrophysics Journal*, Vol. 37, pp. 190–93

Michelson, A. A., & H. G. Gale, 1925, "The effects of the earth's rotation on the velocity of light," *Astrophys. J.*, Vol. 61, pp. 137–45

Møller, C., 1952, *The Theory of Relativity*, Oxford, London

Phipps, Thomas E. Jr., 1986, *Heretical Verities: Mathematical Themes in Physical Description*, Classic Non-Fiction Library, Urbana, IL

Phipps, Thomas E. Jr., 1989, "Relativity and Aberration," *American Journal of Physics*, No. 57, pp. 549–51

Phipps, Thomas E. Jr., 1994, "Stellar and Planetary Aberration," *Apeiron*, No. 19, June

Renshaw, Curt, 1995, "Moving Clocks, Reference Frames, and the Twin Paradox," *IEEE AES Systems Magazine*, January, pp. 27–31

Slusher, Harold S., and Francisco Ramirez, 1984, *The Motion of Mercury's Perihelion*, ICR, El Cajon, CA

Stine, Harry G., 1980, "Faster Than Light," *Destinies*, Feb/Mar.

Sutliff, Donna, 1991, "Why Physics Cannot Assume the Relativity of Motion or an Infinite Universe: Problems with Special and General Relativity." *Phys Ess*, Vol. 4, No. 2.

Van Flandern, Tom, 1998, "What GPS Tells Us about Relativity," posted on the Web at Meta Research, www.metaresearch.org/mrb/gps-relativity/.htm

Wang, Ruyog, 2000, "Successful GPS Operations Contradict the Two Principles of Special Relativity and Imply a New Way for Inertial Navigation—Measuring Speed Directly," *Proc IAIN and ION*, June 26–28

Wang, Ruyong, 2000(a), "Re-examine the Two Principles of Special Relativity and the Sagnac Effect Using GPS's Range Measurement Equation," *Proc IEEE Symposium on Location and Navigation*, March 13–16, IEEE Cat. No. 00CH37062

FOUR

CATASTROPHE OF ETHICS: The Case
For Taking Velikovsky Seriously

Angiras, 1999, *Firmament and Chaos, 1—Earth*. Infinity Publishing, Bryn Mawr, PA

Angiras, 2000, *Firmament and Chaos, 2—A New Solar System Paradigm*. Infinity Publishing, Bryn Mawr, PA

De Grazia, Alfred, Ralph E. Juergens, Livio C. Stecchini (Eds)., 1966, *The Velikovsky Affair*, Univ Books, Hyde Park, NY

Ginenthal, Charles, 1995, *Carl Sagan and Immanuel Velikovsky*, New Falcon Press, Tempe, AZ

Ginenthal, Charles, 1996, "The AAAS Symposium on Velikovsky." See Pearlman, 1996, pp. 51-138

Gold, Thomas & Steven Soter, 1980, "The Deep-Earth-Gas Hypothesis," *Scientific American*, June, pp. 154–61

Goldsmith, Donald (Ed.), 1977, *Scientists Confront Velikovsky*, Cornell Univ Press, Ithaca, NY

Greenberg, Lewis M., 1977 (Ed.), *Velikovsky and Establishment Science*, Kronos, Glassboro, NJ

Greenberg, Lewis M., 1978 (Ed.), *Scientists Confront Scientists Who Confront Velikovsky*, Kronos Press, Glassboro, NJ

Hoyle, Fred, 1983, *The Intelligent Universe*, Michael Joseph, London

Juergens, Ralph E., 1966, "Minds in Chaos." *See* De Grazia et al., 1966, pp. 7–49

Juergens, Ralph E., 1966(a), "Aftermath to Exposure." *See* De Grazia et al., 1966, pp. 50–79

Juergens, Ralph E., 1977, "On the Convection of Electric Charge by the Rotating Earth," *Kronos*, Vol. 2 No. 3, February, pp. 12–30

Lyttleton, R. A., 1961, *Man's View of the Universe*, Little & Brown, Boston.

McCrea, W.H., 1960, *Proceedings of the Royal Astronomical Society Series* AV 256, May 31

Pannekoek, A., 1989, *A History of Astronomy*, Dover, NY

Pearlman, Dale Ann, (Ed.), 1996 , *Stephen J. Gould and Immanuel Velikovsky*, Ivy Press Books, Forest Hills, NY.

Pensée, 1976, *Velikovsky Reconsidered*. Collection of articles from the magazine. Doubleday, Garden City, NY

Ransom, C. J., 1976, *The Age of Velikovsky*, Kronos Press, Glassboro, NJ

Ransom, C. J., and L. H. Hoffee, 1972, "The Orbits of Venus," *Pensée*, 1976, pp. 102–109

Rose, Lynn E., 1977, "Just Plainly Wrong: A Critique of Peter Huber, Installment 1." See Greenberg, 1977, pp. 102–12

Rose, Lynn E., 1978, "Just Plainly Wrong: A Critique of Peter Huber, Installment 2," See Greenberg, 1978, pp. 33–69

Rose, Lynn E., 1993, "The Cornell Lecture: Sagan on a Wednesday," *Velikovskian*, Vol. 1, No. 3, pp. 101–14

Rose, Lynn E., 1996, "The AAAS Affair: From Twenty Years After." See Pearlman 1996, pp. 139–85

Rose, Lynne E., 1999, *Sun, Moon, and Sothis*, Kronos Press, Deerfield Beach, FL

Rose, Lynn E., and Raymond C. Vaughan, 1976, "Analysis of the Babylonian Observations of Venus," *Kronos*, Vol. 2, No. 2, November

Sagan, Carl, 1979, *Broca's Brain*, Ballantine, NY

Sagan, Carl, 1985, *Comet*, Ballantine, NY

Savage, Marshall T., 1992, *The Millenial Project*, Empyrean Publications, Denver, CO

Sherrerd, Chris R., 1972, "Venus' Circular Orbit.," *Pensée*, 1976, pp. 132–33

Sherrerd, Chris R., 1973, "Gyroscopic Precession and Celestial Axis Displacement," *Pensée*, 1976, pp. 133–36

Talbott, George R., 1993, "Revisiting the Temperature of Venus," *Velikovskian*, Vol. No. 3, p. 95

Van Flandern, Tom, 1993, *Dark Matter, Missing Planets, and New Comets*, North Atlantic Books, Berkeley, CA

Vardiman, Larry, 1990, *The Age of the Earth's Atmosphere: A Study of the Helium* Flux, ICR, El Cajon, CA

Vardiman, Larry, 1993, *Ice Cores and the Age of the Earth*, ICR, El Cajon, CA

Velikovsky, Immanuel, 1950, *Worlds in Collision*, Doubleday, NY

Velikovsky, Immanuel, 1952, *Ages in Chaos*, Doubleday, NY

Velikovsky, Immanuel, 1955, *Earth in Upheaval*, Doubleday, NY

Velikovsky, Immanuel, 1966, "Additional Examples of Correct Prognosis." See De Grazia et al., 1966, pp. 232–45

Velikovsky, Immanuel, 1982, *Mankind in Amnesia*, Doubleday, NY

Velikovsky, Immanuel, 1983, *Stargazers and Gravediggers*, William Morrow & Co., NY

Wilson, Robert Anton, 1995, *The New Inquisition*, New Falcon Pr, Tempe, AZ

FIVE

ENVIRONMENTALIST FANTASIES: Politics & Ideology Masquerading As Science

Bailey, Ronald, 1995 (Ed.), *The True State of the Planet*, Free Press, NY

Baliunas, Sallie, 1994, "Ozone and Global Warming: Are the Problems Real?", West Coast Roundtable for Science and Public Policy, Dec. 13

Baliunas, Sallie, 2002, "The Kyoto Protocol and Global Warming," Speech to Hillsdale Coll, February

Baliunas, Sallie, Arthur B. Robinson and Zachary W. Robinson, 2002, *Global Warming: A Guide to the Science*, Fraser Institute, Vancouver, BC, Canada

Beckmann, Petr, 1976, *The Health Hazards of* Not *Going Nuclear*, Ace Books, NY

Bennett, Michael J., 1991, *The Asbestos Racket: An Environmental Parable*, Merril Press

Bennett, Michael J., 1993, "Exposing the Big Myth About Cancer," *Insight*, January 4, p. 23

Bennett, Michael J., 1993(a), "A Pointless Stir Over Asbestos," *Insight*, September 13, p. 33

Carson, Rachel, 1962, *Silent Spring*, (11th printing, April 1970), Fawcett World Library, NY

Claus, George and Karen Bolander, 1977, *Ecological Sanity*, David McKay & Co., NY

Cohen, Bernard L., 1983, *Before It's Too Late: A Scientist's Case for Nuclear Energy*, Plenum Press, NY

Cohen, Bernard L., 1990, *The Nuclear Energy Option*, Plenum Press, NY

Dobson, Gordon M.B., 1968, "Forty Years Research on Atmospheric Ozone at Oxford University: A History," *Applied Optics*, Vol. 7, No. 3, pp. 387–405

Edwards, J. Gordon, 1985, "DDT Effects on Bird Abundance & Reproduction." *See* Lehr, 1992, pp. 195–216

Edwards, J. Gordon, 1992, "The Lies of Rachel Carson," *21st Century*, summer, pp. 41–51.

Edwards, J. Gordon, 1993, "Malaria: The Killer That Could Have Been Conquered," *21st Century*, Summer, pp. 21–35.

Efron, Edith, 1984, *The Apocalyptics: Cancer and the Big Lie*, Simon & Schuster, NY

Ellsaesser, Hugh, 1978, "Ozone Destruction by Catalysis: Credibility of the Threat," *Atmospheric Environment*, Vol. 12, pp. 1849–56, Pergamon Press, UK

Ellsaesser, Hugh, 1978(a), "A Reassessment of Stratospheric

Ozone: Credibility of the Threat," *Climatic Change 1*,
pp. 257–66, D. Reidel Publishing, Dordrecht, Holland

Ellsaesser, Hugh, 1991, "The Holes in the Ozone Hole, II,"
Cato Institute Conference, *Global Environmental
Crises: Science or Politics?* Capital Hilton, Washington,
D.C., June 5–6.

Ellsaesser, Hugh, 1992, "The Great Greenhouse Debate." *See*
Lehr, 1992, pp. 404–13

Elmsley, John, 1992, "On Being a Bit Less Green," *New Scientist*, October 17

Epstein, Samuel, 1971, Statement. Official Transcripts., Consolidated DDT Hearings, E.P.A., Washington, D.C.

Ginenthal, Charles, 1997, "The Extinction of the Mammoth,"
The Velikovskian, Vol. III, Nos. 2 and 3, Ivy Press, Forest
Hill, NY

Grant, R. W., 1988, *Trashing Nuclear Power*, Quandary House,
Manhattan Beach, CA

Hayden, Howard, 2001, *The Solar Fraud: Why Solar Energy
Won't Run the World*, Vales Lake Publications, Pueblo
West, CO

Hayden, Howard, 2002, "Grievous Hazards," *The Energy Advocate*, Vol. 7, No. 5, December, Pueblo West, CO

Hogan, James P., 1988, "Know Nukes," *Minds, Machines, & Evolution*, (Baen edition, 1999) Bantam, NY, pp. 213–331

Idso, Sherwood, B., 1992, "Carbon Dioxide and Global
Change." See Lehr, 1992, pp. 414–33

Jukes, John, 1994, "*Silent Spring* and the Betrayal of Environmentalism," *21st Century*, Fall, pp. 46–54

Kerr, J. B., and C. T. McElroy, 1993, "Evidence for Large Upward Trends of Ultraviolet-B Radiation Linked to
Ozone Depletion," *Science*, Vol. 262,
pp. 1032–4, November

Lehr, Jay H. (Ed.), 1992, *Rational Readings on Environmental
Concerns*, Van Nostrand Reinhold, NY

Luckey, T. D., 1980, *Hormesis with Ionizing Radiation*, CRC
Press, Boca Raton, FL

Luckey, T. D., 1992, *Radiation Hormesis*, CRC Press, Boca
Raton, FL

Maduro, Rogelio A., 1989, "The Myth Behind the Ozone Hole
Scare," *21st Century*, July–Aug, pp. 11–19.

Maduro, Rogelio A., and Ralf Schaurhammer, 1992, *Holes in the Ozone Scare*, 21st Century Science Associates, Washington, D.C.

McCracken, Samuel, 1982, *The War Against the Atom*, Basic Books, NY

Molina, M. J., and F. S. Rowland, 1974, *Nature* 249, p. 810

Pease, Robert W., 1989, "Holes in the Ozone Theory," *The Orange County Register*, June 25

Pease, Robert W., 1990, "The Gaping Holes in Big Green," *The Orange County Register*, October 29

Penkett, Stuart A., 1989, "Ultraviolet Levels Down, Not Up," *Nature*, Vol. 341, September 28, pp. 282–4

Pike, Tim, 1979, "The Great DDT Hoax," *Fusion*, June, pp. 60–8

Robinson, Arthur B., 1994, "Ozone and Ultraviolet Light," *Access to Energy*, Vol. 21, No. 5, January

Robinson, Arthur B., 1997, "Global Warming," *Access to Energy*, November

Robinson, Arthur B., and Zachary W. Robinson, 1997, "Science Has Spoken: Global Warming Is a Myth," *Wall Street Journal*, December 4

Sanera, Michael and Jane Shaw, 1996, *Facts, Not Fear: A Parent's Guide to Teaching Children About the Environment*, Regnery, Washington, D.C.

Scotto, Joseph, et al., 1988, "Biologically Effective Ultraviolet Radiation: Surface Measurements in the United States, 1974–1985," *Science*, Vol. 239, Feb 12, pp. 762–64

Simon, Julian, 1981, *The Ultimate Resource*, Princeton Univ. Press, Princeton, NJ

Simon, Julian, 1990, *Population Matters*, Transaction Publishers, New Brunswick, NJ

Simon, Julian and Herman Kahn, 1984, (Eds.) *The Resourceful Earth*, Basil Blackwell, Oxford, UK

Singer, S. Fred, 1994, "Shaky Science Scarier than Ozone Fiction," *Insight*, March 28, pp. 31–34

Singer, S. Fred, 1997, "Global Warming: The Counterfeit Consensus," Interview by The *Intellectual Activist*

Singer, S. Fred, 1997(a), "Failed Predictions"—review of Paul Erlich's *Betrayal of Science and Reason*, Book World Review, July, p. 272

Singer, S. Fred, 1999,"The Road from Rio to Kyoto: How

Climatic Science was Distorted to Support Ideological Objectives," Presented at the Symposium "An Assessment of the Kyoto Protocol, Georgetown International Environmental Law Reform, April 15

Smith, Lee Anderson and C. Bertrand Schultz, 1992, "Global Cooling, Scientific Honesty, and the NSF," *21ˢᵗ Century*, Winter

Stevenson, Robert E., 1996, "An Oceanographer Looks at the Non-Science of Global Warming," *21ˢᵗ Century*, Winter

Tomkin, Jocelyn, 1993, "Hot Air," *Reason,* March

Weber, Gerd R., 1990, *Global Warming—The Rest of the Story*, Dr. Boettiger Verlag GmbH, Wiesbaden, Germany. Distributed by 21ˢᵗ Century Science Associates, Washington, D.C.

SIX

CLOSING RANKS: AIDS Heresy In The Viricentric Universe

Brink, Anthony, 2000, *Debating AZT: Mbeki and the AIDS Drug Controversy*, Open Books, Pietermaritzburg, SA

Caton, Hiram, 1994, *The AIDS Mirage*, University of NSW Press, Sydney, Austria

Craddock, Mark, 1995, "HIV: Science by Press Conference," *Reappraising AIDS*, Vol. 3, No. 5, May. Included in Duesberg 1996(a), pp. 127–30; also in Duesberg 1995, pp. 481–507

Craddock, Mark, 1996, "Doesn't Anybody Read Anymore?" *Reappraising AIDS*, Vol. 4, No. 11, November

Darby et al., 1989, "Incidence of AIDS and Excess Mortality Associated with HIV in Haemophiliacs in the United Kingdom," *British Medical Journal*, No. 298, pp. 1064–68

De Harven, Etienne, 1998, "Remarks on Methods for Retroviral Isolation," *Continuum*, Spring.

Duesberg, 1992, "AIDS Acquired by Drug Consumption and Other Noncontagious Risk Factors," *Pharmacology & Therapeutics*, No. 55, pp. 201–77. Also included in Duesberg 1995, pp. 223–377

Duesberg, 1995, *Infectious AIDS: Have We Been Misled?* North Atlantic, Berkeley, CA

Duesberg, 1996, *Inventing the AIDS Virus*, Regnery, Washington, D.C.

Duesberg, 1996(a), (Ed.), *AIDS: Virus or Drug-Induced?* Kluwer, Dordrecht, Netherlands

Fumento, Michael, 1990, *The Myth of Heterosexual AIDS*, Regnery Gateway, Washington, D.C.

Geshekter, Charles, 1998, "Science, Public Health, and Sexual Stereotypes: Comparative Perspectives on AIDS in South Africa," April 25 presentation

Hodgkinson, Neville, 1993, "Epidemic of AIDS in Africa 'a Myth,'" London *Sunday Times*, March 21

Hodgkinson, Neville, 1996, *AIDS: The Failure of Contemporary Science*, Fourth Estate, London

Johnson, Christine, 1994, "The Role of HIV In AIDS: Why There Is Still A Controversy," *Praxis*, Vol. 8, Summer–Fall

Johnson, Christine, 2001, "Why the 'AIDS Test' Doesn't Work in Africa," *Rethinking AIDS*, Vol. 9, No. 1, January

Lanka, Stefan, 1995, "HIV—Reality or Artefact?" *Continuum*, April/May

Lauritsen, John, 1990, *Poison by Prescription*, Asklepios, NY

Lauritsen, John, 1993, *The AIDS War*, Asklepios, NY

Lauritsen, John & Ian Young (Eds), 1997, *The AIDS Cult*, Asklepios, Provincetown, MA

Maggiore, Christine, 2000, *What If Everything You Thought You Knew About AIDS Was Wrong?* AFAA, Studio City, CA

Malan, Rian, 2002, "AIDS in Africa: In Search of Truth," *Rolling Stone*

Papadopulos-Eleopulos et al., 1993, "Is a Positive Western Blot Proof of HIV Infection?" *Bio/Technology*, June

Papadopulos-Eleopulos, Eleni, Valendar Turner, John Papadimitriou, Harvey Bialy, 1995, "AIDS in Africa: Distinguishing Fact and Fiction," *World Journal of Microbiology and Biotechnology*, Vol. 11, pp. 135–43

Papadopulos-Eleopulos, Eleni, Valendar Turner, John Papadimitriou, John Causer, 1996, "The Isolation of HIV: Has it Really Been Achieved? The Case Against," *Continuum* Supplement Vol. 4, No. 3, Sep/Oct

Philpott, Paul, and Christine Johnson, 1996, "Viral Load of
    Crap," *Reappraising AIDS*, Vol. 4, No. 10, October
Ransom, Steven, and Phillip Day, 2000, *World Without AIDS*,
    Credence Publications, Tonbridge, UK

Index

F

Kronos, 218, 221
Kyoto Conference, *See* Global Warming

L

Lamarck, Jean Baptiste, 14
Lancet, 295
Lanka, Stefan, 317
Laplace, Pierre, 64, 179, 202
Larrabee, Eric, 181, 183, 185
Laser and Particle Beams, 89
Laws of motion, *See* Newton, Sir Isaac
Le Carre, John, 225
Leibnitz, Gottfried, 335
Leipzig Declaration, 245
Lemaitre, Georges, 67-68, 78
Lenz's laws, 137
Lerner, Eric, 87-91, 108
  plasma focus and scaling laws, 86-87
  star formation, 89
LET, *See* Lorentz Ether Theory
Levine, Herbert, 292
Lewis, Gilbert N., 139
Libby, W., 176
Light, 48, 52, 66, 72, 74, 77-78, 90, 335
  aberration, 134-35
  bending by mass, 140, 148, 166
  emission and absorption, 120
    re-emission, 134-35
  L. microscope, 281
  spectra, 65
  tired L., 74, 93
  See also Radiation Redshift
Light, velocity of, 119-26, 131,
  135, 139, 145
  ballistic theory, 120
  constancy postulate, 124, 130
  faster than, 145-48
  from Maxwell's equations, 118
  Michelson Morley experiment, 123-26
  privileged frame, 120-21
  transparent media , 120-21
  upper velocity limit, 126
  See also Ether; Relativity
Linear, Non-Threshold model, 289
LNT, *See* Linear, Non-Threshold model
Local Supercluster, 103-04
Logic, deductive and inductive, 12, 196
Lorentz, Hendrick, 123-25, 131-33, 138,
  143, 145
  L. Ether Theory, 131
  L. transforms, 123-24, 138-39, 143

Lorna Doone, 241
Luckey, T.D., 288
Lucretius, 63
Lundberg, G.A., 183
Luther, Martin, 337
Lyell, Sir Charles, 20, 22 64, 173,
  175, 180
Lyshenkoism, 328
Lyttleton, Raymond A., 201

M

Macbeth, Norman, 31, 33
Mach, Ernst, 106
Mackay, Charles, 225
Macmillan Company, 168-69, 171
Macroevolution, 18
Maggiore, Christine, 301, 325
Magnetism
  celestial, *See* Celestial dynamics;
  Plasma Universe, physics of, *See*
  Electrodynamics; Electrostatics
Malaria, 262-65, 269, 284-85, 319, 323
  M. mosquitoes, 262-64, 277
  eradication programs, 264-65, 269, 277
    cutbacks, 269
  symptoms, 263
  transmission, 264
  See also DDT
Malthus, Thomas, 229
  neo-Malthusianism, 228
Manetho, 155
Manna, 208-09
  Sagan, 209-12
Margulis, Lynn, 9
Mariner 2, 177, 184, 212-14, 220
Mariner 4, 187, 210
Mariner 6, 199
Mariner 9, 187, 210
Mariner, Mission to Venus, 184
Markarian, 101
Marklin, George, 132, 135
Marmet, Paul, 93, 108
Mars, 160, 163, 165-66, 180, 197,
  203, 209-10, 219
  ancient deities, 160, 163-64
  atmosphere, 210
    neon and argon, 166
  Earth encounters, 163-64, 166,
  180, 197, 210
  motion, 187
  polar caps, Sagan, 209

idealistic view of, 3-4, 333
outsiders, 334-36
S. based on faith, 9, 40, 54, 76, 171,
183, 189, 271
scientific vs. legal debate, 270
social and political structure, 5, 50-51,
230, 270, 336
See also AIDS; Catastrophism;
Cosmology; Environmentalism;
Evolution, Theory of; Philosophy;
Relativity
Science (magazine), 86, 89, 176, 177,
184, 189, 196, 199, 218, 238, 260, 262,
271, 284, 295, 314
Science and Environmental Policy
Project, 244, 255, 262
*Science Awakening II, The Birth of
Astronomy*, 196
Science fiction, 3, 106, 146, 234, 259, 339
Science News, 213
Science News Letter, 169
Scientific American, 184, 218
Scientists, 3-5, 27, 50, 55, 72, 166, 172,
176, 181, 185, 191, 199, 210, 217, 227,
228, 240, 244-46, 249, 255, 258,
268-69, 272, 295, 314, 331
advocacy positions, 169, 191, 240,
246, 269, 270
and common perceptions, 90, 115,
117, 285
and Velikovsky; *See* Velikovsky,
Immanuel
authoritarian, 149
defending doctrine, 6, 15, 19, 57,
109, 114, 153, 214, 333
environmental and environmentalist
S.s, *See* Environmentalism
EPA DDT hearings, 271-76
forensic S.s, 55
human nature, 65, 265, 333
surveys re. global warming, 233, 247
social S.s, 183, 246
training, 73
See also, Science
Scientists Confront Velikovsky, 194, 216
Scotto, Joseph, 260
Scranton Bird Club, 277
Seitz, Frederick, 247
Selection, 14-15,17-20, 29, **31-34**,
44-46, 54, 175
adaptive variation, 14-15, 18, 32,
35-36, 38, 46, 48

artificial S., 14, 34, 43
bacterial, 42-44
circular definition, 33
conservative force, 17, 29
horse toes, 27, 29
imaginative speculations, 32
limits, 18-19
not a source of originality, 34-35, 38
only mechanism for naturalist-
materialist philosophy, 32
peppered moth, 33-34, 42
pesticide resistance, 43;
See also Evolution, Theory of;
Genetics; Mutation
Selikoff, Irving, 293
Seneca, 161
Seyfert galaxies, *See* Galaxies
Seyfert, Karl, 99
Shapley, Harlow, 168
Shakespeare, William, 53
Sheba, Queen of, 156
Shishak, 157
Shklovskii, I.S., 212
Sierra Club, 268
Silent Spring, 266, 268, 277, 282, 286
Silk, Joseph, 61
Simmons, S.W., 265
Simpson, Gaylord, 45
Singer, S. Fred, 245-46
Siwalik Hills, 174
Sky and Telescope, 86
Slipher, V.M., 65
Smallpox, 9, 304, 319
Smith, P.V., 176
Smoking, 290, 293, 295, 311
Sober, Elliot, 54
Social change, ; *See also* Cosmology
and society
Social scientists, 183, 246; *See also*
Scientists
Society for Interdisciplinary /studies, 221
Socrates, 52
Solar System, 71, 80-85, 148, 162,
165, 167, 171, 179-80, 185, 198,
201-03, 219-21
angular momentum, 80-86, 117,
180, 187, 198-99, 204
comets, 197, 202-04, 209, 211-12
electrical forces, 78-81, 167, 179,
185, 199, 204, 219-20
formation, 78, 82, 87, 91-92, 180, 201,
208, 217